WHEN OTHER PEOPLE SAW US, THEY SAW THE DEAD

Edited by
Lauren T. Davila

WHEN OTHER PEOPLE SAW US, THEY SAW THE DEAD
All stories within are copyright © 2023 their respective authors. All rights reserved.

"The Repetition Tango" by Alicia Thompson first appeared in the Los Angeles Public Library's Short Story Dispenser in 2019. All stories appeared in the original edition of this anthology, published by Haunt Publishing, Edinburgh, Scotland, 2022.

Published by Outland Entertainment LLC
3119 Gillham Road
Kansas City, MO 64109

Founder/Creative Director: Jeremy D. Mohler
Editor-in-Chief: Alana Joli Abbott

ISBN (paper): 978-1-954255-59-3
ISBN (eBook): 978-1-954255-60-9
North American Rights
Created in the United States of America

Editor: Lauren T. Davila
Copy editor: Alana Joli Abbott
Galley Proofer: Stephanie Scott
Cover Illustration: Mina Martinez
Cover Design: Jeremy D. Mohler
Interior Layout: Mikael Brodu

Printed and bound in the United States of America.

Visit **outlandentertainment.com** to see more, or follow us on our Facebook Page **facebook.com/outlandentertainment/**

— TABLE OF CONTENTS —

PRAISE FOR
— *THEY SAW THE DEAD* —

"A haunting and poignant anthology. The gorgeous voices within culminate to create a memorable work. These stories of grief, love, fear, and ghosts cut deep; the authors have infused Gothic elements in their own unique way, and the shadows of each tale will linger in the reader's mind long after reading. A stunning addition to the horror canon."

Sara Tantlinger, Bram Stoker Award-winning
author of *The Devil's Dreamland*

"Beautiful and heartbreaking, *They Saw the Dead* is one of those rare anthologies without a single subpar story. From start to finish I was fully immersed in the collection's world of darkness, lost loves, and ghosts. A much-needed collection of diverse stories from BIPOC."

Diversity in Horror

"Terrifying and thought-provoking, this anthology is perfect for fans of small stories that pack a big punch."

Hannah Whitten, author of *For the Wolf*

"Grabs you by the throat from the very first story. As you navigate from one twisted world into the next, you'll find yourself on an adventure—visiting cold lakes and houses with huts best left alone, receiving notes and letters that warn and welcome you at once. Every so often, you'll flip a page and find a story that is indelible—both quietly horrific and so beautiful. Brace yourselves—this anthology is deliciously, meditatively, dark."

Bhavika Govil

"A delicious anthology of stories from authors of color across the globe. Within these stories lie the horrors of colonialism and the loss of identity and home, but also the beauty and humour found and created through community and love; memories of shared meals and music; and magic which heals, takes vengeance, and empowers. This collection is bursting with some of the most exciting voices in contemporary dark fiction. These stories will challenge you, make you heartsore, and leave you feeling richer for the reading."

Katalina Watt, author

"At once blooming with rage and gentle with memory. From rotting, ravenous colonisers to the creeping ghosts of generations past, stories of fantasy, folktale, and horror come together to create something truly haunting in this powerful collection."

Andrew Joseph White, author of *Hell Followed with Us*

— CONTENT WARNINGS —

The publisher has made every effort to accurately reflect the content in this book. Any omissions are accidental and the publisher's own.

CONTENT WARNINGS A-Z

Abuse: Blood and the Bottomland; Headmaster; The Candlemaker's Daughter.

Alcohol: Blood and the Bottomland; Sight; The Mountain Air.

Blood, gore: Clockwork; For Evermore; Headmaster; Hollywood Nightmare; In the Bone Fields; Poppy Tea and Hearty Pie; Reincarnated Rose; Smoke from a Flame; The Candlemaker's Daughter; The Guilt of Rosalino; The Mountain Air.

Bullying: In the Bone Fields.

Colonialism: Clockwork; Headmaster; Poppy Tea and Hearty Pie; The Guilt of Rosalino.

Death: Acheron's Lesson; Clockwork; Every Soul Will Taste Death; For Evermore; Headmaster; In the Bone Fields; On the Shoreline; Poppy Tea and Hearty Pie; Reincarnated Rose; Sight; Smoke from a Flame; The Candlemaker's Daughter; The Ghost of Creek Hill; The Guilt of Rosalino; The Mountain Air; The Veil and the Cord.

Drug abuse: What the Wind Brought with It.

Loss of a loved one: Acheron's Lesson; Every Soul Will Taste Death; In the Bone Fields; On the Shoreline; Reincarnated Rose; Smoke from a Flame; The Ghost of Creek Hill.

Manipulation: Clockwork; For Evermore; The Candlemaker's Daughter.

Mind control: For Evermore.

Misogyny: Clockwork; On the Shoreline; Poppy Tea and Hearty Pie; The Candlemaker's Daughter.

Pregnancy: Blood and the Bottomland.

Racism: Blood and the Bottomland; Clockwork; Headmaster; On the Shoreline; Poppy Tea and Hearty Pie; The Candlemaker's Daughter; The Guilt of Rosalino; The House by the Dell; Yama-Uba.

Sexual assault: Headmaster; The Mountain Air.

Slavery: Blood and the Bottomland; Poppy Tea and Hearty Pie.

Suicide: Headmaster; The Ghost of Creek Hill.

Torture: The Candlemaker's Daughter.

Violence: Headmaster; The Candlemaker's Daughter; The Mountain Air.

CONTENT WARNINGS BY STORY

Acheron's Lesson: Death; loss of a loved one.

Sight: Alcohol; death.

Clockwork: Blood, gore; colonialism; death; manipulation; misogyny; racism.

In the Bone Fields: Blood, gore; bullying; death; loss of a loved one.

The Mountain Air: Alcohol; blood, gore; death; sexual assault; violence.

We Have Always Lived in the Projects: None.

Headmaster: Abuse; blood, gore; colonialism; death; racism; sexual assault; suicide; violence.

The Repetition Tango: None.

Blood and the Bottomland: Abuse; alcohol; pregnancy; racism; slavery.

Smoke from a Flame: Blood, gore; death; loss of a loved one.

The Candlemaker's Daughter: Abuse; blood, gore; death; manipulation; misogyny; racism; torture; violence.

Reincarnated Rose: Blood, gore; death; loss of a loved one.

For Evermore: Blood, gore; death; manipulation; mind control.

Hollywood Nightmare: Blood, gore.

On the Shoreline: Death; loss of a loved one; misogyny; racism.

The Guilt of Rosalino: Blood, gore; colonialism; death; racism.

The House by the Dell: Racism.

The Veil and the Cord: Death.

Poppy Tea and Hearty Pie: Blood, gore; colonialism; death; misogyny; racism; slavery.

What the Wind Brought with It: Drug abuse.

Yama-uba: Racism.

Dream House: None.

The Ghost of Creek Hill: Death; loss of a loved one; suicide.

Every Soul Will Taste Death: Death; loss of a loved one.

— INTRODUCTION —

Representation matters.

Representation on the page and behind the page matters. I've always believed that it is crucial for authors to be as diverse as the characters we see represented. Marginalized authors still do not have the same opportunities as those from historically privileged backgrounds. If marginalized authors are published, they often find success only by writing literary works focused on racism, immigration, death, or other hot-button issues. However, what about the BIPOC (Black, Indigenous, and People of Color) authors who want to write genre stories? Romance or fantasy or Gothic horror?

Historically, Gothic has been extremely white-/male-/cis-centric. So, when conceptualizing this anthology, I couldn't help but wonder—what would a Gothic horror collection look like through a truly diverse lens?

In this collection I've gathered twenty-four stories that engage with "the Gothic" from authors under the broad umbrella of BIPOC. Each story accesses the Gothic from a particular racial standpoint specific to its author. Many of these authors are intersectional beyond BIPOC identity, whether in terms of religion, sexual orientation, disability, or otherwise. These are stories, reimagined or original, about haunted houses, intergenerational trauma, lost loves, and more. Spanning cultures, continents, and backgrounds, this anthology is one I envisaged as escapism in its purest form.

"Gothic horror reminds readers of one eternal truth: death will find us all. But instead of running away from this often-feared condition, gothic stories embrace it, and even reveal in it a sort of beauty. Death is not prejudiced, and the voices of BIPOC writers add breadth and depth to a subject that affects us all." —Daphne Dador

"Horror has always meant to challenge and speak in twisted metaphors of our real-world fears, but what do those fears look like outside the standard paradigm? That's why we need a diversity of perspectives: to feed the curiosity of both our own fears and the fears of others." —Desiree Alvarado

"A lot of gothic stories are tied to European roots, and diverse writers are needed to expand this scope. They bring in stories that underrepresented folks can actually see themselves in. With our anthology, we're reimagining the landscape, applying a myriad of experiences linked to identities that aren't usually in the spotlight."—Emily Hoang

"I used to think Gothic horror was a genre only white people wrote about white characters, but I now realize the thoughtful and symbolic nature of the genre: an amazing avenue for confronting the frustrations faced as a WOC and the history of my family/ heritage/culture." —Nisha Addleman

"For centuries, gothic horror has looked the same. Crumbling Victorian mansions sitting forlornly on forgotten patches of countryside, or precariously on foggy sea ledges. But while these mansions often manifest as characters in themselves, what they represent is universal. Diversity in gothic horror allows us to explore each quiet room and hallway tucked away in our own cultures. It changes the landscape, but not the sense of isolation and loneliness. It reminds us that while what haunts us may look different, the manifestation of our fears is one place we will never be alone." —C.M. Leyva

I thank all the writers for trusting me with their work. I hope this anthology haunts you long after you turn the final page.

Lauren T. Davila

— ACHERON'S LESSON —
by Adam Ma

The hardest part about carrying your body into the dinghy was navigating the darkness. My hands fumbled with every task. It was frustrating, but the night was as much a shroud as it was a hindrance, lending me the confidence to do what I wouldn't have been able to achieve were I exposed to light. It was far from the only stroke of luck I had been blessed with.

The docks were empty, and I knew this place well. The owner was a friend of the family. Their small metal boat had been left close to the water and was easy for me to push off the rack and into the river. I stole the motor from their shed, snapping the lock with a pair of bolt cutters I'd brought from home. I took gas and rope. Every step of the way I wondered what I would say when I got caught. I expected barking dogs, or searchlights, or a scream to startle me from my work. In the end, I was the one to break the silence as I brought the motor to life and steered the boat upriver.

I'm sure they've called the police by now, but it doesn't really matter. It's the middle of the night, and I'm hours away.

I have lived near these marshes my whole life, but at this moment I am an intruder. The low whirr of the engine cuts through the chirping and screeching of insects and forces the water to clap unevenly against the bow. I have only a vague sense of what direction I'm taking us in, but I cling tightly to the idea that I know what I'm doing. Any action right now feels better than how useless I felt standing alone in our home.

I wish I could talk to you, but I can't stand to see the way you are now, tightly wrapped in blankets and bungee cords. I don't remember how long it took to bundle you this way. The moment I look down at your cloth cocoon, questions begin to surface. I don't want questions infiltrating my thoughts at this moment. The most I can handle are facts.

You are dead, but a part of you is alive and is burning so vividly within me that I cannot understand your absence. Your heart is still, but I can still feel it beating heavily against my own. You can't speak, but I can still hear your voice so fresh in my mind. You passed quietly, alone, during your sleep. That's what's driven me to this place. There is no one to blame for your demise, and the very idea of that frustrates and infuriates me. Something horrible has happened to you, and there's nothing that can be done.

There are rules for approaching death, but those laws and traditions feel so far from me at this moment. Every time I look at you my mind wanders. I'm trying to recall stories my grandmother used to tell me. I'm not special. Everyone has a grandmother with stories. We grow up learning all kinds of useless superstitions. Some of it becomes a habit, like holding your breath when you pass a grave or keeping your feet off the cracks in the sidewalk. Other memories you recall only when you're living in the moment. When you're moving, you leave the broom behind. Sneezing with food in your mouth invites illness. Flowers bring good tidings, unless they bloom too early, or fade too soon, or if you find them tangled in vines, or if you find them too far under a willow's shade. Rules upon rules, all circumstantial.

As my grandmother would tell it, there is a power in running water. Places where the world of the living and the dead meet, where spirits can more easily flow from one realm to another. She claimed she saw her father once, smiling and thankful, days after he had passed. It was sunrise, and I remember the tone of her voice when she told me how terrified but thankful she was to be able to catch one last glimpse of him. She watched him step across the water, heading deep into the marsh, but, fearing the boundary between life and death, she chose to watch his spirit fade into shadow. When I asked why she didn't go to him, her answer was simple:

"It was just his spirit. His body was long gone. I had gone there to pay my respects, and he was only stopping by to say goodbye."

The story reached me in such vivid clarity. Once buried you'll be lost to me, and I can't bring myself to think that far ahead. Ten hours ago you were still with me. Fifteen hours ago we were making weekend plans. Our last meal at a shared table was over twenty hours ago. Every second pushes us further apart. How fast can a spirit travel? How long before the current takes you away, permanently, to a place I cannot follow? Your body rests at my feet, bundled and safe from the calculated, modern procedures that would strip you of your humanity and seal you from my touch. For now, I have saved you from that fate.

Together we travel upriver, to find that missing piece of you that's slipped away.

It is several hours into our journey, and I have not seen the sun. In its place is a moon that should have begun to fade into the distance. I am beginning to suspect that I have crossed a threshold and time has lost meaning. The celestial orb above is too close in the sky to be the moon I am familiar with, and it lights my way with a shimmering silver glow that radiates across a sky of pitch-black night. I cannot see the stars. They have been swallowed by this foreign body, and, without them, my way is lost.

A large part of me is relieved. My missing daylight and this lunar fallacy are something immediate that I can worry about. I don't have to pay attention to how still you rest. I slow my pace across the wetlands by dropping the motor to its lowest setting, gently pushing my stolen vessel across the water. My attention is turned in every direction except to what lies within my boat, and in searching for my destination I am met with oddities that strike both fear and comfort in my heart.

There's a stench in the air I can't pin down. These wetlands have always smelled terrible, but what clogs my nostrils doesn't feel green. It smells old. Noxious. I have a faint suspicion of the source, but as my boat cuts ahead in this endless mire, I find myself still tethered to science and reason. It is too soon for rot to bloom in you. I fold a shred of cloth over my mouth and continue guiding us ahead while my eyes scan for the source. I keep clear of whatever may be hiding within the reeds and steer ahead through open water, where I am confident this vessel can glide unhindered.

We drift in the glow of the silvery unmoon, and I catch a glimpse of something in the water. That glinting light gave it the appearance of stone, but the closer I approach the more clearly I can recognize the form of a woman. Her body is an iceberg, only partly afloat across the mire's surface. Her skin is pale and stained in hues of green from the water's grasp. The way her head is tilted across the surface, face half exposed to the air, reveals her state of being. Her eyes are open, unblinking, occasionally dipping below the chop of murky water disturbed by my presence. I keep myself from approaching any closer. Her presence feels wrong, though I am the intruder here. My vessel glides past, and I can see her moss-tinted pupils follow my path across the water. I closely watch her chest in search of the rise and fall of shallow breathing, but can find only a still lifelessness betrayed by her unblinking gaze. The woman is not the only body I see. There are more, some caught in the reeds or tangled in the roots of marsh trees like insects trapped in a wooden web. They are clothed, or naked, or mummified in bundles of fabric long drained of color by time and exposure to the water's eroding touch. I steer to avoid them where I can. Where I can't, I close my eyes and try to ignore the sound of their forms striking and scraping against the aluminum hull. The farther I press, the more these abandoned bodies begin to dot the landscape. I know in my heart they are loved ones whose partners did not have the resolve to venture further. It is a sign that I am on the right path, and I refuse to fail.

I press ahead as the small motor of my vessel sputters to a halt. I do not feel like it should have died so soon, but I am in no position to argue. I'm forced to draw up my oar and row as steadily as possible. I guide us ahead, parallel to the shore. Close enough that I could turn and find land, though truthfully I do not wish to step onto it. Something moves between the mud and the trees. I've seen pale corpses disappear between the reeds. Without the whirr of an engine filling the air around me I can hear the agonized snap of bark echo across the water as something beyond my sight pushes through the trees.

I am tired, but time seems meaningless in this place. Drifting across these waters where so many rest eternally, I hesitate to give myself any sort of reprieve. I keep my gaze focused ahead. An object in the distance is beginning to come into view. Two massive trees unlike any I have seen. They've grown up from the mire on an island of rock and mud, curling and twisting their entwined branches as though they've been shaped by an unseen hand. Their boughs bend apart and arch back together to form an uneven portal or gate. It is impossible to make out any more detail from where I row, but its existence in my path must mean I am close to the end.

The water here is thick with bodies. So many have been left behind. I think the current passes them along to the base of these trees, leaving them mockingly adrift along the muddy shore so close to their destination. I'm forced to paddle through them until the bow of my boat sinks into the muck, and my body freezes in place as I realize I have been deceived. Pale flesh from twisted limbs and gnarled fingers breach the mud, revealing the true composition of this island. It is rock, and flesh, and mud, and bone, and I do my best to ignore what I'm stepping on as I drag our stolen vessel to shore. You seem heavier now than you were at the start of this journey, and my burning arms struggle to pull your body up from the floor of the dinghy. It seems a sacrilege to let any part of you touch this grime-coated place, but I cannot avoid it. Your cloth-wrapped legs splash into the water's edge as I pull you onto this macabre shore.

I can inspect the gateway now. Both trees twist and intersect at their canopy to create an imperfect circle. Resting through the portal between the bark is a foggy haze my vision cannot penetrate. I do not know what to do, but dragging your body closer seems to be the only option I am left with.

I hear a man's voice before I realize how uncomfortably close he is to me. His unseen approach startles me into clutching your body to my breast as if you could protect me. I have never seen this stranger's face before, but his voice is gentle in a way I do not trust. It is like speaking to a dam. Every word is carefully selected to slip past his lips. He is draped in a dark cloak so clean it's as if the mire itself refused to touch him.

"What brings you here?" he asks.

I am hesitant to say. I no longer know what fables can be trusted, and I have a deep fear of any creature longing for my words.

"Is that your lover? Do you intend to bring them back to life?" He gestures to the gate ahead of us. Like a fool, I answer.

"Yes. How does it work?"

"Their soul could be returned if you bring them to it. Pass their body from one side to the other. Be careful not to touch it."

"Are you here to try and stop me?"

"I have no intention to step in your way. I am just a traveler, and it is only in good fortune that we are able to meet this evening. You must miss your companion greatly, to have carried them so far."

"I do."

"And what will you do if you pass their body through that gate and they return different from what you remember?"

The stranger is asking questions I never thought to consider, and I am instantly resentful of the implication. You had passed in your sleep. It was peaceful but unjust. I wasn't ready. You couldn't possibly have been ready to leave what we had built together. It seemed so obvious that you would want to return to me.

"That's not fair," I say.

"Death often changes the spirit."

"You don't know that."

"Death has already changed you."

My fingers grip the cloth that wraps you, and at this moment the weight of your body feels like a foreign thing. I don't want to speak of myself again. Instead, I ask, "Who did you lose that brought you here?"

"I've lost many. But no one, in particular, has brought me to this place. Unlike you, I am welcomed here as a denizen among the living and the dead. I've been here many times before. You are not the first mourner I have found carrying a loved one to this place between life and death."

"I am mourning," I admit. "I want more time. I wasn't ready for this."

"That's understandable."

"I feel so alone. I don't know how to make my heart stop hurting. I know this is supposed to be part of a process, but I don't want any part of it. I don't want to see my family. I don't want to hear that I'll be okay. I don't want to talk to anyone, or relive memories, or explain what things I'll need to keep, or donate, or decide to throw away. I don't want to throw anything away. I don't want to let go if it means being alone. Not after all this time of searching, and making mistakes, and building. We built everything together. I don't feel strong enough. I don't want to let any of it go."

"So you would bring them back because you're afraid of being alone."

"No. Yes. I'm not afraid. I just don't want to be like this. I don't want to feel this way. And I know everyone will tell me this won't last. I don't care. The thought of this sadness lasting for days or weeks makes me wish I was dead. I don't want this to be how our story ends."

"Sweet child." I hear a pity in the stranger's voice that wasn't there before. He moves closer to me, and under the silver light of the unmoon I can see this man is nothing human. There's no warmth in his complexion. He glides across the mud in a smooth motion that makes no more sound than a feather's fall. "The spirit is empowered by the history of those who touch our hearts. You have proved this by coming here, to where the living do not belong and the dead do not linger. You made the journey alone, but did you not draw from the strength of their enduring memory to reach this place?"

I look down at you. I am not ready to let go, but I know what I am holding onto isn't quite you anymore. I am scared to forget the components of you that have become such a tremendous part of me. Your laugh. Your warmth. All the small habits of yours that built their way into my life, for better or worse.

"I don't want to move on," I say.

"Then don't. Keep them with you. Take them wherever you go. Grip as tightly as you can, but do not carry them as you do now. Heed my wisdom. I am a creature that survives by drawing strength from others. You see me now as transcendent. In truth, much like you; I cannot survive alone. We rely on others to unlock the full potential of our spirit, but, in my experience, the weight of someone else's love should never be a burden to you."

The mire is silent beyond the beating of my heart. I see the bodies of those who were left behind in this place and lock eyes with one whose gaze rests pointed in my direction. I think of how forgotten they must feel. Abandoned.

"Can you help me?" I ask the stranger. Solemnly, he does.

Together we raise you back into the boat. The stranger helps me lay you down, and we gently push you back across the water. I cannot carry you any farther, and I dare not risk the thought of passing you through this gate only for you to return as something different. This compromise feels wrong, but to see you lying abandoned with these forgotten souls feels like a violation of our love. Instead, your body slowly drifts away. I have to remind myself it's just your body. You're not in it anymore. It isn't you. The real you is beyond the gate I cannot touch.

I ask the stranger where he is going next. He tells me he's traveling away from this place and lets me know that I am welcome to join him. I don't know what options I may have. I should be afraid, but as I stand in this moment, I feel numb to fear. There is something about the stranger that calms me. He seems immune to this kind of pain. Or perhaps he is so accustomed to experiencing it that he knows a secret to navigate grief that I cannot comprehend. Whatever his reason, I am envious. He says he is immortal, and I believe him. I am building the courage to ask how he manages to carry such a weight. He has found a way to live on with sorrow, and that is a gift I desire. I believe it's a gift he's willing to impart.

I take a final look at your resting place as you drift across the water, then together we leave the gate behind. I am longing to be by your side, but, despite a yearning to run and drown myself in this corpse-laden nexus, I force my gaze ahead. I know that with my death our love would only be forgotten. Instead, down this path, perhaps I can survive with the memory of you resting deep in my eternal heart.

— SIGHT —
by Shakira Savage

The Mississippi sun followed Eres everywhere he went Saturday morning, like he had a target on his back. Heat burned the nape of his neck as he trekked the Piggly Wiggly parking lot, his last stop before he could return home.

A handwritten sign on the automatic doors informed customers that, unfortunately, the air conditioner was out. With that in mind, he decided to keep this trip short. He threw things in his buggy as fast as he could remember them: a gallon of milk, leg and thigh quarters for supper later, collard greens, a loaf of bread. And beer. His cousin Tyler had drunk the last Natural Light.

"Eres?"

The aggressive spinning sounds of barrel fans in the store made it hard for Eres to hear. He could have sworn someone was calling him.

"Eres."

The voice seemed disembodied, until it grew closer, repeating his name over and over again. Eres peered over his shoulder and was startled by the appearance of his elderly neighbor, Lora.

"Sweet Eres, I always knew you were special."

Lora smiled gently, wrinkled cheeks rising high and nearly closing her eyes. She approached him, pulling her favorite purple cardigan closed.

"Hey there, Miss Lora."

As she drew closer, a sudden chill ran up Eres's body and raised goosebumps and hair on his arms. It was an odd sensation, considering the hot interior of the store on an even hotter day. He checked above him for a vent, in hopes that the air conditioner was back up and running. It wasn't.

"What are you doing out here?" asked Eres.

Lora didn't have a handbasket or buggy. She didn't seem to be shopping today.

"Oh, I'm just passing through."

"You, uh, need some help? I can give you a ride home." Lora chuckled to herself and started to walk away.

"I'm already headed that way," she continued, with her back turned toward Eres. "Gotta go home and rest. Yes Lord, home and rest."

Eres raised his brow. "Well, I'm cooking later. I'll bring you a plate, all right?"

By the time Eres called out, Lora was already rounding the corner, still muttering to herself, *"Home and rest... home and rest..."* Lora lived alone in a house built before Eres was a twinkle in his father's eye. He knew her mental health had been declining in recent years, and he checked on her very often. On cooler mornings, they'd sit on her porch and drink black coffee as she told stories of times past. She was still pretty sharp for an ageing woman, but he had never seen her like this before.

Eres found their interaction peculiar, but he put it to the back of his mind and finished shopping. All he could think about was going home and resting.

The road leading to his home was narrow and could barely accommodate two cars at once. By the afternoon, the road was so crowded he could hardly drive down it to reach his own residence. Vehicles were parked in various carports and ditches all along the way to Lora's small house.

Had Eres not seen the gleaming black hearse, he would have thought they were having a party. People from around town stood in Lora's yard, speaking quietly to one another. Tyler was among them, soaking up information. He threw his hand up at Eres as his truck pulled into the driveway.

Had something happened to Lora *that fast*?

Tyler jogged over and caught Eres as his feet hit the pavement. "What's going on? What happened?" Eres asked frantically. Tyler sighed and stuffed his hands in his pockets. "It's Miss Lora. She's gone."

"How?" Eres knitted his brow in confusion. "When?"

"They say her son found her about thirty minutes ago. EMT said she might have been dead since this morning, though."

"That's not...that's not right." Eres glanced over at the adjacent yard as the funeral home attendants rolled a covered stretcher out of the house. Lora's son followed with a tearful face, purple cardigan draped over his arms.

"Death ain't right, but it's fair. That's what Ma'Dear used to say anyway." Tyler wiped sweat from his brow and leaned on the hot truck. He quickly recoiled and rubbed the red spot already forming on his arm.

"I just saw her at the store," Eres started, lowering his voice to a whisper. His eyes were still focused on the covered body being roughly loaded into the hearse. "I just fucking saw her, Tyler. She even had on that damn sweater!"

"Are you sure?"

"I'm positive."

Eres noticed his hands shaking when he reached for his grocery bags. As they entered the house, he passed the case of beer to Tyler, fearing his tremors would break the glass bottles.

"You know what this means, don't you?"

Eres jumped at the slam of the hearse door. He busied himself with putting food away and refused to look back outside. He was afraid he might see Lora again, lingering among the living in her own front yard. And if not Lora, maybe one of the many apparitions that had haunted him through childhood.

Eres had his first sighting at the tender age of seven. It was Molly, a classmate with dishwater-brown pigtails and a dirty face who would never play with him during recess. She was struck by lightning one stormy spring.

The teachers tried to explain what had happened to Molly in the most gentle, age-appropriate way, but young Eres had an almost innate understanding of death. He understood what happened when fish went belly up and knew what it meant when buzzards circled roadkill. Molly was gone and she wasn't coming back.

Until the day she did.

Their first supernatural encounter was on the school playground, and this time she *did* want to play. It spooked the other kids to see Eres rolling a ball to no one and the ball rolling back. Among the first-grade tattletales and naysayers, Tyler was Eres's first believer. And even though he was unsure of where Molly actually was, he played along too. Based on his classmates' reactions, Eres decided it was best not to tell anyone else. Since then, it had been his and Tyler's little secret.

After Molly, there was Mister Jim, the man who sold fruit under the bridge. Then Pastor Jones, who preached tent revivals every summer. Miss Callie from the corner store. Soul after soul he'd spot wandering the earth and searching for home.

When lines became blurred and Eres struggled to tell the living from the dead, he tried his best to pray "the sight" away. He pleaded to any god that would listen and laid himself on many different altars. It took time and tears, but he learned to separate himself from it, from them, so that he could live a normal life.

It was becoming clear to Eres that normal days would soon be a thing of the past.

Tyler left Eres alone with his thoughts and peered through the screen door. The hearse with Lora's body had long pulled away, but people still gathered on the front porch to comfort one another. Behind him, Eres popped the top on a beer and let the cap sing as it hit the tile floor. He drank down nearly half the bottle with one gulp. Tyler took his cue and did the same. He let the silence settle between them before speaking again.

"Your gift, Eres. It's back."

Eres finished his last swig beer and rolled the glass bottle in his hands. He sighed and lifted his head to look outside to the yard next door. On the front porch, in her favorite rocker, Lora sat among her unsuspecting relatives. She pulled her purple cardigan closed and smiled, wrinkled cheeks rising high and almost closing her eyes. Lora waved. Eres reluctantly waved back.

"Yeah. I guess it is."

— CLOCKWORK —
by Desiree Rodriguez

I woke to the sound of a ticking clock.

I felt strangely cold, a shiver passing through me like creeping fingers. Intimate and unwelcomed. I reached out to my new husband, who slept peacefully next to me, the rise and fall of his chest a comfort to my panicked heart. The countryside, he had told me, would take time getting used to. It was naturally cold here, and I was just unused to the change in climate, he assured. I reached out, touching his hand; he was always so much warmer than I was. No matter where I went in the manor, a place that had yet to truly feel like home to me, I remained cold.

Even here, in our room, the walls felt unwelcoming. I was a stranger still to the embrace of Mejias Manor. Perhaps I was too young, as the servants whispered in tiny echoes that circled around me as I walked the halls. Perhaps I was too lowly, as the groundskeeper once complained to the winds. Perhaps the color of my skin, a rich brown, was too exotic for the high society of parliament, as one of my husband's assistant engineers has pondered over blueprints and streamed smoke. Perhaps, perhaps, perhaps.

Perhaps it would just take time, as my husband once said gently, pressing a kiss to my lips and quieting my fears. A kiss so sweet it had swept me off my feet during our courtship, a whirlwind fairy-tale that grasped me by the wrists and flew me above the sky. When he proposed, after months together, in secret on our own little island, the ocean itself was no match for the clarity and sparkle of the diamond he placed on my finger. I had been overwhelmed with joy, a joy that felt faraway now.

Displaced and stolen within the air of the manor. The doors locked at every corner, and all that was left was the sound of a ticking clock that I could not find, echoing throughout the seemingly endless halls.

In the light of day my husband was often away at his workshop, tinkering away at some new steam-powered project for the royal family. He never told me what he was working on, and when I asked, he would merely smile, rub his fingers over the knuckles of my hand, and ask me instead of my adjustment at our manor. I was given free reign of the grounds, which were large and encompassing. Almost their own world, an island of greenery, wood, metal, and large black gates encasing everything within.

The grand spectacle that was the Mejias Manor was at its center, surrounded by tiny towns of stables, servants' buildings and steam-powered machinery. A large forest wrapped around the back half of the manor grounds, and my husband's workshop was a lighthouse where the shore of the cultivated landscape ended and the unbridled forest began.

"Is there a new maid?" I asked my husband as we sat for evening tea. I didn't very much like tea, but my husband assured me I would get used to its bitter taste with time.

He looked at me, puzzled.

"I saw someone today, though only from afar." I had been walking along the crest of the manor's grounds and the beginning of the forest's edge.

I was beginning to feel so lonely here, the months passing by so slowly, and yet the seasons didn't seem to change with them. Was it always to be winter here? Was I always to feel cold when my husband was away from my arms?

I had found a strange sort of longing for the woods, an echo of a memory of a dream. I thought about the vastness of the forest before me, an ocean that would drown me if I were pulled in.

Nothing but vast, endless greenery, and the setting sun drifting beneath it. The forest had reminded me of our honeymoon. The bright greenness of the jungle around us, the humidity sticking to our skin. They hunted game on safari, burning red under their hats and laughing uproariously under a blazing sun. Though, no, no, that wasn't quite right, was it? Their honeymoon had been—

"Did you see her face?" he asked, interrupting my thoughts.

I shook my head.

I had only her silhouette—a floaty little thing. She had been dancing through the trees, and I had only just caught a glimpse of her hair, the curve of her cheek, and the shine of her shoes. It was almost as though she had no face at all, and yet I couldn't remove my eyes from her. Something had captivated me about her, a sense of elegance, a charismatic quality to her form.

"Then you probably imagined it, darling. The fog around here, it gets quite thick during the winter, plays tricks on the mind, that it does." He patted my hand and we shared a smile.

Yes, of course, she was just a specter in the fog. Nothing more. The servants at the manor would not speak to me unless I spoke directly to them, and, even then, they would not look me in the eye. It was strange and disorienting. The times our eyes did meet, they were cold, as cold as the winds that blew through the black gates of Mejias Manor itself. A distant sort of cold, detached and a bit frightening. It was as though I was a misplacement, a being not meant to be there at all. If it was hatred, I could perhaps understand.

Before my husband came to me, I was nothing. I had no one. A life not worth remembering at all. He stole my heart away with his smile and gentle eyes. I was probably of lower class than them, yet here I was now, a Lady. Did they believe me to be arrogant? And yet, I found myself more jealous of them, longing to be included, or offered a friendly smile. My husband was always away, off in the distance, either at his workshop or gone on business. We had spent so much time together on that faraway island of our romance that it felt like a dream now. Blurred around the edges, the memory kept me company in the sprawling hallways. Our island romance, yes. We had our honeymoon there as well, did we not? A beautiful ocean, the white sands, a small village—

I could hear the ticking clock again.

My feet moved to follow the sound, chasing it as a moth does flame. Searching for warmth on a cold winter's night, I flew. And saw her again.

The specter.

My lonely, lovely specter.

She was dancing a waltz on the ballroom floor, elegant, beautiful, and yet each step cried out with a deep sadness. Despair radiated off the glint of the red of her ball gown. Fragile, breakable, and secret.

She looked at me, with no eyes, no mouth, no discernible features, face smooth like marble, when her face began to crack where her mouth should be. Jagged shards fell from her marble face like puzzle pieces to the floor. She took a step toward me and screamed.

I woke to the sound of a ticking clock. My husband looked down at me with a concerned furrow to his brow, one of his hands gently rubbing the skin on the back of my neck.

I lifted my hand to gently rub the crease in his face away. He should never look so distressed; he was my heart, my comfort. His touch on my neck, his other hand pressed against my chest where my heart beat, kept me stable and warm. He was so very warm.

"What happened?"

"I saw her again," I said.

He sighed. "Darling, we've been through this."

We had, and each time since the first time he assured me she was nothing but a trick of the wind, a flash of smoke, a shadow lining the hallways. Yet, how many times could a shadow merely be a shadow before it became a companion? My faceless, tragic, lovely companion.

"But I did see her," I said again.

We didn't often disagree; in fact, before my specter appeared we had never so much as had an argument. My husband was so attentive, how could I be anything less? He was so loving, so worldly, and I was so lucky to have his heart for myself.

For a moment my husband pressed his thin lips together, and then squeezed the back of my neck with gentle pressure. "Let's get you to bed. We'll fix this in the morning."

I nodded, feeling cold in my joints, and an even deeper cold had settled into my bones. Suddenly, everything ached, and it was difficult to move. The last thing I heard was the echoing sound of a ticking clock.

I told my husband in the following weeks how much better I was feeling. In a way I was. My body seemed lighter. My joints moved with a renewed smoothness as I played the piano at my husband's request one night. My laugh lifted out of my chest freely and I soaked up each smile he bestowed upon me.

"You are my heart," I had said. "You are the reason my heart beats each day and each night." He kissed me then and I felt his love. A deep, all-encompassing feeling, drowning me in its depths and carrying me further and further into the warmth of his smile, his eyes, his hands. Each wrinkle on his face belonged to me, each cut or callus on his palms belonged to me, and each beat of his heart was mine to covet. In each way that he was mine, I was also his.

So yes, in many ways I was feeling better. And yet, it was the first lie I had ever told my husband. For I had not stopped seeing my specter, nor had the sound of my ever-echoing clock abandoned my footsteps.

I felt my mind escaping me. Was the isolation of the manor stealing away my sanity day by day? I was too afraid to voice this thought to my husband, too afraid of losing him to my own growing sense of madness.

My husband would say, "You seem agitated, darling." And with a gentle touch of his hand on the back of my neck I would feel better. He could cradle me to his chest, and I would bask in the warmth of his body, the sound of his beating heart lulling me into a deep sleep. "Do not worry," he would whisper, "we shall fix this too."

When I would wake, my body felt lighter, but my memories seemed hazier than ever. The soft ticking of a clock wailed its way underneath my door, pulling me from my marriage bed. My husband had left before the sun rose, going to the city for business. I left the warmth of the bed, barefoot, and stepped into the hardwood hallways of Mejias Manor.

My husband came and went, but I could never recall a time when I too had left the grounds. I was always tittering on the borders of the woods, gazing at the black gates, which had begun to look like bars. Or following the sounds of a ticking clock, knowing they'd lead me to my ghostly companion.

I spotted the flutter of her dress, the sunlight hitting its edge and making the whiteness gleam like crystal, contrasting with the smooth brown marble of her skin. This time, she was barefoot as I followed her, her rambunctious curls bouncing as she ran ahead of me. She disappeared through a door—the library.

I entered, wary.

Was she simply my imagination? But no, I had seen her, over and over. She chased my steps and dodged my eyes, hiding her identity. Revealing herself only in glimpsed, hazy shadows, a dream of a memory before me.

I walked through the vast bookshelves, unsure of what exactly I was looking for, when I spotted a book on the ground. I flipped through its pages, some yellowed with time, some ripped from the seams of their binding altogether. It appeared to be a recounting of the Mejias Manor construction, along with some family history. A woman named Verita had written about her family's conquest of an island nation in the far west. Of a primitive people, of how the Mejias family—her husband's family—had provided them with new life, a civilization. Her nephew, Christopher, had even taken one as his wife, much to the family's shared dismay. Christopher, my husband's given name.

The ticking clock grew louder, as if its hands were reaching out to wrap around my throat. Why wouldn't the clock of the manor stop hounding my steps like a wolf, starving and crazed? Was this Christopher my Christopher? But I had never heard of an Aunt Verita before, nor a previous wife. Christopher was alone in this world, like I was. That was why we were meant for each other, two lone beings standing against the tides. Yet there was something in the corner of my mind, a glint of rainwater drifting down a windowpane, too quick to catch yet.

A flash of white, a flicker of shadow; my specter was beckoning me to follow once more.

Outside we walked, me following the sad fluttering of the woman's white dress, knowing that with each step there would be truth at the end of this path. A truth I wasn't sure I wanted to know.

She led me to my husband's workshop. I crept inside. It was empty. He must have taken his assistants with him to the city. I glanced about, but my tragic specter was nowhere to be found.

Quietly I searched my husband's office, picking through the secrets of his domain. There were blueprints and, though I did not understand them fully, they seemed to depict the construction of a mechanical heart made from clockwork and steam.

Then I saw it; sitting on his desk was the picture of a woman—me.

Yet, she wasn't me. She had the shape of my face, but her nose was wider, her eye-shape ever so hooded, more so than mine. She was a version of me, less perfect, but so much more beautiful. More real. She must have had a name, a beautiful name, a name erased and purposely obscured.

A door creaked open, but I could not hear it above the sound of the ticking clock. I pressed a hand to my chest, right above my heart.

"Welcome home, my husband."

He stood before me, imposing in a way that was both familiar and strange to me. Absently, or perhaps protectively, I covered the back of my neck with my hand.

"Why are you here?"

"Why did you not tell me about her?" I asked, holding up the picture of the woman, my ghost, my true companion throughout this endless winter.

He sighed. "I hadn't meant for you to find out this way. I didn't want you to feel..." He took a step toward me, holding open his arms. "Your adjustment has been so difficult, my darling. I didn't want to burden you with the fact I had a previous wife."

"What happened to her?" Though inside the dream, the memory, I already knew the answer.

"She died. Wandered off into the woods one winter's night. When we found her the next morning she had passed."

She had died cold, running through the woods toward the black gates of Mejias Manor.

"Yes, yes, you did lose her." I stared at the picture in my hands. Even now, he lied. "But it was because she ran away from you; the Lady Yuisa, former wife of Lord Christopher Mejias."

He stood, silent, this man I no longer knew.

"You met on an island, the island your family sought to conquer. You stole her from her village." I could feel tears well up in my eyes at the recollection. The beautiful memories of white sands, and a gleaming ocean. Not memories of a wondrous honeymoon, a fairy-tale romance, but memories of a *home*.

He stepped toward me once more, arms still open as if welcoming me to run into them. Insanely, the temptation was still there, even after the truth of my heart had been revealed to me. Sitting there on his desk outlining the truth in black ink.

"Now, darling," he said, but I didn't want to hear his voice any longer.

"You stole Yuisa away." My voice began to tremble. "You stole *me* away!"

I was Yuisa, or was once. Now I was merely a clockwork puppet. I pressed my fist to my ticking heart. Beneath my skin was nothing but gears, wires, wheels, and barrels, making up my mechanical insides. I was a mechanical dream in the shape of a person, made from steam and clockwork.

"I saved her. I saved Yuisa from a meaningless life as a dirty island peasant."

"You killed her soul and called yourself a savior, and when she died you replaced her with me."

"I thought we fixed this," he said to himself frustrated, as if I wasn't even there. And I wasn't. Not truly. I was a shadow, a memory, a false image created by a man who loved an idol instead of a woman. He had turned away, looking at his walls of blueprints and diagrams and mechanisms. His hand pressed to his chin, pondering over a difficult equation, the equation of how to fix me. How to make a better clockwork model, one that was an improved version of Yuisa. One more palatable to his society, with blue eyes, lighter hair, a smaller nose but no less exotic. A puppet wife, who wouldn't run away, who wouldn't challenge or condemn him. A clockwork woman he could tinker away at and rebuild whenever he wanted, *how*ever he wanted.

I took a breath and closed my eyes. I could see those shores again, clearer than before. The shores of my island home, the white sands and mountains that my feet once knew so well. The warmth of the air sticking to my skin. A woman, my mother, calling my name over the salt-scented air.

"Maybe you are right, my husband. You can fix me, can't you?" I said, opening my eyes to peer at the reality before me.

He walked closer and gently placed his hands on my shoulders. His fingers slowly creeping toward the back of my neck. "Of course, my love, I just need time and I can get it right. I can get *you* right."

I placed a hand on his chest and smiled. "My heart was meant to be yours." Every gear, every wire, every cog that was within me was built by his hands. "And your heart..."

I pushed through his chest; flesh and bone alike gave way to the strength of my grip. Maybe this newfound strength came from the clockwork gears of my body, the machine parts, clicking and turning, that kept me alive. Or maybe it came from the freeing feeling of truth, of the strength found in knowing my own name.

"...is meant to be mine."

He gurgled, a wet, grotesque sound, as this man, my husband, my captor, my darling, my tormentor, stared at me, at the heart that I held in my hand.

I crushed it, and, finally, the ticking of my own stopped. At peace, and warm.

— IN THE BONE FIELDS —
by Anuja Varghese

T he farm where Devika and Revika were born could not be found on any map. It existed—real as its broken-down boards and its long-abandoned barn, groaning against the howling winds sent forth from Lake Eerie to batter the field and rattle the rusty silo. Yet the narrow road on which it sat veered off from the highway like a wayward gravel snake seeking to shed its skin in private. It was an hour's drive, at least, from the nearest ghosts of civilization, and double that in the winter when drifts of snow made the access road virtually impassable.

The farm hadn't always been in such a sorry state of disrepair. Devika and Revika's grandfather, one Mohan Chakraborty, had first arrived from Pondicherry in 1969, one of hundreds of migrant workers summoned from the subcontinent to work the fields of a barren country turned fruitful for a few blessed months each year. Back then, the barn, and the house in its shadow, had been bright red, shining at the edge of an expanse of green surrounded by a white fence. Along with the corn, the melons, the pumpkins, and the potatoes that Mohan planted in the stingy ground, he nurtured a budding romance with the farm owner's fair-haired daughter. They were married, and the farm passed into the young couple's care. They tried for many years to have a child with no luck, until, one day, while she was weeping in the grass, the field whispered a solution into Devika and Revika's grandmother's ears. She listened, and, though she got what she desired, the farmhouse got something too.

Devika and Revika's mother proved to be a flighty creature who left the farm as soon as she could and returned round, with twin girls in her belly. There was no record of her death, nor her mother's before her. There were no witnesses, save a cracked mirror and the moon, to a terrified young woman and her father praying to all the gods they knew, as two tiny, blue babies lay in their arms, cold and silent. Who can say what deal was struck so that, in the morning, four dark eyes opened and the house was filled with the cries of newborns, alive and well, wailing their motherless woe at the remnants of the winter storm outside.

In his heart, Mohan knew that his daughter should have been returned to ash, the ash released into water, into air. But the fields had called her, as they had called her mother before, had compelled him to bury their bodies, half rotted by the time the earth was soft enough to open, and he had obeyed. Two gravestones marked their resting place, the only small patch of field he dutifully tended and cleared of brush, the rest of the land falling to neglect and decay. He shut up the room of the house where the thing nobody saw had happened and set about raising the twins, Devika and Revika, as best he could.

They grew as girls will if left unchecked, curious and bold, two bright flowers reaching for the sun. In appearance they were exactly alike, but in nature they could not have been more different. Devika took after her grandmother, capable and quick, born with a love of the farm in her bones. Revika, on the other hand, was willful and wild, resentful of the ramshackle farm that was not even worthy of its own marker on the map. They took a bus to and from the little country school in the nearest little town that the highway passed, except when it snowed and the single side-winding road to the farm was lost. Eager though they were to be invited to birthday parties and into town for movies and milkshakes, children have a sense for strangeness, and they had few real friends. The distance others kept drove Devika closer to the land, and she grew determined to restore the farm to its former glory. By contrast, Revika grew restless and began to dream of adventures somewhere far away. The farm, for its part, heard the yearning of their young hearts, and, after many years dormant, decided to deliver them a gift.

It began during the summer the girls turned twelve. The days were long, and the girls became bored with books and bike riding and watching their grandfather mutter his grievances at gravestones that were unmoved by his grief. Devika had availed herself of a box of tools found rusting in the barn and roamed the house, looking for things to fix. Revika followed, sullen, not looking for anything at all, other than her chance to escape. Perhaps that's why the farmhouse chose to make its magic known to her first.

"Devi, did you hear that?"

Devika looked up from her tinkering with the broken banister at the top of the stairs. She cocked her head and listened, then rolled her eyes and went back to her work.

Revika followed the sound, a soft sort of scraping, to the end of the hallway, to the door that had always been locked. The knob turned smoothly beneath her palm and the door swung open, inviting her into the musty space of a bedroom draped in heavy sheets and coated from corner to corner in a thick layer of dust. Devika appeared behind her, peering over her shoulder.

"How'd you get the door open?" she asked.

"I didn't," Revika replied, already making her way into the room.

Devika hesitated. "Are you sure we should be in here?" The room felt removed from the rest of the house, darker than it should have been, despite its shuttered windows, in the middle of the day. A sheet covering a chest of drawers fluttered, although there was no breeze, and they both heard again the soft scrape of a drawer opening, a gentle thud as it closed again.

"That's weird," Devika said, pushing past her sister to pull the sheet away. They watched as the top drawer slid open and remained that way. An invitation.

Devika looked inside the drawer, which was empty, then got on her hands and knees to check if either the floor or the chest itself was slanted. Meanwhile, Revika pulled sheets free of a writing desk, a wooden chair, and an oval mirror attached to the chest of drawers. She traced her name in the dust on the mirror's surface, revealing as she did so the cracks that spiraled out from its center, like a spider web woven into glass.

"Do you think this was our mom's room?" Revika asked. They knew almost nothing of their mother, other than where she was buried, out in the field. Revika turned, wide-eyed. "Do you think this is where she died? Do you think this room is haunted?"

Devika stood, hands behind her back, and nodded. "I think it's definitely haunted," she whispered, "...by rats!" Gleefully, she thrust forward a recently dead rat discovered beneath the chest of drawers, dangling the rodent's corpse in Revika's face. Revika shrieked and stumbled backward, falling onto the bed and raising another cloud of dust. Drowned out by Devika's cackling and Revika's complaints, neither of them felt the farm—the barn and the house and the fence and the field—shudder with wanting, barely holding its hunger at bay. But it was a patient thing. It could wait.

Devika tossed the rat into the open drawer and held up in her other hand a small bit of curved wood, flat on the bottom, jagged on top. "It's not haunted, idiot. It's the '90s, not the 1800s or whenever ghosts are from," she said. "The chest is missing a foot, see? That's why the drawer won't stay shut." She dropped the broken piece into the drawer for safekeeping and slammed it closed. "I bet I can fix it. I just need to find some glue. Now, let's get out of here before we get caught!"

Devika ran down the stairs, buzzing with the excitement of finding a secret room. Its oddness was only due to it being unused, and, even if the furniture was useless, a secret was a special thing to have. A gift.

Revika stood to follow her sister, but movement in the mirror caught her eye and she turned to look. A flash of dark hair, familiar eyes, a gaping mouth; half woman, half bone. Revika frowned and looked again and saw that it was only her own reflection, fragmented by cracks. She left the room, closing the door behind her. The glue was forgotten when dinner was served, and it was only the next morning, when their grandfather was tending the graves and the girls could return to the room unnoticed, that they heard the scratching from inside the drawer. Devika pulled it open and a rat scampered out, skittering over the drawer's edge, before tumbling to the ground and escaping out the door.

"I thought that thing was dead!" Revika exclaimed.

Devika closed the drawer. "I guess it wasn't," she said, even though she knew that it was. That it had been and now was not. The broken leg too was gone, and Devika didn't need to check to know that it was in its rightful place, made whole, or something like it.

"When did you fix the leg?" Revika asked.

Maybe it was because she had been placed in the drawer first on the night she and Revika were born, and died, and were born again (or something like it), that Devika understood the farm for what it was. She looked in the mirror and made with it a pact. "This morning," she replied. "Before you woke up."

So, they set about tidying the space, and, for a while, delighted in the shared deception of a room that was meant to be locked, but had opened, somehow, just for them. They shared their summer secrets there, kept their treasures hidden there, but, before she went to bed each night, Devika always made sure to check the top drawer for anything her sister might have left behind. She wanted no cause to tempt the house into transformations that could not be explained.

At summer's end, they went back to school, and the room, being just a room in a dilapidated house on a long-dead farm, was no longer of interest to Revika. The room became Devika's alone, and she used it to make the house whole. Into the drawer went the banister's broken spindles. In went bits of faded red board, peeling off from the slowly rotting barn. In went a pair of baby bunnies, mangled by the mower's blades. In went soil and seeds and bug-infested vegetables and bird-eaten fruit. And everything that went in came out the next morning something new, something better. For all these small favors, the house asked nothing in return. It was biding its time, watching the girls ripen.

Years passed and Devika and Revika took the bus to the little high school in the nearest little town. Revika made new friends, age and beauty and distance from the farm all helping her blossom into someone new, someone better. The boy who washed dishes at the town's only restaurant was named Miguel and, when he called Revika on the phone to sing to her in Spanish, Revika felt like she was falling in love. Devika too listened to Miguel's recorded songs, and imagined him smiling his dimpled smile at her, and felt too like she was falling in love. But her secret made her doubly suspicious, doubly strange, and Miguel never saw her, never knew how she felt, a weed left to wither in a sunflower's shadow. She was bound to the farm, but she was lonely and wanted what her sister had.

One day, when fog rolled in thick over the field and spring held the farm in its damp grasp, Devika had finished her planting and was returning to the house when she met Revika, skipping down the porch steps. A pick-up truck idled in the driveway, filled with Revika's friends, ready to head into town. Devika took a deep breath and mustered the courage to call after her: "Hey, can I come with you?"

Revika looked back at her sister, startled. They spoke little these days, and Revika assumed her sister was content playing farmer, hiding in her secret room. She heard her friends snickering in the truck and she hesitated. "Sure," she said, "Go get changed. We'll wait for you."

Devika hurried into the house and stripped off her overalls and boots. She changed into jeans, then a dress, then back into jeans, and, as an afterthought, dabbed a drop of Revika's perfume on her wrists, behind her ears. Miguel might like that. From outside, she heard the truck's engine revving. "Wait!" she cried and rushed down the stairs, running out the door just in time to see the truck pulling away. The horn honked and the boys in the back of the truck laughed as she ran after them.

In a moment of desperation, Devika grabbed her old bike from the side of the house and hurtled forward as fast as she could. But rain had made the road slick with mud, and Devika was only halfway to the highway before her wheels slid out from under her, sending her flying into the dirt. Her face hit hard gravel, and she felt a tooth jar loose as her mouth filled with iron. She spat the tooth into her hand and picked herself up, bloody and muddy and bruised. "Wait," she whispered again, but the truck was long gone.

When Revika returned later that night, she shrugged her shoulders as teenage girls will do, and said, "Relax, Devi. It was just a joke."

That night, Devika crept into her sister's room, and, while she slept, took a pair of scissors to her thick plait of long, lush hair.

It was just a joke, she thought she might say, smug in the face of Revika's ruined vanity. Yet, holding her sister's hair in her hand, Devika felt none of the satisfaction she imagined the act would bring; rather, she felt vaguely horrified at what she had done. She quickly put both lost tooth and lopped-off braid in the drawer and went to sleep, content in the knowledge that both things could be fixed and no one need be the wiser.

Come morning, two things were true: one was that Devika's tooth had indeed grown back out of the soft hole in her mouth from which it had been wrenched—but it had been given back to her sideways, protruding from her lower gum at an odd angle. The second was that Revika's hair had grown back too, but not as it was. Not as it should have been. Her blood-curdling screams brought Devika and their grandfather rushing to her bedroom, where they both stared in horror at the matted ropes of mold-green hair that snaked around Revika's body. She clawed at her scalp and a few maggots fell out, hundreds more still burrowing into the putrid nest sprouting from her head.

"I don't understand," Devika said, but, even as she said it, the answer was clear. The hair she had cut had not been tarnished or broken; it had been midnight black and lustrous, the picture of good health. Hunger had begun to gnaw at the house's patience, and with the morsel of hair it had been fed, laced with jealousy and spite, it knew how to do only one thing.

Devika grabbed her sister's hand and pulled her down the hallway to their secret room. She picked up the scissors and hacked at the hair, which seemed to move with a will of its own, the reeking seaweed-like strands winding around Revika's neck. It grew back as fast as Devika cut it off, something stronger every time, something new. The shutters swung suddenly open and the top drawer slid forward and slammed shut, over and over, punctuating Revika's screams. Their grandfather stood in the doorway of the room he had locked so many years ago and stared at the chest of drawers, at the bed, at the mirror and the face he saw within it. A face that was not his own. "What have you done?" he moaned, and it cannot be said if he asked the question of Devika or of the house itself.

Revika turned wild eyes on her twin, clutching at the hair that strangled her, as her skin crawled with creeping things, falling from her head onto her shoulders, slinking along the back of her neck and into the open holes of her ears. "You did this," she said, and she knew it to be true, just as she knew then why the room had opened to her years ago, and why it would never let her leave again. She saw now what her grandfather saw—her mother's face in the mirror, contorted in a hideous grin. Somewhere behind her, another woman beckoned with fingers made of bone, making new cracks in the glass the closer to its surface she came. Revika backed away, a Medusa gone mad, but there was nowhere to go, and the hair had wound itself so tightly around her neck that she could not even draw breath enough to scream.

"Revika, stop!" Devika cried, reaching out for her, as she stood with her back to the open window and the grey sky, but it was too late. They locked eyes in a moment of shared terror, and then, as if shoved by an invisible hand, Revika tumbled backward and hit the ground with the sickening crack of skull splintering on stone.

The room went quiet. Devika and her grandfather looked down at the broken body seeping blood into the earth. Devika looked sideways at the chest of drawers. "I can fix this," she said.

"No," her grandfather answered. "No more. We will bury her. In the field. Where she belongs. Then we must lock up this room and never open it again." And so it was done. They locked up the room and buried the key with Revika's bones, at the edge of the field, now bursting again with corn and melons, with pumpkins and potatoes and all the goodness the land could provide. Two graves became three and, as Devika sat weeping in the grass, the field, sleepy and well-fed at last, whispered how she might be someone different, someone new. Devika listened, and although she got the thing she wanted, she knew that someday, the farm would wake and want something in return.

Years later, the Chakraborty Farm had yet another record harvest and the little newspaper in the nearest little town sent a reporter with a camera to cover the story. He photographed the farm owner and her husband in front of their bright red barn and gleaming steel silo, enclosed by a white fence. He interviewed their crew of migrant workers and quoted the owner as saying she was proud to have brought the family farm full circle. Finally, he asked her, "Tell me, Ms. Chakraborty, after your sister's tragic death, wasn't it hard for you to stay here?"

She clasped her husband's hand and said, "Restoring this farm was my sister Devika's dream. Now it is our life's work—Miguel's and mine—to keep her memory alive. We hope this farm will stay in our family for generations to come."

The reporter asked the couple to stand just so and smile, and they did—the man all dimples and charm, the woman a beauty, despite one tooth protruding most unnaturally from her mouth. Upstairs, their daughter, a girl of twelve, rolled her eyes at the spectacle and dreamed of a life far away from the farm. Beyond the house, the field rumbled with hunger, and, at the end of the hallway, a drawer scraped open, then closed with a gentle thud. The girl lifted her head and listened. Then she followed the sound.

— THE MOUNTAIN AIR —
by Nisha Addleman

E va was, by all accounts, adorable. Her small build and curly brown hair so often laced with flowers were only complemented by large, brown eyes and a soft voice.

Leon—her lover, as she called him—was a perfect pairing for her, standing a whole head taller, with a dazzling smile that turned heads everywhere they went.

They were inseparable, and for the best possible reason: being utterly and completely perfect for each other. When Eva wanted quiet, Leon wanted quiet. When Eva was bored, Leon was bored. When Eva was feeling handsy, Leon was also feeling handsy.

Eva leaned out the car window, catching snowflakes in her hair and lashes, as they rambled up the quiet mountain road to their long-overdue vacation.

"Careful." Leon rested a hand on her thigh and gave a gentle squeeze.

"You're not going fast." She grinned at him.

With a soft chuckle, he replied: "Because you're leaning out, love."

She ducked back in and gave him a peck on the cheek, then rolled up the window and snuggled beneath his heavy wool coat. Urging the car faster now Eva was safe inside, he smiled at her. "You wouldn't be so cold if you weren't leaning out all the time." She stuck her tongue out. "I like leaning out. And I like stealing your jackets. I don't see a problem with either."

"Neither do I, so long as your head doesn't get taken off by a tree." As he spoke, they sped past a branch that certainly would have taken her head off.

She slipped her hand around his and leaned her head against the window. Catching snowflakes on her tongue could wait until they were at the cabin.

Their vacation abode was atop a steep mountain. According to Eva's guidebook, ravines cut through the landscape, but she couldn't see them through the thicket of pines weighed down by blankets of snow. It was beautiful regardless, and the air was supposed to be better. Visitors always came out feeling happier and lighter. Leon said it was altitude sickness, but Eva liked to believe it was something else.

Something special.

She inhaled, feeling like she could get out and dance in the snow. That wasn't particular to the air—snow always made her feel like that.

"Look!" Leon pointed down the road, where the wooden building was coming into view.

Two cabins sat near each other, their dirt driveways forking apart for privacy. Their own rental loomed in front of them, while the other only peeked through the trees.

"Do you think there's anyone there?" She pressed her hands to the glass.

"I don't know." Leon slowed as he reached the driveway and peered up the other. "Maybe we'll find out."

Eva nodded back at him, and he turned onto the driveway, winding up the hillside to their cabin tucked in the thicket.

The cabin's interior was massive and gorgeous—an open floor plan bookended by large staircases. In the middle was a large sitting room, trapped in a forgotten era with floral couches, a fireplace and an old radio, which Leon was busy trying to understand while Eva explored.

"Do you think there's a phone?" Eva walked up the stairs, trailing her fingers along wooden railings.

Leon only let out a hum, too absorbed in the radio, which Eva was beginning to suspect was broken.

She went through the first door, finding a master bedroom with a spacious balcony overlooking the front door. Attached to the bedroom was a large bathroom. Eva giggled with delight at the huge bathtub—big enough for two, she noted. Leon would surely enjoy that after the long drive.

She wandered onto the balcony, where she could peek over the trees and see ravines ravaging the landscape, just as the guidebook said. Drawing in a deep breath, a smile slipped across her lips unbidden; she felt she could fly.

Apart from the lone road cutting through the trees—and the other cabin barely in sight—there was nothing for miles.

"Hello!" a man called.

She looked down the driveway to see a couple walking up, about the same age as her and Leon.

"Hello!" She waved to him, leaning over the railing. "Are you staying over there?" She pointed toward the other cabin.

"We are!" The man grinned. "I'm Victor. This is Hannah!" He motioned to the smiling woman beside him.

"I'm Eva!" Eva held up a finger, motioning for them to wait. "Let me get Leon and we'll come out front."

Leon was about to head out the front door when Eva skipped down the stairs. "Who is it?" He reached for the doorknob.

"Our neighbors!" Eva caught his elbow and followed him out.

"You must be Leon!" Victor held out his hand and introduced himself and Hannah.

"Are you two on vacation?" Eva squeezed Leon's arm and leaned in, curious about her new neighbors.

"Yes! We've been here a week. It's wonderful." Hannah let out a delighted giggle.

Victor nodded down at her, letting out his own laugh. Their eyes were wide and their cheeks flushed. Eva wondered if they were drunk, though she couldn't blame them. This was the perfect place to drink too much and get too cozy.

Leon flashed his dazzling grin. "Great! We should get dinner together one day."

"Oh yes!" Hannah caught Victor's arm. "Wouldn't that be nice?"

"Lovely!" Victor nodded.

The couple giggled again, and this time Eva was certain they weren't sober.

Victor squeezed Hannah's hand. "Why don't we let you two settle in. Wander over whenever you'd like! There's a path there linking our cabins."

Eva saw the narrow clearing between the trees and clapped. "Wonderful! We'll stop by soon, then, won't we?"

"Yes, we will!" Leon agreed.

Victor's smile widened, giving away his excitement. "Don't hesitate. We only have each other out here, so if you need anything, we're just next door."

With that, Victor turned, tugging Hannah along as she waved goodbye. The two fell into a fit of laughter again, clutching each other and trying to stifle their joy as they disappeared between the trees.

"Drunk?" Eva looked up at Leon.

"Most certainly." He closed his eyes and heaved a breath. "Or it's just something in the mountain air."

That evening, as Eva ran a bath, Leon smoked on the balcony and watched puffy, grey clouds meander past the stars. She hadn't told him she wanted him to join her yet, but, being the doting lover he was, he set up the now fixed radio—he had taken the entire thing apart and put it back together in an hour—and helped her light candles.

"Leon." Eva stuck her head out and smiled at him. "Come here."

He raised an eyebrow, looking over her as she let her robe drop from her shoulders, and batted her lashes.

"Oh." He stubbed out his cigarette in an ashtray and sauntered up to her. "What's this?"

"The tub. It's so big."

He let out a hum and cocked his head to the side. "And you're too small?"

She nodded, puffing out her lower lip and tracing one finger down his chest.

There was no need for flirting. They had been together for years and he could tell what she wanted from the way her eyes flicked across his body, but they played the part of coy lovers anyway, still finding a thrill in it after all this time.

"Then I must join you." He pulled her to the bathroom, popping open the buttons on his shirt, kicking off his shoes, throwing off everything until they were at the edge of the tub and he could help her out of her robe.

He sank into the water, letting out a sigh and dropping his head back. "This is nice."

She lowered herself in front of him, leaning back against his chest and tracing patterns in the water with her fingertips. "This is perfect."

He let out a hum as if agreeing in a tired sort of way. After driving for hours, he was surely exhausted. Before he could drift to sleep—as he was wont to do in warm baths—she twisted around and drew him in.

He pressed his lips to the base of her throat; her head dropped back, and she let out a soft sigh, his hands meandering across her body.

He had just started drawing more moans from her when they were interrupted by a distant scream.

Eva jerked upright, and Leon snapped his attention to the half-open window.

"What's going on?" Eva clutched his shoulders.

"It sounds like they're fighting." He braced one hand against the edge of the tub as if ready to leap out.

Eva gnawed on her lip, and they listened. The fighting grew worse. Louder. Angrier.

Then it stopped.

Eva looked at Leon, and Leon looked at Eva. Should they do something?

Laughter erupted, jarring the couple and drawing their attention to the window again. Leon's lips pressed into a thin line as the hysterics grew.

"They're odd, aren't they?" Eva let herself relax.

Leon nodded, leaning back and looking up at her. "Very." The laughter abated. Silence fell like a thick blanket of snow. Eva leaned in, pressing her forehead to Leon's and smiling.

"Where were—"

Moaning. Pleasureful and loud moans drifting in through the window.

Leon reached out, switching on the radio to the crackling jazz channel, masking the sounds. "You were saying?" He smiled up at her.

She squirmed as he pinched her thigh. "Where were we?"

Eva sat inside reading and listening to the rhythmic sound of Leon chopping wood outside.

After a few nights of fighting, then laughter, often punctuated by the sounds of pleasure, he had gone to talk to Hannah and Victor at Eva's request. All he had said was they could hear them talking, prodding to see if everything was fine. Victor and Hannah said it was just their night-time walks and they had a bad habit of being loud. They would keep it down. It was enough for Eva and Leon, though they still worried about the fighting.

The door flew open, letting in a burst of frigid air and flurries of snow.

Leon grinned like a child. "It's so wonderful out there." He kicked the door shut and trudged across the room to drop an armful of wood by the hearth. Raised in the mountains, Leon was ever the woodsman at heart. He moved to the city—where Eva met him—for university, and loved the hustle and bustle, but he could never let go of his love for the outdoors.

He pulled off his coat and dropped beside Eva on the couch, tugging off his boots. "Hannah asked if we'd like to have dinner at their cabin the day after tomorrow."

Eva nodded, marking her page and closing her book. "Sure. They seemed fine when you spoke to them, right?"

"They love giggling, but they were perfectly nice. They seem loving together too. Isn't it just so wonderful here?" He switched back to their original topic. "It's the air or something. It's different in the mountains."

Eva nodded. "Fresher, certainly."

Wrapping an arm around her shoulders, he grinned. "Come here."

She leaned into him, ready to snuggle against his chest, but he caught her chin and lifted her face to kiss her. Kiss her deeply and remind her all she meant to him.

He loved that. Passionate kisses and deep eye contact. Pulling her closer and nuzzling the side of her neck. Things that showed her he loved her. Regardless of whether or not it ended with his fingers down her underwear, his only true desire was that she be there with him in everything.

But he didn't do anything so seductive this time. Instead, he let go of her, smiling and standing up. "I'll cook us dinner."

"*You?*" Eva clutched her chest.

As romantic as he was, Leon didn't care for cooking. Maybe he would mill about as she cooked or chop a few vegetables or stir a pot. An entire meal, however, was entirely out of character. "Yes, me!" He threw his head back and laughed.

"And will it be more than cheese and crackers?"

"We have salami and olives too." He winked at her, kissing the top of her head and slipping off to the kitchen.

She offered to help a few times, but he would wave her off, happily humming to himself like a changed man. This was a change she didn't mind. She liked cooking, but she loved being spoiled. And he didn't serve cheese and charcuterie with crackers. He made a pasta aglio e olio with a simple steamed fish on the side. Not a difficult dish, but he made it well, and Eva was impressed with his pairing.

"Do you like it?" He gripped the edge of the table and leaned forward like a worried child.

"I love it!"

He let out a long breath and settled back. "Maybe I'll cook more."

She lifted an eyebrow but didn't object. How strange that he would pick up cooking after swearing he hated it.

Eva had trouble sleeping, and she lay on her side looking out the window while Leon slept soundly behind her. He didn't snore—thank goodness—but she could hear him breathing and she liked that. A reminder he was there, so even when she couldn't sleep she was happy.

She snuggled into her pillow and closed her eyes. When she thought she was drifting off, she heard Leon whisper.

She hummed softly, questioning the incomprehensible syllables, and he repeated them, but she still couldn't make it out, and opened her eyes to see him standing outside on the balcony, facing the window.

But he was behind her. She could hear him and feel his arm pressed against her back. So how was he in front of her too?

And that certainly was Leon on the balcony. She knew him too well to make a mistake.

She blinked and he was closer, his mouth moving as if muttering to himself.

"I can't hear you." More curious than anything else, she sat up. He didn't speak up, so she got out of bed and moved toward him. Every time she blinked, he was a little closer, until his palms were against the glass. She reached out to press her hand against his, the cool pane separating their touch.

And she listened.

"Evie's so pretty," he whispered, repeating the phrase as if it were a Hail Mary and he a sinner.

She let out a soft laugh. "What?"

"Evie's so pretty." The phrase echoed around her.

His fingers sank through the glass, intertwining with hers and pushing her back into the room as he stepped inside.

"What are you doing, Evie?" Leon's voice came from behind her, solid and grounded.

She turned to look back at him. "I don't know." She looked out the window, blinking and squinting, unable to recall why she had gotten out of bed or why her hands were raised.

"Come back to bed."

She paused to look at the mountains. The view was so pretty.

Leon was up late, smoking one cigarette after the next and listening to the news, when Eva went to bed. She could hear the murmur of the newscaster updating the latest baseball scores—the one hobby Eva didn't share with Leon—but she liked the sound of radio news.

The white noise lulled her into a daze and clouds blocked out the moon, casting the room into pitch black.

Leon whispered, his voice wrapping her like swathes of velvet. "You didn't turn off the radio," she mumbled.

He moved closer and farther. His voice next to her ear and across the room. "Evie's so pretty."

A hand gripped her waist and she giggled. Another slid up her arm. More and more hands gliding across her skin. One between her legs, one along her breasts, one inside her mouth.

"Evie's so pretty," he whispered from above her. "Evie's so pretty." At the foot of the bed.

Beside her. All around. A singular point of noise emanating from behind her right eye, but, outside, the whispers screamed: "Evie's so pretty."

"Eva!"

She jerked up, skin slick with sweat and Leon gripping her shoulders.

"Are you all right?" His grip loosened, but his eyes widened.

"Y-yes." She never remembered her dreams, but she knew this one made her heart race, so she flung her arms around his neck. "I've been having weird dreams, I think."

"Me too." He rubbed her back and kissed the top of her head. "It must be the mountain air," he joked.

If it was the mountain air, it left a sickening feeling on her skin, like she needed desperately to bathe. Finding little solace in his jest, she wrinkled her nose, but nodded anyway, and reminded herself it was nothing more than a bad dream.

Hannah and Victor's cabin was similar to Eva and Leon's, in that it was stuck in an era where radios with knobs existed, and furniture was upholstered in floral print. The whole mountain, in fact, seemed removed from reality, and Eva didn't like that.

But she did like the scents wafting from the kitchen.

"It smells delicious! What are you cooking?" Eva sipped on wine with Hannah while Victor told Leon how disappointed he was that the radio didn't work. Leon was quick to start fixing the old box.

"French onion soup and a slow-cooked pork shoulder." Hannah lifted the lid off a pot and motioned to the pork surrounded by a simmering red-wine sauce.

"You've been cooking all day then!"

Hannah waved off the comment. "I love it."

"Me too." Eva set aside her wine. "Do you mind if I use your restroom?"

"Not at all! It's just down that hall. The last door." Hannah seemed less odd that day. *Sober*, Eva thought. She and Victor must have had a bad habit of drinking too much wine and being too loud and that was that.

Everyone had bad habits. Leon smoked. Eva tugged at loose strings. Hannah and Victor drank too much.

Eva relieved herself and freshened up, pausing to bat her lashes at herself in the mirror and giggle. Thus far, Hannah and Victor had been wonderful hosts—like old friends, even. The company and free-flowing alcohol helped Eva forget about her sleepless nights. This would be a good night, she was certain.

As she stepped out into the hall, she ran into Victor standing motionless and staring at her.

"Oh, I'm sorry. I didn't mean to make you wait." Eva motioned for him to move past her, but he didn't budge.

She wasn't sure what to do and took a step toward him only to hear him muttering to himself.

"What was that?" She leaned in.

"Evie's so pretty." He stared at her unblinking, repeating the same phrase over and over. She knew the phrase, but from where, she could not remember. Regardless, it seemed an odd thing to say.

She gave him a weary "Thank you." She was uncertain if she should thank a man saying the same thing again and again, but it *was* a compliment, and she had the manners of any good girl who studied at Catholic school.

He reached out and grazed her arm with his fingers. "Victor!" Hannah called.

Life snapped back into Victor's eyes, and he seemed a little lost when he looked at Eva.

"Victor," Hannah called again, "help me set the table!" "Excuse me." He furrowed his brow before walking back to the kitchen.

Eva followed a safe distance behind and saw that Leon had gotten the radio to work and set it up in the kitchen to play jazz. "Come, Eva. Let's eat. I've put your wine just over there." Hannah directed traffic like a good host as Victor set out plates and silverware, stealing glances at Eva that she pretended not to notice.

He didn't do anything throughout dinner. He was amicable and kind, well versed in conversations and easily excitable; Eva wanted to enjoy his company but couldn't.

The dinner, however, was delicious. Hannah was a wonderful cook and said she would never pass up an opportunity to show off. However, she abhorred sweets. Thus, dessert was chocolate mousse made by Victor.

"This has all been delicious." Eva reached out to Hannah.

Hannah held Eva's hands between hers and offered a sweet smile. "You're too kind."

"And I want that mousse recipe." Leon leaned one arm over the back of Eva's chair. Unlike Hannah, Leon loved sweets.

Victor chuckled. "I'll write it up and bring it over tomorrow. How's that?"

"Perfect!"

Hannah tugged on Eva. "You're so pretty, you know." Her eyes grew wide.

"Thank you." Eva bit down on her lip. The compliment didn't feel like one anymore—even less so now Hannah kept pulling her in until she had to stand up and lean over the table.

"Evie's so pretty." Victor was beside her, touching her shoulder and marveling. Eva couldn't look at him. She didn't want to see his vacant gaze.

Hannah repeated: "Evie's so pretty."

Eva gave Leon a desperate look, but he only watched as if in full agreement. Like it was perfectly normal to be half bent over a dinner table as their hosts repeated the same thing in unison. She didn't understand how any of them thought this normal; it brought a glisten of frantic embarrassment to her eyes.

Eva gave a brusque yank to retrieve her hand from Hannah and sank back into her chair with a nervous laugh. "It's late, isn't it?"

Leon checked his watch, and much to Eva's relief, it *was* late. Eleven p.m. to be exact. They said their goodbyes, which Eva kept short and out of arm's reach, then headed out.

Eva was just about dragging Leon down the path back to their cabin when she stopped and whipped around to face him. "Why didn't you do anything?" Her eyes were full of tears and her chest jerked to hold back a sob. "That was humiliating!"

Both Leons cocked their head to the side. Why were there two of him?

She hiccupped and her eyes darted between Leon and...Leon. "They were just being nice, love." He reached out to her hand—the Leon on the right—no, he was in the middle now.

They were three.

Four.

Five.

"Why are there five of you?" Eva scanned over the group. Each did something different. One held her hand. One circled her. Another rocked back and forth on his heels while the remaining two leaned against a tree.

"Five?" Though she heard only one voice, all their mouths moved. "There's only one of me." They stifled a laugh.

"I'm not feeling well." She pulled away and started down the road.

"Eva!" He lost the battle for his composure and started to laugh, calling her name between his fits and rambling behind her.

It wasn't until they were back at the cabin that he contained himself. "I'm sorry. I should have stopped them."

"You know Victor cornered me in the hall." Inside, she pulled off her coat and kicked off her boots.

"He did?"

Eva nodded and turned away. "I'm going to change."

"Love, wait! I'm sorry!"

She didn't like this new Leon anymore. These new Leons. All eight of them.

When Eva finished changing, she went to the sitting room, where only one Leon stood staring at the fire.

She walked up behind him, wringing the front of her robe. "Leon? We should talk."

"Evie's so pretty," he whispered.

"W-what?" She took a step toward him, dreading what she heard.

"Evie's so pretty," he spoke louder, turning to face her. He clutched a drink in one hand and held a cigarette in the other. This would have been a common sight if it weren't for his vacant, wide-eyed stare and his repeating of that damned line.

"You're scaring me, Leon."

"Evie's so pretty!" He let out a laugh and downed the rest of his drink.

The glass slipped from his fingers as if he forgot he was holding it and it shattered on the wooden floor.

"Come here, Evie!" His voice grew harsh—a tone she had not once heard from him before.

"Stop it!" She backed away.

He took a long drag from his cigarette. "Come here, Evie!" Smoke curled from his lips as he spoke and his cigarette fell, his hand still hovering in front of his mouth like he didn't notice. He grabbed for her, but she slipped away, turning and running.

"What are you doing?" She made for the stairs, hearing him cackle behind her as his footsteps quickened.

"Evie's so pretty! *Evie's so pretty! Evie's so pretty Evie's so pretty Evie's so pretty!*" He was like a doll with a pull string in its back, but the string was jammed and he was saying the same thing over and over, again and again. *"Evie's so pretty!"*

He darted up the stairs behind her, snatching her ankle and tripping her. She caught herself on the stairs, but he was upon her, not noticing how she yelped in pain when he grabbed her wrists too hard.

Her cries were lost on him, and he tore at her robe. Tears streamed down her cheeks as she pummeled his chest, but her fighting was met only with the same laugh and the same call: *"Evie's so pretty!"*

"I don't want this!" Summoning all her strength, she shoved him, and he slipped back.

He didn't try to stop his fall, instead tumbling down the stairs and slamming onto the wooden floor, where he lay limp and smiling.

Eva stole the chance to pull shut her robe and hurry to the master bedroom. She locked the door, wedged a chair beneath the knob and ran the hottest bath she could.

Sitting in scalding water and silver moonlight, she listened to Leon's laughter echo through the house.

"Eva? Oh God, Eva. I'm sorry!" Leon's voice woke Eva early in the morning. "I...I don't remember anything from last night after we got home. I'm so sorry."

"Go away!" Eva pulled the blankets over her chest. He must have tried the doorknob already to find it locked, and thus started apologizing.

"Love, I am so sorry if I hurt you. Please, just tell me what happened. I'll make it right."

"I don't want to talk about it."

He let out a sigh. "I'm so sorry, Eva."

"Go away."

He sucked in a breath, relinquished the fight. "Right. I'll be downstairs." It took a moment for him to walk away, as if he wanted to say more, but thought better of it and left.

Eva collapsed into a heap on the bed and cried. She cried harder than she ever had. She didn't know if she could get over this.

But the man behind the door had been the old Leon. The Leon who liked deep kisses and hated cooking. The Leon who apologized and cared.

She hugged her knees to her chest and watched the sun rise. Would her Leon still be there when she left the room? She didn't know. But she had to get up as her stomach growled and the sun rose well above the horizon.

A cigarette dangled from Leon's fingers, and he was staring at the radio, as if neither smoking nor listening, when she came down. He looked up at her, keeping his head bowed and his lips tilted in a frown.

"I want to leave," she said, as her foot came to rest on the ground floor.

"Of course." He turned off the radio and stubbed out his cigarette.

"Today. *Now.*"

"I'll pack." He rose to stand, but didn't make to move, as if he didn't want to take a step toward her. "I'll pack everything. You just get breakfast." His voice was desperate, trying to fix everything with hushed tones and perfect answers.

She pressed her lips into a thin line, tugging her robe tight across her body. She would have to burn the robe after all this too.

He noticed the motion. It had been a long time since she hid her body from him, and the act was enough to make him pale. "All right." She turned on her heel and went to the kitchen to make herself a fried egg and dry toast, then ate it, wedged in the corner and watching him through the bedroom door as he put their clothes back into their bags and found his keys.

"I think that's everything." He came down the stairs with their bags as Eva was cleaning up.

"Good."

"I left a change of clothes out for you." He stood so far out of the way and beside the wall like a child in trouble.

"Thank you." The nuns would be proud of Eva's manners.

She heard him make his own breakfast as she went upstairs to dress. She waited until she could hear him cleaning his plate to come down again and toss her robe in the fire.

"What are you doing?" His mouth snapped shut as if he already knew he shouldn't be bothering her, but it was too late.

Her eyes narrowed on him. "Let's go."

Eva snapped on a smile as she saw Hannah and Victor walking from the path joining their cabins. As uncomfortable as they made her, she would end things without too much friction for her own sake—she didn't feel like fighting.

"Good morning." She brushed her curls with her fingers.

"Leaving? I thought you had another week." Victor held out a scrap of paper with his mousse recipe on it.

Where Leon would typically come up with an excuse, Eva spoke up instead. "I haven't been feeling well, so we've decided to go back."

"It'll do that," Leon added, setting the bag beside the car and taking the recipe. "The mountain air."

Eva hated those words now; neither mountain air nor altitude sickness nor whatever anyone called it caused the type of things that Eva had experienced. Of that she was certain, but no one needed to know about the eight Leons or the assault or "Evie's so pretty."

Victor gave a wide grin that bore too many teeth. "Stay." His gaze was fixed on Eva. "Stay with me, Evie."

"No, we really should be going." She bit down on her lip and his eyes darted to her mouth. He reached out as if "no" weren't in his vocabulary. As if he couldn't even hear her.

"She's so pretty." Hannah's head lolled to the side, and Leon let out a soft laugh.

Victor grazed Eva's shoulders. "Evie's so pretty."

Now faced with all of them closing in and staring, Eva thought she would be sick.

Leon jerked her back, stepping in the way and shoving Victor. "Stay away from her." His voice was ragged and his lip curled back. The tendons of his jaw flexed. His eyes went vacant. He was slipping again.

Victor stumbled, slamming into Hannah, and the couple began to laugh, shoving each other back and forth. Despite Leon's protective stance, he laughed while backing Eva toward a stack of firewood.

Hannah slammed her fist into Victor's face. His eyes widened with mirth as he rolled his weight forward and hit her back. They fell into a brawl of biting and kicking and scratching, at which Leon laughed harder. Eva inched away as the fight moved closer. "Evie's so pretty," Leon whispered, and Eva knew that they had to get out. She had never been more terrified or frightened in her life, but she felt a bubble of laughter trying to fight its way up.

Hannah stumbled and fell. Victor pounced on her, snatching up a rock and smashing it into her face. But she kept laughing, even as her teeth broke and her nose was smashed in.

When Hannah fell silent, Victor pushed himself up from the ground and smiled at Eva. "Where are you going, Evie?"

"Evie's so pretty," Leon repeated.

"Evie's so pretty!" said Victor, ambling toward her like he was drunk, reaching out and grabbing for her.

Backed into a corner, with Leon rocking back and forth while laughing and Victor lurching toward her, Eva grabbed an axe wedged into a stump and—before she could think—swung it hard into Victor's face, hacking open his cheek and half his mouth with a sickening crack. She wanted to laugh, yet she knew she couldn't.

He slid off the axe, what was left of his face still grinning up at her. Leon had gone silent and now gaped at the carnage.

Eva dropped the axe like she would a burning coal and grabbed the keys from Leon. "Put the bags in the car, Leon." She looked away from Victor and swallowed.

Leon glanced at the bodies as he moved, but he did as she said. "Get in the car." She climbed into the driver's seat, trying to ignore the blood slick on her hands and face.

He slid into his seat, still staring at Victor and Hannah bleeding across the snow as they drove away.

He seemed so empty as they started out, but the farther they wove from the cabin, the more his breathing came back and his eyes softened. Halfway down, his shoulders slumped forward. At the bottom he dropped his head into his hands.

Eva didn't try to speak to him, not even when she pulled over, running to a nearby snow drift and using it to wash her hands and face. The snow burned her skin, but she had to get the blood off. She scrubbed herself raw with snow, trying to banish the image of Hannah's smashed-in nose and Victor's hacked face.

The car door opened and closed.

She didn't turn around; she kept scrubbing until her skin was too frigid and her fingers too stiff to go on.

"Eva?" Leon's footsteps crunched up to her and he knelt down. "Here." He pulled out a handkerchief and held it out to her, but she didn't take it, fixing her gaze on the snow drift. "Why don't I remember half of our trip?" His voice was soft and gentle, much more like himself. "I don't even remember getting in the car."

She couldn't meet his eyes.

"Eva..." His voice fell to a whisper. "Why did you burn your robe?"

She swallowed to keep from crying, trying to ignore him.

"I'm so sorry." His voice trembled. "I just wish I knew. I...I can guess I hurt you, but I don't know how."

She looked up at him. Tears streamed down his cheeks and his hands shook. He looked like he would be sick. He looked how Eva felt.

"You attacked me." She found it hard to check the anger in her voice. It wasn't him who had done that, but it was him all the same. She hated it and wished she had forgotten too, but she couldn't.

He stared at her, the color draining from his cheeks as he churned over what she said. Disgust first crossed his face, then confusion. His mouth moved as if to deny the accusation, but he stopped himself and, at last, sorrow shrouded his features. "I did... what?"

She couldn't say it again, instead pressing her lips into a thin line as he covered his mouth.

"I am so, so sorry. I'll do anything. I'll cook again—god, I don't know why I was cooking but I'll do it. I'll take you anywhere you want to go. Eva, I'm sorry." He dropped his head into his hands, sobs shaking loose from his chest. "I'll make it right. I swear."

She stood up, sucking in a shaky breath and holding out the keys to him. "You can start by driving us home then. I want to lean out the window."

WE HAVE ALWAYS
— LIVED IN THE PROJECTS —
by Danny Lore

Bee's cell phone vibrated on the couch next to her, and it made her think about how her walls don't have their own beat.

She checked her phone and realized she'd been fixated on the lack of a beat long enough to have her sister send her four texts, her mother three, and to have reduced her mom to actually calling, like some kind of cavewoman…or overly concerned mom.

"Hey, sorry, I was…"

Bee looked around the apartment; it had stark eggshell walls, the only break from the patternlessness a small dent in the doorway where the movers had clipped it with the new couch. Her couch. Her and her roommate's new couch. None of it seemed right, especially as whatever collection of things she had was in boxes around her. Sparse, unopened boxes.

"…unpacking," Bee offered, after a moment.

"Ah," her mother said, and there was a sudden wash of warmth on the other line, such pride and encouragement that Bee almost

regretted the move already. "Right, makes sense. Sorry, I just...
with you out the house, it's so quiet here."

Was it? Bee twisted so that she could reach up and place one
hand flat against the wall. No pulsing radio sounds from next
door, or thumps from a basketball dribbled upstairs. Just smooth,
cool flatness. "Hillary is there."

"I know that, Bee, but it's different without your noise." Bee had
only moved into the new place last weekend, and she wanted to
point that out, but something about the wall made her stop. At first
she thought it was a rare moment of understanding her mom, the
way that different people had their own noises, just like different
places had noises and silences and ebbs and flows.

"What's wrong, honey?" Her mother's concern was the only
reason that Bee realized she'd yelped.

"I, uh...nothing," she said, stuttered. "I just thought I heard
something."

"It's the new place," her mother explained immediately. "That's
one of those new Manhattan buildings, and you know they don't
creak and groan like they do up here in the Bronx. They're built
different."

"Yeah, that must be it," Bee said. "I actually have to go. Geni and
I are about to order food."

She rushed her mother off the phone, with proper pleasantries
and assurances she'd call back in the morning, leaving her alone
in the apartment again. Bee put her phone down, placed both her
hands flat against the wall. She closed her eyes, searching with her
palms and trying not to listen to the sound of her own breath, the
sound of her heartbeat as it raced.

There was a thrum, a beat like a loud block party down the
street—except it flowed across the wall. Bee could *follow* it, she
realized, as she opened her eyes and allowed her hand to trace the
vibration.

With one hand pressed against the wall, she climbed off her couch, following the sound. She wondered why she couldn't see it, why it didn't ripple out past the path she followed, why it didn't reach her ears as she felt the force of it with her fingertips. Bee left the door open when she stepped into the building's hallway. The beat flowed upward, along the edges of her doorframe. Beyond that, there was nothing to feel underneath her hands.

But there were *shadows*. So many shadows!

The hall looked as if it was beginning to drown in them. They stretched into every corner and flicker of light. When there was no light left, the shadows climbed atop one another. There were no limbs, no eyes, no features, just shadow over shadow, darkness covered by darkness, pooling at the sides of her doorway.

Bee slammed the door shut, locking it behind her. She collapsed onto her knees, barely feeling the impact.

There was no beat. No sinister shadows. Just her breath, silence. It was all *out there*.

"We're so happy to have you, Beatrice," Claudine Matthews was saying. "You're our first paid intern, you know." The emphasis, Bee heard, was on the "paid" not the "intern." "It's really important to us that we help young people with potential rise up to meet it."

There were a million things that Claudine was saying, and that she didn't say, but Bee was fixated on the way the woman's perfectly tailored pink blazer and black skirt felt dated. Or was that back in style? Or worse—was it the woman's attempt to look far more fashion-forward than she was, skewing in the blazer's brightness just over the line from retro to out of touch? Bee felt bad, instantly. She was supposed to be excited about this opportunity— it was why, after all, her parents had helped cover half of the rent in Manhattan. The rising up, the social mobility. It didn't matter what she thought about the woman's blazer, or about real estate, or anything like that: her professor had made the introduction, spoke highly of Bee as someone who could do *so much* with her aptitude.

Aptitude. She'd been hopeful that they'd stop using that word when she got into college, but no, she'd learned in her freshman year that people who were friends with women like Claudine might never stop using it.

"So, the first week or so, we really want this to be about acclimating you to the office and its routines. Normally, I'd say you can ask me anything, but unfortunately your on-boarding is coinciding with my one vacation of the year—so, tomorrow, I'll introduce you to Taylor Jacobs, and you can ask him anything. He's really amazing; we wouldn't be able to run without him."

At the idea of being passed off, Bee's stomach twisted. Another new person. She smiled back at Claudine. "That sounds great! I can't wait!" She hoped that she sounded sufficiently grateful, the way her dad had mockingly said that people like Claudine liked them to be. She modulated her tone slightly higher than how she talked at home, hoped that the force of her smile flattened the accent she'd tried to leave up in Pelham Park.

Claudine beamed back at her. Behind her, Bee almost saw the woman's shadow stretch out of proportion and take on a tinge of pink.

At night, the night before Geni was supposed to move her stuff in (Bee felt awful, having lied to her mother about when Geni would arrive, but she'd needed some time alone in the apartment, to get used to it—besides, she'd done plenty of lying about Geni already: they were school friends, not a roommate found online, of course they'd seen each other in person a bunch of times, don't be ridiculous, Mom), Bee heard the beat again.

Felt it, really, against the balls of her feet as she took a step. She felt the beat, almost tapping along to it, until she remembered there was no reason to be hearing a beat right now. She was alone, she didn't have any music playing. Beyond that, this wasn't a neighborhood whose floors thrummed with beats at three in the morning; that was for back *home*, and Karaoke Carlos who kept belting Dominican ballads at all hours of the night. That beat felt alien here, and she couldn't help but remember the first time she'd heard it in the apartment. It was too dark to really differentiate shadow from darkness.

She turned on every light in the apartment, just in case. As she finally sat on a kitchen school, she pulled her feet up off the floor, like a small child who realizes the monsters might see the tips of her toes.

Bee did not look toward the door. What if the shadows were creeping in, this time, welcomed by the beat?

Taylor Jacobs was the kind of bland handsome that Bee saw in mid-budget melodramas, with hair that might curl with another half an inch of growth, a decent smile, and nothing about him to differentiate him from almost any white man she'd met during her college years. She knew he came from a good family before he opened his mouth. When he did speak, she thought of hundreds of conversations she'd had with her girls back uptown, Deanna and Fatimah, about the kinds of boys that you dated once you decided you weren't ever going to end up staying in their neighborhood.

"Look," Fatimah had scolded Deanna, "you can like Felix all you want, but him and his brothers are staying in the hood for *life*. You wanna be living Felix's mom's life 2.0 in ten years?"

Deanna had made a face. "You say that like I'm supposed to hate it here. If I wanna head out, I've got a MetroCard. But not every man here's a fuck-up."

Fatimah's mouth had pressed together tightly, and Bee was tempted to tell Fatimah that she sounded like *her* mother. Instead,

Bee had changed the conversation. Whoever she ended up with, Bee hadn't yet gotten so far as figuring out an imaginary place to settle down with her future wife or husband.

Taylor talked about filing systems and then offered Bee out across the street for coffees. She made a joke about him being younger than she'd expected, the way Claudine talked about him. Taylor laughed and said that he started interning with the firm at the end of high school. Claudine, Bee found out, was Taylor's aunt.

A car passed, its windows rolled down, the radio blaring loudly. It came with a bass beat that made Bee's breath catch in her chest. It almost made her miss how pained Taylor became at the sound, the way his face distorted with the vibrations of the song.

It was mid-laugh, and his laugh, for a moment, became *too sharp*. Bee refused to accept how his mouth distorted, moving as if parts of it stretched, pinned back on a board without blood and pins, yanked in every direction. He didn't scream. He ground his teeth, lifted his hand—which Bee refused to accept grew razor sharp as well—to his temple.

Bee stared at Taylor as the car rounded the corner and the sound vanished. His features and limbs stretched back to normal. He finished a very human laugh.

He asked how she was enjoying school. Bee stared at his shadows and waited for them to return to normal.

Geni texted Bee that night. Family emergency, she said. It would be a few more days.

Bee started to text back: Is it quiet where you are? How dark are the shadows?

She caught herself, deleted every word. Instead, she said: Don't worry. Take your time. Your new home will be here when you're ready.

She put a chair against the door after locking it, but that just ended up another shapeless blob in the middle of the night, another thing for shadows to cling to.

In her sleep, there were bachata melodies and her dreams smelled like oxtail.

Bee tried to stand on the steps, but they didn't do that here.

Or, rather, *she* didn't do that here, because she wasn't stretching to go on a run, or planning to walk a dog, or push a stroller. When she stood on the steps, she was too young, too unestablished. Even the ones that smiled and nodded her way seemed startled by her existence, and their acknowledgement crawled up her skin like the shadows that kept closing in every night when she came in from work.

But there was sunlight here, sunlight seeping into her skin as she tried to listen to the neighborhood. Nothing sounded right here. The children were too quiet, and so were the adults. There were dogs, but their owners weren't on beat.

Not that there was a beat to be on beat to.

She finished drinking up the sunlight and suspicious side-eyes and went back inside.

When she called her mother, they talked about how great the apartment was. How the internship and classes were such a leg up on everyone else in the neighborhood. How Bee was so happy to have taken that chance and moved downtown.

Bee kept her eyes on the strip of light from under her front door. As the sun set, the light beyond the door was blotted out by shadows. Her voice pitched a little higher, her accent a little flatter, as she agreed with her mom again and again.

It was so much quieter here, after all. The only sound that invaded her thoughts was the beat, thrumming by the doorway, tapping through her foot.

She talked too much about the silence. That was what her father finally said, in a huff of frustration. If it was so *quiet*, watch a TV show, he told her, blast the radio. Make a *friend*, her mother pleaded.

Bee explained that she had friends.

She had Geni—who had extended her stay at her parents again, and they still hadn't met one another, but she did send her half of the rent along to the landlord.

She had Taylor—that *boy* at work with the warping smile, but he seemed to put up with her.

She had Claudine with the pink shadows—no, that was her *boss*, not a friend, even with the large, sharp grin.

She had co-workers, although she didn't tell her father how they had distanced themselves from her because she talked about the silence *there* too. Insisted it followed her there too.

Bee was invited to lunch with her co-workers. Taylor sat on one side, with Bee's knee almost too close, and her voice modulated a smidgen too much. They all stared at her as she sunnily described her life. Not one of them noticed how quickly their shadows jerked toward her, a Swiss army knife of bladed shadows focusing on her every word. Bee forced herself to sound even more cheerful, to blunt the edges.

One of her co-workers suggested she go to the doctor. Her insurance wasn't like the shadows, though; it didn't stretch that far. Another suggested she use headphones. She decided against explaining why that wasn't an option, because she was only starting to realize it herself: it wasn't a *real* beat, it wasn't an actual bass drop, and that wasn't enough. She was starting to suspect she'd been wrong about the beat heralding the shadows.

Bee had assumed that the beat and shadows were both out of place, but as those sharp shadows shuddered as she tapped her toes under the table…she started to wonder if the beat was trying to keep the shadows away.

The shadows, she suspected, belonged more than she did.

She worked late, and Taylor offered to give her a ride home. No one in Manhattan drove a car, so it confused her, until he explained he lived in Brooklyn. Ah, right. That made sense. She accepted.

He played music in his car, but it was all acoustic guitar and watery drumlines. She *liked* it, but today it was wrong. Flat. The lack of vibration made her queasy, but she blamed it on bumps in the road. She leaned her head back, closed her eyes.

The road steadied, and then the bumps *changed*—she'd forgotten what familiar speed bumps felt like, how she knew the distance between one and then the next left turn. She could count out the seconds between the green lights and red ones.

She thought the windows were closed, but the smells filtered through regardless. Barbeque and pies, all freshly made by uncles and aunts who all spoke over each other, loud and cackling. The heat of the sun was split sharply in a diagonal across her face where the tree over her favorite bench only partially offered shade.

The queasiness was gone, and a heavy bass drop replaced it. She smiled; she remembered this song, remembered her and her girls dancing to it when she'd caught Felix looking back at her. She tapped her foot.

The car jerked to a stop, and her eyes shot open. The queasiness was back, the bass migrating up to the nape of her neck. Taylor was speaking, but like so many voices recently she didn't *hear* it; the words didn't penetrate.

But the beat was still there, and his meaning was clear.

She smiled. She would love for him to walk her upstairs. It was so *quiet* in the apartment without her roommate there yet.

Taylor came upstairs with her, and they stood at her door. He was speaking about how much Claudine liked Bee, and how everyone was sure that she had a bright future already. It had only been two weeks, but they could all easily see her sticking around after her internship if she keeps "this" up.

Bee didn't know what "this" meant, or how to keep it up. Her smile in response felt almost as sharp as his sometimes was. The bass beat twitched the baby hairs on her neck, like the time she got in trouble for lying back against a too-loud speaker. It buzzed without the painful roar in her ears. She thought that the sound and vibration were one and the same, but she was wrong.

She leaned herself against the wall, her palm pressed against it, and this time the beat pulsed down her arm, pushing against the wall as if it wanted to push her away from it. Taylor was still speaking. The beat continued, the only thing in the whole building, on the whole island, that remained on beat.

And then the shadows started to creep in.

It started above them, at the corners of the ceiling. Bee thought she apologized, explaining that this was the longest she'd been in the hallway since that first night, but she didn't know what Taylor's response was.

How could she, when it was the very shadows above them that seemed to distort his mouth and peel it backward?

The darkness kept layering, one shadow over another, until the ceiling could no longer hold the weight. Bee hadn't known the weight of a shadow until now, and she looked up at the way they oozed down, a thick sludge that poured down over Taylor's head.

Taylor still spoke, even as he sharpened at every corner of his body, until there were corners that Bee had never seen before, until there were claws and blades dressed up in the finest

Brooklyn-meets-East-Side fashion. Until that beaming smile was a blinding headlight, and Bee squinted to see past it.

He was *part* of the shadows, it dawned on her. That was why Taylor's face jerked in every direction, and Claudine's shadow had tinted pink, and maybe Geni *knew*, maybe she'd discovered the truth about the shadows and couldn't bear them and their beat anymore—

No, not their beat.

Bee saw her hand against the wall, felt the thrumming in the wall, and saw the shadows didn't touch the wall there. Hadn't touched her yet.

That first night...the shadows kept from the doorway. The shadows crept at the edge but did not touch her when she heard the beat. When the car had passed by her job, Taylor's shadows were laid bare, but they had not touched her.

They were part of the shadows. They were part of the silence. The beat...the bachata and the melodies and the smells, those kept it at a distance, kept these hunting, creeping shadows from moving in close. She sucked in a breath.

Unlike Taylor's words, she heard her own breath. She let it sync with the familiar beat. She reached out, and her hand touched Taylor's shoulder.

The shadows twitched first. Then they *exploded*.

Their explosion was what she thought space must sound like: an absence of sound as layers of darkness shattered and blew away. There was a young man underneath, a man who must have been Taylor, the same Taylor who had driven her home, and yet... He seemed a little realer. A little tired. His shrug and smile a little less sharp.

"I'm actually thinking about moving back home," Bee heard herself say. Her voice had never sounded so strong. "It may involve breaking the lease and a longer commute, but I think it's worth it. I miss my neighborhood."

"Really?" Taylor's response was surprised, as if she'd shattered some illusion he'd had about her. "Every time I've had to drive through there it's always been so *loud*." She heard his response, but did not care about it, as she closed the door.

She felt the beat again, and it was in her pocket. She pulled out her phone. Deanna was calling, and Bee couldn't wait to catch up.

— HEADMASTER —
by A.M. Perez

K aiènhne iónkiats."
My name is She Has Brought It Over.
"Kanienkehá:ka niwakonhewentsiò:ten."
My nation is The People of the Flint.
"Wakeniáhten."
I am Turtle Clan.
The words are a lullaby. She repeats them at night, every night, reminding herself of who she is and who she is not.

She is *not* Mary. She has the bruises to prove it. For all the times they call that name—*Mary*—she refuses to look at them. She will not answer to it, and she speaks her true name in a whisper. In the institute—the *Mush Hole*—a word spoken in Kanienkehá is worth a lashing.

At night, with her back sore against the thin hay mattress in its hard wooden frame, Kaiènhne closes her eyes and recites her name to herself. She recites all that she can remember of her language, her clan, her family. With eyes closed, she fights the urge to shiver beneath paper-thin sheets. The other girls' breathing is short and stifled, a chorus of trembling exhalations rattling like fall leaves carried by the wind. Kaiènhne imagines those leaves and their colors, the colors of the world outside the unforgiving walls of the institute.

"Kaiènhne iónkiats. Wakeniáhten."

As she recites her mantra, she pictures Ka'nisténhsera. The woman's face is a canyon, rough and light brown and lined from old rivers, old stories that carved age and wisdom into her skin and earned her position as Clan Mother.

Ka'nisténhsera warned against forgetting. She reminded Kaiènhne that stories are all their people have, all that they are. Words give life. And, someday, Kaiènhne would be the one passing stories on to the next generations. She must remember them, must recite them. *She Has Brought It Over*. It is in her name.

"Tell me a story, Ka'nisténhsera." Kaiènhne whispers the words in her native tongue, hiding her lips beneath the sheet, afraid of being caught even in the darkness.

The deep wrinkles around Clan Mother's eyes and mouth crease when she smiles. Around her, the leaves shudder their tiny breaths. "I will tell you the story of the Sky Woman."

Kaiènhne shakes her head, trembling at the chill of encroaching winter. "No, Clan Mother, you told me that so many times. Tell me something new. Something..." She shivers again, and says, "Chilling."

The old woman smiles and tells her tale, weaving together with words the image of an angry spirit, an angry soul, vengeful, abused, cold, and insatiably hungry. Growing claws, blood-red eyes, thick hair black and flowing like a raven's wings. Born of betrayal and cruelty, set to devour those who wrong it. In her dreams, Kaiènhne hears Clan Mother's tale.

The Kanontsistóntie's, the Flying Heads, will rise in the face of betrayal, to seek vengeance and death. But they are cursed, and, from the moment they rise, their hunger for human flesh can never be satiated.

Two burning red coals stare down at her like eyes, surrounded by thick wires of black. The face is twisted, deformed, thick vines of veins pulsing under ice-blue skin. Its jaw is unhinged, open, gnashing, bloody teeth in rotting black gums. Its neck is severed, blood and sinew dripping from its open throat, fragments of bone protruding from its neck like talons.

Kaiènhne shoots upright, gasping. Her blood is ice in her veins, her skin prickling, but the monster in the room is not the one she saw in her dream.

Among the chattering teeth and trembling breaths around her is a quiet sob, a rustle of sheets and a low groan.

The girls' quarters are arranged like the rest of the Mush Hole—intent on keeping them apart. A wide, long room with wooden boards built up in rows. Each bare bed is pressed up into a corner, and, despite the room's overall size, the girls are broken up. The beds are in pairs in parallel. The children cannot gather, laugh, play or share stories.

In the darkness, Kaiènhne sees the shadow of a man wrestling a girl in her bed. She knows the girl who sleeps across from her only as Alice, a child too frightened and too battered to even whisper her real name.

Fear does not protect her.

Usually, the headmaster and teachers would take them to the basement to torment them, where their screams and sobs would fade into the rumble of the boiler. The Reverend is not a patient man; he can't be bothered to wait the few minutes it would take to move Alice from the shared quarters.

Her stomach clenching up, Kaiènhne starts to move, but she knows better, of course, than to interfere. To try and stop it would only earn them both more pain. She has burn scars for her defiance, hours and days lost to the darkness of the closet where she has been left to starve for merely speaking, and where other children with too much defiance had been left alone so long, by the time the door was opened, their bodies were stiff and cold.

Kaiènhne pulls her blanket over her head, squeezes her eyes shut and covers her ears. The sounds of the man's grunts and the girl's whimpers make her wish for dreams of the Kanontsistóntie's instead, the flesh-eating monsters. But dreams do not come to replace this nightmare.

In the morning, Kaiènhne dresses in her uniform, a long dress buttoned up to her throat and accented with a pinafore. Her once long black hair is cut and styled at her shoulders, and she ties the bow into her hair, which helps her look exactly like the other girls and nothing at all like herself.

As they walk out in lines to lunch, Kaiènhne passes Alice's bed. The girl lies there still, despite the teacher at the door demanding they move. Kaiènhne pauses. "Alice," she hisses in English, in case the teachers are listening, though it tastes sour to call a girl by a name she knows isn't hers. "Come on."

Alice's puffy eyes stay fixed on the ceiling, her body stiff in the bed. She does not acknowledge anything. Her face is streaked with tears, her hair ruffled.

The woman at the door snaps, "Mary, let's go."

Kaiènhne lingers longer, defiant to respond to that name. But still, as the teacher begins to march into the quarters, she finally turns and hurries off after the other girls.

Breakfast is, as always, a bowl of grey slop that stinks of mold and turns her stomach. Though they are kept separate, Kaiènhne eyes the boys across the room. Among them is one she knew once, before they came here. They call him Joseph here; she does not remember his real name, but he came here with her. They played as children once, back when they still saw their families, still used their names and were free to laugh and speak and be together. She might have known his name, but she has forgotten it, and since the day they were taken—their parents deceived and their families broken—Joseph has been too afraid to tell Kaiènhne his name.

His eyes find hers. Bruises around his protruding cheekbones, bruises on his knuckles. He is, like her, one of the oldest students here. She knows the staff drag the boys to the basement and make them fight, placing bets on them for entertainment. Joseph is the biggest of them all but, every fight, he loses. The heavy shadows beneath his eyes tell of a late night, no doubt scrubbing his own blood from the floors. His collar is buttoned tight around his throat, his once long hair trimmed and styled short.

Kaiènhne suspects he throws the fights, allowing the other boys to win. She wants to ask, but the teachers do not let them near each other, don't risk that they whisper to each other in Kanienkehá.

A woman slams Kaiènhne's hand down beside the rotten porridge. She begins to scold her, but she calls her Mary, so Kaiènhne doesn't listen. She looks at the bowl before her, the mush for which this place earned its nickname, holds her breath, and eats.

Alice doesn't come to breakfast. When she thinks of the girl's face that morning, Kaiènhne closes her eyes, and sees two hot coals like irises staring back at her, gnashing teeth below them. In the afternoon, Kaiènhne takes laundry out across the snow to the washing building. Many of the clothes are stained with blood and vomit and piss. The wash house is crowded and cold, littered with uniforms and bedsheets and coats in piles or hanging on lines. She scrubs her hands raw in the deep basin of water, trying to wash the stains out. She hangs the uniforms to dry under the cover of the wash house, anticipating snowfall. She removes yesterday's dried clothing from the outdoor lines and folds them carefully into the basket, tracing the lines of the dress hems with stiff and aching-cold fingers. There are browning stains among the girls' undergarments, some from the older girls' monthly bleeding, but others from the Reverend and the teachers, the things they do to the girls in the boiler room.

Kaiènhne stares at the wood line as the sun dips beneath it. She thinks she sees birds in the trees, black feathers moving from dead branch to dying tree. When the shadow moves again, she swallows, exhales, and hurries back to the building, feet crunching on the snow.

The main structure of the institute is a massive, looming building, full of long halls and rooms of every size. The front half of the building and the classrooms are decorated with fine art and oriental rugs and perfectly placed antique furniture for guests to marvel at. But the sleeping quarters, the dining hall, the rooms where the children are punished, those are stripped to their bare, wooden bones, and left to the mold and the bugs. Kaiènhne passes other students in the halls going about their own chores, lowering her head lest the teachers become angry with them, accusing them of speaking in the devil's tongue. Kaiènhne makes it back to the girls' quarters with the basket of clean, folded laundry.

Her breathing is labored. She finds her mind flying back to the tree line, the flash of movement behind it, the nightmares of last night, both real and imagined. A deformed head above her bed, and another above Alice.

The beds themselves are haunting, even empty. Kaiènhne walks past them, stepping through row after row of isolated sleeping cubicles to the linen closet at the back of the room. She reaches for the handle and the door swings open.

Two bare feet swing in front of her. Kaiènhne slams it shut.

The clean clothes fall around her as the basket hits the floor. She falls among them, ice in her blood, heat in her eyes, sobbing.

"Mary, what are you doing?"

Her head turns unwittingly to the doorway. The Reverend stands in his black suit, tall and slender like an elm tree. Haunting and dark like a summer storm. His eyes are pure blue icicles, as frozen as his heart. "I'm s-sorry, Sir." Kaiènhne's voice shakes, her hands scrambling for the dropped laundry. "I tripped, I d-didn't mean to..."

"Never mind that, girl," he snaps. "Alice has gone missing. Have you seen her? I fear she may have tried to run."

Kaiènhne swallows a heavy lump in her throat, imagining the skinny legs swinging to and fro in the closet behind her. "No, Sir."

"Hm." He shakes his head. "Say a prayer for her, Mary. The snow has begun to fall. A winter storm is coming. She won't make it far if she runs."

Kaiènhne nods. "Yes, Sir."

When he walks away, she gathers up the clothes quickly and throws them aside, rushing down to the kitchen. The room is full of hot steam and busy hands, pans clattering. It stinks of the mush in here, and the ingredients that litter every counter and hang on the walls are as moldy and spotted as the slop they make.

Joseph enters the kitchen suddenly, squeezing through a narrow back door and between a pile of wooden boxes, his sunken cheeks red from the cold. He carries firewood to the burning stoves, his hands calloused from his chores, from scrubbing blood off floors, and from digging shallow graves along the tree line and beside the lake where their kin lie nameless. Kaiènhne wonders if he would one day dig a grave for her, too, where she would lie forgotten.

Kaiènhne rushes past him, out the door into the snow. Outside, a pile of sharp tools rests on freshly chopped firewood. Dim light from the kitchen makes the metal glow. Her hands hover over the objects: hatchets, saws, and knives.

"Mary, what are you doing?" Although his English is clear and almost fluent, Joseph's voice is distinct from those of the teachers and staff—he speaks without confidence, tone low and uncertain.

Kaiènhne turns to face him and speaks clearly in their native tongue, telling him the truth with no hesitation. "They won't find her," she says. "She's dead. I need your help."

His dark eyes go wide and his face pales. "Alice?"

"While they look for her, find me in the girls' quarters. Please."

He is not her family, but he is of her tribe. She remembers him when his hair was long and wild, his eyes bright and free. She hopes it is enough.

She takes a long knife from among the tools and hides it in her skirts, hurrying back inside. The kitchen workers don't mind her, their eyes focused on chopping and tossing ingredients into large pots over the fire. She rushes back along the wooden floors, over carpets and past paintings and bookshelves filled with bibles and histories that are dead and written rather than alive and told.

Upstairs, she reaches the room and closes the door behind her, breathing in and bracing herself before opening the linen closet.

It is Alice, hanging by her bed sheets, which are tied to the ceiling and wrapped around her delicate neck. Alice is far from the first dead friend that Kaiènhne has seen or touched, but it may be the first time any of them was brave and angry enough to die in their own way.

Kaiènhne knows then what she must do, why there is a knife in her hand.

She climbs the shelves in the closet, cuts Alice down and spreads the sheets across the floor beneath the girl's frail body. Her face is purple, bloody black eyes bulging. Unwrapping the sheet from the girl's neck reveals purple marks along her throat. Kaiènhne runs a hand along her own chest, up to her throat, to the suffocating buttons on her dress.

Leaning over the girl, whose name she doesn't know, Kaiènhne whispers a prayer to the Creator, the Sky Holder, and to the Sky Holder's brother, the Bad Spirit, Flint.

"I am sorry," she says in the language of Flint, her eyes burning, hands trembling. "I don't know your name, but I'm sorry. You're right, death is better than this, better than watching our names die, our stories, our language, our culture die before us. So please help us. Please come and help us."

She takes the knife to the bruises on Alice's neck, holds the girl's body steady with her other hand, and presses the blade into her flesh.

Blood squirts and stains the white sheet deep red. Kaiènhne grunts as the knife gets caught. Cutting a throat is hard, tougher than she imagined. She saws into Alice's neck, hand shaking, feeling chunks of skin and muscle against her fingers. The sight of it turns her stomach as the blood and flesh tears and rips under the dull knife. The smell of iron hits her with a wave of nausea.

Kaiènhne squeezes her eyes shut and begins to sob, hands shaking, feeling the blood on her fingers soaking into the fabric of her dress. The flesh splits, but cutting through the bone of Alice's spine takes all the strength Kaiènhne has.

The knife bites against the floor beneath the girl. In her mind's eye, she imagines Alice's head, disembodied, opening its jaw to devour her.

At that moment, the door swings open. Kaiènhne gasps.

But it is only Joseph. He stands in the doorway of the girls' quarters, for which he would be brutally punished if he were caught. Still, he came when asked.

At the sight of Kaiènhne, face wet with tears, covered in blood and kneeling before a beheaded girl, he cries out in such shock and horror that he forgets himself and speaks their language. "Mary, what have you done?" Blood drains from his face. "Have you killed her?"

Kaiènhne shakes her head. "She killed herself. I found her, but I need your help. And my name is Kaiènhne."

He swallows but doesn't offer his own name in return.

"Please, there can't be much time. I need you to take her body to the boiler room and burn it."

"Why?"

Kaiènhne's eyes are wild. Swallowing bile, she wraps the body in the sheet it's in and covers the head in a clean dress inside the laundry basket.

"We'll be caught." He switches back to English. "What will they do to us?"

"What more can they do?" Kaiènhne wipes her face of sweat, blood, and tears with her sleeve.

Trembling, Joseph asks, "Are we cursed?"

She doesn't answer.

He comes to lift the body carefully, wrapped in the bloodied sheets. She leads the way out, checking for any sign of the staff. They go separate ways on the first floor, Joseph heading toward the basement and Kaiènhne to the double doors that lead into the grand institute. At the entrance, she spots one of the teachers coming down the hall, about to round the corner and come face to face with Joseph and the body he's struggling to get into the stairwell.

Kaiènhne shouts, demanding attention in her own, forbidden tongue. Her mantra: "Kaiènhne iónkiats! Kanienkehá:ka niwakon-hewentsiò:ten! Wakeniáhten!"

The teacher spins toward her, a furious scowl across her pale features. "Mary, you will speak English!"

Joseph pauses for one panicked second and then uses the distraction as an opportunity to hurry out of sight. "Kaiènhne iónkiats!" Kaiènhne cries out.

Furious, the woman marches toward her, and Kaiènhne bolts out the door.

She runs toward the washing house, the woman shouting after her. The white snow glows in the darkness of night, but there are a few teachers and staff outside, searching for Alice, at least until they forget her as they forgot the others, the children whose families will never know what happened, whose remains they trample daily. Kaiènhne will not let Alice be forgotten. She sprints to the tree line and throws the basket into the woods.

She hears the crunch of Alice's head hitting the snow, and the noise of it tumbling away, lost in the darkness.

A hand grabs her with force. She turns to meet the pale eyes of the Reverend, the angry teacher standing with arms crossed behind him.

"You know better, Mary," he says coolly.

He drags her back inside, past the grand front hall, and the dining hall, and the kitchen, and toward the back of the Mush Hole, where classroom doors line the halls. But he forces her to go beyond that, passing a row of antique vases and extravagant French paintings. He is taking her to his office.

"In all the years I've been head of this institute," he says, "I have never dealt with a more defiant and rebellious child than you, Mary." He presses his fingers deep into her flesh to leave bruises. The stink of the dinner fades into a scent of dust and old wood— the core of this building. He pulls her toward his office. "You know, we are trying to teach you children, educate you, *civilize* you. But it seems that some of you refuse to be helped. Perhaps you were too old when we found you."

Her body is trembling, her mind screaming.

"Perhaps you are just too far gone. Perhaps some of you children will always be savages, born and bred—it is in your blood."

They are alone in this hall. They have gone far beyond the usual punishments, the old damp closet where she has been locked for days, the classroom where they burn and shock her with batteries, the boiler room. "Where are you taking me?" she demands.

"Alice is missing," he says. "She was a good girl; I can make you a good girl, like her."

Kaiènhne pulls against him, digging her heels into the ground, bunching up the carpet under her feet, but he is too big, too strong. His grip is iron and stone.

"Your people were monsters. The way they raised you, they taught you nothing of the world, nothing of how to live, how to behave like a young lady should. I will teach you."

Something in the darkness moves. She starts, her head turning to follow the movement. The shadows shift down the hall as he drags her through the door into his office. A single dim lamp on a writing desk casts a sinister glow on his narrow features. He leaves the door ajar and throws her into the shelves, books shuddering in their dusty bindings.

"Alice is gone because of you!" Kaiènhne says.

He slaps her hard across her cheek. "You will address me with respect, girl!"

She is used to being hit, but it stings all the same. The door behind the Reverend creaks. The shadows move into the room as he moves toward her.

He pins her hands against the wall, his long body curving down over her, a cage of limbs surrounding her. She struggles, crying out, "Sátka'w!"

Again, he strikes her. "You will speak in English, and only when spoken to!"

She spits in his face.

Shock, then fury, burns in his eyes, and he is so fixated on Kaiènhne that he does not see the door swing open behind him. She goes pale with fear. It floats over his shoulder.

The bloated, bloody head glides on black hair like wings. Glowing eyes, claws made of bone, teeth like dull knives. It comes in behind him, silent and hungry.

He assumes the fear in her eyes is for him. "I will teach you respect," he hisses.

Kaiènhne goes still, her gaze beyond him. "My people had enemies long before your people arrived."

"Of course you did," he spits. "You were savages, killing one another."

"They called us something else," she says. "You call us Mohawk. It's from a word from their language, but do you know what it means, Reverend?"

"I do not remember asking you a question, Mary."

The head floats up behind him, close enough that his pale eyes go wide when he feels a coil of the monster's hair on his cheek.

"Man Eater!" Kaiènhne pushes him with all her might.

The Flying Head's teeth gnash down into his shoulder. He screams.

The head bites into his arm. He falls to the ground, and it flies over him, jagged talons scratching him open, ripping into his flesh, his gut, as he lets out a gargled scream.

Kaiènhne is frozen in fear, watching the man's guts spill from his belly as the monster devours his flesh. She backs toward the door. When she reaches it, the monstrous head turns.

Alice's face is in there, somewhere, but lost in rage and violence and torment. Her eyes are fire.

Kaiènhne slams the door shut and runs. She hears it slam again behind her. The head is hunting her, looking for the one who didn't help her in the night against the Reverend, the one who betrayed her by leaving her to his whims, then dishonored her body and spirit. Kaiènhne knows this, she knew the monster would come with an insatiable hunger for all who wronged it. She races past classrooms, past the dining hall, where children choke down their stinking excuse for a meal, down to the boiler room, and finds Joseph, shaking and rubbing his hands on his trousers. The basement is full of heavy metal tools and steam and coal and screeching pipes so loud it's hard to hear a child scream among it.

"Kaiènhne?" Joseph says, and for the first time in years she hears her name on lips that are not her own and she wants to cry for the joy of it, but she has no time.

"We must run," she shouts above the noise. "Go, get the others, take what you can, and tell them to *run*."

Her eyes find the door to the boiler. Despite the heat that burns, she begins to unscrew it, begins to open the hatch to the burning coal inside.

Before Joseph can ask her more, a piercing cry echoes from the stairs. The head comes, larger and more twisted than before, bloating up to an unnatural size and shape. Blood dribbles down its chin, its jaw snapping open and shut.

Joseph whispers something under his breath.

"It is here for me," Kaiènhne exclaims, trying to pry open the hatch. "Please, hurry, get the others outside!"

The Kanontsistóntie's moves toward her, so she runs again, moving around the boiler. Joseph takes the chance to run as the head turns to follow Kaiènhne. She finds a wrench and swings it at the head, but the head easily flies above her reach, then swoops down and grazes her shoulder with its teeth.

Falling to the floor, Kaiènhne barely avoids losing a chunk of flesh. She crawls away and a burst of steam explodes from a nearby pipe, burning through her dress and leaving a blister on her arm. The Kanontsistóntie's moans and flinches back from the heat.

In that moment, Kaiènhne rushes to the hatch of the boiler with the wrench as the Kanontsistóntie's screams, jaw unhinged, swollen face swooping down over her. With a pop of metal, she pries the hatch open, hot coals spilling out onto the floor around her feet. She stumbles beneath the head, and it hits the boiler, making the whole structure shake, and a piece of coal flies up and hits its veiny blue flesh. The head hisses and flies away from the burning heat of the fire, to a damper, colder corner of the basement.

Kaiènhne's breath catches, her heart in her throat. She stares at glowing red eyes in the shadows, the glowing coals at her feet. Somewhere among the ashes, she knows, is Alice, but she pushes the thought from her mind and dances over the coals, her skin burning.

Kaiènhne races to the tools along the wall and grabs a shovel. She scoops a pile of the hot coals, red and glowing just like in her dream, and runs, losing a piece of coal here and there as she hurries up the steps. The Flying Head screeches behind her. Kaiènhne rushes to the front of the Mush Hole, where the stink of dinner and the smell of burning coal mix with old, damp lumber. Antique clocks and shelves line wooden walls, wooden floors groaning beneath her feet. The Kanontsistóntie's flies, its bone talons poised to tear into its next meal.

The air around her whistles as the head swoops in and Kaiènhne spins, jamming the shovel into its unhinged, unnatural, bloody mouth.

It swallows the hot coals and a screech pierces Kaiènhne's ears so loud it shakes her bones and makes the walls of the institute tremble.

The monster continues to scream, falling to the floor. Its veins erupt through its skin, oozing black blood, smoke pouring from its mouth. It bursts into flame, screaming. The smell of rot and burning flesh fills the air.

The wooden room ignites.

The fire spreads fast, catching every curtain, every carpet, every wooden beam around Kaiènhne. She runs, an echo of wild shrieking around her. The basement's support beams moan, and wails of human horror mix with unnatural cries as the fire spreads throughout the institute. She runs through the door, with flame licking at her heels, and reaches the snow outside.

Fifty children are gathering at the tree line, Joseph among them, as the teachers inside the building scream. Some of them have already escaped; others burst through the door. Another can be seen in a window, banging bloody fists against the glass as a shadow with red eyes descends upon and devours her, only to be consumed by fire.

Kaiènhne heads for the trees, the rising smoke over the crumbling institute at her back. Though she is dizzy, she goes to the others in the woods. They are small and frail, but they have survived much already. They can survive more.

Something snags her foot, and she falls into snow.

The Reverend clutches her leg and pulls himself up over her.

His eyes are bloodshot, red like the monster's, hungry for vengeance.

"You cursed us, you savage!" he hisses. "You did this. You brought this over to us because you would not listen. Demon! Devil! You are not human!"

His hands find her throat, ignoring the spilling of his own guts. He is too far gone, a dead man already, with only enough strength left to break Kaiènhne's neck.

She claws at him, but it doesn't faze him. He is in shock. He cares about nothing but killing her.

"You brought this curse!" he spits again. "Devil-worshipping *savages!*"

Her vision begins to fade; her arms lose strength. A knife finds the Reverend's throat.

Joseph's face emerges beside the Reverend's as he cuts him from ear to ear. The once frightened boy speaks clearly. "Skahiónhati iónkiats."

My name is Skahiónhati.

"Wakathahio:ni."

I am Wolf Clan.

"Ongweh'onweh ni'i."

I am a real human being.

— THE REPETITION TANGO —
by Alicia Thompson

I saw me again, getting off the train. I looked beat down as hell. This was the fourth time I'd seen myself out in the world in the past six months. The sightings are picking up.

I didn't even recognize myself the first time. It was more of a nagging sensation as I brushed through the steel doors of the Metro train. She was frumpy and fat, swathed in baggy, over-stretched pants that rose too high above her socks. A floppy blue tunic top completed her ensemble. Her chocolate-colored skin looked washed out and unhealthy and her liberally grey hair was pulled tightly back in a messy bun. I touched her as I was going in and she was coming out. My swinging arm slid momentarily against hers. Gooseflesh erupted all over my body. I barely turned my head in time to catch a glimpse of her profile. The doors closed and I saw her standing on the edge of the platform staring at me through the filthy window. She was me, all right. As I walked home in the dusk air, I realized she had been wearing clothes I had seen in my closet just that morning. I couldn't sleep for two days after that. I had to be imagining the whole incident. It just wasn't possible...right?

The second time I saw me I was buying a coffee in a Starbucks. I hadn't gotten one in months, but I was walking down the street and decided a hot mocha would hit the spot. I pushed open the door, walked up to the line, and stood behind myself. I didn't realize it was me at first. But something about the back of the head and the slumped shoulders sounded an alarm in my mind. Prickles enveloped my entire body, just like the first time. I slowly backstepped until I was far enough away to turn and flee. Adrenaline pounded through me until I was sitting in my living room, trying to appear nonchalant under the gaze of my husband's eagle eyes. There was another version of me walking around out there, and I didn't know why.

She scared the daylights out of me today. I went out onto the balcony for some air and looked down ten floors below. There she was, standing in the middle of the circular driveway, tilting her head back. She had on my purple sweater with the hole in the back hem and those damn high-water black pants. Her hands were planted on her hips, and I could see by the way she rocked slightly from side to side that her legs hurt, just like mine do. What does she want? There can't be two of us here at the same time in the same place, can there? It doesn't seem natural. Well, crap. Maybe she'll just go away.

I wake up at 3:11 a.m., drenched in sweat. I feel like I can't breathe and I'm trapped in a small space. As I sit up, gasping, movement in the corner catches my blurry eyes. A dark shape is lurking there, pressed against the wall. Fear instantly squeezes my heart.

"Who's there?" I cry out.

Beside me, my husband stirs and grumbles. "What is it?"

The shape is gone. I stumble out of the bed and lunge for the switch on the wall. Warm yellow light fills the room, and I can see that nothing is there. But the thing is, I can still feel it. Can still feel *her*. My husband rolls over, pulling the comforter over his face. I flip the light off and go into the kitchen for a drink of water. On the way back to bed, I hesitate at the apartment door and eye the peephole. Seconds hang in the air while I debate with myself. Of course, I look. I have to. Slowly, I step up and gaze into the small hole.

She's in front of the door, staring solemnly back at me. Her face is drawn and tired and there are dark circles beneath her deep-brown eyes. She looks mad. I think she's growing impatient with this dance of ours. She turns her head and walks away out of sight. I sigh. I lean my forehead against the cool wood. What am I going to do? I don't believe she will go away.

It's 2:00 p.m. on a Wednesday. I'm sitting on a concrete bench in Vista Hermosa Park, overlooking downtown Los Angeles. The sky is cerulean blue. There are no clouds. The sun is warm, but not too warm. The winter air still has a bite of cold in it. I'm watching a sparrow hop about on the grass. A shadow falls over my face and I look up. It's me. She sits down a few inches away. My eyelids droop in the bright sunlight. I have a headache. I can feel me looking at myself sideways. I'm too sleepy to turn around. She leans in close to me, and I shiver. Tiny electrical prickles flare over my entire body as she whispers in my ear.

"It's funny, you know. The sun is white here."

— BLOOD AND THE BOTTOMLAND —
by Michelle Mellon

The letter was delivered on her eighteenth birthday: June 19, 1971.

The knock at her apartment door was an unwelcome surprise, so she stayed quiet until her visitor had presumably gone away.

Hours later, as she was leaving to celebrate by herself at the movies, she found a cream envelope lying on her doormat.

Her name appeared in elegant script on the front. Several minutes later, after her hands had stopped trembling and she could open the envelope, she saw a letter inside addressed to her and her alone. Miss Clara Mae Elwood.

It was from a law firm, informing Clara she was sole heir to a family estate. They requested she take possession of the land and plantation house or advise them on a sale and dispensation of the resulting proceeds. She laughed at how overly officious it all sounded, but it seemed too elaborate a joke and she couldn't think of anyone who would put in this much effort for a mere prank.

Clara waited through the weekend before calling the firm's telephone number. After the second ring she was preparing to hang up when the receptionist answered and transferred her to one of the partners. He confirmed the contents of the letter and the names of her parents. But Clara remained skeptical; any search of public records would have details of the car accident that claimed their lives and sent her to the orphanage.

The orphanage. She had pushed it out of her mind for the past two years, ever since she'd run away, surviving by squatting in abandoned buildings and doing odd jobs for local businesses. Eventually she'd become an employee at a boutique, saving money until she could get an apartment, then a used car. She didn't go out much, and, though the people at the boutique were friendly enough, she didn't allow herself to have friends.

Not after the orphanage. Not after the teasing of the other kids when the administrator made a habit of calling her to his office, alone. Not after the wardress dismissed Clara's accusations against him and shamed her until she had no choice but to run away. Trust was a mountain between Clara and humanity that she was willing to leave unconquered.

Yet, as she refocused on the lawyer's voice, she heard what sounded like relief. The orphanage had apparently been no help, even suggesting that she had probably met an unfortunate end. The firm had hired a private investigator to find her in the months leading up to her eighteenth birthday. As much as she'd lived her life without believing that good things could happen to ordinary people, Clara started to believe what he was telling her. In mere moments she had gone from inner-city orphan to heiress. She had survived all the wrongs, and something might actually be going right for her. Clara felt just like the heroine of *Jane Eyre*, her favorite of the old novels she liked to read from the library. But when she hung up the phone, she wondered if a true heroine would feel as terrified as she now felt.

A week later her hands gripped the steering wheel, the tires on her ratty car churning a rhythm through unfamiliar stretches of country miles instead of stop-and-go city blocks. The drive from D.C. to Southwest Virginia wasn't that long, but Clara had been squirreling away payphone change anyway in case she needed to make an emergency call.

She had the address, basic directions, and a road map unfolded on the front passenger seat with the route marked in highlighter. So far, the drive confirmed what the lawyer had said about the property being in the middle of nowhere. Clara had never seen so much space that was so full of nothing.

But then she began noticing rolling hills and wildflower meadows and ponds and fields with occasional livestock and wildlife. Before she knew it, she arrived at the end of a long lane lined with massive weeping willow trees. She was here.

At the end of the packed-dirt lane, Clara entered a circular driveway and parked her car in front of the house. Instead of a sprawling southern structure with ornate columns like she expected, the house before her was more of a grand farmhouse. Three stories tall, large and square, with a full wraparound porch. She spied a much smaller, single-story version of the farmhouse in the distance, through some trees. It was undoubtedly the caretaker's cottage. The lawyer told her that, apart from a brief occupation during the Civil War, their firm's periodic visits and historical society events, the main house had been empty for nearly a century.

Surely the caretakers would notice any activity, then. And Clara feared they would come greet her before she had time to absorb her surroundings. So, she left her bag in the car and hurried away down into the greenery that flanked a large creek running parallel to the entrance lane.

She had been to city parks and even lived near the National Zoo, but this area had its own special feel. It was as if the green banks had at some point risen until they filled the sky before settling back down, leaving a lingering sense of the earth's omnipresence and the smell of rich soil. According to one of the books Clara had read in advance of the trip, the area around the creek was known as the bottomland. It was highly coveted because, even though it was treacherous during a flooding season, it was otherwise the most productive land in the valley.

On the other side of the creek, in a field, a pond rippled with an unfelt wind. A bank of clouds moved in and, feeling a slight chill unrelated to the weather, Clara walked the main lane back toward the house. The willow trees were now bowing and bouncing in the same wind that had disturbed the pond. The branches seemed to sing or sigh in their flight; she couldn't tell which. It was as if they were caught between a welcome and a warning.

Clara picked up her pace until she crossed the oval of grass in the center of the driveway and stopped to look up at the house. She was eager to enter, yet anxious as she approached the glass-paned double doors. There had been few things in her life to look forward to, and many more to disappoint. Hope was something new to her.

She took a deep breath, grabbed one of the door handles, and turned it. As expected, the house was unlocked in anticipation of her arrival. She stepped inside. Despite the obvious tending by the caretakers, the air inside felt heavy and ancient.

Clara was struck by the polished wood floors and wall panels. She walked around and looked at the elegant old furniture and peered at artwork in the gloom because she wasn't yet ready to acknowledge that pulling open the drapes was her right as the mistress of the house. But she soon found herself in tune with its rhythm. Like the house had been waiting for her and had finally taken a great cleansing breath of its own.

She heard a noise and returned to the foyer, expecting to find one of the caretakers. Instead, Clara looked up to the top of the stairs and, to her disbelief, saw herself descending. It was like those times she practiced in the mirror, trying to emulate the heroine of a century-old novel in the slight tilt of the head, the mysterious smile, and the way her arms hovered away from her body like beautiful birds with clipped wings.

One step. Two steps. It was five steps before she shook her head at how silly the thought was. She was not standing there watching herself approach. The girl coming down the staircase had cream-colored skin, much like the envelope nestled somewhere in Clara's bag. The girl wore a pale-green full-length gown that flattered both her figure and her emerald eyes. Her honey-colored hair was piled loosely atop her head, with two carefully escaping tendrils on either side of her freckled cheeks. No, definitely not Clara. She imagined herself descending the same stairs in the same gown. It might flatter her figure, but it would contrast against almond skin, not ivory, and large hazel eyes. And her hair was not arranged in careful disarray. It sprung from her head in an unshaped black Afro with a mind and landscape all its own.

Clara was so lost in musing that she hadn't realized the other girl had reached the bottom of the stairs. Then suddenly she was there, reaching for Clara, snaking small, cold hands around Clara's wrists, with a grip that sucked the breath from Clara's lungs. Darkness squeezed in from the edges of her vision and she fell to the floor. When she awoke, there was a moment when the darkness still hovered. It was as if death had made itself known. And she realized she'd feared it all her life—feared its power to erase without remorse. It had come into the light to claim her, and it was reluctant to let her go.

"Welcome back, Clara," said a voice outside her field of vision. And with that, the darkness was gone.

"I'm Sinia. The caretaker," the voice said, moving before Clara could turn her head to find it.

The woman now standing before her was older, darker skinned, with her hair cropped close to her scalp. Something about the woman felt familiar, but as much as Clara wanted to know what had happened to her, she didn't know that she could trust Sinia. She might not believe Clara, or she might be involved in whatever had happened earlier. Clara thought it might be wise to ease into that discussion.

"It's just you for all of this?" Clara waved her arm beyond the realm of the bed on which she lay, intending to indicate taking care of the cottage and the main house and the surrounding land.

"It's just me," smiled Sinia. "Just like it's just you. Again."

"What do you mean?"

"You saw someone in the house, didn't you?" asked Sinia.

"Yes. A girl my age. A white girl. It seems silly," Clara hesitated, "but at first I thought, well, I thought—"

"She was you?"

"How did you know?"

"Clara, let me tell you a story."

The letter was delivered on her eighteenth birthday: June 19, 1861.

The knock at the door was a manservant, waiting with the letter lying on a tray in his hand. She picked up the envelope with some trepidation as she dismissed him and retreated into her room. It was too soon to hear from her brother, who had foolishly left to join the army after the battle at Fort Sumter.

She would have made a better soldier than him, and knew it was only a matter of time before he ran away or was killed.

As she studied the stationery, she recognized it as her father's finest. She should have felt flattered, but as she opened it and read its contents there was little solace in the beauty of its form. The address inside exactly matched the outside. No "dearest daughter," then, nor ever after. The letter stated that she, Miss Eugenia Jane

Elwood, was no longer a member of the family and in three days' time she was to take her belongings and vacate the estate.

It seemed her mother had confessed her role in concealing Eugenia's recent indiscretion—that indiscretion being a larger blow to family honor than the deception surrounding it. To flaunt his hypocrisy and derision, her father also stated that, should anything happen to his son and heir, he would affirm the paternity of the young boy resulting from his own liaison with one of their house slaves. And the first female descendant of *that* line would inherit the house and land.

Eugenia burned with shame and rage, but she had no time to waste with a tantrum. She calmly placed the letter on her bedside table and dressed in simple clothing suitable for an outing. She left the house as if she were going for a walk. Once beyond the range of any spying eyes, Eugenia ran across the field, through the family graveyard, and into the neighboring settlement of freed slaves.

The house she sought was at the end of a short dusty path, slightly off center from the makeshift settlement square. It was, in fact, the exact place where she'd gone to remedy her pregnancy. This time her need was greater, and her purse bulged with compensation accordingly.

"A poison and a curse?" The woman inside whistled and sucked her teeth, weighing her words. "I am a healer. I don't know why you have the idea that I would help you in this."

"You took one life for me already. What difference is two more?" Eugenia spat.

"It makes a difference to me," countered the older woman. "And what makes you think I did what I did for *your* sake?" she asked as she forced the pouch of jewels and coin back into the palm of the young woman. "In this, you are on your own."

Eugenia stalked out and wasted no time making enquiries on the main street. Everyone knew who she was, but everyone also knew how she paid to get her way. She soon found someone willing to prepare her an elixir and place a curse on her father's line of bastards. Eugenia needed no assurances of confidentiality. Even in her disgrace she knew no one would take the word of a colored person over hers.

She returned home and waited, playing the remorseful daughter, certain her father's message was a bluff with no legal bearing. Yet the evening before her presumed departure she saw no relenting. She prepared a farewell tea in the parlor and served her parents the elixir in their portions. By morning, she was an orphan.

Less than a month later, her brother was killed in the battle at Bull Run. And, though it turned out her father's missive had been no bluff, in the country's subsequent upheaval the lawyers allowed Eugenia to remain on the estate until the end of the war. Afterward, she moved into a small cottage several miles away, still intent on recovering her home. But she died of smallpox before reaching the age of thirty.

"That's some story," said Clara. "How much of it is true?"

"All of it."

"How do you know?" Clara pressed.

"There's one sure thing about this place. Blood and the bottomland are interchangeable and immutable."

"What does that mean?"

"Most of us who choose to stay here are related," said Sinia. "So, blood. But there's a terrible beauty to this place, a history of some of the very first Black bodies brought to this continent bound in service here, in the bottomland."

Sinia explained further: "It's the blood of our ancestors and ourselves watering the soil of this land. It's in us, and we're in it. It means we carry the weight of this place and all its stories and we pass them along as a sort of legacy."

Clara sighed. "That certainly sounds more meaningful than how I'm feeling right now. But I don't know that I want this place and all its weight as my legacy."

"Legacy is a choice," said Sinia. "It's fate or destiny or whatever you want to call it that usually holds people back. But I believe you're free."

"How do you mean?" Clara asked.

"Free of Eugenia's curse."

"Which was what, exactly?"

"The boy her father sired with the house slave? Eugenia cursed his descendants to be bound to the bottomland. Not by a love of this place, but because they felt a stifling, unfulfilled obligation. They were to live uneasy lives here and suffer violent deaths."

"Like my father," Clara whispered.

It was Sinia's turn to sigh. "Your father was so much stronger than his forebears," she said. "He met your mother on a trip into Roanoke and that was enough. He left this place and endured the ache and call of the curse and started a new life. I think it was the first step toward breaking its hold."

"The first step," Clara repeated. "There was more to the curse, then, wasn't there?"

Sinia nodded. "Eugenia had no shortage of money to spend, and the witch she contracted for the poison and the curse had no shortage of greed or power."

"Just before you told me Eugenia's story, you asked me about seeing someone at the house. It was Eugenia, wasn't it?" asked Clara. "Is she haunting the house?"

"Not exactly."

In response to Clara's confused look, Sinia clarified: "Remember what Eugenia's father threatened—that the first *female* descendant of his bastard's line would inherit the estate? Eugenia's curse was also meant to prevent any daughters. A spiteful move so that no other woman would become mistress here. But she requested a fail-safe. In the event a daughter was born and returned to claim the estate, Eugenia would claim that daughter for herself and live on through her."

"Wait, you're talking about possession? By a dead woman? That's crazy!"

"A few years ago, men left this planet and landed on its satellite. How crazy is that? How is this any crazier than anything else happening in the world right now?"

"It was you," Clara breathed. "Your voice sent away the darkness when Eugenia came for me. Are you...are you related to the witch that set the curse?"

"No," Sinia laughed. "Folks ran her out of the bottomland once word got 'round about the deaths of Eugenia's parents. But I am related to the woman who first refused to place the curse." She winked.

Clara gasped. "But how..."

"There is no good or evil in magic. Only in the intention behind it. Power is power. It's how you use it—to harm or to heal—that makes the difference. There's an energy in the bottomland, in that blood and love that keeps us here. If you choose to draw on it, you can do almost anything."

Clara thought about when she'd arrived on the estate to a landscape and house devoid of other people, yet she'd sensed movement and energy as she walked through the grounds and entered the house. It was like an undercurrent, or faint heartbeat, that buzzed with a need and a promise. But it undoubtedly came with a price.

"Thank you," Clara said. "Thank you for using it to help me. I could feel it when I first got here. But I don't know if I can use it. I'm afraid that if I stay, I'll somehow end up trapped, like my ancestors. And that somehow Eugenia will win."

"It's not about winning or losing. But if you want to look at it that way, your great-auntie Eugenia has already won. She's kept your kin—and you—from claiming what's theirs."

"A week ago, I was an orphan that no one thought twice about. I was poor, but content. I was alone, but not lonely. Now there's this estate and this community and this crazy history with murder and a curse and a jealous, avenging spirit and now bottomland magic." Clara threw up her hands. "It's all so overwhelming. I don't know what I should do."

"Listen to your heart. Listen to your head. Meet them somewhere in the middle," Sinia smiled. "But it's a choice only you can make."

The letter was delivered on her thirtieth birthday: June 19, 1983.

Instead of Sinia's familiar scrawl on the envelope, Clara opened a note from Sinia's granddaughter, who had taken over the bulk of caretaking on the property the past several years. She was writing to inform Clara that Sinia had passed away after a brief and sudden illness.

For more than a decade Clara had deliberately stayed away. She informed the lawyers the estate would remain as it was indefinitely, with Sinia remaining as caretaker. She and Sinia corresponded regularly as Clara went back to school, received her diploma, then earned a degree in history.

Out in the wider world Clara saw that life was changing at a pace that guaranteed that some things would soon be lost forever. She began traveling, studying stories from small Black communities all over the country. Capturing those moments was what Clara had chosen as her legacy. But there had always been something missing. A hole that she'd tried to fill. First with college drinking, then with lovers she'd easily kept at arm's length with her nomadic lifestyle.

Recently she'd noticed some changes. While standing in the unforgiving sun in some far-removed place, she smelled the earthy scent of the bottomland on her skin instead of her own sweat. On winter days, if the world outside was frozen, she felt the sun-kissed waters of the creek bubbling through her veins. And, while listening to the oral history of a vanishing community, she'd suddenly hear the whispering rush of willow branches, with the language of the leaves becoming clearer each time.

Now she sat down and scribbled a quick note to confirm she would be there for Sinia's funeral. And long after. Clara wanted to learn more about her own stories. Stories that had shaped her life before she ever knew it. Maybe it was the lingering effect of the curse. Maybe it was a synergy with the bottomland that left the kind of kiss on her heart she could never forget. Magic or mood or simple maturity—whatever the reason, she felt she was now ready.

She opened the bottle of birthday wine she'd bought for herself. Her first toast was to Sinia, who had shared many stories in her letters over the years, and had become Clara's one true friend and confidante. Then she toasted her late parents and hoped one day, like her father, she would find the kind of love that was so strong it could even break the bind of a family curse. Then she toasted her great-great-great aunt Eugenia, who shared this birthday with her but had never lived to see her own thirtieth year.

Clara smiled and made a final toast to herself. She was no longer some teenage heroine from a Victorian novel embarking on a new adventure. It was time to accept the signs all around her. It was time to embrace her blood and the bottomland and all that entailed. It was time for her to go home.

— SMOKE FROM A FLAME —
by C.M. Leyva

Gabriella Morales exists only in memories. A place where grief holds souls in a world no longer theirs. Flashes of moments her sister, Sonia, can't move past.

One such memory was an overcast day in the garden of their home in Coconut Grove. Gabby and Sonia were ten, playing hide and seek in the vibrant greens of overgrown brush and behind cracked statues of melancholy saints. An older woman dressed in black and grieving the death of her husband lost her way home, wandering into their garden, her eyes orbs of trapped fog—an inescapable sadness. Bony fingers, dressed in loose rings, reached out to the twin girls. Words escaped her thin lips in a language they didn't understand, sucking the air from Sonia's lungs. She reached for her sister.

"It's okay, Soni," Gabby said, stepping between them.

Their mother rushed over, guiding the woman to the front of the house. But as days passed, the girls' imaginations took hold of the moment now decaying in ruminations tainted by fear. They invented an ominous past for the woman in black, convincing themselves that her words were a curse.

That the brujeria had stained the blood coursing through their veins.

That they had been marked.

Each unfortunate event in their lives became only further evidence of the woman's dark spell.

When Sonia spent two months practicing for her role as Wendy in the school play of *Peter Pan*, Gabby blamed the curse for Sonia's laryngitis on opening night.

When Derek Jackson confessed to no longer loving her, Sonia finding him and Carmen Ortega in the AV closet at school, Gabby blamed the curse for his wandering heart.

But when they watched their mother slowly waste away from breast cancer, Gabby's silence told Sonia what she already knew. The nurses did what they could to provide their mother comfort and dignity in her final days, but the curse took her from them two days before her forty-fifth birthday.

Then Gabby died.

Sonia remains alone in their home in Coconut Grove. Once a prominent ER nurse, now a shell of the woman she once was. Nothing more than a shadow cast against the walls of the vast, crumbling home. A house that no longer feels like a home. The walls shudder on stormy nights like Gabby did as a child. Sonia is convinced that the curse has marked them not just in the world of the living but also in the next. The lingering warmth of her sister still surrounds her, even if Gabby has become nothing more than smoke from a flame.

A world exists between love and death. Gabby's soul remains delicately balanced in between. Her footsteps echo with Sonia's across the red terracotta floors as they wander from room to room. Each day the same routine. Trapped in a world that's nothing more than an echo. An eternal witness to the gradual dissolution of her sister's soul. Sonia Morales no longer lives, only exists, despite the white pill she takes for health and the beige pills she takes for what's left of her sanity.

The harsh white walls trap mirages of family portraits now tucked away. Tobacco-stained ceiling beams hover over Sonia like ribs, protecting the fragile life within. The soft orange glow of the filigree wall sconces mirrors the flickering flame inside her. Straining for vitality, but only one breath away from being extinguished.

The doorbell rings, stopping Sonia and Gabby's footsteps on their usual path. The carved wooden door groans in protest as Sonia opens it.

"Hello! My name is Peter—and I just moved in next door. I noticed your house could use some repairs and wondered if you were in the market for a handyman?"

Peter looks like someone who understands the power of his smile, explaining how he's made his fortune flipping houses. The eagerness in his russet eyes tells her that he sees an opportunity to make a diamond from coal.

She pulls her shawl tighter. The only people who had approached her in the last ten years were enthusiastic men and women looking to buy her home. Desperate to take from her the only thing she has left. Sonia shakes her head, ignoring his outstretched hand. Fear grips her even at the thought of a simple handshake. She isn't looking for a connection. They only end in loss.

"I'm not interested," she says, closing the door.

But each day for the next week, Peter brings her pastelitos and cafe con leche to share in the garden.

"Sonia, this house is a masterpiece. If it's the money keeping you from taking my offer, I'll do it for free. I just want to help." Gabby watches from the empty chair between them as her sister's resolve cracks like the statues in the garden. In the end, his kindness is the only key he needs for Sonia to allow him in. His excitement overcomes Sonia's initial fears, and he immediately goes to work, taking inventory of all the items she allowed to fall into disrepair. But as he labors down the list, Sonia finds herself living in a world between dreams and nightmares. Each mended wall crack re-emerges the next day. Peter stares in confusion, but gives a confident smile, blaming it on an unstable foundation.

Gabby stands next to him, admiring her destruction.

Even after a picturesque day working in the garden together, Sonia and Peter find their freshly planted flowers dead the next morning.

"Must be contaminated soil," Peter says, delicately lifting the wilted foliage.

It took nothing more than a touch for Gabby to watch them wither and rot.

Despite Sonia's efforts to keep the curse tamed—trapped deep within her—she is convinced that it now bleeds into her home. As she sits in the garden tub, struggling to suppress a panic threatening to take hold, she concentrates on the rhythmic drip of the new faucet. It wasn't the plumbing, despite what Peter would probably try to convince her of the next day.

Gabby's finger swirls the water of the garden tub, staining it black, as Sonia teeters on the verge of breaking. For the first time, Gabby thinks that if she can convince her sister to leave their home, maybe they can both move on.

Sonia picks up the phone the next morning, dialing their old friend, Teresa. Within a few hours, Teresa arrives, dressed all in white. A maroon and white headband restrains her once wild curls.

"I've been waiting for your call. I just never expected it to be ten years after your sister passed."

"Has it been that long?"

Teresa's eyes fill with empathy. "She was such a vibrant soul. It's a shame she left us so young."

Sonia's hands tremble, transporting her back ten years to the buzz of the fluorescent lights at the nurse's station of Mercy Hospital.

Her twelve-hour night shift was coming to an end, and she was looking forward to showering and crawling into bed. She hoped to beat Gabby home, so she didn't have to stay awake listening to her enthusiastically replay the events of her evening with friends.

A call came in over the radio. A car accident on southbound I-95.

Sonia looked down at her watch. Gabby would be on I-95 driving home.

A red Jeep Wrangler overturned.

Gabby drove a red Jeep Wrangler.

Three females. One fatality at the scene. One in critical condition. One with serious injuries. Ambulance five minutes out.

Gabby, Clara, and Melissa had gone to the concert together.

Sonia no longer heard the chatter from the nurses around her—not over the incessant buzz of the fluorescent lights. A fog engulfed her thoughts, and she sat, staring but not seeing. Minutes. Hours. Lifetimes. None of them held meaning in the darkness surrounding her. She reached a trembling hand to her stethoscope, draping it around her neck. Her footsteps sank into the floor as she forced herself to the ambulance entrance.

She arrived just as Melissa and Clara were rushed in.

The metallic taste of blood fills Sonia's mouth, pulling her from her memories. She'd chewed the inside of her cheek raw while lost in thought.

Teresa looks away, scanning the vaulted family room. "I can begin the cleansing if you're ready."

It was time.

Teresa places her bag on the leather couch and removes a bundle of sage, lighting it with one of the wall sconces. She closes her eyes and dances from room to room in a trance, her long skirt twirling around her as she sings. Sonia wants to feel something in the moment, to know the Santeria and sage are working. She wants to see the darkness peel from the walls, but nothing happens.

Gabby follows Teresa, feeling a connection between them. Since she passed, it was as if the link between her and the living had severed. Somehow, Teresa has opened a piece of herself to this realm Gabby exists in. It manifests as a glow radiating from the center of Teresa's forehead, drawing Gabby to it like a moth. She reaches out, touching the light on Teresa's brow.

Teresa suddenly stops. Gabby is now looking through her eyes. Her soul stretches to fill the skin, but it isn't her skin. She's a visitor, and the body already fights to expel her. Her eyes lock on Sonia's. The connection they had lost ten years ago, reawakened. Teresa's eyes fill with tears—Gabby's tears—as her bare feet move across the floor, leaving ghostly impressions on the red tile.

"Soni," Gabby says in Teresa's gravelly voice.

Sonia's eyes grow wide. "Gabby?"

"It's okay. I'm okay." Gabby walks forward, bridging the gap between them as their connection grows stronger. "But you're not. It's been too long since you were okay."

Sonia's shoulders collapse as tears flow down her cheeks. "I miss you so much. I never thought I'd feel so broken."

"You aren't broken, though. Cleansing this house won't take away your pain." Gabby lifts Teresa's hand, grazing Sonia's cheek. "It's your soul that needs cleansing. Until you can walk away from me and this home, you'll never be whole again. Can you take that first step with me?"

Teresa's hand wraps around Sonia's, guiding her to the door. Sonia hesitates in the threshold. It's been ten years since she stepped beyond the property.

"I'm scared."

"I was always the braver one," she says with a grin. "Do you still trust me?"

Sonia takes a deep breath and pushes her foot through all the barriers she's created.

The world is so bright and abrasive, but something about the harshness feels cleansing. Like the first breath taken after being submerged underwater too long. The house remains behind them, its tendrils snapping with each step Sonia takes. There's a weightlessness as she looks back at the home they'd grown up in. Teresa's hand disappears and Sonia knows her time with Gabby has come to an end, but the warmth lingers on her skin. There is hope in the moment, and she lets it wash over her, suffocating the cold trapped within. It will take time to learn to live again. Gabby had always been better at it than Sonia, but she would try each day.

Peter slides the last of her boxes into the back of his silver pickup. Excitement radiates from his eyes, and he kisses the back of her hand. Sonia smiles, his adoration filling her with warmth. Her home in Coconut Grove shrinks away in the sideview mirror, and her gaze travels to a box of pictures resting in her lap. Memories now kept safe in delicate frames, allowing her and Gabby to move on. Reminders that, while a world exists between love and death, grief no longer holds their souls.

— THE CANDLEMAKER'S DAUGHTER —
by Amiah Taylor

My mother loved to play with fire. I could see it in the way she held matches in her hands. Sometimes I would catch her striking them and putting them out, as though she liked the smell of smoke. Growing up, we warmed ourselves by the fire and told stories. I would sit on her lap and listen to her heartbeat, memorizing her scent of cigarettes and incense. And she would always leave a candle burning for me in my room. We had an unspoken understanding that I hated sleeping in the dark. So I grew up perceiving flames as my friends. When we left the old country, we didn't take much with us and we were poor. But my mother was determined for us to be more than just down-trodden immigrants; she worked more than one job at a time and slowly amassed enough money for us to open a shop. And of course we sold candles.

Mother taught me how to dip-dye them and set them into different shapes. My favorite part was boiling the sweet-smelling wax and pouring it. It made me feel like a sorceress, transmuting liquids into solids on a whim. And if the candle turned out misshapen, I could always melt it back down and leave the wick to dry. My mother always told me that mistakes aren't mistakes until you leave them that way. Just like I loved the fragrance of her, I loved the fragrance of candles. And making them wasn't just my trade, it was my way of life.

My mother and I were brown in a sea of white. We existed on the periphery of society in that we did not look like everyone else. My hair was coarser than that of the other girls. My lips were more deeply pigmented and so was my skin. Even the palms of my hands were etched with dark lines. My hue was a constant reminder that I did not fully belong, even if people waved at me or greeted me with candor. I understood that I was the buxom girl with long hair and dark skin.

We were different in the thick accents that we still harbored and the strange foods we still cooked. We ate with our hands for a lot of our meals. My mother would sometimes get a craving for okra stew—a meal that had comforted me on many nights when I was feeling homesick.

On one such occasion, she sent me to the market to collect vegetables for the stew. It was a week after my twentieth birthday and just like any other day. Flocks of centaurs were haggling for fruit, a few fairies were playing by the river, and an angry sorceress was trying to scold a child for taking her wand.

In the marketplace, placing round, lush tomatoes into my straw basket, I could feel his stare. Peripherally, I confirmed his presence. It was almost silly to see such a fine and decorated man against the backdrop of the canal and the cobblestones quays with a basket in his hands.

A week had barely passed before he called upon me at my house, joining my mother, Cyra, for tea in one of her fussiest outfits and discussing his intentions. Soon, my mother had it in my head that I could be the next marchioness.

She had visited Madame Moth, a local fairy endowed with psychic prowess and large opalescent wings. A simple crystal-ball reading emboldened her to believe that I was going to be engaged soon to a man of power and status. The madame had prophesied it, and she even told my mother what colors to wear to make it so. "He's looking to get remarried," she purred, braiding my hair into long plaits. "Why not you?"

The motives that led me into the arms of the marquis were mixed. I was happy being an artist, acting as a housewife of sorts to my mother as she ran our candle shop, but I did not know whether the pleasure was genuine or a habit of circumstance. I knew nothing else. I was used to our humble abode and the rose-filled front room and the pots of wax always bubbling, making the air sweet and heavy. My mother was the one who began staring at the roses with discontent, grieving that she could not give me more or place me higher in society. She called me her crown jewel and wanted me married before my beauty began to fade.

So, no wonder she had fallen under the spell of the marquis in less time than it took for the tea to boil. She even asked him to call her Cy. In a high, falsetto voice she sang my praises ceaselessly. First, it was how clean I kept the house, the superbly polished silver and the well-dusted shelves. Then, it was my green thumb, how violets and roses blossomed under my touch. Then it was my cooking, which seemed to compound in greatness by the minute. I listened to it all with a weak, unconvincing smile.

"Océana makes the most tender roast that you'll ever sink your teeth into. The meat just falls off the bone."

Studying the face of the marquis, I thought he knew my mother's game as well as I did, but he nodded politely.

He had a warm, sibilant voice that did not suit the local accent. His temperament seemed well practiced, a distraction from some undefinable, unnatural thing at his center. It was almost as if a record player sang sweet songs from behind his lips, songs that were not plucked from his own imagination. Undeterred, my mother allowed him to visit at least once a week and looked at him approvingly when he began to present me with gifts.

The first gift that he presented was for my mother and me to share. It was a lovely porcelain tea service set, meant to accommodate at least four people. The teapot and saucers were accented with gold trim and hand painted with yellow and mauve tulips.

My mother cherished the tea set above everything else in our home. When she was not dusting the saucers or fussing over them, she was speculating about the price.

"Such fine craftsmanship! Such painstaking detail! This set must be worth more than anything we've ever owned. Just look at it, Océana. You could be the wife of King Midas."

Not a week had passed before a second gift arrived.

It was a hand-carved trunk filled with fine imported teas and two square boxes made of black velvet. Inside were a pair of pearl and ruby earrings and a necklace to match. My mother was absolutely beside herself with delight. When she saw that I had left the jewelry in the trunk, she carried the boxes to my room and sat on my bed. With a smile she fastened the necklace around my neck. It hung at my collarbone and sparkled incessantly. She held my hand mirror to my face, forcing me to look at my reflection. She had tears in her eyes.

When she spoke, it was from a deep, guttural place. "I always wished I could give you more. You have to eclipse me, Océana."

"We don't need pretty jewelry and fancy teapots, Mother; we have each other."

"If we are taking stock of what we have, don't forget the bills. Or the lack of customers and what it costs to run the shop. Don't sell yourself so cheaply."

"I didn't realize I was for sale."

"To be content with vegetables from our garden and our tiny house, when you could live on an estate, it's foolish. Please, don't turn away from what could be a beautiful life."

Looking at my mother, I could see how much she wanted me to be happy, and how badly she wanted me to be open to the attention of the marquis. Woman to woman, she was pleading with me not to repeat her mistakes.

The next time that the marquis visited, he bore another gift. I received him differently: less as an option I could run away from, more as an inevitability. My mother had all but begged me to be flattered by his visits.

My emotions hit me like a succession of waves when he gave me an emerald bracelet that I had seen on his late wife, Aubine.

When Aubine died, it surprised no one. The marchioness was a woman who loved to eat and drink but maintained a chic figure. She would come out wearing makeup and earrings, her heavy black hair piled high on her head. It was not uncommon to see her half-collapsed at a luxurious restaurant, her long brown neck exposed and her wine-stained lips parted in laughter. There was something sumptuous and decadent about her cocoa skin. Drunk on an astronomical amount of red wine, she had lost her footing and cracked her skull on the marble fountain at their shared estate. Like many others, I attended her funeral, albeit briefly, to pay my respects to the late marchioness. It was a closed-casket funeral, during which the marquis seemed tired but businesslike. It seemed surreal to me: if she had survived that calamity, the marquis would not be here and this bracelet would be dangling from her wrist, not mine. "Océana, my sweet, do you like your new bauble?"

Rather than give an answer, I pressed myself against him and kissed his thin red lips. When I drew away, he was smiling.

The proposal came soon after, to my mother's delight.

When he brought me to the manor, it looked like something from a lavish dream. The house itself was a stately three-storied stone chateau. It was preceded by a lush rectangular garden of lavender and sprigs that was parted in the middle by a gleaming pathway.

Inside, the floors were a never-ending sea of swirled marble. On the walls were alternating paintings of war and peace. The windows were receded rectangles angled to show the full magnitude of the gardens. The furniture was made of oak and satin and draped with mink and fox furs.

When I found him sitting on the stairs of the courtyard, shaded by a blooming tree, he looked like some sort of Greek god. Reading, his eyes were focused on the pages, and yet, as if he sensed me, he smiled slowly.

"I trust you enjoyed exploring the estate?"

"You're so blessed to have so much beauty around you."

And with startling clarity, I saw our children running barefoot through the grass. Their small brown fingers investigating everything that thrived around them. The flowers and the trees and the slow-swaying grass beneath their feet. At night, perched on the stairs, I would show them the patterns of the constellations. Outlining all the celestial bodies with my finger.

"Oh no, my sweet. Prayers and blessings have no effect on this house."

I stared, unsure of what to say. The children evaporated.

"If God is not in your heart, what do you believe in?"

An apple dropped into his lap. "Science."

He rose and extended the fruit to me. "Come, I will show you the library. I think you will be spending a great deal of time there."

The library turned out to be one of many. Upon the walls were dozens of preserved butterflies of various sizes. He followed my stare up to an iridescent moth with a wingspan the size of a small bird's.

"Many of them flit through the property and find this to be their final resting place."

"Why are there so many?"

"A variety of exotic flowers grow here. Many of them happen to be poisonous to their species."

"So, death comes to them in the guise of a beautiful flower. Why not remove the flowers?"

"Why not resist them?" he countered. "That is why they are in my philosophy room, darling. Personal agency. Choice."

Frankly, I wasn't sure if his mentality was poetic or damaged.

I softly uttered, "What a price to pay for following their most basic urges."

He waved off my comment, nonplussed. "Would you like to know one of my basic urges—in fact, one that's affecting me at present?"

He did not wait for me to answer, continued anyway. "Hunger."

As he turned away, I could not help but notice how broad his shoulders were, the expanse of his back. I looked at him curiously, and accompanied him for a brief walk, to a shed adjacent to a kitchen garden full of budding green herbs.

The door to the shed had been pulled off by its hinges and propped against a nearby wall. In a pen in the yard, a few chickens were pecking around. My husband gingerly picked up one of the hens and assessed her with a calculating stare. He placed her on the ground in favor of another hen.

"This one will do. Océana, my pet, will you fetch my axe?"

There was a wooden post with an axe lodged into it a few steps away from me, and I felt paralyzed. I looked up to see my husband towering over me, his lips pursed, and I knew that he was waiting for me.

"Is my pretty new wife not ready to get her hands dirty?"

He smiled but it didn't quite reach his eyes.

With all my might, I tugged the axe from the tree stump and nearly lost my balance. It was heavy and sharp enough to cut through bone. Without much grace, I dragged the weapon over to him and set it at his feet. My hands would not stop shaking.

Axe in hand, he headed to the doorless shed.

"Bring the bucket."

He extended the chicken's neck across the wooden post and waited a second, for her to be calm. In a single strike, the axe fell and severed the chicken's neck. A thin and steady stream of blood poured from the wound. I placed the bucket underneath to collect it.

He nudged the bucket toward me. "The plants can't be an afterthought. Feed them."

"With this?" I questioned, gesturing toward the bucket.

A small smile played on his lips. "Oh yes, you must sate their thirst. They love it. It will make them grow big and strong."

As I evenly distributed the red contents of the bucket, I could feel him watching me. It was not so different from the bubbling pots of red wax that I would stir at my mother's shop.

His eyes drank me in, in the same way the parched soil swallowed down the blood. Then, perhaps for my benefit, he began to muse aloud.

"You are a true marvel, if I have ever known one. Beautiful and willing to learn. What did I do to earn such perfect obedience? My perfect Océana."

We ate the chicken that we killed together for dinner. I couldn't shake the dark feeling that we were co-conspirators. He sent the carcass to the kitchen and had the cook prepare us a luscious dinner of chicken-stuffed pies, wilted greens and braised pheasant with olives, and roasted chestnuts. The dessert was sugared cherries and port.

Before long, it was night and the estate was quiet. The talk of butterflies was forgotten and we had long departed from the shed. Despite my husband's comments on resisting temptation, he was very much in the business of spoiling me. As if he liked to watch me struggle to accept the ludicrous wealth he had at his disposal. After a bath together, where I was too nervous to do anything but soak and let him wash my hair, he led me to our bedroom, which was filled with gifts and flowers. There were blue orchids and hydrangeas. There were hyacinths and forget-me-nots. There were orange-centered daisies and tangerine-hued chrysanthemums and buttercups, which gave way to blushing red poppies and scarlet zinnias.

I sighed. It was nearly fatiguing to behold so much undiluted beauty. He had made the room look like a sunset, the arranged flowers transitioning from the afternoon blue sky to the reds and violets of the evening.

"We've been married, my sweet," he smiled, "but not in the eyes of God."

I paused and met his eyes hesitantly. "Do you mock me? You have no such belief in Him."

He sat on the bed with great relish. "Of course not, darling. But I delight in your piety. Especially when one of your religious rites of passage bestows something so sweet unto me."

"And what might that be?"

"Consummation, of course. To become my wife in all things."

I looked at my reflection in the wall mirror. My dark coarse hair hanging at the small of my back, still unruly and damp from the bath. The sheer lace nightgown that clung to my hips and decorated me with indigo satin. The small oval buttons that began at my collarbone and ended at my navel, implying an accessibility to privileged areas. I knew that he was a privileged man. I was unfamiliar with bedclothes such as these, that were supposed to summon desire in a partner. I pictured my old cotton nightdress hanging on the clothesline. I pictured my husband's stark white hands on my skin.

I did not realize that I had been trembling until my husband came to stand beside me and put a steadying hand on my shoulder. And his hands were like the hands of a clock, maturing me. I felt older under his touch, calmer. Less like a child and more like a woman who was feminine and ready.

The marriage was consummated—he took me twice—and I woke up in bed alone.

"Darling?" I called groggily.

I felt around for my husband and realized that his side of the bed was cold. Finally, my fingers brushed a note detailing the reason for his absence. I could hear his voice in the loops and curls of his penmanship:

A thousand apologies. I daresay you will be left idle for six days as I attend to an urgent business matter. Make yourself familiar with Lottie, our phenomenal cook, and request anything your heart desires for meals. I've left you presents, carafes of sparkling wine and endless poetry. My only request is that you bypass the small room on the third floor as you explore. The keys to every room are on the keyring by the bed. You may use every key but the small iron one. Refrain from even looking at it for too long, lest your curiosity overtake your reason. All my love, my sweet, until I return.

With my actions so explicitly policed, I stepped out of bed with some uncertainty. I glanced at the ring of keys. All rooms but one. I supposed that was fair. It was probably a private den where he took his cigars and kept his hunting rifles. Or maybe it was a revealing room full of evidence and sensitive documents.

These were the thoughts that plagued me as I descended the stairs in search of Lottie, the "phenomenal" cook.

Lottie turned out to be a giant snake.

Lottie was a female cobra the height of a fully grown man and wore a red ascot and a chef's hat. I thought it would be rude to ask her how she cooked with no arms or hands. My husband was clearly so rich that he could afford to hire magical creatures to do household chores.

The breakfast spread that Lottie prepared was some of the best food I had ever had the pleasure of eating. There were wine-soaked pears and small artisan cakes, scrambled eggs with chives and root vegetables and many types of grapes. As soon as I could finish one plate, it seemed like another was placed in front of me. I indulged in everything, the fruit mousse, the candied rose petals, and the many breads covered in sesame seeds or walnuts or cheese.

I told Lottie that breakfast was heavenly, that she put my own mother to shame.

Lottie smiled an unsettlingly wide smile and promised that she would make every meal better than the last.

Pleasantly full and newly aware of my loneliness, I offered to help Lottie with the cleaning up

She recoiled in surprise. "The marquis would not hear of it; that's well below your station."

I followed her into the kitchen. "Has my husband been a good master to you?"

Lottie tensed and looked me in the eye for the first time. She seemed to be searching for ulterior motives.

Slowly, the snake said, "Yes, mistress."

"It's just us girls," I insisted. "Is your master a good man?"

Lottie considered the question as she slithered around the kitchen.

Finally, she said, "The master has always done right by me. He's kind and likes a finger or two of scotch each night. His solitude is everything to him."

I asked a question I knew the answer to. "Has he been married several times?"

She nodded. "I believe you're the fourth mistress I've had, ma'am."

I hesitated. "Do you know what's in that room?"

"It's under lock and key. I've never been inside. I wouldn't dare intrude upon his privacy. Us snakes have a saying, sssssa sse si ssss ses siya sssss. It means, swallow your food whole and count your own eggs, not your neighbor's."

Lottie continued. "I do just that. I keep my head down and scrub these plates. When Aubine tripped and fell down the stairs, he stayed in that room for days. I suspect it's a grieving parlor."

"I thought she hit her head on the fountain outside," I said.

"Perhaps I'm mistaken." Lottie's eyes returned to the ground.

"Is that what he told you?"

"I have no desire to contradict him," she said hurriedly. "I— I don't remember, and my memory is quite poor. Let's speak no more of this. Would you look at the time! If you'll excuse me, ma'am, I must tend to the dishes."

Before I could say anything more, she bowed gravely and slithered away.

I retired to the master suite. As instructed, I opened my presents and found many fine pairs of earrings studded with rubies and garnets. There was a tiara and a matching necklace of yellow diamonds. I found sweets and books of love poetry with my husband's handwriting in the margins. I found decadent fruits and exotic bottles of sherry. There were petal-smooth silk slips for wearing to bed and colorful silk scarves for my hair. There was a collection of floral and musky perfumes that I found to be quite agreeable.

All in all, I didn't want for anything.

But then I thought of my husband's compliments, calling me pristine and obedient. That was the measured space he had designated for me. His perfect Océana. All his expectations tightly wound into one woman.

Clearly, Lottie was unreliable. Snakes have been treacherous since the beginning of time and that's all there is to it.

Perhaps I could talk to my husband about replacing her when he got back from his voyage. No need for such blatant negativity and insidiousness in our household. This was a peaceful manor, and any discrepancies could very easily be ironed out.

At the funeral he had confirmed that she had cracked her head on the fountain. I remember his brisk tone and the touching eulogy. I remember the firm texture of the chair I was sitting in and him saying it was a fountain and her drunkenness that did her in. Did he misspeak...or mislead?

I needed to have a reckoning with my own heart and tell it to stop slamming into my chest. I needed to regain control of my own body, which had begun to shake and tremor. I could feel sweat collecting at the small of my back. I could feel an unknown force piloting me.

I knew in my heart that I shouldn't succumb to curiosity fueled by baseless gossip. But my hands didn't know that. My feet didn't know that. And, together, they were moving me closer and closer to the iron ring of keys, pressing the forbidden one into my palm.

It wasn't a crime to just hold it.

And he didn't tell me I couldn't look under the door or through the keyhole. He never said that I couldn't press my ear to the door and just listen.

So, without my permission or consent, my feet led me to the small room on the third floor. The small iron key was warm in my sweaty palm. My back felt drenched. At that moment, it felt dreadful just to exist in my own body. My skin was crawling, the hairs on the back of my neck were standing up, my heart was thudding almost audibly.

Stooping, I tried to look through the keyhole, but my eyes were met with nothing but darkness.

I took a shallow breath and tried to steady my hands, but they were already sliding the key into the lock.

The door noisily creaked open. It was dark inside. The windows were covered with thick velvet curtains of intricate scrollwork. The whole room was decorated in ugly striped wallpaper and the floor was wood paneled and squeaky. The first thing that I took notice of was an overwhelmingly putrid smell, a scent so gut-wrenchingly disgusting that I instinctively clutched my stomach. I saw an enormous bed, two white bathtubs and a table with a full set of dinnerware on it. The room was large enough to be a small apartment.

My eyes took a moment to adjust, and then I saw her. Seated at the table was the mutilated corpse of Aubine. I froze. The dreadful sight rendered me incapable of action. Something inside me called out in silent agony. My throat tightened. I could feel the pinpricks of tears.

There was no doubt that the corpse was Aubine. One of her arms had been cut off. On the other there were long and deep marks, as if the sharpness of a blade had been tested on her skin several times. I shivered, beholding Aubine's sallow cheeks with a mixture of fear and repulsion. Her mouth was contorted in a silent scream. And, perhaps most horrifying of all, there were bite marks on her neck. Not love bites; mouthfuls of flesh had been torn from her collarbone, exposing sinew and bone. The man she married had eaten small parts of her.

Aubine was not alone in this terrible room. There was more than one Black body in a state of decay.

With growing fear came the realization that more than one woman had died at my husband's hands. Upon the great bed in the corner was a lifeless woman. She had long dreadlocks and tribal scars on her face. Her eyes were closed, and her wrists were tied to the bed frame. She lay next to Aubine's missing arm. She was clad in very little more than a jeweled collar. Upon her legs were sheer white stockings and she was wearing fine lingerie of indigo lace and satin. It made me think of my own nightgown. The one I'd been deflowered in.

The third woman had not met a less disturbing fate. She possessed a dark complexion that bordered on blue-black and a large puffy afro. There were large almond-shaped holes in her back, revealing the pink and yellow muscle beneath. One of her arms was bent strangely, as if she was reaching for something. On her thighs were scratches and holes where insects had burrowed. Deep-purple bruises covered the surface of her skin, and around her ankles were rope marks, as if someone had strung her from a tree and used her for target practice. Her disfigured face was the hardest thing to look at. She had large, round, black eyes that seemed almost accusatory, and a blood-stained mouth pried open.

There was another still, a body in one of the bathtubs. She was a beautiful brown woman with a honeyed complexion dressed all in white, like a baby at a baptism. There was something ecclesial about her, despite the circumstances. Her death seemed the most simple, and her body was in the best condition. She could have been sleeping, except that there was a translucent bag over her face, which made her head look like a balloon. She had been suffocated and left as a pretty corpse. I could see the effort made to preserve the woman. The tub was full of ice water, slowly melting. The woman lay there lifeless.

The inexorability of my fate dawned upon me. As I started to back slowly out of the room, a jeweled leash abandoned on the ground—presumably once for the dead woman on the bed—made me stumble. Startled, I dropped the key and it clattered to the ground. I scrambled to my knees to retrieve it, but it was too late. A red stain had imparted itself on the key, as if the metal itself were bleeding.

Two days later, when my husband got home, he was all kisses and flowers, and I felt rigid in his arms. Despite his warm smiles, I could not get myself to unthaw. He was quick to show me the daisies and poppies he'd collected for me at the market in an effort to make me smile. Instead, my stomach somersaulted incessantly.

I looked down and saw that I was clenching my fists so tightly that I had fingernail marks in my palms, and my tendons ached.

He carried me up the stairs, in his arms like a child, and set me down on the bed.

Those same high-thread-count sheets, which had seemed so luxurious and enveloping a few days ago, made my skin crawl. I kept thinking about the corpse in the lingerie. The white stockings. The vacant look on her face. The ghastly scent of decomposing bodies muddied together with women's perfume.

When I started to pull away from him, he held me tightly to his body. His face was exuberant.

Beaming down on me from his great height, he said, "I can't get enough of you."

All I could think about was my body lying lifeless in a bathtub filled with ice. And how I would've brought it upon myself by not seeing the signs. Not heeding the rumors, wanting too much to be my mother's source of joy instead of my own person.

I tried to suppress the glare that was emanating from my face, and he continued heedlessly.

"Every time a wave crested, I thought of the gentle swell of your lips. Was I missed?"

"Yes, darling," I whispered. "You consumed my thoughts... I didn't expect to see you so soon."

"My history of being fastidious has been utterly unraveled. I'm afraid I was quite hasty in my business matters, trying to rush back to you. You're already changing me, Océana."

"And you've changed me, darling...irrevocably." I hoped my voice sounded normal and relaxed.

He lifted my chin toward him for a kiss and, instinctively, I shrank from his touch.

He paused and looked into my eyes searchingly.

"I'm unwell," I said, scrambling for an explanation. "Really, I haven't been out of the master suite all day and all I can keep down is weak broth. You were just so enthused to see me I didn't want to say anything."

"You are not the first wife I've had." He smiled wryly. "Or the second or the third. So I am more familiar with cohabitation than you. What makes it work, my little sweet, is trust."

"Yes, of course," I stammered.

"You should think enough of me to tell me when you are ill. I want you bare, completely free of pretense. Is that understood?"

"Yes."

"I will get you one of my personal elixirs from the medicine room. Just tell me where the keys are."

"No," I almost shouted. "I am actually feeling well enough to get it myself."

"Nonsense," he chuckled. "Produce the keys this instant and I'll procure the medicine."

"They are in the white dresser."

Watching him walk away from me, the air felt palpable. He covered the distance in a few short strides and I could hear the keys rattling around in the drawer. Tears pricked at my eyes and I hurriedly wiped them away.

"Where is the little iron key?" he asked.

"It's an amusing tale," I started. "I was just so tempted to look in that room. The room you said was private."

I could feel him closing the distance between us and I tried to keep my breathing steady. With him towering over me, I felt myself losing my nerve. I lowered my eyes, afraid to face his glowering expression.

He said slowly, "I am waiting to be amused."

"Well," I said. "I knew if I kept the key then I would give over to temptation. So, in a moment of sheer desperation, desperation not to be misbehave, I'm afraid I did something quite unladylike."

"Which was?"

"Swallowing the key."

He clapped his hands together in delight, as if truly amused by my antics. "Oh, my sweet! That key was over a hundred years old, no wonder you're sick."

He continued. "To go to such lengths to keep from defying me is admirable. What did I ever do to deserve such an obedient, foolhardy little wife?"

"I certainly feel like a fool," I said weakly. "A fool with a stomachache."

My husband was attentive to me in my supposed illness. And after a while it was no longer an act. His very presence nauseated me and made me tremble. He rubbed my feet as he told me about his sea voyage, and he helped me to change into a satin robe.

He ran me a bath that he wanted me to luxuriate in, full of flower petals and scented oils. I could smell lavender and frankincense and, despite myself, my body began to soften a little bit. I felt a little more safe. He didn't know that I knew about his wrongdoings, and that was the most important thing.

After soaking long enough for the water to transition to lukewarm, my husband entered the bathroom purposefully, holding a hairbrush.

"Let me help you wash your hair."

Leaning my head back, I tried to breathe evenly as he massaged my scalp. I couldn't help but acknowledge that his hands were so close to my throat. There was a gentleness to him that was completely mismatched with the evidence of his potential for harm. Those women, were they like me...did he wash their hair too?

I was interrupted from my thoughts when I felt his grip tighten on my hair.

"What's that mark on your stomach?"

"Darling, what are you talking about?" I cried out. "You're hurting me."

Looking down at my navel, clear as day there was a red imprint of the key I had swallowed. So red and so vibrant, it was as if I'd created the deep bruise with blood and red candle wax. I was branded with a scarlet letter that I simply could not explain away.

He released his grip on my hair and I was left looking at him blankly, wondering how soon he would hurt me, and why the redness of the key was so visible against the blackness of my skin. How had my act visibly branded me?

His demeanor completely changed. He smiled, but it seemed as predatory as a hyena rearing its head back to attack. "You didn't tell me you used the key before you swallowed it." The corners of his mouth were upturned as he said, "I was just going to make another. But now I am going to cut that one from your stomach."

"Listen," I said, "we should talk about this, darling."

He continued as if I wasn't speaking at all.

Casually, he remarked, "Then, after, I will grind you up and feed you to the barn animals. Better yet, maybe I should use you to water the plants."

"No!" I shouted. "It was a mistake. It was just a mistake!"

He dragged me out of the tub and, in my struggle, I knocked over a vase of flowers. He groaned in agony. He held his face gingerly as if I'd slapped him.

Unaware of how I'd hurt him, I had no time to really think or recover. With all my might, I pushed a crystal lamp onto the floor, and he howled in pain. Wildly and desperately, he was reaching for me, flailing his arms out uncoordinatedly. His face was bleeding, his eyes were dark with pain and his mouth looked torn and bruised.

Suddenly, I understood. He was as old as this manor. He was at least as old as the key. This house was his body, and he was a cannibal, "eating" those women and storing them in his secret stomach. It was as simple as hunger, the basic urge that he couldn't deny any more than the butterflies on the wall of his library. Like a bright and breath-taking flower, he used marriage to lure in Black woman after Black woman, and each one was too ensnared by the beauty he offered to realize how much they'd suffer from his thorns. All he had to offer was vampiric love, and drain them to the last drop. This house was the last remnant of him, running on borrowed blood.

I ran from our bedroom, pushing over or crushing everything I could touch on my escape route. Running into the hallway, I saw three candles and a tray of wine and glasses he had set out for us. He had planned a romantic evening.

I ran toward the candles in the hallway and knocked two to the ground. The drapes began to burn, set ablaze, and I could hear him screaming.

I snatched the last candle and wine bottle and continued down the stairs. I resisted the urge to look behind me, knowing that he must be following me, absolutely enraged and wounded, ready to choke the life from my body and cut out his precious key.

I had to burn the chateau to the ground. The lifeblood of his evil.

Cracking the wine bottle on the ground, I soaked the cushions of the couch in the sitting room with the sweet liquid, and used the candle to start an impressive fire, hearing the animalistic screams of my husband.

The dead woman collector.

Fleeing the chateau, feeling the sun hit my face, I nearly sobbed with happiness.

I made my way outside the manor and wandered barefoot among the trees. My arms were lined with scratches, my hair filled with ash.

Naked as the day I was born, my soul felt bright and fluid, the fierce flame of a candle.

— REINCARNATED ROSE —
by L.C. Star

As her previous clothes burned in the fireplace, Selena Thornton reflected on everything that had happened. The family vacation at the beach in Taboria was only supposed to be for the summer. They had saved up for so long. And everyone but her was slaughtered by the Conclave of Harmony.

They claimed it was because the Thornton family were necromancers, but the Thorntons were in fact channelers. They had nothing to do with forbidden magic.

The Thorntons could communicate with ghosts. An ability as natural as breathing. This power wasn't used to bring back the dead. Rather, it was used to bring closure to others, to send messages back and forth so that the spirits and the living could both move on. It was for peace of mind. But they were still misunderstood to be necromancers.

The Council did not want anyone working with the dead.

And only Selena lived because she was gathering seashells in a cave by the beach—far away from her family.

She had never paid attention to where her hometown was; there wasn't any need to. All she used to do was sleep on the way; she knew it took days to get there, and she never learned the direction until she started to make her way back. She gripped her dress tighter as more tears came.

Selena should have left. However, her grief kept her stuck at the abandoned house. It wouldn't let her up. The grief was too heavy. If her younger sister were around, she'd joke it was because Selena was yet to tie up her long and light-purple hair. But images of her burnt body displaced Selena's smile. If her older brother were around, he'd joke it was her heavy sadness for a spirit. But she would never see the state of his body again. The fire before her made her hyperaware of how she looked; her hair was thick, long, and oily, her skin was dry and full of dirt and oil, and her lips had become chapped and scarred.

Since she had managed to escape the massacre of Taboria, her family's deaths, Selena tried her best to run away and hide, finding abandoned houses and changing into any clothes she could find. She'd burned her previous clothes. For food and passage, she pilfered any items she could trade for coin. Over and over, she had to guess what was valuable to survive.

"I'm close, aren't I?" Selena muttered aloud. "Is that why it's so hard to leave?" She was terrified, terrified that if she stepped back into town she would be executed. Her hands shook in that fear. She couldn't stay there for long. She remembered her mother saying that she had forgotten her grimoire and had to include some new spells. Somehow, the parchment papers had survived rain and humidity between Selena's body and her undergarments. She wanted to honor her mother's wishes. Though she had to make a promise to herself: if she survived the journey, she would grab her mother's grimoire and take care of her family's affairs.

The dress she chose was a bit big on her, but it didn't matter. The white collar almost covered her brown neck and had three black buttons. At the edges of the collar were frills, and black ribbons covered the middle of her chest. The dress was easy over her head because it was big, and, had the dress fitted her appropriately, it wouldn't reach the floor without her nearly tripping over herself; she had to find something to tie the extra fabric behind her. The brown fashion boots she wore had caused her feet to blister and cramp, but she forced them to get used to it. Once she got home, she would make time to treat her wounds and form a new plan of action: to leave Emain permanently.

As her eyes dried up, she felt a presence. Some stray tears ran down her cheeks, and she became hyperaware of her living body. She had been awake longer than the sun had been out, and she had to get moving quickly. She started to suspect, though, that she had long since overstayed her welcome.

She heard a child's laugh.

When Selena turned around, she saw a servant boy. His outfit reminded Selena of the masters and servants she saw her mother work with; however, he was translucent.

A dreamy look was on his face as he ran around Selena.

"You look just like her!" The child examined Selena from all sides.

He started to recite a strange poem over and over, but a line popped out that grabbed Selena's interest: "By the grave I saw the waterways!" A few iterations of this strange poem and the child disappeared, giggling out of existence.

Despite the oddness of this occurrence, Selena felt strangely calmed by it, until she heard the sound of horses' hooves and three people coming in. She realized how much longer she had stayed there than intended. She knew she should have left earlier, instead of sitting there crying as the fire smoldered, but she was frozen in place. The fire had long since gone out, and her previous clothes lay as ashes.

There wasn't much time between Selena getting up and heading out the door, with her items in hand, and the Conclave of Harmony breaking through the door and windows. Selena screamed and dropped her items. The parchment papers were safe in her undergarments, but any items she held, they were gone.

The Conclave—their full name was most ironic—came in wielding their magic powers. Snarls and sickening smiles covered three faces—a man's and two women's—as they tried to get closer to her. Two of them hurled fire and ice at her. Selena threw herself with all her strength to avoid the blasts.

While these witch bounty hunters closed in on her, Selena felt her heart thump and grow in size. She didn't know if she would make it—death had come for her family and she'd only narrowly escaped it then.

There wasn't much time.

The sudden sound of horses crying out alerted all three bounty hunters.

"This way, Josephina!" the child spirit yelled. Somehow, the back door slammed open, almost torn off its hinges. The bounty hunters had turned their heads for a mere moment. And it was all she needed.

Josephina? Who is that?

Selena didn't think after that—she ran out the door the moment the opportunity presented itself.

As soon as she left the house, she gritted her teeth, closed her dark-purple eyes, and prayed. She didn't stop when her legs buckled underneath her, when she stepped on rocks at odd angles, even when a cart came to a panicked halt and someone yelled at her.

"Josephina, get out of the way!" cried a male voice.

The shock of the sight upon opening her eyes almost stopped her in her tracks. She fell to the ground. The horse jumped and brayed in the air, trying to avoid her, spooked just like the ones at the abandoned house. Selena raised her arms to protect herself and cried out, desperately trying to get out of the way.

Somehow, and quickly, the young man calmed down the horse, momentarily ignoring the girl who was so frightened that she wouldn't budge from her spot.

The young man helped her up. He had fairer skin—lighter than Selena's, to be sure—with a healed scar on his left cheek. With black ruffled hair and rich green eyes, he wore clothes very similar to the human priests she had seen on the way to this area. White robes with a huge red cross on the back indicated holy status as a priest. But Selena blinked, realizing he had a small earring in his left ear. He had a handsome face, and the scar somehow enhanced his features. He was much taller than her.

"Are you all right?" he asked, with reserved authority. Once she was comfortable on her feet, the priest let go. The sound of hooves and the shouts of people echoed in the direction Selena had come from.

Selena turned toward the sound and, with her sweat mixing with her tears, held back a sob, trying to catch up with her breath. She turned back to the priest and grabbed his arms as tight as her strength allowed. His eyes widened, and she could tell he wanted to speak, but Selena interrupted him before he had a chance.

"Please, please, please," she started to beg. "They're after me—I'll do anything, j-just please help me!" She realized how clean he was compared to her. When had her hands become so covered in dirt? How crazed did she look to this stranger?

As the priest got his bearings, he managed to get her hands off his arms, dragging her by her wrist to the back of his carriage and up the steps. The carriage seemed to fit only one person, but he forced the door open and grabbed a handle attached to a large board.

"Be quiet," the priest said as he closed the hatch's door and stepped back outside. She heard his footsteps recede and then felt the carriage shake a bit. Selena was surprised at the amount of room this crawlspace had.

Silence gripped her throat, but not her heavy heart, as she heard the steps of the horses. She wished she could thank the child ghost for their help earlier, though the strange mixture of fear and gratitude kept her quiet.

"Have you seen a dark-skinned necromancer come through here?" one of them shouted from their horse.

"I have not," the priest shouted in return. Selena heard him pat the horse who'd nearly trampled her earlier. She tried to calm her breathing, her sobs, her thumping heart; she hoped their senses were dull enough to not pick her up. If there was anything that she allowed to flow freely, it was her tears. "Are you the Conclave?"

She couldn't hear anything other than the sounds the horses made as she placed herself as close to the hatch's door as she could. Desperate, she tried to search for words between the Conclave member and the priest.

Though Selena was still just a student of channeling, she struggled to keep her presence dulled as the men walked around inside the carriage.

While it was difficult to hear the full conversation, it sounded like the priest was doing everything in his power to distract the man from fully exploring the carriage, going by the irritated tone of the Conclave member.

The Conclave member opened the carriage door and she felt the vessel move. Heavy thumps echoed on top of the floorboards and the member started to move through various items in the carriage. Selena didn't know what to expect—did they know about the secret crawlspace? Selena didn't want to die...

Eventually, she heard the carriage door open, and, once again, she moved with the carriage as it shook, shifting off. Her heart crawled up to her ears and thumped along with the heavy footsteps.

"I told you. They're not here. Now, will you please put those items back where they belong? I'm on my way to the next town to take care of the refugees there."

The Conclave member was silent, and then grunted. They mumbled something under their breath, not bothering to do as he asked before leaving the carriage. Selena took as many breaths as she could without creating much noise. She was so close to freedom...and the priest didn't give away her location.

"Are you satisfied? Please just leave. I'll pray to Samher in your name, your organization, for disrespecting a priest such as I."

"You're just a rich boy in disguise. But since you are a priest, we'll leave you alone. For now. If we find out you're hiding that dirty necromancer, you'll have to answer to the Council." Selena nearly jumped out of her skin when this man suddenly raised his voice. He must have grabbed the priest, because she heard the shuffling of clothes and grunts. Eventually, she heard the Conclave member walk away, and the sounds of the horse's hooves fading.

Selena didn't know how much longer she would stay in the crawlspace—most likely a while longer, in case they stalked the priest. Because she had expended so much energy, and because she hadn't had the chance to eat, to breathe, Selena found herself at the far corner of the crawlspace and her body falling asleep. She was shocked when she woke and found herself in the carriage. She sat up straight and grabbed her chest—her mother's parchment notes were, thankfully, still hidden in her undergarments—and looked around her. The carriage was very cramped, and there were boxes filled with miscellaneous items, as the young priest was slowly putting things back, almost done.

He looked somewhat annoyed at her, but there was a gentle look on his face, seeing her stir.

"Are you awake?" he asked, turning his attention away from his duties. "Are you hungry? I have some leftover food from lunch I can give you."

Selena didn't know what to say, but when she realized that the Conclave member was nowhere to be seen, she relaxed a bit. "I'm sorry for troubling you."

"It's not a problem. I'm a priest and I help people. What's your name? You can call me Adam."

She hesitated, but eventually she opened her chapped lips. "My name is Selena." The priest nodded and reached over to grab leftovers and water to give to her, and she ate fervently. "Thank you so much for your kindness. Truly, I appreciate it. I've been running from the Conclave for a while."

"Where are you heading?" He kept his green eyes on her. Heavy and cold, but full, Selena felt settled. It was more food than she had had in a long time, but Adam gave her a gentle smile, putting away the remaining food.

"Ah, I'm heading toward Quickstar. Which is in the direction you were going in. Um, I don't have any coin to give you..." Selena stuttered and hesitated in her speech, once again gripping her skirt, afraid of any strange "payment." The situations she'd managed to escape from were countless. "But if we go to Quickstar and you wait a few days, I can give you coin for food, water, travel and a place to rest."

"You do realize I'm a priest."

Selena nodded. "But this is the best I can offer. I'm not...human, either. So I don't know what penance you require." She looked down and felt her body grow hot. Embarrassment, shame, other emotions collided within her all at once.

"All I ask for is your company, and coin to compensate for the food. My church may not be too happy, but if it's just to the next town over then it should be fine." A soft smile on his thin lips appeared. Selena felt dark.

"My apologies, but may I rest? I didn't think that lunch would make me sleepy." She grabbed her head for emphasis, and the priest nodded, finishing his clean-up.

"Go right ahead. The seat is right there, unless you prefer inside the crawlspace again." He laughed playfully, but softly, as he climbed up to the driver's seat.

On top of feeling tired, Selena didn't want to travel with him openly in case the Conclave continued to watch this carriage; however, she was already stuck there, and there wasn't any other form of travel. Her feet throbbed and her legs ached. Selena had no choice but to stay. She knew she put the kind priest in danger, so, while she was awake, she had to do what she could to prevent his punishment, whatever that might be.

Adam left the carriage and sat in the driver's seat. Once settled, he stayed alert to the periphery, watching for the Conclave, or anyone else who might be watching or following him. It wasn't every day he had such a lovely passenger, even if she was being chased by the bounty hunters.

When this girl ran out in front of Delilah, it certainly gave her quite a shock, but Adam was more shocked—he could've sworn she was Josephina for a moment, before realizing she wasn't. He hadn't realized that he had even blurted her name. Was it the midday sun? Was it his loneliness in traveling? He'd become a priest only recently, and had managed to beg the head priests to let him go on his own—all he was tasked to do was to seek potential locations for churches in this land. As a very small part of a very large plan, humans and other witches made a very shaky alliance: the humans helped the refugees who has escaped the necromancers; in return they could spread the word of Samher.

"So, is there anything in particular in Quickstar?"

He glanced at her with a small smile. Selena eventually joined him in the driver's seat, fully awake and fully alert, as the day went along.

The girl seemed to choose her words carefully. "I'm trying to leave this country," she finally responded. "I just believe it's time to leave."

"Is there a particular reason you're leaving? I won't ask questions about the Conclave. They have their reasons for searching for witches."

"I'm sorry," she said, and Adam was surprised that he was able to pick up her tiny voice. "All I can say is that it's time for me to leave."

Once Selena set her boundaries, Adam decided not to push it further; his curiosity, however, was almost getting the better of him. He managed to keep quiet.

The trip by itself took a day, and the closer they got to Quickstar the more open Selena became. Adam still didn't learn anything from her other than that she too was someone who came from the upper-middle classes. Not as high class as Adam once was, but it was a comfortable life for Selena.

They talked of many things—it was clear that she was educated and had a loving family. Selena never divulged too much about what happened to them, but he couldn't help but wonder. He wanted to prove to the growing darkness in the back of his mind that she was not Josephina.

She was nothing like her.

Eventually, they entered the settlement, and Adam was surprised at how bustling it was, even at night. Selena became excited, and tried to convince Adam to drive the cart toward her house. With a few turns, they eventually make it to Selena's home. The town itself was by the coast, and something prickled at the back of his mind—something between a twinge of familiarity and a twinge of urgency. Something told him he shouldn't stay in the town for much longer. Once they arrived, Adam was relieved that his assumptions were correct.

It was a simple, two-story home that only an upper-middle-class family could afford, to his knowledge. It was eerily quiet—surely, for a young woman like her, she would be missed by such a family.

And nothing familiar, he told himself.

Selena climbed down the carriage and looked at him, with a few tears rolling down her cheeks.

"Um, thank you so much for bringing me here. Please give me a few days to sell some things and I'll give you some coin." Selena tried to calm herself down, but her tears betrayed her once again. "You...you're more than welcome to stay in my family's home and use our facilities until then."

Something wasn't right. Was it the things she was saying? Or was it the ocean air he inhaled? Regardless of the growing cold around his neck, his back, his body, Adam smiled and nodded.

"Just tell me where to park good ol' Delilah." He patted the horse's bottom for emphasis, who blew out her nose and tapped her hooves gently.

Selena directed him to the nearest stable. She would wait for him inside the house.

The young woman dashed into her home and took a quick bath, her first bath in ages. The familiar scents of her family were almost too much for Selena. She wished she could use her magic to summon their spirits, but it could reveal her magic to the priest; worse yet, it could reveal her magic to the town.

Or, even worse, her family wouldn't respond.

Before, most of the residents of Quickstar never questioned how a family of channelers succeeded in their business as they were. Her father was a key member of society, someone who wanted to be on the Council eventually. Her mother was the lead channeler of the family, the one with the strongest magic, and Selena was being trained in the magic under her mother's care.

All they wanted was a vacation, away from home.

Images of her mother's slit throat, her father's frozen body, a blood spot that was once Alvaro, and the burnt body of Martina flooded back to her as she gathered jewels, clothes, and other items of value to sell for her journey. Each memory ached her heart, and she hesitated more and more when gathering her items. But she had to abandon them and this life.

She didn't know how much money she would need, so she had to decide what to come back for later.

How much time did she have left? The Conclave was not stupid; they could hide their presences better than she could. Not even that—someone in Quickstar was bound to report her coming back home to them eventually.

Another knock brought her back to this world once again. She wiped her tears and sighed as she made her way to the door. Behind the door, Adam looked a bit nervous, and he rushed in before she could properly invite him in. Once he entered, he forced the door closed.

"We have to leave. Something about this settlement isn't right. Something's amiss."

Adam sputtered out his reasons in fragments, but Selena couldn't piece it together. She tried to respond to what she could.

"Huh? W-well, I need to give you your coin..."

"Look, we'll travel together. You said you need a safe passage out of Emain, right? Well, we'll need to make some adjustments." He grabbed Selena's dress and let go just as quick. "Cut your hair. Do you have any servants?"

"Uh—"

"It doesn't matter—we'll buy some with the money we'll get. We just have to leave! The sooner, the better!" Adam grabbed her hands and brought them close to his chest. Selena grew red against her dark skin, feeling his warmth against her cold.

"Uh..." Selena didn't know how to take this. "I have so much to do. I have to sell these goods and this house. I have to tidy myself up, pack, and we have to find the clothes in such a short amount of time."

Frustration flashed across his face, but it quickly disappeared and he let out a sigh. He never let go of her hands. "Can't you hurry it up? There's darkness! And the sound of dripping! There's something unholy about this settlement." He tightened his grip and she grimaced slightly at his words.

"For now," Selena said, ignoring his pleas, "take my older brother's room and I'll do my best to sell this as quickly as I can. That's all I can do."

He had to accept her plans; he finally let go of her hands, and Selena excused herself to change her clothes. A frigid feeling started to cover his body; the house creaked and groaned with every movement they made. Nothing in this house was familiar to him, and he couldn't shake the cold away.

Once Selena was dressed in different clothes, Adam had to blink a few times. He thought he'd seen Josephina's short black hair, not Selena's long purple hair. Selena's dark skin had suddenly turned white for a moment; she was no longer a child servant but someone else entirely.

This was a girl of upper-middle class, not poor, and she wasn't a servant. It was a coincidence he saw Josephina standing there and not this young woman, Selena. The ocean's winds were tricking him, and the whispers in his mind started to echo. They were too fast for him to understand, but he shook his head to focus on her.

Even though the sun was setting, Adam took Selena to get her hair cut.

"Isn't this a bit too much?" Selena asked quietly, trying to get used to her much shorter hair. "Your robes would've been enough!"

Adam ignored her whispers as he turned to her, placing his hands on her shoulder. His green eyes widened at the resemblance, and he felt his body sweat, even though the ocean winds blew. He shook his head, reminding himself that Selena was not Josephina. She had dark skin. He had to focus and he had to answer her.

"You're right. Are your ears pierced, Selena?" She nodded slowly as she tried to understand the growing, crazed look in his eye.

He breathed out. "Great, let's get you some earrings. The story between us is that you're a traveling acolyte who was high class all her life and you're not from here."

He patted her shoulders and wandered to the next merchant who sold earrings before Selena could respond.

Something was disturbing Adam's heart, and she had to figure it out before they left. Not only for his safety of mind but for her safety of body.

The sun set for the evening and Selena forced Adam back to the house. She was disappointed that she wasn't able to break free from Adam's grasp to do her tasks, especially since he was so desperate to leave.

Selena wanted to go to sleep as fast as she could so she could wake up from this hellish nightmare. Her family wasn't dead. Even if she could only see them in dreams, she'd see them again downstairs and they'd be alive. Her younger sister, Martina, would run around while her mother scolded her. Alvaro would be begging Father to teach him politics or any new ideas he had. But while Selena struggled to dream in her bed, Adam felt just as restless. The sound of water dripping started to bother him. There was no water around that could drip, yet it drip-drip-dripped.

The next morning, Selena woke up in her bed to find that it wasn't a hellish nightmare; it was real. Her family had been murdered in Taboria and she was the sole survivor. She wasn't aware Adam had less sleep in this house of dripping water and frigid wind.

He had left a note for Selena and, while he patted the horse, he noticed the dripping had stopped. His horse was on loan from the Samher priests, after all, so she was probably blessed.

When he looked at the carriage itself, he noticed that one of the front wheels had been smashed. Whatever caused the wheel to look as it did, Adam took it as a sign of the wind keeping him there. He didn't want to stay there any longer and the smashed wheel mocked his desire to leave. He groaned with anger and—he couldn't help it—stood up and yelled at the wheel as he kicked it.

"Hey, are you in here?" a familiar voice echoed. It pulled him out of his temporary madness, just by a little. He still yelled at the strange wind, but finally he settled when someone grabbed him from behind. They surprised him with their strength, but he found himself struggling in their grasp—he almost cursed at them as he turned around, with green eyes not belonging to him anymore.

Suddenly, he saw Selena against the view of the water. She didn't seem of this world, and his heart stopped when he realized her lips moved. And they moved so familiarly.

"Once upon a midnight splendid, by the grave, I saw the waterways." Words escaped him and only his body reacted to the gravity of this world.

"Sir? Sir? Come on, sitting in this darkness isn't good for you! Let me try to lift you again."

He blinked, seeing an older man instead of a mocking Selena...a hallucination. He had to know the truth about her and her connection to Josephina. He started to sweat under his robes, and the sound of dripping became faster and louder. He couldn't understand what was going on, but he had to get back to Selena's house.

When he arrived, he didn't care if anyone was around or not—instead, he rushed inside the house. He looked through the desks, cabinets, everything he could feasibly open.

And finally, he found a strange book, with many gems on the cover, and a name he didn't bother to read. Even with the book's resistance to being opened, Adam forced it and turned to any and all pages he could find information on. He found notes and spells. Then he saw a page that caused him to drop the book.

It talked about the rules of channeling; the ethics and complicated questions surrounding bringing back a ghost; references to what happened if they turned violent, references to clients' reactions, and what to expect. And the subject of reincarnation.

"That's it! That's it! She's reincarnated!"

Adam had confirmed that Selena was a witch who dabbled in communication with ghosts—a channeler. There was no need to wonder why she had to hide from the Conclave. And she had to be a reincarnation of Josephina—she just had to be! For a moment it felt to him like a dark figure was creeping up his back, and he ran out the door. His body was clammy and the drip-drip-drip became louder with his every heartbeat. He needed air. Adam couldn't be in this town anymore.

He ran though Quickstar—a place unfamiliar to him. Whenever his legs gave out, he stumbled to the ground and crawled. Eventually, Adam seemed to come to his senses, realizing where he was. He stopped, on his hands and knees, almost unable to breath, seeing lines of familiar stones rising from the ground.

A graveyard.

Josephina blew her spirit to his back, in the guise of the ocean winds, and she stood behind him.

Adam looked down at the moss-covered stone beneath his hands, realized he crawled on a gravestone. He pushed away the moss from the stone, seeing letters and numbers reveal themselves to him. When he realized what he was reading, he could no longer move.

Josephina Hamilton 1498–1506

A beloved daughter dreaming with the water lilies.

Had he had his voice, he would have screamed in horror. A harsh flashback came to him.

They were only children when it happened. Adam wanted to swim that morning and wanted to spend time with her—a strange feeling for a privileged son to have for a servant daughter, but it didn't matter. It was at his insistence that they swam—he wanted her to swim with the water lilies. He wanted to have a beautiful backdrop for such a beautiful girl. She dived in alive, and the last thing he ever saw of her was her hand, her small hand.

Adam was a coward.

Only when it was too late did Adam get help. The girl's body was eventually found, and he had to identify her—for his parents, for her parents. And it angered him. He'd hear stories of those who drowned with a feared look on their faces—permanently etched and taken into their graves. But her face was peaceful, a watery and permanent sleep. And it angered him.

"Adam?"

He blinked, and realized that Josephina looked down on him, using Selena's voice again; her dark skin, her hair...she used this lovely girl to torment him. He was still a coward, wasn't he?

The only word out of his mouth was a single name, an unnatural smile stretching over his face.

"Josephina."

When Selena arrived with the other Samher priests, Adam broke her heart. They'd only been there for half a day and somehow, someway, he went mad. There wasn't time to sell her items, much less make plans to sell her home. An accident happened to the carriage while he made strange accusations, the stableman explained, the young girl had no other choice but to report the madness to them.

"We'll take care of him. Thank you so much for giving him to us." A much older priest bowed to her in an expression of remorse. As thanks, the priests gave Selena Adam's religious beads and she gripped them tightly, covering them in her tears. She was looking forward to traveling with him and being with him.

Her mother's grimoire on the floor gave her indication of what he discovered. Selena was shocked to realize that he was probably overcome by the possibility that she was Josephina's reincarnation, not by her family's channeling. There wasn't much to be done about that madness, she feared.

As another token of their embarrassment, the priests gave Delilah and the carriage to Selena. With her shortened hair and the acolyte dressing, it would take a few more days to sell the rest of her items and her home. She was relieved, however, at the rumors that the Conclave redirected their sights to the Dragonfly Witch.

When the day came for her to leave, Selena grasped the rosary beads she wore, to complete her disguise, and clutched them.

"Goodbye, Adam."

— FOR EVERMORE —
by S.M. Uddin

I *'m sorry. I had to,"* were the last words Zara Ali dreamed before waking up in an infirmary bed.

Who had said that? She blinked away the haze from her vision, looking around at the gloomy room devoid of any life other than herself. A dark blur sat on her chest—a single black feather. Presumably it had floated in from the open window nearby.

The school nurse entered. A short woman in a white dress and blue cardigan.

"You're awake," she said, cheery. "What happened?" Zara asked.

"You fainted. Again."

"Fainted?"

She took Zara's temperature. "Right in the middle of the corridor. You've been doing that a lot, haven't you?"

Zara didn't know. She didn't remember fainting. Though she didn't remember much these days. All her memories were slowly drifting away, save for the most random incidents, which she could recall with almost perfect clarity.

The nurse did a few more checks before giving her the option to stay another night. She chose to leave. The smell of disinfectant became stronger the longer she was there, and it was starting to make her gag.

Zara was still drowsy as she made her way to her room. The curious words of the faceless, yet maybe recognizable, figure from her dream were an echo, bouncing off the bare walls before dissolving into the warm light of the streetlamps that streamed through the windows. Though they could do nothing to mask the autumn chill in the long, narrow hallway. Coldness was in the nature of Raven's Eye Academy. It sat tucked away in the shadowy corner of a small, hillside town. Almost forgotten, forever reclusive.

The ever-present silence accompanied Zara as she wondered how she dreamt of people who didn't exist.

Zara sat on her bed after class with a headache. A strange one. As if something was hammering its way through her skull with a dull pickaxe.

"Zara, have you seen the registry forms for the photography club? Miss Walsh is on my back again," said Lily, Zara's friend and roommate, as she rifled through the desk drawers.

"You already gave them to the club president, remember?"

"I'm serious. I need them!"

Zara sat up, confused. "But you did? I was with you. You called the bright orange folder he put them in ugly."

Lily gave her a look. It was her turn to be confused. "Who's 'he'? I'm president of the photography club."

"Since when? It's Nick Cho, isn't it?"

"Who the hell is Nick Cho?"

"You know, Nicholas Cho from class 9b? Angela Cho's cousin." The words were ingrained in her mind like muscle memory, and came as easily as if she were speaking her own name.

Lily scrunched up her face. "What? Angie doesn't have a cousin."

"Yes, she does. You're in the same club. You've spoken to him. I've *seen* you." Zara was suddenly aware of her headache again. She closed her eyes and waited for the hammering to subside.

"Z?" Lily looked at her, concerned. "You told me your memory has been weird lately, hasn't it? You should lie down for a bit. Don't think about it too much."

Zara sighed. "You're probably right." Though she didn't know how a fading memory could create a whole new person.

Zara asked Angela Cho about Nicholas.

"What? I don't have a cousin called Nicholas," she said. None of her classmates knew anybody by that name either.

It made no sense. Zara tossed all night. The name *Nicholas Cho* was branded inside her eyelids, glowing and searing its way through her mind in a painful pulse. Why did nobody know him? He was real. She *knew* he was real. And, to make things worse, her headache had returned.

Frustrated, she sat up. She needed some air. Zara left her room, her mind too full to think about where she was actually going.

Maybe Lily's right, she thought as she walked, feeling the chill of the empty corridors through her thin pajamas. Her memory must be worse than she realized. She had no idea where the sudden loss had come from. Maybe she'd forgotten that too.

The screech of a bird outside pulled her out of her thoughts. Zara found herself to have stopped walking, and, instead, to be looking up at a large painting by the stairs. Just how much time had passed?

William Eldridge Jr., 1738–1782. Zara squinted to read the dull plaque under the frame. Everybody knew his story. The architect behind Raven's Eye, who tragically met his death on the grounds, leaving behind his terminally ill father, William Eldridge Sr.

He was depicted with neat brown hair and a red jacket. Normal, for a painting of that age—nothing Zara hadn't seen in a gallery a million times. But something about it drew her in. Mystified her. Though there was nothing remarkable about Eldridge himself, she couldn't help but admire the talent of the painter, who somehow managed to make him look almost *alive*.

She tiptoed, trying to get a closer look at how the artist managed to replicate such a lifelike glint in his eye. There was something odd about it—it was almost *too* real. What Zara didn't realize was that her headache had gone, and that, when she finally blinked, the life in the painting had disappeared too. It was suddenly nothing more than a flat portrait.

"Hello."

Zara jumped. She'd been caught by a teacher. Though when she'd spun to meet them, she was met by nothing but air. She remained on the spot. Maybe it was too dark to see? Or maybe she was losing more than just her memory?

"Hello?" the voice said again, seemingly from behind her. Zara turned, facing the painting.

"Don't be frightened. I need your help. Please."

Great. A voice in her head. That's *exactly* what she needed. Or maybe someone was playing a prank on her? But the room was so quiet, and empty, you could hear someone breathe from the other side.

"Hello?" she whispered into the air.

"Can you help me?" the voice said. At least her imagination was strong.

"Lily? Angela?" she asked, but gained no response. "William?" She felt stupid. How likely was it that she was talking to a man long deceased?

"Yes! Eldridge Junior. I designed the structure in which you stand."

Zara yelped and jumped back, clapping her hand over her mouth.

"Please! You'll wake that horrible woman with the painful voice. There's no need to be afraid."

Was he talking about Miss Walsh? Zara shuffled on the spot. What do you say in situations like these?

"What are you doing in the painting? Aren't you..." Zara didn't finish. She had heard stories about ghosts who didn't know they were dead, who unleashed their terrible wrath once they found out. Zara didn't want to be on the receiving end of such wrath.

"Yes, child. My body is long dead. Though, thanks to you, I no longer reside in this frame."

Zara took a step back from the frame she was whispering into, embarrassed. "Oh. So, where are you?"

"I apologize. I have taken refuge in a small portion of your mind. I could not stay in the portrait any longer."

"What?!" Zara whisper-shouted.

"Zara Ali?" a woman's voice said. Zara faced the voice and found herself blinded by a flashlight.

Once she regained her full vision, she observed the figure in front of her. "Miss Walsh?"

The headteacher stood in front of her, dressed in a nightgown, with a stern look on her lined face. "What do you think you're doing out of bed?"

"Um, I..." Zara panicked. Spinning an unbelievable story about communing with ghosts would see her to detention, an institution, and some sort of unsavory exorcism. In that order.

"I was getting some water," she said.

Walsh put her hands on her hips and furrowed her eyebrows. "A weak, *weak* excuse. Come on. Bed."

Walsh pointed to the stairs and escorted her to her room, staying right behind her, holding the flashlight to Zara's back like a gun.

"You can expect your outside privileges taken for a week now." That was the last thing Walsh said before dropping her off outside the door.

Zara wanted to argue but had more important things on her mind. *Literally.* She was about to speak when she remembered Lily, sleeping on the other side of the room.

"It's okay. You do not need your voice to talk to me."

The situation kept getting stranger. *"Fine. Get out of my head."*

"I'm sorry, I cannot. I can only seek refuge in the minds of others now."

"Then go to someone else! I don't want you here."

"Alas, I cannot do that either. It has to be you. You were blessed by the raven. You're the only one who remembers."

"Remembers what?" Zara mentally scoffed. Now she knew he was lying. Remembering was the opposite of what she did.

William replied, *"The one before you. They one they call Cho."*

It was as if she had been hit in the face with a brick. How did Eldridge know about Nick? What did he mean *"the one before"* her? Nothing was making any sense. The exhaustion and confusion hit her at the same time, making her lightheaded.

Then the world faded to black.

Zara stood on a grassy hill, overlooking a small village. The sun warmed her skin in a way she hadn't felt seemingly in years.

A small crowd was gathered in front of a large, almost castle-like house, a little way away from her. Like there was an event of some sort. She recognized it—it was the school building. Except the bricks weren't as dull, and the roof was almost *shiny.* This was Raven's Eye before the academy.

The crowd was dressed in long skirts or coats, with bonnets and hats. Where was she? Zara made her way to the front, curious about what it was they were cheering for. In front of her stood a few men, and William Eldridge himself. Almost the spitting image of his portrait.

"I thought it would be easier to just show you," said the William in her head, before she could question anything.

Zara watched, quietly, as the William in front of her hushed the crowd, pointing to two men dressed in black.

"When I created Raven's Eye," William in her head started, *"she was my greatest joy. I took no wife. I bore no children. I spent every waking minute of my life on her design."*

The two men brought out a girl, blindfolded with a white cloth. She seemed to be a regular village girl, judging by her simple dress.

William continued: *"In our village, we had a tradition."*

Zara didn't like where this was going.

"Every year, when a house or boat or something new was built, we would bathe it in the blood of an innocent, believing it would ward away the devil."

"What?!" Zara said.

"It was such common practice that people would offer up their own children. They couldn't afford to care for them, and believed that at least this way they would see their children to heaven."

"Does that mean—"

The girl was forced to kneel, with her head laid on a tree stump, with a shallow bucket in front of it. She was close enough for Zara to see how young she actually was. Though what surprised her the most was how eerily calm the girl was—her movements were slow and clumsy, like she wasn't used to her own body.

"Yes. I'm sorry," William's voice was soft, and apologetic. *"Don't look."*

But it was too late. A sword swung down on the girl. The crowd cheered. Zara stood frozen, with her eyes wide open, not even knowing *how* to process what she had just seen.

The girl's headless body bled into the bucket until it was half full, before it was taken and splashed across the bricks of the building.

Zara was about to let out a scream when the scene melted away, leaving her surrounded by darkness. William appeared in front of her. Except he was different from the one she just saw—the one from the past. This one had deep lines in his forehead, and dark shadows under his eyes. His skin was grey, and he looked moments away from simultaneously bursting into tears and crumbling into dust.

She felt it. It was as if hell took pity on him for what his soul had already experienced. This was the William that lived in her mind.

"This is why I need your help," he said.

"Help you?" Zara said aloud. "Help you what? People died because of you!"

"I'm asking you because I want to be rid of all the blood!" That was the first time William had raised his voice. Zara could see a spark of pain, and anger in his eyes. Though she knew it wasn't intended at her, but himself. *"I had grown tired, and weary of all the death many years ago. But Raven's Eye...the very spirit I breathed into these walls demands it. I cannot stop her. I have tried for a century, yet, to this day, she continues to take. My soul can no longer bear it. I need you to end this cycle."*

Something about what he said unnerved her. The whole situation was horrifying, but those specific words produced a chill she was reluctant to investigate. "What do you mean, *'she continues to take'?"*

Zara opened her eyes. Sunlight leaked through a crack in the curtains, slicing through the solitary darkness of her room.

She knew the answer. It just took a minute for her brain to slowly connect the dots. That's when she realized. He had already told her. The horror froze every ounce of blood in her body.

"The school killed Nicholas Cho."

"Correct."

"And I'm next...aren't I?"

"What?" Lily's voice suddenly piped up.

Zara shot up, looking at her friend, who had just come out of the bathroom. "Nothing." She shook her head.

"How are you feeling? Better? You were mumbling something in your sleep all night. I thought you were possessed!"

Zara laughed nervously. "It was just a bad dream."

Lily nodded, rapidly tying her shoes. "Well, if you're coming to class today, hurry up. I'm saving us seats at breakfast."

"All right, I'm coming."

Lily smiled and rushed out of the door.

Zara waited until she was sure that she was alone before speaking. "William?"

"You're right."

Zara never thought she'd hate hearing those words. How do you even respond to the news that your death is coming? "How are you sure it's me?"

"The one that receives the raven's blessing will be the next to nourish the grounds with their blood. Once a soul is taken, she erases every trace of their existence. It's why nobody remembers your friend, and how, even after all these years, she has never been caught."

"But *how?* A building can't do all that, it's just bricks."

"I'm not talking about just the building."

Zara felt her skin start to crawl. "Then, who?"

"The devilish creature you call Walsh."

"The headteacher?" Zara said. It was true that nobody liked her, not even the staff. Even as the head, she made it her point to inject herself into every student's business. But to think she was an actual *devil.* "But why would she want her own students dead?"

"Someone has to do the dirty work. She and the school breathe as one. As long as it lives, she lives. Raven's Eye gets her endless supply of blood, and Walsh lives for another year."

Zara sat in assembly after breakfast. Staring at the stage where the headteacher stood, preparing for the morning announcements.

She had to kill her. Zara had to kill Walsh, before Walsh killed her. And William taught her exactly how.

A steel knife to the heart, wiped with the blood of one with noble intent, and blessed by the one who was blessed by the raven.

Luckily, she could do it all on her own.

"Zara!" Lily elbowed her, pulling her out of her thoughts. "How long were your outside privileges taken away for again?"

Zara responded absentmindedly. "A week."

"A week!" Lily nudged the friends sitting next to her. "Just for getting up. Walsh is a demon I *swear*."

A devil, actually. All Zara could think about was the plan she intended to put into motion that very night.

When the headteacher spoke she seemed to look straight into Zara, as if she knew what she was thinking in that exact moment.

"Not a single slip, or she will consume your soul," William had told her.

But Zara could do it. Or she had to believe she could. She would break the cycle.

She carried that sentiment with her until the sun went down and, once again, cast Raven's Eye in shadow. Once she was sure that everyone was asleep, she crawled quietly out of bed and pulled out a knife, which she had swiped from the kitchens, from under her pillow.

Under William's instruction, she had already blessed it, and, with the tip, pricked her finger and wiped the blood along the blade.

Still in her socks, she padded across the hall and out of the student dorm. The teachers lived on the top floor. Zara carefully made her way, her shadow stretching in the faint lamplight as she tiptoed up the spiraling staircase, still brandishing the knife. Her breath came out in condensed puffs as she shivered. Zara didn't know whether it was from the cold or the fear.

She emerged into the teachers' corridor, and the shivers took over. Fear. It was definitely fear. Still, she commanded herself to move, and crept up to the room right at the end of the hall, where headteacher Walsh lay asleep.

Her heart started to thump loudly in her chest—the accompanying war drum to her endeavors. The melody to her madness. But no, this wasn't madness. This was survival.

She took a deep breath and, ever so slowly, pushed open the door.

The room was as dark as the rest of the school, and just as cold. The headteacher's silhouette lay sleeping, softly breathing under the blanket, a mere few feet away. So close. So vulnerable.

All confidence left her. Zara's knees started to buckle, and her hands shook violently. She couldn't do this. Person or not, she still looked human.

"I can't do this."

"Calm yourself, child. Yes, you can. It's her or you, remember? You're doing nothing but simply returning this creature back to Hell, where it belongs."

"Sending it back to where it belongs," Zara repeated aloud. The words comforted her, but her heart was beating so loudly she feared the devil would hear and wake up.

She tried her best to swallow her fear. This had to be quick. "Just jump on the bed, stab her in the heart, leave," she told herself.

She bounced on her foot, getting ready to jump.

"One, two—okay wait. One—"

"Please just go," William said.

"Okay."

Zara jumped on top of Walsh's sleeping form, startling her awake. Using Walsh's sleepy confusion to her advantage, Zara raised the knife and plunged it as deep as she could into Walsh's heart.

An ungodly screech escaped Walsh's mouth before dying down. She looked down at the teacher, whose blood stained her face and clothes. Her mouth contorted into a scream, her eyes almost popping out of her head. The life completely gone from them. She was dead.

What had she done?

Zara couldn't contemplate it. This was a good thing. *She did a good thing.* So why didn't she feel good? A strangled sob forced its way out of her as she dropped the knife and pressed her hands to her mouth.

"You have to leave now. Someone will come soon," William told her, panicked.

Zara didn't hear. She felt her thoughts evaporate, and her mind recede into itself as her tears fell down her blood-splattered face.

She didn't hear the noises in the room next door, either.

"Zara, please, now!" William pleaded. Yet Zara still couldn't find it in her to move. She had no self, was an empty shell. *"I'm deeply sorry for this,"* he said.

Zara couldn't bring herself to care. Not when her empty mind was refilled, not when her feet moved on their own and swiftly exited the teacher's room with an alarming grace. She watched it all through frosted glass—only vaguely aware. Zara found herself climbing up the fire escape, right before another teacher's door swung open to investigate the noise. She climbed a little higher and heard the muffled scream.

Soon she found herself on the rooftop. The surface was uncomfortably wet, and the dampness soaked through her socks, but the icy wind felt so good on her hot skin that she could ignore it.

"How did you do that? Take over my legs like that?"

"I apologize. We had to escape."

"I suppose I should thank you then." Zara caught her breath, leaning on the edge of the roof. William spun her around to face the view. Though at that time of night, all she could see was the outline of the trees standing tall and still, as if they were watching her. Waiting.

Her hands braced against the edge, and her legs slowly followed.

Before she noticed what was going on, Zara found herself standing on the edge of the roof, a sneeze away from plummeting to her death.

"What are you doing?" Zara asked. She still didn't have control over her body yet.

"*The final part.*"

"Final part? Get me down. Give me back my body."

"*I cannot. It is almost complete. I just need you to do this last thing for me.*"

"No. William, get me down." Zara struggled to move but shifting her limbs felt like the equivalent of trying to budge a house. They were stuck in place.

"*Struggling will only make it worse.*"

"Why are you doing this? I thought you wanted to end this all."

"*You do what you must. Raven's Eye…she still craves the blood of an innocent. But I need the soul of the guilty. And now, I can find both in you.*"

"That's impossible."

"Zara?"

She spun around, and saw Lily standing by the door, eyes wide and afraid.

"Lily? What are you doing here?" This was the last thing Zara said before she lost control of her speech.

Lily took a step forward slowly. "I saw you sneak out, so I followed you. But when I got up there, you were running out of Miss Walsh's room? There's a whole fuss down there now, Z. What's happening? What are you doing up there? Please, get down." Her voice was shaking.

Zara tried with all her energy to say something, to move her mouth. But her effort was in vain. She was bound by a power that the earth did not recognize.

"*Don't,*" Zara pleaded with William.

Yet he ignored her, and spoke for her anyway.

"I'm sorry, I had to," he said to Lily, in a tone almost robotic, before stepping Zara's body off the edge.

All she heard was a faint scream, then a rush of air that drowned all other noise as the ground got rapidly closer.

"*Thank you for your help,*" Eldridge said, swiftly leaving her mind, and returning her body back to her.

When the next autumn came, Lily woke up in an infirmary bed, contemplating the strangest dream she had ever had, and why her memory had been failing her recently. Though what she found even more strange was the small, black feather lying on her chest.

— HOLLYWOOD NIGHTMARE —
by Angela Burgos

I have always had a good grasp of the difference between dreaming and waking. And all my life I've had a preference for one over the other. Every night I look forward to the next scenario my subconscious will conjure up. Some nights I dream of relatives who live across the country; other nights my dreams are set in bright flower fields extending for miles. I usually sleep deeply through the night, but it is 5:45 a.m. and I am wide awake. My boyfriend kisses me goodbye on his way out to work, leaving me alone with my thoughts. Instead of dealing with them, I commit to silencing my mind and going to sleep. I am dozing off into the precious corners of my mind when the heavy thud of my front door startles me.

Growing up in the same very old and loud apartment building, I have come to recognize the language of my home, to have a sort of sixth sense. If my obsession with true-crime podcasts has taught me anything, it is the importance of listening to your gut when something feels off. And I am definitely awake now. It's almost impossible to shake the feeling that something strange is happening outside my bedroom door. My boyfriend has come back, right?

"Man, what the—"

I pause to collect myself as the rational part of my brain engages; the person who just walked through my front door is the only other person who lives here. He's going to walk through that bedroom door any second now. I'll simply lie here and wait.

My room grows dark, and the world around me feels out of place and time. My bedroom window displays an eerie red sky and fiery clouds, as if the whole world is burning. I've seen this sky before, in another dream. So, this is it, I'm dreaming again. I can hear the creak of someone's footsteps in my living room, can see their shadow at the foot of my door. Whoever is out there is pacing back and forth. I'm starting to freak the hell out. Should I run? Should I hide? I attempt to peel myself from my bed, but the movement triggers a skull-splitting headache that holds me down. I can't move. I can think of nothing else—panicked thoughts and an overwhelming tightening in my chest. Even though, as a young girl, I was prone to episodes of sleep paralysis, each one more cryptic than the last, I have lost all sense of safety: a dark entity has taken over my free will.

Something is entirely wrong. And I'm aware of three crucial things: (1) my boyfriend isn't back; (2) I'm dreaming; and (3), based on the noises coming from my bathroom, I'm not alone. Control of my body starts to return in waves, but the danger outside my bedroom door remains. The noises grow louder with every passing moment as I lie in bed. Kicking noises are followed by loud shrieks of agony. I'm the helpless prey and whoever is behind this knows my fears. I may not be able to see who is tormenting me, but the dark energy settling into my room is more than real. Though my body is confined to my bed, my mind races. I decide to use my voice in self-defense.

My lips part, but no sound escapes. I want so badly to scream out.

"Who are you?!"

"What do you want?!"

"Leave me alone!"

But words do not come.

In my wordlessness I hear another sound: crow-like clicking outside my bedroom window. I turn to it and see a lone crow on my windowsill. And behind it—my chest sinking into itself at the sight—the dark silhouette of a man.

Fear shoots through all parts of my body and wakes me up.

I'm gasping for air. I've just escaped some crazy dream.

I shoot a glance at the window. The crow is still there, but the man is nowhere in sight.

My shock at what has just happened is still present in my body as memories from my childhood flood my mind. I have always believed in the incredible, from aliens to vampires. But now, suspecting that I have just come into contact with a being beyond my understanding has triggered something in me. I come from a special line of people with spiritual gifts; the ability to speak to spirits or see the future is not a foreign concept in my world, so why do I feel so shocked?

The first person to come to my mind after this freakshow of events is my mother. My mother and I have always been close. I look up to her, admire her bravery, migrating from her home country to a foreign land, where her future children could have opportunities she did not. I live in a state of constant awe at her dreamer attitude, choosing to settle in Hollywood, California, of all places. But in my admiration I have detected in her a reservedness, a protectiveness; I can never shake the feeling that she is keeping a secret from me. I am aware that she has spiritual gifts. They are gifts she refuses to talk to me about. Instead, she speaks to spirits in private. Nevertheless, the memories of her waking up in cold sweats are embedded in me forever. I have wiped tears from her freckled cheeks as she mumbled the names of loved ones who have passed away; they have visited her through the night, mostly to bring her comfort.

My mother came from a place that I have always thought was magical. Even though destiny had made it so that we were far removed from our ancestral land, we held the mighty little country of Ecuador close to our hearts at all times. I imagine the two of us as vessels of ancestral power and history, two women bound by our rich and mysterious Ecuadorian life-blood. Which is why I used to try to talk to my mother about my vivid dreams often; I know she experiences something like them too. I need my mother to explain spirituality to me; I need her to explain how worlds can blend together and become one. I want so badly to understand what is real and what exists on different planes of reality.

The dream that I have just woken up from reminds me of a questionable moment from my childhood. My mother and I were watching a classic black and white film, set in Hollywood, of all places. The movie was dark and dreamy, and the Hollywood stars were glorious. More importantly, I recognized one of them. The leading actress had a striking beauty that was unforgettable. She had visited me in a dream the night before. I had watched her dance around my bedroom in the 20s-style dress she wore in the film.

I turned to my mother in a fit of excitement and said, "I know that woman. She's my friend."

"What woman, Annie?" my mother replied.

I rolled my eyes and pointed to the screen. "That woman, Mom. She was wearing the same dress."

My mother's face turned pale and she paused the film.

She looked me dead in the eyes and carefully explained that the film was made in the 1920s, the woman on the screen was Diana Restrappo, and she was dead. She turned the movie off and told me never to bring it up again. I was confused, but I listened. This memory, one that I have repressed for a long time, proves something very important to me. If she was magic then I was magic too. I know that my mother refuses to talk to me about anything spiritual, but the truth is that I'm over it. So, I decide to call her and take back some control of my life.

"Mom, something weird just happened—there was a ghost in my dream. At least I'm pretty sure it was a ghost. I didn't see him, but I heard him."

"Oh, Annie, I really don't think so. Did you watch a scary movie last night? I'm sure that's it."

"What? No! The dream was really weird. Freaky. There has to be some explanation. And this seems like the most logical. Mom, I know some part of you understands."

"You know that not every dream means something, right? As long as whatever or whoever you see doesn't scare you, you will be okay."

I don't know how to tell her that I'm terrified.

I spend the rest of the day reliving my dream, trying to make some sense of it all. As the sun finally sets, I decide that getting out for a walk will be the best thing for me. I choose fresh air over my creepy little apartment for one simple reason: the city will protect me, as it has always done. But the truth is that the nightmare is infiltrating my waking moments, giving my beloved city a menacing, dark aura. As I walk out of my apartment I convince myself that the entity is following right behind me. I hope that walking through Hollywood Boulevard, which is lined with shops, people and the names of movie stars plastered on the ground, will help me find calm in the madness that is my life.

Based on how vulnerable I felt in my dream, I suspect that the source of my terror is in fact a ghost. A freaking ghost. That conclusion makes the most sense to me; I mean, I live in Hollywood, the land of broken dreams and immense heartache. I'm lost in my train of thought when I notice a man dressed all in black at the top of the street. The rhythmic tapping of his feet gets louder and louder as I continue to walk in his direction. A sudden pounding in my chest is followed by a loud ringing in my ears. It has to be my gut signaling impending danger. I stop in my tracks. This man is translucent. The realization that he is some kind of apparition is too much for my fragile mind to handle. I close my eyes in the hope that, when I reopen them, this figure will have dissipated into some kind of mystical abyss.

I open my eyes. The figure is gone.

I decide to take my ass back home; what else am I to do?

I turn around and head back on the same route. I'm on a mission to get home before anything else creepy occurs. But, before I can even finish the thought, I feel fingers wrapping around the back of my neck. The sensation lasts only a brief moment, but my heart stops immediately. I turn around to look at whatever or whoever is standing behind me, but again there is no one. I run home.

Running, terrified, I barely notice that the surrounding town, which I have known all my life, has turned a shade of red. The brick buildings drip blood. The buildings are talking to me now; they cry out the stories of pain that they have been forced to keep confined within their walls.

It is not enough to say that, as I crawl into bed, I am utterly exhausted with my own existence. I am afraid to close my eyes. I am afraid to sleep. But, more importantly, I am afraid to dream again, if that means reliving the same ordeal. I lie in my dark and lonely room, fighting the urge to let myself go into a dream state, into the altered reality where I once felt safest. But the lonely night seems to be winning, and my mind goes quiet. I finally fall asleep to the sound of my leaky bathtub faucet dripping water, hitting its mark over and over again.

I feel something happening again. If the ominous static noise erupting from my bedroom television screen isn't enough to alert me to the danger lurking into my apartment, the burning color of the sky informs me that I am in fact dreaming again. This time I try to wake myself up immediately; one dream of terror feels like enough to me after all. But my efforts to will myself awake are in vain. This new dance between myself and whoever is on the other side of my door has already begun.

The creaking of my front door sends shivers down my spine as I realize once more that someone is in my home. The dark pit in my stomach expands as this uninvited guest makes his way through my apartment. He is intentionally noisy, destroying my belongings and banging on the walls, as if he wants me awake and ready to meet his wrath. He makes his way into the bathroom, where it quickly becomes evident that he is enjoying this torture: he flicks the lights on and off, his maniacal laughter ripping through my home.

I am fed up with his shit. Instead of lying here in defeat, as I did last night, I am ready to make my presence known too.

I use the anger in my body as fuel. I scream. "Get the fuck out of my house!"

The entire apartment falls into a silence that I have created. I cannot help but wonder what he's thinking at this moment.

Is he impressed? Is he plotting? I want to mess with his head as much as he wants to haunt me.

I shut my eyes again, hoping that this time my will to wake up is stronger than the panic running through my body. By some twisted occurrence of fate, or maybe the calculated actions of a lunatic, my bedroom door is slowly opening, showcasing my dimly lit living room. Yes, I've seen enough horror films to know that a door slowly opening on its own is an invitation to a world of creepy, but what else am I to do? How else am I to escape? I gather what is left of my shaken mind and decide to walk through the door. My gut keeps telling me that the only way to lift this strange sort of dream-curse is to run, to run far from the torment between these walls. I walk into a living room that is both mine and not mine. The fresh fruit I bought only two days prior and left on my knock-off mahogany dining table is now a pile of rotten mush that drips onto the floor. The gallery wall I had adorned with beautiful paintings now displays only a single painting: a woman lying dead near a river of blood. I let out a whimper of fear, feeling my arms start to go numb. I know that, before my body is gripped by a horrifying paralysis, I must make a break for the front door and leave this warped version of reality.

My plan to run away is in vain; the ghostly figure clearly has other things in mind. I'm barely able to grip the door handle before my body feels frozen in time once again. I close my eyes and feel cold fingers wrap around my bare waist, one by one.

The fingers slowly dig into my skin, causing me to cry out. There is no doubt in my mind that the individual standing behind me is a being that exists beyond this world but has now found its way into mine. The metallic scent of blood that is now circulating throughout the room, and the heavy breathing I feel traveling down my neck, are symptoms of this crossing over of worlds that I do not understand.

"I have to tell you something."

My heart sinks as the ghost's first icy words linger between us. "I've been waiting a long time to show myself to you. You may not feel ready, but the truth is that you are finally there."

Every word feels like a dagger to the pit of my stomach. I finally muster the courage to speak.

"Who are you?"

Hoping he is distracted in responding to me, I try to wriggle out of his grip. To my surprise, he releases my waist. A gust of air rushes past my body. I turn, wanting to see what this being looks like, and, to my surprise, he has moved. I notice the same orange-red sky, the color of burning flames from my dream the night before.

With a kind of superhero strength you only see in Marvel movies, he leaps over to me from across the living room. He had been standing in the corner of the room watching me cower. He lands in a crouching stance right at my feet, and as he looks up he gives me a devilish smirk. Directly in front of me is the most terrifying creature I have ever seen, this dark figure resembling a man. A very tall figure who seems to chuckle as he steps closer to me. His long black hair has green highlights running through it, his skin is a very pale grey and—oh yeah—he's missing a face. He has a head and lips, yes, but the rest of his head features smooth craters where his eyes and nose should be.

"Wh-where is your face?"

"I don't have one. In this dream. You're not ready to meet me in my entirety."

"What are you?!"

"I'm a part of you, Annie. I'm not a ghost. I'm someone who has known you all your life. I've been with you always. This won't be the first time we meet. I won't let you see my true form until I've broken you."

Maybe it's his weirdly vague statement, but the pent-up aggression in my body is overwhelmingly the star of this confrontation. My shaking fingers get a hold of themselves and slowly start to form into rage-directed fists. I swing at him, even though I have never actually fought anyone before, in a dream state or otherwise. The sensation feels odd, but I keep swinging. I hit him over and over. I hit him and my fear of him withers away. I hit him and I start to enjoy it. I hit him until my agitated chest causes me to stop. I've grown angrier with every swing, but he remains emotionless, which feels like an even greater insult. Am I not worth the effort to fight back? Am I not worth it even now?

"You've lived a lot of lives, and now you've ended up back in Hollywood. You've lived in this apartment before. It's the reason why the city has always felt so familiar to you."

Many things start to make sense at once. But what I'm aware of the most is this: my mother fears her gifts because they take a toll on you. They shift your perception of the world, take you away from a perspective that we try to hold on to so valiantly.

I wait for him to make a move, to do something or say anything, to break the tension in the room. An overwhelming rush of emotions pushes me right back into a rage. The agitation in my chest is only a mild symptom of the heavy weight on my mind. As I stare at the faceless body in front of me, I start to accept that we are connected. I wish I could explain what makes me so sure, but this out-of-body experience has to be proof of something.

The sound of cracking noises above us catches my attention, and I look up. This version of my apartment has turned my old-fashioned popcorn ceiling into a large mirror, and the mirror is beginning to crack.

"We don't have much time left, Annie. You need to know that I'm always watching and waiting for your return."

These words send shivers down my spine; I believe every word he is saying. In my attempts to interpret the dream of the night before, I've failed to understand that I will continue to relive this nightmare over and over. We are not mortal enemies; we are part of each other.

The ceiling mirror cracks further with every passing second. I brace myself, knowing what's coming. Jagged pieces of mirror rain down in my little Hollywood apartment. Sharp edges pierce my skin. I feel every cut. The pain is consuming, but my attention still shifts to my window, to a sound I've heard before, a pecking sound.

With a sudden gasp for air, I'm awake again, and find myself staring into the worried eyes of the crow at my windowsill. I try to take a moment to catch my breath, but emotions and memories are crawling up the cavities of my chest. I feel everything over and over. My lips quiver as I let out the cry of fear and defeat I was about to release within my nightmare. But that's just it, right? It was only a nightmare, something that exists in the realm of my own mind.

The room feels like it's spinning, and my brain feels like it's on fire, as I lie back down.

I have always felt most comfortable sleeping on my stomach. And as I run my hand under the bottom of my pillow there is a sharp pain in my finger. Blood is running down my right forearm; small pools are forming on my white sheets. I accusingly lift my pillow to reveal the cause.

It is a broken mirror shard, and my reflection stares accusingly back at me.

— ON THE SHORELINE —
by Lauren T. Davila

I f she was being 100% truthful, Luna Navarro thought her college roommate was a little strange. While everyone else in their freshman dorm was living it up in L.A. going to rock concerts, movie premieres, Malibu beaches or downtown nightclubs, Mary was poring over oceanography textbooks. Which, like, no one had even declared a major yet, so it was sort of premature. And she rarely left her room, didn't talk about her family, and didn't have any interest in exploring their new town. But even if Mary was a bit strange, Luna still liked her.

Mary would make Luna tea when she was homesick and crying about San Antonio. She took notes for their humanities course when Luna flew home for her tio's funeral their second semester. Comforted her when she found out that he was the last family Luna had. Mary shared that she didn't have anyone either. Oh, and she kept her side of the room super neat. So, when it came time to pick room assignments for sophomore year, Luna asked Mary to room together again. And again, junior year. And the summer they studied abroad in Scotland. And their senior year, off campus.

And everything was fine, normal, easy. Until Luna found the positive pregnancy test in their bathroom right before winter break. She checked the living room, finding her friend sitting on the floor, staring at the wall. Her hair was half curled, but it didn't seem like she realized she had forgotten the other half.

"Do you want to talk about it?" Luna asked, leaning down to adjust her fuzzy Chewbacca socks.

"No."

"Do you want to order in some dumplings and watch Bravo?" Mary nodded, taking a moment to look up at Luna. Her smile was unrecognizable, hollow and terrifying. Luna ordered the food, grabbed a fluffy blanket, and covered her roommate. She fell asleep with the taste of soy sauce on her tongue and the sound of women screaming about money in the background.

When she woke up, Mary was gone.

The only thing left was a cheque for enough to cover rent for the rest of the semester and a note:

I'm sorry. Please don't change your phone number. You were the best friend I ever had.

Luna left the note on the table until she moved out of the apartment months later. She threw it away right before she left.

The notification from Mary popped up right when Luna was rejected from another role. This one wanted her to play some shitty stereotypical Latina a la what's-her-face from *Modern Family*. They asked Luna to "spice up her accent" and Luna had to fight back the urge to scream. A ding from her phone alerted her to a text.

Seeing it was from Mary, she wanted to delete it without reading. Who just throws away four years of friendship and ghosts? But as she went to delete it, she saw the photo attached to the message. Just a small thumbnail image, but enough for her to see the tiny hand.

A baby's hand.

She opened it up, letting out a squeal at the little pink hat.

Baby Rosalie wanted to say hi to her Tia Luna. And Rosalie's mama wants to say she's sorry and she hopes you can forgive her. She needs you. We both do.

Luna sighed, knocking her head against the seat rest. God, she was such a pushover.

She's the most beautiful thing I've ever seen, she texted back, loving the image. *Her Tia can't wait to meet her. And hug her best friend.*

The message was marked as seen immediately, and Luna drove home, humming a little lullaby as the ping of another message came through.

Mary had never been the best communicator in college, and nothing had changed. Over the next five years, Luna got a text every couple months. Usually it was a photo of Rosalie. A story about her starting preschool or finding an orphaned squirrel, or learning to swim. With context clues and a couple of pictures with background, Luna pieced together that they were living in Las Vegas. Far away, but close enough that she could have driven and visited them any weekend they asked. But Mary never asked. It wasn't strange when the messages stopped. Until two weeks after the last message of Mary and Rosalie posing in Marvel superhero costumes at Halloween, she received a call.

Child Protective Services.

A horrible car accident.

Mary no longer a text away.

The custody of one broken-hearted six-year-old child.

Luna didn't think twice. She jumped in her car and started driving. She was able to hold back the tears until she hit the state line. They didn't stop until she pulled up outside the house Mary had called home. She reapplied some drugstore mascara in her mirror and took a deep breath. It hurt to hold it in her lungs when she realized her best friend wasn't breathing anymore. She let her breath out as she rang the doorbell, and it opened to reveal Rosalie. The little girl's eyes were bloodshot, blonde hair in two loose braids with red dye at the ends.

"Tia Luna," she said, wrapping her arms around Luna's legs. She could feel the little girl shaking. "She said you'd come if anything bad ever happened. She said you would always come."

"I'm here, mi florecita." Luna reached down, hoisting Rosalie up in a tight hug, trying to ignore the tears dripping down her neck. She moved across the threshold, walking into her new life. She didn't have another choice. "Now why don't you tell me about this hair of yours?"

"If one more tourist tells me that their room is haunted, I'm gonna scream."

Luna rolls her eyes as Steven walks up to her, slamming an empty tray of margarita glasses onto the countertop. She's been working with him for over two years now and he's her best friend here. He'd welcomed her when she was hired and showed her exactly how to avoid the handsy, drunk guys on the casino floor. He also showed her how to flirt with guests to get more tips, but she doesn't necessarily use that knowledge. She teases him all the time that if his husband only knew that the extra money came from a seductive smile, he wouldn't want it. God, she loves them. They have twins around Rosalie's age, which makes raising a child easier.

"They act like the Luxor isn't the most haunted hotel on the Strip?" she says, tightening her money belt around her waist. "Did they not google that before they booked the room?"

"I mean, I guess not. But, like, beyond the ghosts, this is just creepy! Go to the Bellagio or even the MGM. At least they don't have tepid water and creepy sarcophaguses lying around."

"Sarcophagi."

"Huh?"

"You said sarcophaguses; it's sarcophagi."

"Oh, so sorry. Excuse me, Ms 'I went to a fancy bougie school that taught me the correct plural form of ancient...things.' "

"It's not my fault that I paid attention in my art history classes! And hey, it comes in handy when any of the guests have questions about anything."

"If they ask me questions, I just smile and ask if they want another drink. It's easy. Less stress."

He grabs a tray of refills from the floor manager and turns around to go back out onto the floor. The sound of Egyptian-adjacent music, coins clinking, and raucous laughter beckons to them. But it's cut by the sound of some Lizzo song—Steven's ringtone. He shoves the tray at Luna, who barely has time to grab it.

"Babe, I'm working, you know that— What? Yeah, she's right here."

Luna pauses, feeling that uncomfortable worried feeling wash over her. The worry of having a tiny being to look after. Her mind races. Is Rosalie okay? Did something happen?

"Uh huh, I'll tell her. Okay. Yes, I'm sure. And are wings okay for dinner? I can swing by Voodoo on the way home. Okay, love you more!"

"What happened? Is Rosalie hurt? Does she need me?"

"That was Jadyn. She's fine but she fell outside on the swingset playing with the twins. He was on a work call and he heard her crying. She has a teensy scratch, but she keeps asking for you." Steven grabs the tray back from Luna. "Go. I'll tell Miranda you had to dip. But you owe me."

Luna throws a quick kiss on him, missing his cheek and landing in his hair. He makes a kiss sound back and shoves her toward the door. She slips through the casino floor, weaving around the fake palm trees and wasted tourists at 2 p.m. on a Thursday. Her heels click on the yellow floor, and she takes a deep breath as she opens up the door to the hot Vegas air. Rosalie needs her.

"Mijita, you're fine."

Rosalie sits on her bed, wrapped up in the fluffiest towel Luna could find. She let her soak in the bath for a while, giving her a full shampoo massage. Her eyes were still puffy from crying over the tiniest scratch Luna had ever seen. But she doesn't say anything. It's almost that time of year. Almost the time when everything becomes too much. And Rosalie just cries and cries and cries.

"I fell though. And the twins weren't even there because they'd ran off and left me behind."

"Why did they leave you behind?"

"They wanted to go play a special sibling game. They said I couldn't play with them because I wasn't related to them." She pauses and looks up at Luna, letting out a low sniffle. "I'm not related to anyone anymore."

"Oh, florecita. You have me."

"But you're only here because Mama had to leave. You wouldn't be here if she didn't leave. And we're not even related by blood."

Luna opens her mouth to say it's not true. To say that she is here by choice. But she'd be lying. She would have stayed away forever, content with pictures and text messages, too afraid to intrude. She's only here because Mary died horribly, and Rosalie needed someone. And Mary knew she wouldn't be able to say no to her little girl. There's only one thing she could say that wouldn't sound fake and hollow.

"I'm your tia and I'll always be here. Nothing anyone can do or say will ever make me leave. You have me for life, mijita." She leans down and kisses Rosalie. Although horrible circumstances brought them together, she's so glad she has this girl to raise.

"Can you sing the creation song to me, Tia Luna?"

"The creation song? Really? It's been a while since you've asked for that!"

"I know, I just really want to hear it tonight."

Luna nods, lying beside her and snuggling under the covers. She hums low and starts singing: *How I confound and astound you, to know I must be one of the wonders, of God's own creation.*

She has to concentrate or she'll choke up. This song always reminds her of Mary—dancing around their living room in college, bare feet in her raggedy granny nightgown. She'd sing it off tune, all scratchy and whiny, unlike Natalie Merchant.

Know this child will be gifted, with love, with patience and with faith, she'll make her way.

As she finishes the last chorus, she's met with Rosalie's soft snores. She slips out of the twin bed and into the hallway, closing the door softly behind her. Then, from down the hall, she hears the sound of a pipe creaking and a sudden burst of water. Cursing under her breath, she runs into the master bedroom that had been Mary's.

Maybe it was unhealthy, but she didn't use the room. She lived in the guest bedroom downstairs instead. And she hasn't touched any of Mary's things in the two years since she'd been living here. Which was coming back to bite her in the ass now. Water is every-where in the bathroom. She grabs some old beach towels from the closet and shoves them at the crack in the door, hoping that will be enough to keep it from bleeding into the thick carpet. She reaches under the sink and turns off the water. She'll call a plumber in the morning. But right now, she needs to make sure nothing valuable is in danger of being ruined.

There's nothing in the closet but neat clothes and shoes and a couple of small spiders. But under the bed is a different story. Piles and piles of clear bags filled with what looks like letters and flyers and a bunch of other stuff—things that a water leak can quickly destroy.

She hoists them into her arms and runs them downstairs into the living room. After six trips, almost all the bags are safe. Last one in hand, Luna shuts the door behind her and makes her way back down the stairs. She misses the last step.

She stumbles, bag dropping out of her hands and papers flying everywhere. Letting out a deep sigh, she crawls on her knees, haphazardly shoving them back into the bag. Until one catches her eye.

It's a small movie poster of one of Silas Campos's most recent movies. The one he directed in Mumbai, she thinks. It cost a ridiculous amount of money to produce. He does a movie every decade or so and it's groundbreaking every time. Like, who even was Scorsese if Campos was around? But this print has writing all over it, an ancient scrawl like it was from someone elderly. One line at the bottom stood out to her:

Please come home. We can talk about it. I want to meet your daughter.—Abuelo

In the distance, a clicking sound. It stuttered, like it was pricking out a message in Morse code.

Luna shuts her eyes tight, ignoring the sound. She remembers all the times Mary refused to go to see Campos's new movies. When she skipped his section in their film appreciation class. How she always evaded questions about her family or where home was. Family. It all makes sense now. And Luna knows what she has to do.

She looks down at the flyer and, grabbing her cell, types in the number near the message.

"Hello? I'm calling to speak with Silas Campos. I have some information on his daughter he probably needs to hear."

The clicking fades out into the sound of static—static crashing around her like wild ocean waves.

"Yes, Steven, I'll call every day. And y'all can visit at Thanksgiving. I promise. Yes. Give the twins and Jadyn our love. Mmhmm, pulling up to the house now, so we've got to go. Love you too. Bye."

Luna disconnects the call as she pulls into the long driveway off PCH. Rosalie is asleep in the backseat, a golden retriever stuffed animal thrown across her face. If she weren't sleeping, it would be blocking her view of the sunrise. They'd left Vegas close to 2 a.m. to get through the desert while it was still cool. Luna didn't realize how much she'd missed the sunrise over the ocean the last couple of years until she saw it again. The blues and oranges and pinks that painted the sky. But she couldn't truly appreciate it because she could still hear a clicking noise. She thought maybe it was a spare water bottle clanking around. Or a piece from the air conditioning rattling. But it was getting louder and louder the longer she drove. It's starting to drive her mad, all she can hear as she zips around the freeway interchanges and into Malibu.

"Mama. Mama."

Luna looks in the rearview. She rarely talks in her sleep anymore. But whenever she does, it's just that. Over and over again. Poor baby.

"Florecita, it's time to wake up. We're here." She stirs, pushing the stuffed animal off her.

"Tia, why can't we just stay home? I don't know these people. Mama stayed away for a reason—there's gotta be something wrong with them!"

"Rosalie! You need to be kind. And not judge them when you haven't even met them. Your great-grandfather and uncle are excited to meet you and get to know you! They were nice enough to invite us to stay here and you will be polite at the very least. Please, mija. Neither of us know why your mama wasn't talking to them, so don't jump to conclusions."

Rosalie takes a drink of her water and raises an eyebrow. Well, that's probably the best Luna is going to get.

"Hello, um," Luna says, dialing the callbox. It clicks on, static filling the air. "This is Luna Navarro and Rosalie Nav—Rosalie Campos."

There isn't an answer and, for a second, Luna considers listening to Rosalie and turning right around. Driving through downtown until she gets back to her friends and the Luxor and the desert. But then the gates open and her foot presses on the gas and it is too late.

It's way too late.

"Woahhhh, this is a long driveway."

Luna can't help but agree with Rosalie. It feels like she's driving forever until the driveway empties out and she has to muffle a gasp. The biggest house she's ever seen springs up in front of her. House isn't even the right word—this is a full-on mansion. They get out of the car to stare open-mouthed at the white walls. They aren't stucco but have some fancy texture that Luna is sure some designer created. The white walls shine bright in the sunlight, contrasting with the tropical green of the palm trees and banana leaves. Red brick lines the stairs leading up to a wrought iron gate. There's a brand-new welcome mat that feels entirely out of place. Maybe they put it there just for them.

And god, why can she still hear the clicking?

"You look just like her."

Luna turns around at the familiar voice and has to suppress a gasp. He's smaller in person, frail, and hunched over a bit more than he usually is in press interviews. But she'd recognize the cunning in Silas Campos's eyes anywhere. "Come and give me a hug," he says, opening his arms; they shake a bit. Rosalie steps behind Luna, looking up at her and shaking her head just so lightly.

"Hi, Señor Campos! Thank you so much for inviting us, we—"

"Does she not have any manners? Why isn't she coming to greet me?"

Rosalie tightens her grip on Luna's cardigan, pulling it. Maybe Rosalie was right—there probably was a reason Mary had stayed away. She opens her mouth to tell him off, damn his fame and hospitality.

"Abue, leave her alone," a voice from the shadows says. "She doesn't have to hug if she doesn't feel comfortable."

The man steps out of the light and Luna about swoons. He's tall with sun-kissed skin and freckles splattered across his face. In his white linen blouse and bare feet, he's a dream.

"I'm Ethan," he says, holding out a hand to her. "Thank you for watching over my niece. And for bringing her home. I hope you'll like it here."

The sunrise slips over the top of the house as she takes his hand. Warmth floods her body and she can't tell if it's from the sunlight or from touching him. And then he smiles at her.

Only her.

And finally, the clicking pauses for just a second.

Until he pulls his hand away and it starts back up, and Luna is left to wonder again what exactly she's doing here.

Two months later, she's still wondering.

Luna wants to love it here. It's an absolutely stunning compound: mountains on one side of the house and nothing but endless ocean waves to the other. She has time to send in audition tapes and Silas has given her contacts at his studio. Ethan asks her opinions on his music compositions, and, although she knows next to nothing about it, he always thanks her for her input. And it's not just in her imagination that he keeps finding reasons to hang out with her, beyond just getting to know Rosalie. Morning coffee and surf trips to Zuma and sneaking out to watch the new Marvel movie Silas mocks. And the fleeting touch of his fingertips across her hands.

But she still can't shake the feeling that they need to run back to Vegas.

Well, that is, if Rosalie wasn't thriving here. Rosalie doesn't seem to feel the chill of the ocean in the morning. Or see the dark shadows the palm trees cast on her walls and windows. And god, she sure as hell can't hear the constant clicking.

The ENT doctor couldn't find anything wrong with her. He said it must have been psychosomatic. But it's all she can hear, crescendoing, especially at night. And tonight it's almost unbearable. She leaves her bedroom, grabbing her robe before slipping out toward the kitchen barefoot. It echoes around her in the dark house.

Click. A crash of the waves. Click. Waves. Click. And then— She lets out a curse as she stubs her toe and hits the wall in the hallway off the living room. She pauses, waiting to hear if she has woken anyone up. When she doesn't hear anything, she readies herself to continue into the kitchen. Make herself some chamomile tea and convince herself she just hears things. But then she sees a low glow of light from behind the panel in the hallway she knocked into. And the girl who was raised on a steady diet of Nancy Drew novels just can't help herself. She pushes the panel aside and enters the small room.

It's no bigger than a mudroom, stuffed with old movie posters and some broken chairs. But two things catch her eye. One is a portrait leaned up against the far wall. It's a picture of the most gorgeous woman Luna's ever seen in her life.

It's the epitome of Old Hollywood glamor. A woman stands on a red carpet, half in the light of the paparazzi's cameras and half in shadow. She's in a tight emerald mermaid dress, red lipstick contrasting with her brown skin and dark hair. One arm is outstretched to the light, to where a young girl stands a couple of feet away. The young girl is the spitting image of the actress. A small note is taped to the bottom of the frame: "*Bianca and mi sirena.*"

Click.

A bright light flashes and Luna throws her hands in front of her face. The outstretched hand of the woman is burned into her vision. Once her sight returns to normal, she glances at the corner where the light came from. And then she walks over, slowly, avoiding the papers and debris around her feet. She bends down next to the old movie projector, broken into pieces. And as she puts her ear right next to it, she hears the click again. As if the movie projector is starting up.

And then a woman screaming.

She runs, slamming the panel shut behind her.

She slips back in bed, hearing the click and the crash of the waves and all she wants to do is run and never stop.

Rosalie shakes her awake, interrupting the projector clicking she hears even while sleeping.

The fourth time this week.

And it's too damn early to hear about ghosts.

Luna groans, reaching out to pull her into bed. Maybe if she cuddles her, she won't have to wake up and help her. But Rosalie snatches her hand away.

"I can hear her again, Tia."

"Mijita, there's no one there—I promise."

"Why won't you believe me? She's down there on the beach. She's walking up and down the sand. I think she's hurt because she won't stop crying."

"Florecita, I've checked every morning you see her. And there's no one there."

"Maybe you just can't see her because of the fog. But she needs us to help her."

"Mmhmm. That must be it."

Rosalie leaves the room and Luna swears she hears her say something about the woman calling her.

But she's back asleep before she can overthink it.

"She was so young there."

Luna startles. She's in the paneled room again, trying to figure out why she can hear the broken projector. But Ethan is only looking at the poster.

"Oh, the actress in the photo? She's gorgeous!"

"Yeah, her too, but I was talking about the little girl. My abuela took my mom to her first Oscars. Silas put the poster here because it makes him sad to look at it. After what happened to them."

"Wait, what happened?"

"My abuela died in a boating accident off of Catalina. She was on a trip with some of her childhood friends. And then my mom died too. I don't remember much about her because I was so young."

He moves toward Luna, running his hands through his hair and plopping down in front of her. His ratty sweater and piercing eyes are almost enough to distract her from the clicking.

Almost.

"She died and Mary vanished. I barely remember either of them besides the fact that they had matching dimples."

"What about your mom?"

"She drowned. Right out back actually. It was the night Silas received the Academy Honorary Award. She must have drunk too much at the afterparty and we think she probably slipped off the balcony in the living room. Abue found her the next morning on the shoreline. I was still sleeping in my room and Mary was just...gone. She was probably like twelve? Maybe she'd just turned thirteen? I can't even remember. It's been that long."

"I'm so sorry, Ethan."

They sit in silence, legs almost mingling in the middle of the room. It's comfortable, sitting here with him. He's calming for Luna. Every time they interact, he makes her feel like maybe she can find peace here.

"How did you even find this place? Abue has had it sealed up since I moved back after college."

"I'm not too sure. It was like something was calling me here. Oh, and the panel was open."

"Well, I'm glad you found it. And that you had a chance to meet them."

They both turn to the picture.

And for a second, Luna swears Bianca turns around and looks at her, hand outstretched. As if she's asking for something. Asking for help.

And then the clicking of the projector starts up again and she has to fake a smile at Ethan as they head toward the kitchen.

"Luna! Luna!" She wakes up with a jolt. The sun is just rising and she can see the fog lingering heavily outside her window. Ethan crouched at the foot of her bed. "Rosalie's missing!"

She throws back the covers and grabs her robe, running down the hallway after Ethan. They search the entire compound top to bottom. They are heading into the ravine at the side of the property when they hear the police sirens and dart back to the house.

"Officer, what happened?" Ethan asks, out of breath. Luna doesn't hesitate but lunges toward Rosalie. She's in one of the police officer's arms, sopping wet and wrapped in a flannel blanket. "The Coast Guard found this little one in the ocean about 100 yards down the shore. She was hysterical, yelling about trying to find the crying woman. She was barely afloat and if we'd found her a couple minutes later—"

"Well, it's good we have her back," Silas interrupts tersely. "Thank you for finding her, officers." He ushers them out, signs a few autographs and slams the heavy wooden door shut. The sound echoes down the hallway and back to the living room. Ethan flinches.

"What do you think you were doing?" Silas whispers, bending over Rosalie. "Do you know what would have happened if the press got a hold of this? If they figured out that the girl I took in was so reckless?"

"Excuse me, but don't speak to her like that! She's a child! She's terrified and hurt and she doesn't need you saying that—"

A crack sounds out and Luna reels back, clutching her cheek in the spot where Silas has slapped her. She should have run when she could have. Rosalie starts crying, hiding behind Luna's legs. The click of the projector starts up in her mind.

"Don't even talk! This isn't your child, and *we* aren't your family. You shouldn't even be here. You're only here because she wouldn't come without you. Otherwise, you'd still be working in that trashy casino in some slutty outfit for tips. I can make it happen again if you aren't careful."

"Don't touch either of them, Silas," Ethan says. "Or I'll call those officers back and make sure they bring some reporters with them to see you carted off in handcuffs for abuse."

Silas doesn't say a word, just coils up and goes after Luna once more. But before he can hit her again, Ethan lunges forward to throw himself in front of Luna and his niece.

The clicking crescendos as the windows to the balcony slam open. They turn toward it and Luna lets out a scream.

A woman the spitting image of Mary sways in the doorway. She's dressed in a slinky gold dress down to her ankles and holds a statue of a movie projector in her hands. She's sopping wet. And pale. So very, very pale.

"Mama?" Ethan questions wildly.

But before she can answer, the room goes dark and a vision fills the space. Nighttime and the Santa Anas are whistling through the air.

A younger Silas slams the front door shut, yelling at the woman in the gold dress. She tears off her jewelry and her Jimmy Choos, throwing them at a familiar poster of her mother hung on the wall. She tries to claw off her dress, but it won't come off. She's yelling, mascara tears rolling down her face, as she gestures to her father— for something that time has hidden from view. Luna notices a young Mary in her pajamas crouched toward the back of the couch, watching everything. The woman grows more agitated as her father screams louder, growing red in the face. She maneuvers toward the windows, opening them to the ocean. As she takes a deep breath of the salty air, a huge wave crashes against the house, spraying her.

But that isn't the only thing.

Silas looses his award in a rage, throwing it at his daughter as if to knock some sense into her. But his aim is wide. Or maybe it's true. The statue strikes the back of her head and she slumps, toppling over the railing and into the ocean below.

Luna watches as Mary turns and runs out the door, bare feet digging into the gravel.

The scene dissipates as sunlight returns to the room. The woman floats lightly toward them, passing the three until she's hovering in front of a stunned Silas. She reaches out to him, anger and sadness warring on her face. Then, softly, she places the statue in his hands.

It becomes solid and he sinks to the floor, gasping a couple of times until silence. Ethan runs over to him and checks for a pulse.

"Call 911, Luna! He's not breathing."

But Luna is still as the woman floats toward them. She gestures to them, but no, not to them. Past them.

Luna spins and lets out a gasp. It's Mary. She's floating in the hallway, in a light yellow dress, hair loose down past her back like it was back in college.

Mary's smiling and peaceful as she moves toward them. She reaches out a hand to Luna, and for a split second she swears she can feel the warmth of Mary's skin. But then she's gone. Dropping a lingering kiss on Rosalie's forehead, she moves to her mama.

A bright light fills the room as they walk toward the balcony and vanish into the early morning Malibu fog.

And then it's only Rosalie crying and Ethan muttering on the phone.

And in the silence, Luna realises she can't hear the clicking anymore.

Ethan and Luna watch as the contractor pulls out of the driveway. One lone brown brick flies off the back and slams onto the concrete.

Luna reaches down, holding it in her hand.

"This is the last thing to remember all of them by. Do you want to keep it?"

"No. I think it's best we don't keep any reminder at all." Ethan grabs the brick and walks through the newly remodeled compound. It's filled with laughter—Rosalie and the twins playing outside. She spots Steven and Jadyn making something in the kitchen for all of them for dinner. The house is filled with happiness now and the shadows of the palm trees don't feel stifling.

She follows Ethan outside, down the steps and to the cliffside.

They linger for a second, staring down at the high tide. "What are we looking at?"

Luna sighs as she feels Rosalie slip her hand in hers. The three of them together on the cliffside.

"Nothing, mi florecita. Just looking at the ocean with your tio."

"It looks really pretty today. Not foggy or anything. I like it." She smiles and squeezes Luna's hand. "I like being here with you. With my family. Can I borrow your phone? I want to play our song."

She runs off with it to plug it into the stereo.

Luna smiles at Ethan as he winds up and chucks the brick into the ocean, then grabs her hand.

It disappears beneath the seafoam with a little plop. And then there's nothing but the sound of seagulls and the laughter of the children.

Not a constant clicking or a distant scream.

Luna hears nothing but her family and the future. And the sound of the Natalie Merchant song filling the air.

It sounds just like home.

— THE GUILT OF ROSALINO —
by Gerardo J. Mercado Hernández

B orikén island, now called Puerto Rico, caresses the sky with its mountains and hilltops shrouded in emerald and jade; their valleys hold the echoes of birds, frogs, and secret things. Rivers take serpentine paths, curving along ancient woods and roads; from the inner valleys they reach their end at the beginning: the sea.

Sitting on a washed-up tree trunk by the end of the riverbank, Rosalino watched the ocean unfold below the changing sky. He gazed at the orange tongues of fire overtaking clouds barely hanging above the horizon. He felt the cool sand under his bare feet and took in the smell of salt water, the crashing of the waves below the neighboring lighthouse's cliff. His arms trembled from those lost hours in the woods, and now from holding the icon. The awful chanting that hounded him returned, drowning out all but the song of the sea.

Murder. Murder.

Turning around he saw the evergreen mountains and thought, as he always did, of the island's past, of the Taíno. Those first inhabitants braving the Caribbean Sea, arriving and thriving below its mountains, watered by the rivers and fed by the oceans. They would've hunted for turtles and fish right along that very bank. He tried to hold on to those visions of a past paradise but always those Spanish galleons landed, and with Death invading on horseback, Borikéns Taínos were exterminated. Chained and killed.

Murder. Murder.

He held the cemí tightly for a moment, beholden to it, terrified of it—of what he'd done, and those that'd watched—but he thought again of what was broken, and placed the idol at the river's edge without another thought. He watched as it was swallowed by the ocean. The voices of the past fell silent and, finally, the present washed over the old man. Rosalino did not see any ships, or swords, or chains, just the same familiar beach, rolling into forever. Across the river he saw the moving specks of beachgoers—anonymous blurry silhouettes. He felt the evening wind carry the sounds of life, and heard the song of crickets and coquís harmonize under the choir of swaying trees atop the ancient soil. As the Sun descended below the horizon, and he began walking home, Rosalino thought of where his little idol would go before Bill Jacobs, that newest of invaders, returned for his blood.

Some Taínos from Borikén believed that humanity came from the nocturnal home of the Sun: a cave.

Atabey, chief goddess, ruler of all horizontal waters, had prohibited humans, at that time strange animals that no one knew well, from coming out of that deep place. The woodpeckers had gossiped that it may have been the Sun and Moon who had given them life and song, but that their bodies had been molded by Atabey's trickster son. The son who so often undid the work of Mighty Jukajú, his twin, who brought order to the world; thus, the great goddess, worried what mischief the strange ones may cause, ruled that they were to remain deep within their cave, far below the mountains of Borikén.

Walking below the last of the sky's orange, Rosalino mumbled angrily to himself while keeping close watch of the shuddering woods, trying to recall from which direction the intruder had arrived in the morning. There was no bridge linking the eastern banks, he thought, and there was no engine noise either; the jackass must've left his car on the western bridge. Rosalino continued much the same as he passed that familiar congregation of palms, willow, and pines—all dancing on time with the rhythm of the sea winds.

"How else could I have reacted!" he yelled into his right hand. Below the bending forest canopy an army of shrubs, wild grass, and small trees were trapped in rapid cycles of violent curtsies. *Nod along and smile while he* robbed *me?* Rosalino continued to himself. *For* what? *Beachside condos with* pools? *Where turtles nest? Goddamn killer. Killer.* In his rage the old man tripped on some tangled branches and fell. Before he stood up again, Rosalino saw a familiar face stare back at him from the shadows of the trees. He briefly considered looking behind them, dreading to see those *other* watching eyes, but didn't dare look away from the staring bird. It was another of his cemís, an earlier effort, the size of a garden gnome, made from superglued cans, chicken wire, and bird bones he'd found on his walks. For the second time that day that cemís had moved, and with it the thin veneer of his calmness, the assurance that it might have all been a horrible dream, fell. The old man simply stumbled backward, and stopped only when he reached the wet sand.

From his new vantage point he saw his house, showered in that last of the dying amber light, and Rosalino ran, wiping sweat away from his brow, watching the familiar transformation to dusk. His legs ached, the sands making a momentary hell for his legs, but, in the distance behind him, he heard that terrible ceaseless chant once more, and he pushed onward, until, for the third time that day, his cemís had moved, forming around his home a potter's field of idols and gods and dreams. His lungs on fire, Rosalino threw up his morning coffee, but continued, carefully, onward.

The shadows of the dancing trees stretched along the wooden walls, grasping at his windows and door. With his eyes the old man traced those reaching fingers to their hands and arms and bodies; he thought of those paths leading back to hidden places, between the branches and leaves and roots, and of those who walked them. He gazed at those earlier attempts to connect with his ancestors as he passed them scattered around his home, trapped in some combination of mute anger, tearless crying, and wordless shouting. Though it had been decades since his grandmother had paid for art lessons, he'd made dozens upon dozens of the idols. Like the Taíno, he'd made them of stone, wood, sea shells...or whatever other materials he could find. Cemís could be made from a great deal of things—even bones. Hurrying up the steps into the one-room, one-bathroom affair, he saw its single thin power line move ominously in the wind. He whispered a small hope that the line would hold, recalling those other visions, from his lost time, in those calling woods: himself strangled, buried six feet under a gloating Jacobs' newly minted asphalt parking.

Rosalino went inside, turned on the headlights, and all was silence. Looking down, he saw the broken shards of his grandmother's cemí—courtesy of Bill Jacobs and to no avail: the haunting voice remained. Looking up, he saw a pack of cigarettes—his grandmother's brand too—and settled for the long night.

One day, after mastering the rains, mighty Jukajú walked by the solar cave and heard humanity's cries. He listened to their sad songs, and their

desperation to escape; the birds had told them of the sky and the moun-tains; the coquí frogs told them of the jungles and rivers; the Sun and Moon told them of the world. As their celestial parents did, so too did the cave people create, and those first cemí were given shape from the stories of nature.

Jukajú felt such love and pity in his heart for those who were family, and so he called for a great snake to let all of humanity, one by one, climb out of the cave, through its body, and onto the open earth beneath the sky.

It had been nearly seven thirty in the morning when Bill Jacobs, skin blistering and drenched in sweat from his journey across the beach, barged unannounced through the front door, interrupting Rosalino's breakfast. Thinking himself a hunter, and hungry from the walk, he circled the old man, talking while he took stock of the shelves brimming with assortments of sculptures and books. He discovered that Rosalino was a retired English teacher, who enjoyed watching nature and perusing the spirituality and self-help section of the bookstore. When Bill finally found himself seated, he began to pick away at the scrambled eggs and buttered bread that Rosalino had yet to touch, and, for the better part of an hour, the American pressed the old man to sell his land.

"Honestly man, look at this piece of crap shack, wouldn't you rather live in a big house? Old timer like you? Hell, you ought'a have a nice-looking gal around too."

"I already told you. I like living alone and I'm not selling my home. Not now, not ever, goddamnit. Please leave. I've been a very polite host. I served you breakfast. I'm sorry I don't know more about that historical period you mentioned, but now, truly, I have important things to do." Rosalino tried not to let the big man see his trembling hand, tucking it in the wood-carving bag he'd grabbed—the one with the new chisels.

When Bill's near-permanent smirk finally wavered, he looked at the 'Rican up and down, and remarked on his old sweat-stained shirt, his badly-trimmed beard.

He'd been promised this would've been easy. He was promised that these people quickly caved.

"You know, old timer, this was supposed to be easy. Damn, I thought you were gonna be hopping mad with *gratitude*—someone in your *circumstance* should know a good thing when they see it. Think, a lil' bit, just a bit—it's not that hard—about what I'm offering you. Now, be reasonable—this is a good thing for you, for your people. I'm gonna build you all a goddamned inspirational monument—don't you care about your island?"

A splinter of time later, Rosalino's shaking hands had transformed into flying fists as he yelled, "You bastard pig, get off my land!"

His left hook made Jacobs take a step back. Bill, betraying his red-hot anger only for a moment, quickly, but intently, slicked back his thinning blonde hair, pointed at Rosalino with a finger gun motion and, without warning, pushed the cemí nearest to him—a flat plate made of stone with the Moon's petroglyph—onto the hard floor. The serene god's face lay broken and shattered.

"Be seeing you, old timer," said Jacob before departing. "Why don't you try some Dutch courage for that lil' shake of yours?" slamming the door behind him.

However, one old man, upon reaching the snake head, was frightened, and he beat its head with a loose rock. The blow was fatal, and so the snake fell down, along with the old man and those behind him, back down into the bowels of the earth. Jukajú was infuriated by this death, and so made it rain for many days and nights, until the cave was at the bottom of a new sea, and those great mountains around it became Borikén—Puerto Rico.

"Senile shithead," Bill murmured to himself, seeing Rosalino run from god knows where and back into his little dingy shack. In all his years in Puerto Rico, Bill had never heard a voice raised against him, let alone an insult. It wasn't a feeling he cared for very much. Was it a crime to want to add to this sad, sad little corner of the world? Ingrates—all of them—he concluded. He'd even had the grace to explain that this was a family affair. Should've let the Spanish keep them. He wondered where the old man had been, looking at his ugly garden as if it concealed the devil. Surveying his future prize, Bill had stayed long enough, and close enough, to see the old man stumble out of his house and begin his journey into the unruly jungle east of his home.

Taking his chance, the American has used the overgrowth as cover, approaching the seemingly dazed septuagenarian. He noted the others' disjointed dance and terrified expression, watching his surroundings as if it were a great and terrible beast on the prowl, stalking him from behind the veil of trees; for a brief moment, Bill thought he'd seen a strange-looking bird shimmer, like reflected sunlight, before flying off into the lush emerald canopy. Bill reconsidered his improvised tactic and cursed himself for leaving his gun in the car, for as soon as he'd looked away, the old man had gone into the thick of those wild-looking woods.

Returning after a brief visit to his motel room and grabbing some moving money (and a portion of the mini fridge's contents), the would-be land developer saw no clue as to the old man's trail or behavior, and so Bill went into Rosalino's home. Finding nothing of importance, he grabbed a book that called his eye, and proceeded to wait in his car, just out of obvious sight, and began his long wait.

Hence, consider yourself a world—you the patchwork prism of its Gods and Devils—its creator and destroyer, read the little stolen book. The azure-colored binding made the contrasting ochre-colored pages seem like gold, and, from there, he began to read. William had never heard of the esoteric book, titled *Stars Below, Waves Above: Strange Conceptions & Convergences*, or of its author, R. Eustakio Serrano. Inside, the pages spoke of *those* places, those half steps between the senses, the schemes and metaphors beyond the horizon's line and death's dreaming door. It reminded Jacobs of some hermit mages he'd read about years ago, locked away in their towers communing with magic, pulling living shades and shapes into the world. He'd sometimes enjoyed reading through such subjects himself, on occasion, and was frankly surprised that someone as sorry-looking as the old man owned such a pretty little thing.

Thinking of Rosalino's shaking fist rekindled Bill's ire. *If anyone's a leech it's you lazy brown ingrates,* he thought, *feeding off people like me... I shouldn't be surprised at their cockiness; honest to god, they probably can't even fucking help it. With all that goddamned mixing,* he thought, *these poor hicks probably can't even hold a thought for longer than a minute—goddamn...maybe that's why they're always smiling.*

"Frankly, these people are penniless children: naive, uneducated and eager to be saved," his Rincón man had said. "Just offer up some chump change and work your way down—they'll be eating right out of your palm."

On that advice, Jacobs had invested in raw materials, machines, and workers, emptied his bank account and borrowed money from certain people...

Do they even know *what they have?* Bill Jacobs wondered. He thought of Wilhem Jacobs, one of his ancestors, a member of the 1709 British invasion of Puerto Rico, who, after its failure, settled on a plantation in the British colonies. Wilhem took with him a vision of a tropical Eden, a place brimming with lush jungles and living mountains, where green angels sing in flocks and the deadliest snake is but a charming ornament. How could Jacobs, upon seeing the promised land of his family history, ignore what was now so obvious to him: this enchanted island, where the waves ever rage against the vastness of the sky, had been meant for him. *Consider yourself a world—you are its creator and destroyer...*

Jacobs could already see it in his mind, sprouting like a castle, rooted permanently like a mountain itself, and him, seated at the top, looking down at creation. As his fumes dissipated, he settled, waiting, as all her children do, for the night to shroud the world, and for his hunt to begin. It was a shame, really, to be back doing this sort of manual work; he'd even found the old man charming at first—in an exotic kind of way—locked away in his shack, filled with ugly odd sculptures and bundles of esoteric books. Still, it's an eat-or-be-eaten kind of world, Bill knew, and he'd gotten used to dining big.

As Bill continued to read through the blue book, he thought of lockless doors while, far below the churning waves, Rosalino's idol found itself within caves that hadn't been there before; around it, slithering in those deep and terrible waters, were bodies, meshed together, desperate and hungry, and all followed the voice inside the cemí—its maker's.

Some Taínos from Borikén believed that, as Jukajú's rain filled the mountains, the old man who had killed the snake began in his grief and shame to sing. He cried of his crime and repentance, of deep and terrible things, of high and hopeful things. The rest joined him, and their song rose through the flooding caves to the highest trees until that newly born Borikén knew the song. It was at that moment that the nameless trickster, mighty Jukajú's brother, took pity on those he'd shaped, and so, when his brother's rain had almost filled those caves, he commanded the dead snake's blood turn them into great beings in the form of sea snakes, naming them protectors.

Rosalino's mind shuddered as he took another mouthful of wine and smoke.

Don't you care about your island?

Blowing smoke toward the ceiling, he turned the question over and over in his mind. It had ushered in all of his resentment for all those sins against Borikén by the Spanish and the Americans. Torture, human experimentation, genocide—even speaking the "wrong" language had been a crime. Borikén's cry of *"Justice!"* had made him throw that punch. He'd never shouted at anyone before, not really—especially not at a white man. He didn't need to know history, though he did, to understand how swift and terrible the world could be if you were from the Caribbean, shouting and demanding. Outside, the coquís and crickets continued their melodies, declaring the Moon's domain. Rosalino's house was shrouded in shadows; he'd turned off the ceiling light, and only through the garden's suffused lunar light could Rosalino see about him. Resting on his homemade shelves were his creations, those idols of chango ravens, sleeping turtles, screaming bats, watching frogs and praying supplicants.

Unlike the Taíno, Rosalino didn't have the sacred cahoba herb, nor a priest to guide him during the shaping of a cemí; instead, Rosalino had created his own ceremony from what he'd learned from another tribe in the central mountains, history books and the island's folklore, and, in cases of utter uncertainty, he had elected to be inspired by his *other* books. Rosalino's ritual began by going out to where sand met soil. He felt that was a special place, just as dawn and dusk are special times: birds sang more richly, the mountains seemed more serene, their peaks whispered with the stars, trading secrets for favors and gossip. From *that* spell of life those sacred curtains of everyday life, for everyone, would lift. Opening himself, becoming a vessel for the currents of strange impulse that dictated his walks and turns, his eyes and ears, he collected everything that asked to be taken. After his explorations, he returned to an open table below the shade of the trees; from there he would help the cemís gather their forms. He'd let his hands work with rage and loss, with hope and wanting; in return, he would tell them what had befallen their beloved island.

The clouds began to gather around the Moon, and he looked closer at the cemís below. Rosalino wondered if he'd been wise to create with resentment and pain, if he hadn't betrayed something sacred by his action. In truth, Rosalino had no idea if he was honoring his ancestors, making a mockery of them, or cursing himself, but he yearned for that connection; he'd needed to feel those roots—*their security*—and so, when the other destroyed his grandmother's only remaining heirloom, it had left Rosalino a hollow vessel.

His first instinct was to pick it up, but furiously shaking, he carelessly cut his finger on one of the sharp edges. Lush droplets of blood fell into the broken shards. As the retired teacher stared at his bleeding finger, the sounds of nature filled that newly made space inside himself, and a new sense seemed to overwhelm him. The rolling waves roared at his doorstep, the trees scratched and wailed at his walls like unknown creatures. *He comes. He'll come. They always return*, a voice suddenly said. It was warm and heavy, familiar and ecstatic; it came from the trees and their shaking leaves, from between the thunder of the waves, the shifting sands, the sounds of animals.

The voice too came from the bird of prey he'd finished creating last week, and Rosalino knew then that it *must* be Borikén speaking.

Murder comes. Murder comes.

The bird idol, strainfully, almost painfully, began to move, ruffling the layered cans like feathers. It was struggling to reach the window. There Rosalino saw small dancing shapes, moving in a circle around his house, coming and going from the shadows of the trees where his screaming and crying idols stood. He saw the sky turn to a deep and saturated blue. The Sun had lost its most potent rays, and, alongside the Moon, the two of them were as giant shining eyes. The cemís around him had continued to shift positions, looking at him while they made a path toward that unruly patch of the wild woods. It was only when Rosalino looked back at their faces, contorting and shifting, their disjointed parts coming alive like the birds, that he realized that his own body was moving to some unheard song, following their trail into parts unknown.

He followed it until the trees became too clustered together, their canopy blocking out the strange blue sky and its celestial lamps. He began to crawl along tall blades of grass, the army of trees clinging so tightly they almost seemed like a cave. Those few animals he'd encountered unsettled him, looking at him without running away, almost as if they expected an apology. Borikén's voice never left him, and had begun to warn him of the intruder, how he was to come again; between the openings in the grass, Rosalino was shown visions of white hands around his throat, and evil towers rising above his home and body.

Eventually, he made it to a hollow domed by the trees, cleared of grass—to the heart. No light passed through the tops of the trees, but from the spaces between the roots warm light peered into that place. In the middle of the hollow was a pale white wood, as if it had spent years in the ocean. He realized he was still carrying his carving tools. The wood began speaking to him.

Murder. Murder.

"What body? What shape?" he'd asked himself, unwrapping his tools from their hiding place. Around him, burrowing lizards and toads had come from their hiding places; even a woodpecker was present as he began his work. They began to sing, but he listened only to the voice inside the wood, as he'd done before, but not as he'd done before.

What body? What shape?

His body began working before his mind followed; only as the face began to take shape did he remember—the story of the snake guardians—and soon he remembered those opening words from his little blue book: *There is a hidden place, hidden not from some senses unconquered or undiscovered, hidden without being secret, layered between chance and fate and wanting, always waiting to step out from within dreams and visions, from within those veils between ecstasy and dread. Hence, consider yourself a world—you the patchwork prism of its Gods and Devils—its creator and destroyer.*

Birthed under that strange light, revealed in that secret place, was a face of lidless oblong eyes, a gaping mouth, long, and filled with baleful fangs; its serpentine neck coiled perfectly around its powerful belly, showered in crimson droplets.

The wind howled and a choir of birds sang. The rushing of the waves echoed below the setting Sun, and Rosalino was back, sitting next to the river, under a mangrove's shade. Confused and in a brief panic, he looked back and briefly saw three people, one woman and twins—men—staring back at him with sad eyes. They shared a gaze for a moment, but, turning around, he began to walk toward the river, holding his newest cemí.

Murder. Justice.

Staring at the empty space on his shelf at home, he finished the cheap, tasteless wine and watched a light mist rise from the sea. For a moment, flashing before his eyes, the mental image of a horrified Jacobs being torn limb from limb by powerful jaws. Rosalino smiled briefly before hearing a faint rustle of leaves and sand. Rosalino turned to the window and noticed that the arrangement of cemís had changed: they were all gone.

Murder. Murder.

After so many years in front of a crowd, teaching distracted kids and annoyed teens, he'd nearly developed eyes on the back of his head. When Rosalino turned, cooing by the empty space on the shelf next to the door was his bird of prey, returned, now fully flesh and wire, sitting and crowing, looking straight at him.

Justice. Justice.

...consider yourself a world—you the patchwork prism of its Gods and Devils—its creator and destroyer. Lost between the blue book's pages, Jacobs had been absorbed in its knowledge. He read how the soul's inner cosmos can seep into the world and shape it, break it, mold even time and space. Bill Jacobs could already feel the ocean breeze cooling his hot skin from a day of tanning, he could see his European guests lounging about their tables, drinking, singing, dancing—all for him, because of him. There, where the dead man's house still stands, he'll put the very first stone for *Jacobs' Enchanted Island, Resort & Casino*, a monument among those ancient mountains, like a king, a new William the Conqueror; he will march through them, bathing in its rivers, enjoying the Eden put before him. Yes, he'd put it to good use, his own little paradise, just the one task left, and what was a little death for a dream? His contact had already texted him the police contact he was to call in a few days' time. When it became too dark for him to continue reading, Bill marked where he left off, and decided that his moment was at hand. Grabbing his knife and gun, he stepped out of the car only to see that the little house was gone; the trees, like watching giants, so close together—closer than he remembered—had utterly blocked the Moon's light. He turned and looked around, searching for any familiar sights, but he'd been swallowed wholly by the shadows of the night. The tempo of the waves was just a tiny echo beyond the unseen horizon, but Bill decided to simply move in the direction

his headlights pointed at; hidden or not, the house was a straight-forward path away, and nothing could change that fact.

"What's a little death for a dream," he repeated under his breath, walking under the gaze of silent watchers.

The earth was drenched in muddy waters, the curling grass gnawed at his ankles and, more and more, he found himself tripping over things on the way.

He recalled the old man's ugly sculptures scattered around his property. He'd given their ugly faces the finger on his first visit. He tried to recall exactly where they had been placed, but after a few more minutes of walking, he stopped. He should've reached the house minutes ago. How many minutes? He wasn't sure, and his car was no longer visible. As he took stock, Bill realized that those shapes he kept bumping into had been transforming on his journey; from kicking stone and metal, he began to feel the intruding shapes as taut, with an almost organic shuddering at his touch, and, in one wicked instance, warm. It was then that a soft hissing came from the branches, and Bill wondered if there were any big snakes on the island. Swallowing his tension, he pictured his wrecking ball tearing down the ugly little house while his skyscraper took its place among the mountains, with him in the topmost room. Now calm again, Bill continued on his way, making a mental note to tear down all of those ugly trees, replacing them with a nice civil garden.

Consider yourself a world, he reminded himself, *creator and destroyer.* Jacobs had taken a few more steps when a flutter of wings made him stop again. A second later, teeth like jagged knives bit down on his ankles, crushing both muscle and bone. He let out a thundering scream and fell on his back with a thud that took the wind from his lungs. He tried to draw his knife and, instead, spilled the contents of his pocket on the muddied ground; as vaguely humanoid hands restrained him, a hissing melody neared him. Sprawled on the floor, he fought desperately, but grabbed only dirt and grass, his attackers offering no quarter. The hissing sound had returned with a vengeance: it was around him. He prayed for some light, and the Moon answered him, shining down upon them all. Bill Jacobs saw his captors, chimeras of flesh and wire, holding him under the watchful eyes of nightmares: snakes looking straight at him.

Bill Jacobs wondered how something with so many rows of teeth could sing like a person.

Murder. Justice. Murder. Justice.

The bird had continued to chant while Rosalino observed through the window, even as *they* swarmed his ankles like maddened worms, and a great choir of birds, bats and frogs swelled the night with life.

Justice. Murder. Justice. Murder.

Suddenly, from within the tangled forms, something damp emerged and was propped in his lap. It was wet and wooden, and, as he felt around, he recognized the familiar shape—he'd placed the idol on the river only a few hours ago. Rosalino heard a scream, but didn't dare move, or close his eyes. As the slithering forms departed, he remembered those words again: *...you the patchwork prism of its Gods and Devils—its creator and destroyer.* He heard another scream, strained and gurgling, then quiet; the chant remained only for a moment before returning to silence.

Justice. Justice. Justice always comes.

Rosalino found a set of car keys, and a blotch of blood, a few feet from the house, when dawn marked the end of the night.

The blood, he decided, would disappear within a day. Instead, he focused on the car those keys opened, parked behind a line of trees a few yards away. On the passenger's seat he found the book he thought he'd lost—a copy he had left from one of his self-publishing stints. He began to read the poem on the marked page:

> When those nights of pain and dread rule, Pronounce what you wish in verses your own. No desire or fear, but the passing of pain.
> Repeat and proclaim, till your shadow ascends, Unveiling just once a cure unconcealed.
> Then speak, and ask, before idly you mask:
> What cosmic veil do you wish to unmask?

After he finished reading, Rosalino sat and thought of the cemí with the baleful fangs and the caves below the Caribbean archipelago. No birds sang as Rosalino's shivering cry rippled through the morning cold.

— THE HOUSE BY THE DELL —
by Lauren McEwen

I didn't want to be out in Cedar Bluff that day, but Latrice had guilted me into it.

"Seriously, Arialle, it's not enough for us to just be a part of this organization. We also have to use our social standing for good. To support the community and set an example for other students," she'd droned on, sounding like a brochure.

And yes, when I'd joined a sorority, I knew I would be expected to do more than just go to parties and brainstorm creative ways to torture new pledges. Honestly, other than the "life-long friendships and connections" that I was supposed to be able to make, the community service was a huge selling point for me. I'd always liked for people to see me as a nice person. A do-gooder, someone to be admired and emulated. And that was exactly why this happened to me. My need to be liked.

So, that afternoon I was busy knocking on the doors of elderly people on a list of names Latrice had printed out for me that morning. I bore holiday snack baskets, each full to the brim with things like pralines, oranges, peppermint sticks and pretzels. The kinds of treats my grandmothers would force on us whenever we visited them close to Christmas.

I'd had these visions of me making an elderly friend who I would visit every other week. We would drink hot tea and play checkers on Sunday afternoons, she would teach me her most prized recipes, and, when she died, I would tell everyone how much she had meant to me. It sounded like a good story.

And that was what led me down the winding driveway at the end of the road. For the longest time, I had been looking for Ms. Henrietta Williams' house; the address was 2769 Galloway Road, but it took me forever to find it. This street was far more difficult to navigate than the others. The road wasn't particularly winding, but the house numbers jumped, with no real rhyme or reason to them. Almost like there were houses missing, or they were numbered completely out of order.

Most of the lawns were carefully manicured, but when you approached the homes it was clear that they were in major need of repair. Chipping paint, rotting wooden stairs, clogged gutters full of weather-worn holes. The kind of maintenance that older people often let slide because they either don't have the energy or money or they've just gotten too old to care about living up to a home-owners association's exacting standards.

When I knocked on most of the doors, I was initially met with skepticism, as if they had forgotten about the baskets altogether. It had been at least a month since we'd picked up all the sign-up sheets our chapter had placed at churches, senior centers, and grocery stores around Henderson, so I figured they must have forgotten about it.

Everyone seemed afraid that I was there to sell something or to inform them that one of their utilities was about to be shut off, but, after that initial awkwardness, they accepted the baskets with a polite smile.

Ms. Henrietta, as I'd already come to think of her, was the last on my list, and for the life of me I could not find her house. In fact, I'd almost missed her name completely. I only caught it after doing a third and final scan of my list.

Judging by my GPS, her house was at the end of the road, but I'd driven down the street three times already only to be met with a dell filled with long-dead leaves and rocks and a strange little structure sticking out of one side, almost like the top of a turret, as if a house had either sunken completely underground or been built beneath the earth.

It was strange, but Cedar Bluff was the oldest Black neighborhood in Henderson. A lot had happened there over the years. In fact, it was the setting of one of the first stories I'd been told about my new temporary home during my freshman year. One of the girls in my dorm was from the area, and one night, while we were exchanging ghost stories, she hit us with one that kept me up a few nights.

The first home in the neighborhood was built in the 1920s, smack dab in what my Black Studies professor told us was considered the "nadir of race relations in the United States." Lynchings and murders and strange disappearances haunted Black people all over the country, but here, for some reason, the residents had been able to stay relatively safe. A few tense exchanges and threats were made here and there, but, for the most part, the white folks across the way left Cedar Bluff alone. That was until a little boy named Richie and a little girl named Tabitha from the neighborhood went missing for two days in the summer of 1937. When the local police made it clear that they weren't going to bother searching for two little Black children, the residents of Cedar Bluff took matters into their own hands. Armed with pistols and baseball bats, they combed the neighboring forests, knocked on doors and even waded in the muddy waters of Crescent Lake.

Most of the women stayed behind to protect the kids and elderly, but, as legend has it, Richie and Tabitha's mothers broke from the group to seek the help of an older woman who lived down the road. The rumor was that she was something of a witch, and, although most of her neighbors would have typically steered clear of that kind of thing, the two mothers were desperate. No one could tell you exactly what the old woman had done, but, sure enough, that evening, those kids came walking down the middle of Chester Street in one piece.

Nobody knew what had happened to them—both children claimed to have lost all memory of those two days—or how the old woman had managed to bring them back, but they knew what happened next: bad luck befell several members of Tabitha and Richie's families. There was sickness, car accidents, investments that went belly up before the ink was dry on the paperwork.

Eventually, the last of their relatives moved away, and that was all anyone ever heard of them. When I first heard the story, it had made my skin crawl, a feeling that stuck with me for days. If it was true...what had happened to those children while they were missing? How did the old woman, whose name everyone seemed to have forgotten, save them? And what could their families have possibly done to bring about so much misfortune? I'd almost completely forgotten about that story. I'd been here only a couple times: once to attend Easter dinner with my friend Brittney's family, once on a tour of Henderson during freshmen week. The place struck me because, despite the obvious toll that time had taken on some of these houses, you could still see how much pride had been taken in building them all those years ago.

Most of these homes had been built by amateurs, with blueprints bought from Sears Roebuck, which was a must, given that most architects and contractors at the time were white and generally unwilling to construct new homes for the families in Cedar Bluff. Many of the houses had undergone renovation in the years since.

Porches, new wings, and back decks were added. Sheds and tree-houses and play sets were erected in back yards. The homes grew with their families and, now that only the oldest, most settled residents were left behind, the neighborhood had a somewhat eerie quality. It felt like time had finally begun to move on without them.

A little way down the road I'd passed by a charred shell of a house. I wasn't sure how it had burned down, but there was a little memorial wreath right out front, surrounded by weather-worn stuffed animals and old candles. I didn't even want to imagine what might have happened to the family that lived there.

I promised myself that I would give up after my next try. There was no way in hell that Latrice could make me feel guilty after I made literally four attempts to reach this lady's house. That's when I saw it: an ancient metal mailbox in front of a long, narrow driveway. It had been so close to her neighbor's box that I'd missed it, and the house number that had been painted on the side was almost completely faded. On the far side of the driveway was the dell. The drop-off looked impossibly steep, and I was too afraid to drive my car up to the house for fear that I would go over the side.

I checked the clock on my dashboard. It was already past four. The sun had been setting earlier and earlier with each passing winter day, and I was past tired, but I hated the idea of Ms. Henrietta making small talk with one of her neighbors and finding out that she was the only one who hadn't received her basket.

So, I parked my car, put on my gloves, and began the trek up to the house. Despite the chill, the day was beautiful. The sky was bright blue, with hazy, swirling clouds. Most of the trees had lost their leaves weeks ago, and the ones lining Ms. Henrietta's walkway stood tall, with their highest branches stretched upward, like hands raised in surrender. I'd felt a little nervous the entire time I'd been handing out baskets, but I'd chalked it up to feeling burnt out after having met so many people in such a small window of time.

The feeling of foreboding that I got while walking up Ms. Henrietta's driveway felt sudden at first, but, looking back, it had been lingering just beneath the surface the entire day. I'd had an anxious feeling in the pit of my stomach, like the springs inside me were wound too tight, but I'd written it off as nerves. I'd spent a whole day trying to make good impressions on strangers, after all. As I made my way down the packed dirt path, though, the skin on the back of my neck tingled and prickled. It was the feeling I got when I looked outside a window at night, like any moment I was bound to see something I shouldn't.

"Just keep walking, Arialle. You're going to drop off this last basket and head back to campus. No big deal," I whispered to myself. *"And do not look down at the dell,"* said a voice inside my head. I wasn't sure where that came from, but I picked up my pace and fixed my eyes on Ms. Henrietta's house.

Cursing myself a bit for being ridiculous, I trudged on, but the prickling sensation grew stronger, until it felt like a thousand eyes boring holes into my back. I reached for the back of my neck, trying to rub away the sensation, but it was hopeless. It began to occur to me that something about this place was not right. Yes, I was alone, and I was cold, but I was also terrified in a way that I'd never been before. The air around me seemed colder than it had only moments before, and I didn't hear any cars rumbling off in the distance or any squirrels scurrying through the dead leaves. The bushes on the left side of the driveway were overgrown and— despite the cold—thick, bright green leaves were clinging to the spindly branches.

Good cover for a predator.

I felt like I'd been walking for several minutes, but I was afraid to turn around to see how far away I was from my car. I was wondering exactly how Ms. Henrietta managed her way up and down this driveway to the mailbox each day when another thought slipped into my head, this time in a slick voice that was decidedly not my own: "When she's allowed to leave."

I'd never considered the phrase "a chill ran down my spine" to be literal until that very moment. But it wasn't as though it slipped down my back with ease. It was like someone dumped cold water over my head. I felt it down to my toes, and the shock of it made me spring into a run.

The closer I got to the front door, the faster I ran. I hadn't heard birds before, but suddenly their cries were deafening, like they were all chirping at once, a shrill chorus. By the time I made it to Ms. Henrietta's walkway I was nearly out of breath.

I hadn't made it to her porch before she opened the door. As soon as I saw her, everything shifted. The birds began chirping at a normal volume, my heart rate began to slow, and my stomach finally stopped doing somersaults. I looked around for a moment, confused and a little embarrassed.

"Hi there, baby. How can I help you?" Ms. Henrietta smiled. She was, in a word, beautiful. Her deep-brown skin was softly wrinkled and glowing, her smile warm, and she had absurdly high cheekbones. I guess in taking it all in I stared for longer than what is socially acceptable, because she cleared her throat pointedly.

"I'm sorry! Hi! I'm from Henderson College. You signed up to get one of our holiday baskets?"

"Oh, yes...I almost forgot about that. Thank you for bringing it all this way. Would you like to come in to warm up? It's chilly out here."

Normally, I don't make it a habit to enter the homes of strangers, but I accepted her invitation without a second thought. Something about her felt familiar, but I couldn't exactly put my finger on it.

Plus, I needed to get my bearings after that walk. I was still feeling a bit unsettled.

"I was just about to make some coffee. Would you like some?"

"Yes, thank you," I said, suddenly aware of exactly how cold I was. I burrowed my gloved hands further into my coat pockets.

"Come on back. It's a lot warmer in my kitchen," Ms. Henrietta said, laughing.

When I stepped inside Ms. Henrietta's kitchen, a feeling of déjà vu swept over me. Everything about it was familiar—the two-basin copper sink beneath the window, her lacy white curtains, the small red brick fireplace in the breakfast nook, the array of crystals sitting on the windowsill—I had been here before. I was sure of it.

"You remember?" Ms. Henrietta gave me a knowing smile as she went over to the cabinet to pull out a couple of coffee cups.

"Remember what?" I asked, jumping a little at the sound of her voice.

"Remember me and this house. It's okay, Arialle. I'll explain everything. But first, get yourself comfortable. You've been riding up and down this street all day."

"How did you—"

Ms. Henrietta laughed, but it wasn't mocking. It was amused. "We go a long way back, little girl. Me and your family."

"My family? But they live in California. That's, like, clear across the country."

"They do now," Ms. Henrietta said. "But not always. Go ahead and take off that coat. We need to visit for a little while."

I sat down in the chair she'd motioned to, taking off my coat and staring at the room around me. I just knew that I had been here before. It made absolutely no sense, but I knew exactly where Ms. Henrietta kept her sugar, her flatware—I even knew that she was going to offer me a piece of homemade pound cake to eat with my coffee.

And the more I looked around, the more uneasy I became. I had been here before. It was impossible, but yet I had never been more certain of anything in my life. Me and Ms. Henrietta went way back, and I was not sure whether or not I was happy about the reunion.

"I'm so glad you finally came to see me. I was worried that it would get to be too late for you."

"Ma'am...I don't mean to be rude, but I don't remember ever meeting you. How do you know my family?"

"I've thought a lot about this moment over the years. I figured I'd try to gently jog your memory with little hints and stories, but we're almost out of time. You're about to turn twenty-two, are you not?"

"How did you—" My eyes were probably as wide as the sky. Ms. Henrietta chuckled at the expression on my face, but this time I found her amusement far less charming.

"Just like I said. I know your people. But we don't have a lot of time to be here messing around. Give me your hands."

"My hands? What are you going to do with my hands?"

"I'm going to show you what you can't see. Yet. It'll help us to move forward."

I was reluctant, but I have to admit that I was also very curious. Everything about Ms. Henrietta, her home, even the smell of her cake, I knew it all. I even knew that the fear I'd felt when I was walking up to her door served a purpose. If she was offering me answers; I supposed that I should accept them.

I offered my hands to her, and Ms. Henrietta interlaced her smooth, thin fingers with my own. When our palms finally touched, it felt like the wind had been knocked out of me. As soon as I caught my breath and was able to look around, I realized that I was still in the old woman's kitchen, but this time, I was alone. And not only that, but it was also nighttime. Hours must have passed.

Fear rushed over me like someone had poured a bucket of ice water over the top of my head, but curiosity forced me out of my chair. Slowly, I crept out of the kitchen and toward the living room.

As soon as I walked up to the front, I heard a frantic knocking at the door. I jumped at the sound, and then I flinched again when Ms. Henrietta came walking up behind me.

"I'm sorry. I was just looking for you," I started to say before I realized that Ms. Henrietta didn't seem to have noticed me at all. Instead, she was walking straight to the door. As soon as Ms. Henrietta opened the door, two women began talking to her in a rush. Their panic was so palpable that it took me a moment to really look at them. Everything about them— their hair, their jewelry, their clothing, even their makeup—was old-fashioned. It reminded me of the way people dressed in the old movies my dad loved. They both wore starched collared shirts and A-line skirts that stopped at their stockinged knees. Their carefully pin-curled hair was frizzy from the humidity.

"You have to help us," one of the women said, reaching for Ms. Henrietta's hand. Ms. Henrietta accepted the touch, gently tightening her fingers around the other woman's hand, but she had yet to invite them inside.

"I've heard what's happened and I'm sorry. I understand that you want your children back, but there's always a price to magic, and if I know anything about the two of you…you won't be willing to pay it."

The other woman spoke up then, determination in her voice. "I don't care what the cost is. I need my Tabby back. I can only imagine how afraid she is."

As soon as she said that name, it clicked. Judging from their clothes and hairstyles, this had happened in the thirties. These had to be the mothers of the two missing children from the tale my floormate had told us freshman year. But how could that be when Ms. Henrietta was there, looking the exact same way she had when I walked into her kitchen this afternoon? The thought sent a chill flooding down my spine.

"Yes," Ms. Henrietta said sadly. "They are both afraid and very alone. I felt it yesterday morning, as soon as I woke up. My whole body was soaked in it."

The two mothers looked at each other with a mix of apprehension and horror. It was clear that, while they had heard rumors that Ms. Henrietta had powers, they must not have been prepared for her to say things like that. If Ms. Henrietta noticed their discomfort, she didn't let on. Instead, she set her mouth into a firm line and nodded a couple of times before speaking.

"Yes, yes. You two come in. We must work quickly if we are going to save these children's lives."

"Their lives are in danger?!" said the first woman, Richie's mom.

"I'm afraid so," said Ms. Henrietta, leading them into the kitchen. "But it isn't too late. I can sense them, so that means they're still with us."

"How can we get them back?" sobbed Tabitha's mother. She pulled a handkerchief from her purse and began wiping the tears off her face.

"Well, it will take a spell. And I'll need a little of your blood to do it. Because this is blood magic. It might take a toll on the two of you, so there are certain protections you must take for many months after. We're about to touch something old. Something deep. And even if we're doing it for the right reasons, if the three of us don't make sure we are as careful as possible...I hate to think of what kind of evil could latch onto us."

The two women looked at each other, silently weighing their options. Richie's mother spoke first. "Whatever I have to do to save my baby, I will do it."

"Same for me," said Tabitha's mother, finally taking a seat at the kitchen table.

Richie's mother jumped, as if she'd only just realized that she was still standing, and grabbed a seat of her own.

"I am going to gather a few supplies from around the house, and then we will begin. And whatever God you pray to, I suggest you start calling on 'em now."

As soon as she left the room, I felt the air go out of my lungs again, and suddenly I was back in the kitchen, staring into Ms. Henrietta's molasses-colored eyes.

"What was that?!" I cried, as soon as I could speak.

"I had to show you what we're dealing with. I figured it was easiest if you could just take a peek at my memories."

"I saw. And if I'm being honest, I'm terrified, but I still don't know what it has to do with me."

"Well...for starters, the little girl that was missing? Tabitha? She was your great-grandmother."

A chill flooded down my spine for the third time that day. "What?! How?"

"I'm sure your grandparents and parents didn't believe the old story. Hell, if I hadn't lived it, I'm sure I wouldn't believe it either. But it happened." Ms. Henrietta's tone wasn't unkind, but it was firm. She wasn't trying to convince me of anything. She just expected me to believe her.

"Tabitha's mother, your great-great-grandmother, came to my house that night and asked me to save her child. I did so, and I warned her, and Richie's mama, about the price that we would all pay if they weren't careful. And for a time, they were. But as the months went by and they had their babies there with them—healthy and whole—they started to get careless. Life started to get in the way, and they forgot to put the red brick dust along their entryways, and started to think they didn't need their protective charms."

If it hadn't been for that little trip down memory lane she'd sent me on, I probably would have questioned it more, but, deep down, I knew that she was telling the truth.

"So, that evil you warned them about? It came after you."

"Yes, and every member of those two families, starting when they hit the age of twenty-two."

"But why—"

"That's how old your great-great-grandmother was when she came to see me," she said simply.

I nodded, trying to take all of this in, but something was still nagging at me. "But, nothing happened to my mother at this age."

"You sure about that?" Ms Henrietta asked, knowingly. "You ever asked her about her first husband?"

"Her first what?!" Never in my life had my mother said anything to me about her having been married before my father.

"I figured. She never told you. But your mother's first husband died when she was carrying your big sister. She lost that baby, poor thing, and she and your grandparents all moved out to California. I think they knew by instinct that they needed to get away."

"Was that...the price my mama paid?" I asked.

Ms. Henrietta nodded sadly. "Fortunately, they got away from town, but with you being back here...I'm worried that it's going to come for you, and fast."

"What is it?" I asked.

Ms. Henrietta took a breath, and I could tell that she was trying to think of the simplest way to explain this to me. "When you do powerful magic, you open a door. Hungry, angry things will try to sneak in if you don't guard against it."

"Like, spirits?" I asked.

"Yes, spirits of the dead. But also things that never walked the Earth."

"You mean...demons?" I asked, trying my best not to let my voice crack.

"I'm sorry," said Ms. Henrietta. It was both an apology and an answer.

Now it was my turn to nod. I understood that she was trying to protect me, but there were still a few things that didn't completely add up. "But...how do I know you?"

Ms. Henrietta smiled. "Oh, you used to visit me when you were a little girl. In your dreams. You were just the sweetest thing."

"I used to what?" I asked, but then the memories began to slip back in, like they were waiting to fall into place. Ms. Henrietta's house was like a recurring good dream I'd had. We would drink hot cocoa and she would tell me stories. Good ones. Fairy tales and old legends. The kind of stuff I ate up when I was awake. Over the years, the dreams had stopped, and I'd forgotten all about her.

"I was sad when you stopped visiting me, but I understood. You were growing up. If a child with magic like yours isn't taught to nurture it, they lose it."

"I have magic?" I blurted out. Somehow, this was the moment I started to wonder if Ms. Henrietta was doing okay mentally.

"I'm not losing my mind, and I'm not making this up. Here," she said, grabbing a cookbook from a shelf in her kitchen. She leafed through it until she found an old drawing.

When I held it in my hands, I was in complete disbelief. There, on the page, I'd drawn a picture of me and Ms. Henrietta, holding hands and smiling. In the bottom right-hand corner, I'd signed it -Arialle, with a little heart at the end, my trademark in elementary school.

I swallowed, taking it all in. But then I had another thought. "If you were there with my great-great-grandmother in the thirties... how are you still..."

"Alive?" Ms Henrietta laughed. "I borrowed a little time, here and there. I was planning on letting myself die about seventeen years ago, but then you started visiting me and, well, I figured you might be just the one to end this thing. I want to go to my grave in peace."

I looked at her in disbelief. About an hour ago, I was just a sorority girl trying to finish up a little community service and, now…it was all too much to handle. I started to get up from the table, but Ms. Henrietta grabbed my wrist.

"You cannot ignore this. I know how badly you will want to, but the curse is already beginning to come for you. I saw the spirits closing in on you when you walked up my driveway. They were creeping out of the dell."

When she said that, my stomach dropped about five inches. "I knew it. I knew something was down there. The whole time I was walking up, I felt it all around me. I—"

"I know, baby," said Ms. Henrietta, patting me on the hand. "But you're strong enough to beat this. It's going to take some work, and we don't have that much time, but you are here for a reason."

"Did you do some sort of—some sort of spell or something to get me to come to Henderson?"

For the first time, Ms. Henrietta looked angry at me. "Absolutely not. I could never do that, knowing what might happen to you if you got here. This is where you are *supposed* to be. Sometimes, things inside us guide us on our way. We can't always see it or sense it, but it's there. Sometimes people call it fate, or your purpose, but there isn't a soul on this earth, even me, who can mess with that force."

"I am supposed to be here? Fighting evil with magic? Ending a family curse?"

"I know it sounds ridiculous, but, deep down, you know that I'm telling the truth. I saw it all over your face when you walked in here. You remember it all, and some part of you knows that you are exactly where you are supposed to be."

And, although I wanted to deny it, to get up, walk out the door, sprint to my car as fast as my legs would take me, I knew that she was telling the truth. Before I could come up with another excuse, I picked up my coffee and took a long sip. After a few moments of silence, I placed my cup down on the table, looked at Ms. Henrietta, and nodded.

Again, she smiled that knowing smile. But this time, I managed to smile back.

— THE VEIL AND THE CORD —
by D.C. Dador

Growing up, there was a church near the city of Manila where a peculiar marriage occurred. My Tita witnessed the ceremony and, since then, it's become a tale passed through the generations, particularly the night before family weddings.

The church is still on the island if you visit the village where Tita and I were born. It stands on the same site as it has for four-hundred years. Built in the tradition of a Spanish mission and guarded by worn statues of anguished saints, it's not hard for any passerby to conclude that the old church, crowned by a solitary bell tower, is full of ghosts of the past and their stories. The wedding Tita recounts was quite the surprise because it was considered a fast engagement, announced shortly after the bride returned to her native village.

For the bride, Señora Corazon, this was her third marriage. For the bridegroom, Señor Rivas, who the villagers had long ago resigned to the fate of an old bachelor, it was his first.

At seventy, Señor Rivas was a private man who lived alone. Hailing from a prominent family, he led the life of a lonely scholar with no purpose. He was known to be generous during village celebrations, and would pay for treats like a roasted lechon or pancit noodles, but the town's benefactor often failed to attend.

For most of his life the villagers whispered about the melancholic Señor Rivas. Some pitied his upbringing as an only child caused by a wrathful island hurricane. Others conjectured that there was a family history of mental illness. According to the village's most superstitious, demon worship was most likely the cause of his eccentricities. The village leaders conveniently attributed his quirks to his genteel but idle life. Only one in the village could claim more years than Rivas.

The elder recalled a time long ago when Rivas's life resembled some form of happiness, but many believed the memory to be contrived, or, if true, fleeting, for—sadly—no one could imagine such a state for the lonesome Señor Rivas.

The bride, Señora Corazon, was a complete contrast to her third bridegroom except in age. Born a poor village girl, but a beauty most of her life, she was known to be lively and never lacked company. When the news spread of her first engagement to a wealthy man from the city who was twice her years, it came as no shock.

All accounts point to a happy arrangement, and she a model and dutiful wife, until he passed suddenly in a tragedy, leaving her with a great fortune and great grief.

Soon after, she was wooed by a handsome Southern courtier who had fewer years and less money. Ignoring those who counseled her, she married again and was promptly whisked away to Cebu. It was widely rumored that her second marriage was the opposite of her first, and, after decades of unkindness, she was relieved to become a widow again.

Given her last marriage, it was remarkable to many that the notion of marrying again, especially so quickly, could occur to Señora Corazon. Some villagers admired her as a woman able to make the best of her situation; others ascribed it to her inability to be alone. Of those cynical opinions, a couple of imaginative souls speculated yet another reason for her haste: being childless through two marriages, the Señora could not remain beautiful vicariously through a daughter—she therefore refused to grow old and unsightly until time, as it always does, won the battle suddenly and swiftly. Nonetheless, the vanity of youth remained. Most villagers agreed that the bride proposed the engagement because the wedding was organized swiftly, in the manner of someone with experience. Soon the rumors of a past romance blossomed, leading many to conclude that Señora Corazon was motivated to recapture her youth by uniting with an old flame. How Señor Rivas, with his irrevocable desire for a private life, was convinced to wed was a mystery. Some foolishly guessed that he aimed to steal his bride's fortune, although he was already well off; others speculated that he was exacting some sort of revenge, or, worse, that they were possessed by demons. Fear of the super-natural led many to pay close attention to the betrothed's desire, accompanied by a generous donation to the church, to participate in a pre-ceremony ritual practiced more widely in their youth. Tita recalled the spectacle of the nervous young priest—Father Francis was new to the parish—piercing the bride and bridegroom's frail chests to draw blood. As the red drops collected in a bowl of rice, it reminded everyone of their advanced years and impending deaths, rather than unity and a long life of wedded bliss, as was intended by the ritual.

Naturally, the intrigue of their union was at its highest on the day of the wedding. On that day the church opened to the entire village, which of course attracted many spectators. Those attending knew that Señor Rivas, despite his solitary life, would sponsor a bountiful fiesta to celebrate, following the ceremony. However, the pews weren't full of fiesta revelers alone, but also the curious and romantic, including Tita when she was a young girl.

The ceremony started with the squeaky wheels and stomping of horses' hooves of several kalesa outside. The church's front door burst open, unveiling the jubilant bridal party, whose effusive presence reminded Tita of engkantos from the old tales. Immediately, the villagers whispered how the party, composed of beautiful young people, hailed from the city. None were family members or traditional sponsors typically seen in the bride's party—an unintentional reminder of the bride's lack of family and vanity at once.

Though the bridegroom's party was absent, the bride's entourage proceeded down the aisle with the same enthusiasm as they entered the church. Their steps were light and joyful, as if they were at debutante's cotillion, not a church. The gorgeous dresses of the time—the elegant lace, the high butterfly sleeves, the billowing skirts—enchanted all in the room, who'd never seen such an ostentatious display of wealth.

After the last pair took their position, a hush befell the room. There at the top of the aisle stood the bride in the finest and most expensive gown, complete with a crown of fresh flowers and a beautiful lace veil that trailed the length of a chapel. Her withered hands gripped a grandiose bouquet so full of exotic island blooms that it must have taken some effort for the frail woman to carry. Many openly admired Señora Corazon's breathtaking ensemble but whispered privately that her attire appeared to be a style fit for a maid far younger than her years. The entrance was so buoyant that only a few noticed the ominous event that accompanied it. When the bride entered the church's threshold, the bell swung heavily in its tower, tolling its deepest, loneliest note. *Bonggg.*

"Jesus, Mary, Joseph! What an omen," a friend whispered to Tita, who promptly made the sign of the cross. "That ring is meant for a funeral." She shuddered, imagining a ghostly Señora Corazon floating in her white gown.

But without a care in the world, the bridal party paraded until another solemn note rang out. *Bonggg.* The ground shook and this time the bride's attendants noticed. Their advance wavered, and they shrieked and held one another, their bright glow diminished like the ancient sun god Apolaki closing his eyes.

A lone shiver ran up Señora Corazon's spine, as if the bell's toll struck her heart and awoke her from a distant memory. A visible gloom descended upon the church, but the bride's courage was admirable. Her eyes widened and focused on the altar. If she noticed that her bridegroom was not there waiting, she showed no emotion. Composing herself, while her attendants were in shock, she took the lead and glided calmly up the aisle amid the stares of the admiring and the shocked.

The church bell continued to toll in the same woeful tone, as though a fresh corpse was on its way to the grave. *Binggg. Bonggg.*

"Father, my young friends quiver," said the bride, with a wry smile, to the young priest at the altar. "Though many weddings begin with genial chimes, the tune often changes to an unhappier note through the course of marriage. Perhaps my somber start means a brighter end."

Father Francis hesitated before responding thoughtfully. "My child, this strange occurrence reminds me of some of the old traditions we observe at our weddings, such as the unity candles, the veil and cord. Symbols used to infuse life and death into the wedding ceremony, to remind us to cherish the living sacrament of marriage and the finite time we have in this world. Thus, this funeral toll provides further illustration of the sanctity of today's affair."

Though calm in his presentation, the priest was seen whispering to an attendant and nodding toward the bell tower's door. Meanwhile, the bell continued to toll mournfully, diminishing the exuberance normally on display at weddings, until whispers whipped through the pews like an oncoming typhoon.

The villagers near the windows reported a funeral procession creeping along the road, conveying the coffin of a dead man to the church, while the bride awaited a living one at the altar. Immediately after, the procession was heard at the door. The bride clinched the arm of one of her attendants.

"You frighten me, Señora Corazon," whimpered the girl. "Jesus, Mary, Joseph, what is the matter?"

The bride, as pale as if she's seen a ghost, crossed herself. "I just had a frightful thought that my bridegroom would arrive, accompanied by my first two husbands to sponsor our union.

"Look," cried a villager. "The funeral is the bridegroom's party!" As she spoke, a dark and somber procession entered the church.

First came an old man and woman, he with a black armband around his white barong blouse, she dressed all in black with a lace veil shrouding her face. Pair after pair followed, each couple as stunted and morose as the first.

As the procession proceeded down the aisle, the bride shuddered, recognizing them as old acquaintances from her youth. They advanced toward her as if rising from their graves to claim her as their companion.

While these aged mourners progressed, it was clear from the reactions of the villagers that something sinister was being concealed by the bridegroom's party. When the ghostly procession approached the altar, each couple separated, until there—at the center—appeared a figure worthy of the funeral procession and the church bell's death toll. It was Señor Rivas at last!

The bride's knees weakened seeing him attired for the grave. Dressed in the finest barong, but barefoot, as was the custom for the dead. He carried a box of gold to be buried with, because he had no living relatives to give it to. But for the smoldering fire in his eyes, the man stood as motionless as a corpse, until he addressed the bride in a voice in harmony with the bell's solemn tone. "Mahal ko," he said. "My love, our funeral procession is there." He pointed with his lips. "Let us be married and then to our graves."

The bride's horrified expression only made her look like a dead man's bride. Her lavish bouquet fell to the cold stone floor.

As the bell's ringing ended, an awestruck silence hung over the crowded church.

Finally, the young priest stepped forward.

"Señor Rivas," he said conjuring an air of authority. "Your mind must be agitated by the unusual circumstance. Let us delay this ceremony, so you may rest."

The bridegroom scoffed. "Rest? Yes, but not without my bride. You may say this scene is madness, but had I attired myself as a groom and forced my old lips to smile, that would have been real madness. I say I am properly attired, but not my bride." Here, my Tita always told us, she was awed by Señor Rivas's logic. Given the couple's advanced years, the bridegroom's somber funeral presentation, in contrast to the bride's finery designed for youth, was more appropriate.

The bridegroom paced toward Señora Corazon with a ghostly stare as she covered her face. "Ang lupit!" she groaned.

"Cruel?" Señor Rivas echoed. The fire in his eyes raged. "The Lord, or the god Bathala himself will judge which of us has been cruel! In youth it was you who deprived me of happiness and hope when you married your first withered husband. You took away all the joy and meaning in my life. Even when he passed on and you were free, you married another. From that day, I walked through this world aimlessly and without care. But now, after fifty years, when I have identified my tomb, and am ready to rest there, you call me to the altar? When other husbands have enjoyed your youth, you join me when our days are numbered. Therefore, I have requested our old friends to ready our funeral procession, and come to wed you, as with a burial service. Don't you see? This way we may join and enter our next stage of life together." As the bride considered her bridegroom's words, she could be seen glancing outside the church window, a far-off look in her eyes. My Tita speculated it was then she saw her husbands of the past treading the churchyard outside and calling her to the afterlife. Next her gaze fell on the attendants: Hers an entourage of young courtiers she could barely call friends, his familiar ghosts of her past.

Slowly, Señora Corazon's eyes lit and her face transformed to reflect the reality of her years. The vanity she displayed walking down the aisle vanished. She seized her bridegroom's hand.

"Yes," she declared. "After all these years, you have finally opened my eyes. I proposed our marriage with a callous and vain desire to chase the fleeting happiness of youth. To be the young maiden in love again. How blind I was to the truth of my worldly state. Today you propose what neither my first nor second husband could provide. You offer me a timeless love larger than life itself, which I accept. Forgive me, Rivas? For now I see how foolish I was all these years."

Señor Rivas looked into her eyes, wiping away his tears. "Buhay ko. Beloved of my youth," he said. "Today's public display was a result of the despair that has been tormenting me since you returned home, reminding me of all that I have lost, and maddened me. Will you forgive me?"

"Yes, mahal ko," the bride whispered.

The bridegroom grasped her hand. "My Corazon, let us wed as lovers who were separated through life but meet again as we leave it."

"I am ready," the bride replied.

Father Francis, under the watchful eyes of the village, conducted the ceremony with fervor and determination. He bid the couple to light their wedding candles. The candles, one on each side of the bride and groom, sprang to life with a fragile, solitary flame. It was not lost upon the spectators the superstition that, if one of the candles blows out during the rite, the person beside it will die before their spouse.

The bridal party placed a lace veil over the kneeling bride and bridegroom, and wrapped a cord around their collars in a figure eight, as several in the pews shuddered. The veil cloths the pair as one and the cord symbolizes eternity. However, for Señor Rivas and his bride, eternity has a darker meaning.

After the veil and cord, the bridegroom handed his bride a pouch full of thirteen coins—a promise that he will always look after her. "In this life, and now the next," said Señor Rivas.

And so, amid the tears and bittersweet sentiment of the crowded church, was solemnized the union of two immortal souls.

When the marriage rite was finished, with cold hand in cold hand, the Married for Eternity ascended the aisle as the church's bell tolled again.

And of their own accord, the solitary flames of the unity candles extinguished together.

— POPPY TEA AND HEARTY PIE —
by Adaline Jacques

What do you mean we'll have to wait?!" The room went silent after his outburst. He was towering over his own mother, staring down at the greying hair on her scalp.

"Walter," his mother said sternly, knocking her cane on the floor. "Clean up that mess. Now!"

"Not until you answer my question," Walter retorted. He pulled his handkerchief out of his breast pocket, wiping red-hot sticky tea from his sweaty hand. "Why do we have to wai—"

"I will not be answering anything until you clean that mess up!" his mother said, her stern words rising to a shout, as she stared into her son's eyes.

Walter stood there, breathing heavily, his face growing even redder. He averted his gaze from his mother, only to discover the scene that he had caused. Pieces of a broken plate were wedged in a dropped slice of layered cake. A red and white china cup had tipped over on the mahogany table, its tea spilling onto the expensive rug, browning its rich red. His siblings, and Briar Anne Lee, and the other patrons of the harbor house—they were all watching him. He saw their focus shift from the messy waste of food and up to his reddened, angry face. Then back to the mess. And then back to him.

He dropped onto the floor the fork that he was gripping ever so violently. He huffed as he let himself fall backward into his seat. "You," he said in a hushed tone, looking Briar Anne Lee up and down. "You're the shopkeeper. You clean up this mess."

His mother looked up at Briar Anne, her dull grey eyes apologetic and solemn. Her frown deeper and more wrinkled than before. She was watching to see what Briar Anne would do. What course of action would she take in response to his vile and childish behavior?

"You wouldn't have done it right anyway," Briar Anne huffed.

She snapped her fingers. A pale-faced maid whipped her head around, tipping back the wine bottle before it overfilled her patron's cup. She bowed with an apology to him before coming to her boss's side.

"Clean it, Mary." The maid nodded, running off to the kitchen for a wet rag.

Briar Anne turned her attention back to the old mother, a warm smile on her face. "Go ahead, Mrs. Williams."

Mrs. Williams shook her head in disappointment, her head down, her gaze falling into her lap. "Not until everyone agrees to let me talk. Uninterrupted."

Her children all looked at each other. They all glanced at Walter. He rolled his eyes, his cheeks and temple still beet red after his outburst.

"We will, mother," said Effie, Mrs. William's eldest.

"All right," Mrs. Williams said plainly, gazing past the heads of her children at the wooden wall of the house. "My mouth has become dry from all of this reading. Briar Anne, please read it. In fact, make sure to read everything, from the beginning."

Briar Anne nodded, another bright smile on her red lips. "Of course, Mrs. Williams," she said. "But first..."

She bent over, placing the letter down on the table and picking up the cup of tea. Her sips were audible to every individual in the room.

"It's bad practice for the owner of such an establishment to eat food before her patrons," said Lilian, tapping her teacup with her fingernail to make her disapproval known.

"It is also bad practice for a married woman to look down a lady's dress," Briar Anne said in response, a challenging look in her rich-brown eyes. "I'd imagine your reason for doing so isn't from a place of envy."

Lilian's face became as red as the velvet couch they were sitting on. She turned her face away with a "humph," embarrassed, and fiddled with her long locks of light-blonde hair. Briar Anne shrugged, finishing off her tea before bending back to stand upright. She picked up the letter again, her delicate dark-brown fingers unfolding it. She cleared her throat before reading again.

"The will reads as follows..."

"'I, Watson Williams, am writing this Last Will and Testament, so that my living family may know what parts of my estates, life's earnings, and other belongings will go to each member. I hope that anyone reading this will forgive me for the informal manner of my words. I am currently laid in my bed, stricken with a sickness that will soon escort me to the gates of heaven, whether I am ready or not. I am in a race against time, making sure that everything is in order. I would hate for my own flesh and blood to fight over such things as trinkets and money. Lord knows our name has suffered enough at the hands of internal conflict and public controversy...'"

Briar Anne paused to look up at everyone, to see their reaction to the sentence she had just read. Just as she suspected; a mixture of shock and shame. Walter's face was turned away. He looked as if he were watching the churning waters of the sea, but it was clear that his father's words stung him the worst. She made a valiant effort to not let anyone at the table know that she found this whole ordeal amusing, working hard to straighten the corners of her smile. "Continuing," she said, clearing her throat again.

"'Firstly, Lilian Martha Williams. My beloved daughter, and youngest child. I understand that you and your husband are going through a hard time in your marriage at the time I am writing this. If this rift between you is persisting, I think my gift to you will serve as helpful. The old farmhouse will do for you two. The farmland and livestock are still good to use. You and your husband are an opportunistic bunch; I'm sure you will make use of—'"

"That old rickety farmhouse?!" Lilian shouted, dropping her cup onto the head of the maid who was cleaning up Walter's mess.

The poor pale-faced maid shouted, hot tea scalding her scalp and running down her hair, as Briar Anne stared Lilian down. "Your mother asked for silence," she said sternly, before going back to reading.

"'Luther Williams,'" Briar Anne said, almost as if he was calling him to attention. The man was resting his head in his hand, and his elbow on his knee, drifting off into a tired daze as the proceedings droned on.

"'My youngest son. My most average, and yet adequate, son. You always remained the most level-headed, a necessary trait that helped this family keep its sanity through many scandals and debacles. I leave you with our seaport house. As you may well have realized, it is near a well-known town that sees a lot of tourists and business. I'm sure you'll find use for it.'"

Briar Anne looked up to see his reaction. He didn't seem particularly surprised or enthused. Only slightly awoken by the news of his newly awarded estate.

"'Clifford Williams. My son, you have proven to be a disappointment for the entirety of your adult life. You used to be a star student. One of my proudest achievements in life was siring you. Unfortunately, such a sentiment has passed prior to my own passing. You are not responsible, nor trustworthy enough, to possess any of my estates. All you will receive is your grandfather's rapier. Try to have it only on display, and not in use.' Wow. That was quite seething."

"Father always had a knack for seething, darling," Clifford said to Briar Anne, with a smug, drunken grin, as he pushed his disheveled ginger hair back with one hand. "He was always so uptight, so mean with his words."

"And yet you were always so ready to have a smart remark, instead of heeding your father's 'mean' words," Mrs. Williams spat at him. "Continue with the damned letter, Briar Anne."

"Yes, Mrs. Williams." Briar Anne nodded before clearing her throat to continue.

"'Effie Williams. My darling daughter. You've always been a help to me, and to others. Your altruistic nature is something to admire. Your insistence on letting the Lee family take over the farmland in Jamaica, albeit an out-of-line insistence on your part, proved to be for the better for everyone. I am proud of the woman you have become.'"

Briar Anne paused for a short while. She scanned the words on the letter up and down, seemingly confused. After a few seconds of scanning, she seemed to give up, sighing as she continued to read.

"'Walter Williams, my—'"

"Wait just a pace, Briar Anne," interrupted Effie, looking just as confused as her. "What do I get? What did it sa—"

"'Walter Williams!'" Briar Anne continued. "'You are my eldest son, and thus my prime heir. You are already aware of the high expectations I hold for you; you have never failed to meet them. You, of course, will become the owner of our mill, and will become the next head of our milling company. And, of course, Elizabeth

Williams, my wife, will receive all the money that I held in my name.'"

Briar Anne shifted the paper up in her hands. She scanned the bottom of the last page, only to find that she had read the last words. "That's all of it."

"Aw come now, don't stare at me like that," Briar Anne laughed softly, as she swept her gaze over the Williams children, all staring angrily at her.

"I am not the one who wrote these words. I'm simply the messenger. You already know how your father feels about me meddling in your family's internal affairs, having me read this letter was already a step too far."

"Then let us read it," Effie said bitterly. She stood up and snatched the letter out of Briar Anne's hand, looking her up and down in disgust. "I'd imagine you...*colony folks* aren't the best at reading."

Briar Anne stood frozen for a moment, her hand held out in front of her despite no longer being in the possession of the letter. She simply stared at Effie, watching as the eldest Williams daughter read through the entire letter over and over again. It was amusing, somewhat. But she had no time to waste.

There were preparations to make for tonight's dinner.

"Make sure you scald the mold for the water ice, we're going to need that later today. While you're at it, scald all the cutlery. I forgot I have one more steak I'll need to carve and cut up. In fact, have Scarlett scald all the equipment, if she isn't busy in one of the rooms with a patron. Also, Mary, love, your scalp is still sticky."

Briar Anne dipped a rag in a bowl of lukewarm water, wringing it out before stepping over to the pale-faced barmaid. She walked up behind her, not minding that her bosom was pressing up against her back as she patted her scalp lightly with the wet rag. "That should make it slightly better," she smiled.

"Father said it was always bad practice to fraternize with your workers."

Briar Anne looked up to see that Walter was now in her presence, staring down at her with an ugly sneer, as he stood on the staircase leading down into the kitchen.

"You're not supposed to be down here," Briar Anne huffed, placing her hand on her hip. "Dinner is not ready yet; why are you here?"

"I have every right to be here," Walter retorted as he stomped in. "My father helped you build this lowly harbor inn—his money was family money."

"Ah, but you see, you just said your father helped me with his money. Money he gave up and quickly made back in his own lifetime. That money is not included in your will."

Briar Anne sighed, shaking her head at the eldest William son. Tapping the barmaid on her shoulder, she whispered something to her. Something that turned the barmaid's face even paler. She frantically nodded, collecting the equipment that was to be scalded, and quickly made her way out of the kitchen.

"Anywho," Briar Anne sighed, turning her attention back to Walter, a smug grin on her face. "Just because your father helped me to build this inn doesn't mean shite," she giggled. "If anything, he owes my family."

"Oh, here we go again. You're lucky that Father even let you come with the rest of our family, so that you could finally leave that lowly islander life behind. You act as if you're one of the Williams, but you're not. You don't even have the family name like the rest of the…servants—"

"Slaves," Briar Anne interrupted. "A good number of them were still slaves, until several years ago. And yet they still worked for you, for barely passable payments!"

"Oh, quit your complaining; we gave the property to you lot once we—"

"Again!" Briar Anne interrupted once more. "Again with attempting to include yourself in this story. You didn't do anything. In the years that I've known you, you haven't done anything worth remembering. All you did was enjoy the spoils of your parents' wealth, while also making your siblings' lives living hells, unique to each one. You're nothing without your predetermined status as a Williams. One could grow rich from being hired to do the things you're unable to do for yourself. I know this much from your wife. She often carries the look of someone being constantly robbed of their valuable time and energy. I bet that's why you're truly bitter about your father giving me the funds for this inn. It reminds you of the free labor you no longer have. I can only imagine how much worse it will get, once you realize you'll have to pay your mill workers. What a horrible nightmare for your sorry, posh arse," she glowered.

Briar Anne's eyebrows raised in surprise at Walter's expression. He was seething mad. Redder than before. Breath hot and filling the room with its stench. "You..." he growled. "You absolute whore!"

Walter had raised his hand high, seemingly ready to strike Briar Anne. But now it was frozen in the air. The rest of his body was also frozen in place, as Briar Anne held a butcher's knife to his chest, touching where his heart was. The two stood in silence, and she twisted the knife around in place, making it spin on his chest. Walter could feel the sharpness of the blade tip on his skin. One push and she could pierce his heart. He stood there, silently praying that his heart would stop beating so fast.

"You remember my signature recipe, yes?"

Walter looked up from the knife to meet the ominous gaze of Briar Anne's dark-brown eyes. "Signature recipe?"

"My 'Hearty Pie,' I called it!" she smiled, pulling away the butcher's knife from Walter's chest, holding it by the hilt and playfully bouncing the blade on her mahogany bosom. "It was...well, as the name implied, a meat pie made with the heart of any variety of animal."

"What, that's what it was?" Walter exclaimed in shock and disgust. "Disgusting!"

"Oh, so the heart of the animal that your steaks and liver come from is disgusting, but not said steaks and livers? You Englishmen are so wasteful, God bless your ostentatious souls. You seemed to like those pies, before you knew the contents of them. You especially liked the beef and goat Hearty Pies."

"Yes. Yes, I did. They were serviceable meals," he admitted begrudgingly. "Those pies were resemblant of peasant food back at home, but they were tasty."

"Well, the peasants here love them. In fact, I want you to taste tonight's pie."

She walked past Walter, placing the butcher's knife down, carefully out of his reach, and reached into the nearby oven. From it, she pulled out a tray of tiny, heart-shaped pies. She fanned them with a wave of a clean cloth to speed up the cooling process. Then she delicately scooped a fork under one of the pies, careful to not ruin its perfect form, and placed it onto a small red and white dinner plate. "Bon appétit," she smiled, though her mood was still unreadable.

Walter said nothing in response. He simply picked up the little heart-shaped pie and bit into it. He chewed it for a while before speaking again. "It's greasier than I remember."

"Eh, the heart belonged to an older animal," she shrugged.

"Well...it's good either way, I suppose," he shrugged back.

"Good," she nodded. She picked up the butcher knife again, now bouncing it on her palm. "Do not let my current moment of kindness let you think that I forgive you. I do not appreciate being threatened with violence within my own establishment. Especially when my own crime is not letting you use me to vent and berate, like you always used to do..." An awkwardly long moment of silence hung in the air between the two. Long enough that the pale-faced barmaid returned with another girl, a maid with dark-red hair. The two stood in the doorway, looking between Walter and Briar Anne—noticeably, mostly at Briar Anne. Their look was one of concern and confusion, as if waiting for orders.

Walter cleared his throat before taking a deep breath and standing up from his slouching position against the countertop. "Well, thank you for the taste of tonight's dinner. You won't have to worry about me, however. I'm leaving this establishment. I need to prepare for the transition of power within the milling company. It wouldn't be a good look if I waited longer than necessary. Excuse me, ladies."

Walter walked over to the two maids. Neither of them moved an inch. The pale-faced maid simply crossed her arms, and the red-headed girl simply crossed her arms, both staring Walter down.

Walter scoffed at the two women. "Of course such repugnant girls would be hired at an establishment run by the likes of Briar Anne. You two probably stand as the white alternatives of friends from her home. Move at once, wenches."

He violently pushed the shoulder of the pale-faced barmaid. She looked up, frightened by his sudden, harsh course of action. In response, she thrust her leg up and kicked Walter in his gut, sending him falling to the floor with a violent grunt of pain. He had no time to register the agony of being kicked in his stomach and falling on his back, as the red-headed girl immediately jumped on him, pinning him down to the ground with surprising force. He struggled, yelling, "Let go of me," but she only tightened her grip. "Help! HELP! These women have me pinned down! Please, help me no—"

Walter's screams for help were quickly stifled. Briar Anne's red boot heel was jabbed between his jaws. Briar Anne was able to both feel and hear the crack of a tooth when she stuffed his mouth with her foot. She stood over him, her dark-red dress lifted high enough that she could watch him cry from the pain of a violently cracked tooth.

"Oh, I am so sorry, Walt," she said with a look of pity and amusement. "I hoped that this would be painless for you, just like it was for the rest of your family. But, unfortunately, you decided to attack my beloved Mary. I do not take kindly to that, especially given your history."

Briar Anne reeled her head back for a moment, lifting her hand to cover her loud yawn. "Oh dear, I am growing tired before I get to make tonight's poppy tea. That is no good, no good. I hope you will forgive me for having to speed through this whole ordeal.

"You and your living family are the only living heirs of the Williams family. But given a certain...recent development, you are the last living heir. But that soon will change. There is an extra letter. A letter addressed to me, and to me only."

Briar Anne shifted the butcher's knife from her left hand to her right, and used her now free left hand to pull a piece of paper from her bosom. She unfolded it, cleared her throat, and began to read.

"'I, Watson Williams, am addressing this letter to a young woman, and former servant, Briar Anne Lee. I am aware of the mistreatment that you and your family have faced under my ownership all those years. I will not go into detail, as I am running out of precious time as I write, but I must let you know that I am sorry. No number of deeds I could do would diminish the guilt I feel in regards to you lot. Thus, I will give you this promise: once every current heir of mine dies, you will receive half of all inheritance discussed in the letter addressed to my family. However, in the event that my heirs don't have heirs of their own, you will receive all of the inheritance.' Oh, it ended there. Must've been when he finally saw the light."

She looked back down at Walter's sorry face. His face was now almost puce, not only with blood welling up from his broken tooth but from the puffiness of excessive crying. It seemed that he was crying even harder and louder, despite having a heel buried in his mouth.

"Really?" Briar Anne asked, a giggle escaping her mouth out of sheer disbelief. "That's what makes you cry, truly? Other than pain, the inevitable loss of your precious money is what makes you upset? God, you are pathetic.

"Well, it doesn't matter anymore," she shrugged, now holding the butcher's knife with both hands. "It's clear now. All I need to do is make sure there will be no future heirs left behind. No one cares for the infamous Williams family, so no one will miss you. You're the last Williams left, so this will be a breeze. Not to mention, you already approved of the Hearty Pie I served you. So, if I can make your mother's heavy, greasy heart taste good, then I needn't worry about how your siblings' taste. Not even Clifford's drunken self.

"Now, sweetie," she said, grinning down at Walter, as she lifted her boot from his mouth. "I cannot damage the goods, of course. The goods in question being your ugly, probably rust-brown, twisted heart. So, you will have to be okay with a blow to the head."

Walter was rendered powerless. The once proud and tall heir of the Williams and Co. Milling Company was now lying down on the dirty kitchen floor, screaming for his life. He could do nothing but look up at Briar Anne Lee as she swung her large knife down onto his skull.

WHAT THE WIND
— BROUGHT WITH IT —
by Margaret Elysia Garcia

T he wind blew hard outside the window of Pilar's trailer, and she imagined the pine trees swaying so fiercely that they cracked and toppled onto the tin roof, crushing it in and killing her instantly. She was sitting up in bed and trying to do her homework as the wind bellowed and shook the single-wide with such fierceness. She put her laptop down and got out of bed and went to her altar to light the Our Lady of Guadalupe candle for comfort—and in case the wind knocked out the powerline once more.

Thump. Thump. Laughter.

"Let's get out of here..." came the hurried whisper from the stairs outside Pilar's trailer, which she shared with her father on the outskirts of a tiny forest town. The sounds of footsteps were swallowed in the muddy yard and a truck peeled out onto the highway and a chorus of laughter floated on the already menacing wind.

The lights flickered.

Pilar thought she heard—something. It was hard to tell with how strong the winds were beating the branches of the trees beside the metal roof. She didn't like to go to the door when her father wasn't home. He'd called to say he'd be late over an hour ago and it worried her when he drove alone late on the mountain roads in his old truck. Maybe he bought groceries and needed her to help bring them in from the car. Maybe that's what the sound was.

"Papa, is that you?" she yelled toward the front door, but there was no answer. She turned off her music and closed her laptop, heading through the living room to the front door. The trailer was dark except for the plastic thrift store clock that hung on a nail through the wood paneling next to the wood stove—it was an Our Lady of Guadalupe clock; the stars in her robe and the rays of sun behind her shined and the clock was always five minutes off no matter how many times it was reset. Pilar opened the door cautiously; her ginger cat, Pablito, pushed his face through her legs and hissed at something on the doorstep. Pilar turned on the light to find a big dark burlap sack on her doorstep.

"Papa?" she cried out, but his car wasn't there, and she'd never seen that sack before. She pushed Pablito back inside and closed and locked the door. She pulled her phone from her back pocket and texted her mom.

You busy?

I was going to bed. What's up?

Papa's not home yet. Can you come over? There's something weird...

I'll be right there. Let me just tell grandma.

Pilar's mother lived a few miles away with her own mother, Lydia, who didn't like to be alone anymore but also hated living with people. She needed someone to stay with her. Pilar's mother seemed to be the only one immune to her grandmother's demanding presence. Her parents had divorced five years ago and she opted to live with her papa because three de Luna women was too much for any one household, and she liked Abuela Lydia better when she saw her less often. Abuela Lydia was particular about everything, and if you crossed her you would never be welcomed in the house again. If you had a problem with someone and even casually mentioned it in her presence, she would offer to put curses on the person. She had cursed a priest, who was then transferred out of the parish, and the owner of the grocery store, who had dropped dead of a heart attack not long after Abuela Lydia cursed him for ignoring her requests for better-quality meat.

Pilar's cheerleading teammates thought Pilar was joking when she told them about her grandmother. But Pilar never joked about Abuela; she feared, like everyone else in the family, that Abuela would curse her too. Abuela had no problem cursing someone, and if you came to her and said, "Abuela, that boy's life is already shit, no need to curse him anymore," she'd still curse him, for she never thought anyone truly learned their lessons and that today's American parents were too weak on discipline.

"Pilar seems spooked by something, Mama. I'm going to go over and check it out. Be back soon."

"Is someone messing with my girl? Do you need a—"

"Aye. No, Mama—no one needs your curses."

"Ha. That's what you think," said Abuela Lydia, handing Elena a charm made of white feathers. "Bring her this."

Elena pulled up to the trailer and noticed the burlap bag in the moonlight. The moon was full the night before, but she pulled a flashlight out of the glove compartment along with a pair of disposable gloves.

"Pilar! I'm here."

Pilar opened the door and pointed to the bag. "It was just there. No note or anything. Should I bring it in for us to look at?" Pilar motioned toward the mouth of the bag to pick it up.

"No!" Elena shrieked and slapped the bag away before Pilar's hands could touch it. Pilar stumbled backward. Elena turned on the flashlight and motioned to Pilar to hold it and shine it down on the bag. Elena put on the gloves and opened it. "Never bring something into your house when you don't know who it's from. Bring it into your space and the curses will be in your home and take over." Elena sniffed at the bag and began spilling the contents on the steps. Pilar had trouble believing all the folk wisdom of her mother and grandmother, but she didn't dare cross the de Luna women either. They were almost always right in the end.

"Pilar? What's school been like this week?" Elena asked as she pulled the bag onto the muddy yard and opened it wide, a little away from the trailer.

"The same as usual. The teachers are mostly good except the one racist teacher who won't call on brown people. The yahoos were their yahoo selves—no worse than usual. And cheer has been great. Why?" Pilar asked.

"Someone's trying to curse you—and it's not your abuela this time."

"Stop it, Mama. You're freaking me out," said Pilar, but she had a hunch that her mama was right. She'd had a fight a few weeks back with Sol, who already graduated but couldn't get it together. Pilar had snuck out when her papa was asleep and partied with her friend. Her friend seemed different then. Louder. A little manic and much, much thinner. That night, Pilar had gotten a ride home with another friend and agreed with her that their newly graduated buddy was probably on something. Pilar hadn't seen her since. She didn't really fight with the girl, she just quit hanging around, and Pilar's absence was super loud. The girl called Pilar out and Pilar de Luna did what all de Luna women do: she spoke her mind. Told her everything she really thought. "I told Sol she was becoming a crack head. Because she is. And I don't want any part of it. I'm not going to let her drag me down with her," said Pilar to her mama. Her mother barely heard her. She was pulling out chicken feet and the butts of black candles. There were dollar store Halloween decorations in there that were burnt at the edges.

She pulled out a small doll that looked like Pilar and had an X drawn on its forehead. There was the death card from a well-used tarot deck and a giant plastic rat that, for a split second, looked real.

At the bottom of the back was a pile of animal scat and Elena almost gagged and was thankful that she did not touch it accidentally. She screamed, not in fear but for vengeance.

"It's Sol, Mama. It has to be. Look! There's a pair of jeans in there I left at her house a while back," said Pilar.

Elena picked up the doll that looked like Pilar and took an eraser out of her purse and got rid of the X on the doll's forehead.

"Pilar. I'll throw this all away. You just go in the house and wait for Papa." Elena took up the burlap bag and tied it up, leaving out the doll. She placed the burlap in a plastic bag and threw it in the back of her truck.

"Mama, what are you doing with this? What the hell?" said Pilar standing there in her doorway.

"I don't want to talk about it now. I gotta get rid of this. Keep that doll safe—that's an entirely different procedure," Elena said. "Go in the house. You don't need to see this yet." Elena jumped into the driver's seat and took off in her truck while Pilar stood there on the top step.

Pilar did not go inside. She watched as her mom drove her truck up to the cemetery hill above their small hamlet. She watched nervously as the pine trees swayed back and forth above the powerlines. It would, she knew, be safer inside the trailer. But why was her mama not shocked at the bag? And why bring the bag to the cemetery?

Pilar put on her sneakers and a hood, zipped it all the way up and set out on foot to follow her mother.

Elena lugged the burlap bag onto a blank gravestone in the family plot. She pulled a box of matches from her purse, little white candles in glass containers, some clear, and some with saints' faces on them. Elena was always prepared. She returned to the truck and trudged back up the cemetery hill with a fire extinguisher.

Elena circled the burlap bag with the white candles and lit each one before tossing the final lit match onto the burlap. Elena stretched her arms out to the moon and lowered them to her side and gestured toward the burlap bag as it caught fire. Elena's long hair blew around her in the wind, and as Pilar approached, she was astounded at the sight of her mother, who no longer seemed like her mother at all. Normally Elena looked a little conservative, with her hair in a tight ponytail or bun. But this Elena wore her hair down and wild.

As Pilar climbed the hill to the cemetery, she heard Elena singing a song in Spanish that she had never heard before. Pilar couldn't make out the lyrics. Her Spanish wasn't too great anyhow. The sounds of the song on the wind made the hair stand up. As she reached the family plot, Pilar began to get scared. She'd not seen her mother's brown eyes look cloudy bluish white before.

"Aye, Pilar. Go home. You don't need to see this. I'm just purifying, getting the bad juju off the bag."

"You just burned some of my clothes."

"I just saved your life, Pilarita. Whoever did this is not your friend. And they don't know shit about proper witchcraft. Gavachas. Probably learned spells online."

"What? There's no such thing, Mama." Pilar looked closely at her mother, whose crystal necklace was shining in the firelight. Her mane of thick hair seemed longer than usual and it tangled in her fingers as Pilar stretched out her hands to touch her mother. Her eyes seemed larger and wilder and scared. Pilar thought of backing away from the grave, and possibly going to stay with her crazy born-again aunt, who seemed really sane and not scary right now. The wind blew hard again but didn't seem to disturb the flames. Elena turned to her daughter and yelled for her to stand next to her and hold onto her dress. A crack of thunder broke the sky and Pilar stood there terrified, unable to move. She felt someone push her and she was suddenly holding her mama at her waist tightly as if her life depended on it. Elena called on the angels and saints and on Tonatzin, the original Lady. Pilar felt the presence of someone else behind her. A flash of lightning. The sound of trees cracking and falling—and then stillness. Pilar turned around and her Abuela Lydia stood there behind her, smiling in relief and holding the doll from the burlap bag.

"You're almost sixteen. You would have found out in a couple of months anyhow," said Abuela Lydia de Luna. She placed the doll on the spot where the burlap bag was now ash. She placed her hands above the doll and it shimmered like a star in the moonlight and disappeared.

"Find out what... that you... you're... a..." Pilar could not bring herself to say it.

"We. Not me. We," said Elena. "Brujas," said Abuela Lydia.

"That should be enough. Mama, hand me the fire extinguisher. Don't want a forest fire. This wind is incredible," said Elena.

"Just like that? We're witches?" Pilar said. She stretched out her hands and looked at them for a sign and saw nothing.

"Oh my love, really. How could you not know?" and turning toward the smoke-filled remnants of the burlap bag she added,"Pilar, the bag was a curse. The curse was for you to fail in school and for you to turn out no better than they are. The curse, judging by some of the contents—especially the doll—was to get you into an accident. And also? Mi'ja, I think they just wanted to be jerks," said Elena.

Abuela Lydia took in a deep breath and exhaled. "The pendeja is parked at the waterfall in a black truck. There are other people around. Laughing," said Abuela Lydia.

"That is where Sol likes to party. But you guys, I don't think she wanted to kill me, I think she's just an asshole and trying to get back at me," said Pilar.

"She tried to curse you and she doesn't know what she's doing. It wasn't a harming curse; it was a killing one. I'm so sick of Gen Z YouTube witches. They read half a book and watch reruns of *Charmed* and somehow they think they're witches. Do you have anything of Sol's?"

"Not really."

"Think, Pilar." Pilar stared at her mother without blinking. This did of course make sense when she thought about it. People tended to leave her mother and grandmother alone and never got into arguments with them and indeed changed their tone if the women went near. Pilar reached into the pocket of her hoodie. She remembered letting Sol borrow it. It hadn't been washed yet, had it? Pilar pulled out two paper clips, a lip gloss, a gum wrapper, and fingernail clippings. It wasn't her lip gloss or her fingernail clippings.

"Bingo. Aye. So trashy. Perfect though," said Elena. She placed the nail clippings in the gum wrapper and put it on the monument above the grave. She took out a black candle and lit it and called Sol's name. It was like she was singing the name as both a warning and a verdict. The moon seemed to shine brighter on their faces. The wind picked up again and blew the dead pine needles around their feet.

The three witches stood on the hillside overlooking the town and listened. The wind stopped. An ambulance siren could be heard, heading toward the highway and the trailhead near the waterfall.

"That should do it," said Abuela Lydia, and then, in a scolding voice, "Pilar, help your grandmother to her car." As they walked down the hill toward the truck and the car, Pilar arm and arm with her grandmother, Elena with the fire extinguisher under her arm, they saw that downed trees from the storm had fallen around the trailer—none of them on the trailer. The logs looked like they were forming a circle around the place. Protecting us, Pilar thought.

As the three women approached the two vehicles, an old Chevy truck approached them. It was Pilar's papa, Henry. Home. Finally. "You three all right? There are downed trees everywhere. And judging by all the fire and ambulance vehicles at the trailhead, looks like something went down at the falls."

"We're fine," said Abuela Lydia. She looked at Henry with stern eyes. His face changed then. As if he forgot what he was saying.

"You hungry, Enrique? I brought over a stew," said Elena, as if it were perfectly normal that the three women would be standing in front of the cemetery in the late hours of the evening on a weekday night.

"Yes. Thank you," said Henry to his ex-wife. They went back to the trailer and stepped over the ring of trees. They heard emergency vehicles whipping by without their sirens on, the way they do when there's no longer a reason to rush to the emergency room.

— YAMA-UBA —
by jonah wu

The trees peered in like eternal sentries through Grace's window. They had always lived at the edge of the forest, so by now Grace could name all its inhabitants—hawthorn, hickory, aspen, red versus white oak, all the various pines that erupted with new needles every spring. But now it was fall, so they were shedding the old growth, and the grassy clearing behind the house that hedged in the unruly trees was now covered in the stuff. All dead, brown, and spiny. Claire hated it with an obsessive passion.

From her second-floor vantage point, Grace could see that her mother was still outside raking away the arboreal refuse, undeterred by the late hour. Illuminated only by the back porch lighting, Claire's hair shone like corn silk. So brittle it looked like it could break if you pulled it hard enough. Even at fourteen, Grace felt that everything about her mother was frail: body thin enough for the bones to show, skin pale enough to catch the sun's ire in just under twenty minutes. Her personality, too; Claire herself called it an *inherited neurosis*. "Your damn grandmother," she had once said while sucking belligerently on a cigarette, "and her damn grandmother, and hers—all the women in the family came out with a screw loose." It was an exaggerated folktale until it wasn't. On the days it wasn't, Grace tried her best to melt into the seafoam of her dreams.

Which is why Claire, empowered by whatever righteous fury fueled her brain this time, spent her evening clearing dead pine needles from her back yard. And if Grace watched closely enough, she would see Claire briefly startle and turn toward the woods, as if a fleeing shadow had snatched her attention, and stretch out one shaking, pointed finger—a warning to stay away.

The house was so old and drafty that Grace kept the space heater blowing in her face all night, though it always dried out her throat and made her head achy.

In the seam between rest and reality, Grace glided; her eyes were closed, her mind coasted along a formless stream, but every force outside her body knocked at the door and tried to force its way in. Noises, an errant light, anxieties. A being creaked up the stairs and appeared outside her room, bundling blankets between its arms.

"Grace." Claire sat down at the edge of the bed and nudged her daughter's shoulder, a little blank triangle stuck out like a cliff against the air. Again: "Grace."

Grace mumbled something and peered thinly over at her mother, who said, "Grace, don't sleep with the heater on." And promptly reached over to switch it off.

"'M cold," the girl complained, tugging a corner of her quilt further over herself.

"That's why I brought you these blankets," Claire said, unfolding the squares of fleece she'd brought upstairs and spreading them across the bed. The weight came down in a heap over Grace, warm like a hug. "And, for Chrissakes, wear thicker clothes to sleep. Better?"

"Mm. Thanks, Mom."

"Anything for you, love." A pause, and then Grace felt the bed shift as Claire leaned in to pull the hair out of Grace's face. "Gracie, don't be mad at me. You remember what I told you, don't you? About my family." She couldn't be sure; the last time she had regaled her daughter with the tales about the Watersons had been when Grace was still in elementary school, and disguised as bedtime stories.

"Long, long ago, your grandparents and their parents and their parents before them, lived peacefully on this large plot of land. The money came in like water and fed us fat like happy pigs. But then we discovered something about the land here wasn't right. Something nasty. It killed everyone, one by one, and then trapped me here alive, wouldn't let me leave. The curse was in our blood, you see. And that's why I didn't want you to share my blood. I thought you would be safe. For a long time, it was just the two of us, and we didn't need anyone else, and I thought we were safe. But the woods, the woods, they have come alive again. I know you love going out there and learning the names of the trees, but you can still see them from your window, can't you? So, can you promise to be good? And do as I say? Gracie?"

But her daughter had already fallen back asleep.

She sighed and sat back, though her eyes stayed fixed on Grace's hair. Underneath the careful caress of her hand, it splayed in one uniform wave against the pillow, powerful like a dark ocean. Hair so thick you could tie it into boating knots. Captured midnight, Claire had it called it once. It was a black so deep that it was exactly the same color as it was in the grubby Xeroxed photo square that accompanied the adoption papers. And that little pinched face. Full of uninherited features that arrived from thousands of miles away. *My baby*, Claire had cried the first time she held the child. Hers, something clean and unsullied, free of old hexes, had finally come into her life.

Grace's dreams had been turbulent that night, though she couldn't remember the exact shape of them in the morning. In second-period U.S. history they'd had a pop quiz, and she circled A for all the questions she didn't know the answer to. Probability held that she'd get a quarter of them correct, and that was enough for the score she wanted.

She was an honors student without even trying; as a freshman, most of her classes were with schoolmates who were two or even three years older than her. It was cruel how, despite having a white mom, she somehow still fell into the Asian student stereotype. Of course, there weren't even any other Asian students to compare with. There were a couple of Black kids at her high school, and maybe someone with a Spanish last name. But even they, who could've been her compatriots in another story, were people Grace avoided. She didn't know why. If she was frank with herself, maybe she'd say that she wasn't quite ready to scrutinize what it meant to be not-white in a place full of white people. But she wasn't ready for *that* admission either.

Instead, two months into the first semester, Grace spent most of her time alone. It wasn't an entirely new situation, anyway. The townsfolk had always gossiped unkindly about her mother behind her back, and their house was so far situated from the residential neighborhoods that Grace had grown up having never attended a single playdate. A kind of record, she was sure. She spent her entire childhood reading, which probably had in a way contributed to her studiousness, and now her early adolescence frittering away time on the internet, which, to Grace's delight, detracted from her ace student persona.

At lunch, she sat at the table near the entrance, which attracted the least attention, as everyone usually made an immediate beeline for the food, and kept her nose behind an open book. None of the local bookstores had what she wanted, so she had ordered this manga online. Its crisp, clean pages still smelled like the cardboard box it was shipped in.

Some white girl, a sophomore probably, plopped down into the chair next to her, coming in close. The abruptly new presence made Grace jump in her seat. The girl smelled like a magazine perfume sample. Her clothes weren't dissimilar in vibe.

"Hey, that's Japanese, right? What you're reading."

"Uh...sorta. It's manga."

"Wait, I know what to say. Konnichiwa," the girl said.

Grace stared at her. The worst part was that the girl's expression was completely guileless; Grace imagined her learning the word on an online forum or something and subsequently styling herself as a worldly woman. Grace turned away.

"I'm not Japanese," she muttered, shame taut.

"Crap, sorry! What are you, then?"

Sometimes Grace thought about isekai. Getting yanked into another universe and all that. She didn't like reading about it in manga because otherwise she'd wish it were real. "I was adopted from China."

"Oh, wow. Ni hao, then, right?"

"Yeah, I guess."

The girl beamed. "That's so cool. I told my cousins that I went to school with an Asian chick and they didn't believe me." The wan lunchroom lighting reflected like a knife off the manga cover, which was adorned with the image of a carefree girl dressed in a sailor uniform, posing at the artist's disposal. Sometimes that's just what Grace wanted to feel: escape. All the books populated with girls named Sakura or Misako and where no one ever asked them what they were because they just *were*. "Anyway, it's really cool that you read that stuff," the girl was saying, slipping her leg back up over the chair. "I always found it way too weird." She gave a little wave before retracting all of her body, slinking into the mass of bodies like a needle dives into the haystack.

Grace closed the book and set it down in front of her. She'd already read the whole thing on a manga-sharing site seven months ago, anyway. There was no use retreading something that had already happened.

Seventh-period ecology was usually her favorite, but this was a lecture Grace didn't want to sit through. She'd already read ahead in the textbook, so as Mr. Halwell droned on about the hidden network that existed beneath the soil of all forests, she had her phone in her lap, discreetly messaging a friend from Germany, who was just going to bed in their time zone.

She wanted to vent about what happened at lunch. Mr. Halwell's hoary, halting words came: "An underground web of roots and fungi that communicates information between the trees." *Guess what, some stupid white girl said ni hao to me, like I'm just some game to score points on.* But they wouldn't really understand what she meant by that, either, so they went to sleep without hearing about it.

"Miss Tyler." As the bell rang, Grace tried to fade into the throng of students exiting the classroom, but no such luck. Halwell already had his eyes on her. "Miss Tyler, I'd like a word with you." She hung back, nailing herself against the door jamb as a kind of insurance.

"Yeah?"

Mr. Halwell was deep into his seventies, at least, and moved in such a way that seemed like he was always asleep. But Grace liked him as a teacher, a little funny and never unfair. "I know you know the material, but I wish you'd at least pretend to pay attention during my class."

He sat down at his desk and started marking papers without looking at her. "Sorry."

"And Grace, I really think you can score better than a 70 on the quizzes." He glanced up. His smile looked tired. "That's all."

"Sorry," she echoed herself, but this time quieter. Her long hair hid her shame, and she would have left quickly if she had not heard her name called again.

"Grace." Mr. Halwell's voice, just moments earlier a gentle rasp, now echoed throughout the classroom as if it were coming from the bottom of a well. As if it were not coming from Mr. Halwell at all. A chill lit up the back of Grace's neck. If she were to look behind her, now, would she be opening the door to something she can't shut back in? *"Grace,"* it came again, and the resounding boom compelled her. She turned; somehow the movement of her head had changed everything; it was still daylight but somehow the shadows were very wrong, they were everywhere, all over Mr. Halwell's face. When he spoke, the words slurred loose and sloppy from his tongue, as if he'd just been drugged. "The forest near your house. Be careful. There's something very old out there."

He was looking directly at her, but she could only see the whites of his eyes. "Mr. Halwell?"

"Something old that stalks the land…not evil, no, but a wronged thing, in search of…"

Grace turned tail and ran out the door.

The forest crept into the old house at night and found Grace sound asleep. Her body had dissolved into the mycelium and suddenly she could feel every tree, every lichen and moss, edging for dominance in the wild vein of her thoughts, pulsing. Every nerve an open livewire. Violent green.

"Grace." Her mother clicked her teeth. "Don't just stare at your breakfast. Eat fast, we have to go soon."

She groaned but shoveled in the eggs accordingly. Grace hated these biweekly trips into town, which were always accompanied by an arbitrary list of errands and made worse by her mother's smoking habit. Claire would hang her cigarette hand out the window but the car would stink of nicotine anyway. Always shopping at boutiques for clothes Grace didn't need and dwindling away the scarce amount of money left to them by Claire's dead relatives. It was like her mother had to make a show out of it, parading how *well-adjusted* the both of them were, even though it never stopped anyone from speaking ill of them.

The town was so small that everything happened on a single street, flanked on both sides by neatly ordered buildings made of colonial brick. At the mouth of Main Street sat a large sign with the town's name emblazoned in garishly large letters, and next to it a much smaller plaque commemorating its original inhabitants, the Mechkentowoon people. As if to say, sorry we made you vacate the land and move to Wisconsin instead. We hope this metal plate of craven words suffices in exchange.

"That shop's new." Claire pointed down the way at a storefront decorated with colorful flag banners. "Let's see what they have."

"Do we *have* to?"

"Grace." Claire's frown was resolute. "You need a new coat for the winter. Let's go."

They spilled into the shop unceremoniously. The place was so new it still smelled like the clean, white paint that covered its walls. Claire pulled her daughter along from rack to rack, entreating her daughter to peruse their contents, but Grace couldn't keep her eyes off the woman behind the counter. She was beautiful, yes, but what was even more incredible was that she looked like Grace—the jet-black hair and the thin eyes everyone always made fun of. Not exactly the same, of course, but close enough. And no one else in town was ever *close enough*. Their distinct features, the ones they bore as instant markers of difference, disappeared as soon as they came into the room together. It made them belong to *each other*.

Finally, when Claire had exhausted all the shelves and given up on forcing any new clothes on her daughter, she disappeared into the fitting room, leaving Grace all alone with the woman. Nervous, Grace poked at a nearby hanger. It squeaked.

Their eyes met. "She's your mother?"

"I know, we don't look alike," Grace cut in, on edge.

"No, I get it." The young woman shook her head. "Trust me, I get it. I have POC friends with white parents too." She smiled. "What's your name?"

"Grace," she murmured.

"Grace—what a pretty name. I'm Hana." She propped herself up on her elbows. "I guess it's rare, huh."

Grace frowned. "What is?"

"Another Asian American person around." Hana's laugh felt like a private joke. "Judging from your stare."

She remembered the families of Asian tourists who sometimes rolled into town for the summer, but they had always been separate, distant, a whole entity that moved outside her. "I mean, they're *around*, I guess, I just don't really..."

Claire pushed open the fitting room curtain. "Anything work for you?" Hana asked.

"No, nothing. Nothing at all." Claire sniffed and draped the clothing across the counter in one messy heap. "Come on, Grace, let's go."

Her mother made a quick march toward the door, but Grace was slower to match. She cast another glance back at Hana, who cast her a conspiratorial grin.

"This place isn't forever for you, Grace." It was a whisper, but Hana's voice carried across the room, an arrow aimed for the girl's ears only. "Look, even in small cities you'll find your own people. You're in New York, after all."

The drive back home was oppressive.

Thick with cigarette smoke; and Claire in a mood, railing against newly imagined enemies, like the woman at the wine and cheese shop who *looked* at her like *that*, the elderly couple walking their schnauzer, the little boy who had run into her legs full force and hadn't stopped to apologize.

"And *why* did the girl at that shop talk to you like that? I can't fathom..."

Grace sat up in the passenger seat. "*What* girl?"

"You know," Claire turned her wrist in circles, sending smoke everywhere, "that girl, at the new shop. The first shop we went to."

"The *Asian* girl?" Grace huffed. "You can say it, Mom, it's not a slur."

"Watch your tone, young lady." The car pulled up on their lonely street, buckling from the gravel underneath its wheels. Claire threw the spent cigarette out the window and pushed the gear into park. "I didn't like the way she talked to you. As if..." She pursed her lips. "Well, it wasn't her place. Making you sound like a statistic. Utter nonsense."

With that, Claire pushed the door open, balancing her heels over the rocky driveway to the front of the house. Grace got out too, but kept one hand on the car door. She watched her mother dig for the keys in her bag.

"Gracie, don't just stand there."

"You always do this."

Claire turned around. "Excuse me?"

"You always try to tell me I'm not Chinese. That I'm just your daughter, or whatever." Her eyes began to brim with tears. "But look at my face! I *am* Chinese! Whatever you think I'm not, that's what I am!"

"Oh, for—" Claire crossed her arms. "Come inside, Grace, we're not discussing this. It's time for dinner."

"No."

"*No?*" Claire repeated.

Grace gritted her teeth. "Why won't you let me go into the woods anymore?" Her voice was low, dark. "You know that's the only place I like to be."

"Is *that* why you're angry with me?" Now she was glaring too. "Listen, Grace, I thought we agreed. You would be a *good girl,* and you would do what I said."

"I don't *want* to be good!" Grace's eyes were feral now. "I don't want to be what you want me to be. I— I didn't even want to be *here!* In this stupid town!"

"Now listen here—" Claire clomped down the front steps, finger jabbed in Grace's direction. "You listen to me, baby, *I* saved *you.* How dare you speak to me like that—"

Grace broke into a run, eyes bleary. But she knew exactly where she was going. The forest.

From behind, she could hear her mother screaming, words like *I'm sorry!* and *Come back!* carried by the wind, but by the time Grace cleared the back yard grass, it was already too late. Her legs pumped faster and faster past the trees: white pine—aspen—hornbeam—white pine again. The massive fungus beneath the earth thrummed joyously. *You'll find your own people,* Hana's words came. *This place isn't forever for you.*

She started to laugh, laugh wildly, drunk on the brisk air. So, this was freedom! This was nature, and wilderness...this was the ancient magic of all living things, finding anchor in her heart. Happiness burst out of her like a laser kissing its target. Bent at the waist, she didn't even try to catch her breath, not even when the whole right side of her clenched in pain.

And yet the farther into the forest she went, so too grew the inchoate, irrational fear that tagged alongside intoxication. She became confused. Why was she here? Why had she run away from home? The argument with her mother already felt so long ago and now she couldn't remember her own name...the trees sang to her and lured her down a path of their own design, somewhere no one else had ever gone. Tugged her in until her feet stopped to meet the leering lip of a long, deep tunnel.

The tunnel was devoid of light; in fact, it swallowed and ate up any light that came near it. Impossibly, she could see into it—down at the very end sat an aged, wooden chest overgrown with moss. Slowly, she stepped inside the tunnel. Not because she wanted to. She didn't have a choice. Like her body was playing out a story she didn't know the end of.

She walked and walked the whole length, and, when she could walk no farther, she opened the old chest. She was not prepared. Could never have been. What lay inside glowed with an ornery greed and pulled taut on all of her bones until she could not move at all.

The tunnel was long but grew longer and stretched for miles and soon encircled the entire world, squeezing it tight for sustenance. Behind her, out of the pitch blackness, a thing emerged. It was a very strange thing. It was a creature wearing a long, black cloak, and on its face it wore a cracked Noh mask. The cloak fluttered, even though there was no breeze. Underneath the cloak, the no-breeze revealed nothing at all.

The strange thing snaked its long, nonexistent arms around Grace. The embrace was protective, as a mother does with a child. It felt warm, though there was no warmth at all, like you could sink right into it, like it was full of all the furies you never voiced for yourself, and all the sorrows that had no place to go, so you squashed them down until they grew into something quite remarkable indeed.

Grace began to cry.

— DREAM HOUSE —
by Emily Hoang

*R*eader, you have to understand, it was no one's fault but our own. If you are reading this, it means that the terror we hoped to avoid has caught us. Before our departure, I left a series of notes throughout the house. One thing you must remember is to read these notes only in the daytime. Do not ever—

"Meeka, whatcha got there?" June pulls the sheet of paper out of her little brother's hands.

"Hey! I'm not done yet! Give it back!" Michael—Meeka—jumps up and down, trying to reach for the paper June is holding in her outstretched arm.

"Read what? You've only just started reading the big kids' books." June puts her hand on Meeka's shoulder to hold him while she scans the sheet.

"Nuh-uh. My teacher said I'm ahead of the class."

"Where did you find this?" June flips the paper over, looking for signs that this is a trick.

"It was in there." Meeka turns toward the closet.

They approach and Meeka points at one corner. "Inside that hole."

June takes out her phone. She crouches down toward the corner and turns on the light to examine the hole. It's nothing more than a small cavity in the wall, barely large enough for a mouse. She gets up and looks at the note again.

Meeka uses a finger to push up his glasses and asks, "What does it say at the bottom, Junie?"

June crumples the paper and puts it in her pocket. "Nothing you need to worry about, kid. It's just a prank. Now, come on. Mom's gonna be mad at us."

Although the family moved into this modest home of four bedrooms and three bathrooms a couple weeks ago, they have been taking their time unpacking. Most of the boxes for the kitchen and living room have been emptied. The sun's rays shine through the house, and the house's windows play a game of catch, trying to grasp all the different hues.

Meeka and June return downstairs to lift the last boxes labeled with their names to their respective rooms. Almost every other stair creaks as they walk up and down. The railing will eventually need to be replaced; some screws are missing, making it unstable. Their mother, Min, is in the kitchen cleaning, and their father, Joe, is clearing up the back yard. The kitchen is newly renovated: untouched appliances, shiny floor tiles, and smooth slabs of marble counters. When it gets closer to the evening, they come together in the kitchen and start making dinner. Joe washes his hands and the vegetables in the sink. Min is by the kitchen island, heating up a pot on the stove.

"Did you hear about our neighbor?" Joe asks.

"How one of their kids had to stay behind a grade?" Min turns to wash her hands.

"I think that's the kid across the block. Our neighbor, Ms. Lim, moved out." Joe places the tomatoes and string beans next to the stove and takes out a cutting board and knife.

"What? Then are we getting new neighbors soon?" Min checks on the broth and looks over. "Remember to rip the ends off the string beans."

Joe starts cutting the ends. "No, she's not selling. She left the stove on and it started a small fire. Her other neighbors had to come and help put it out."

"That's terrible," Min says. She checks the stove and sees that the flame is still strong. "Was there a lot of damage? I didn't see anything when we moved in."

"No, thank god it was just a baby fire," Joe says. "A neighbor said it damaged only a small part of the kitchen."

"And this was before we moved in?" Min stands near him and looks over at one of the string beans. "Don't cut too much. There won't be any string bean left."

Joe readjusts the beans. "Yeah. It scared her enough to move into one of her kids' houses."

"Well, I'm glad she's not alone anymore," Min says. "But that house is just going to sit there."

Their conversation causes Min to look over at the stove and the broth. The fire is a lot smaller than what she saw a minute ago. She wonders if she lowered it while Joe was telling the story. She turns the knob to raise the heat, making sure it's not too high. Houses are a safe place until they aren't anymore.

The light from the windows changes from the bright yellow of the afternoon to a peachy orange. As the day reaches the evening, the doors quiver between open and closed like teeth chattering when a body shivers.

All of them are at the dinner table. Joe eats a bánh cuôn and puts his chopsticks down. "Are you kids done with your rooms? Do you need anything else?"

"We might go to Home Depot tomorrow to pick up some more lights," Min says.

Meeka chews on something for what seems to be minutes. Min sees him stop chewing for a moment with food still in his mouth. He looks over to see what his sister says.

"No, I think I'm okay, Dad." June wipes her mouth with a napkin. She takes another bánh cuôn.

"Me too," Meeka says, with his mouth still full.

"Eat more beans, June." Min is grabbing some of the garlic string beans to put into June's bowl.

"Thanks, Mom," June says in a monotone.

"Meeka, I'm almost done cleaning up the back yard," Joe says. "We've finally got some space to throw around a ball."

"Uh-huh, sure, Dad." Meeka lets his glasses drop as he keeps his eyes on his bowl. He takes a sip of the tomato broth.

Joe and Min exchange a glance, but don't say anything else. For the rest of dinner, they eat mostly in silence, with the TV running in the background and the occasional sound of soup-slurping. It's a windy night. Doors vibrate and the wind murmurs as it passes through the windows.

After dinner, Meeka and June help clear the table. June takes care of the dishes while Meeka wipes the table and takes the trash out to the back yard. Joe is watching a drama in the living room. He feels a draft and looks over to see the sliding door to the back yard open. He gets up. He swears it was closed and shuts the door tight, making sure to hear the click of the lock. Min is upstairs, taking a bath.

Before bed, June decides to decorate her room. She glances over at the corner where the note is still crumpled in her pants. She tries to focus her attention on the blank wall in front of her. She is planning which photos to tape up. She decides to alternate photos of her family and friends from back home. In this new life she is about to create for herself, she worries whether she'll meet anyone similar.

In his room, Meeka plays a game on his iPad. Like June's room, Meeka's room is mostly bare, waiting to be filled with past and future memories. Near his small window, the books in the bookshelf are the only details in the room that reveal any evidence of his occupancy.

Around eleven, June stands by his door and tells Meeka good night before walking through their shared bathroom and closing the door to her room.

"Night!" Meeka yells.

He waits to hear the second door close before reaching to put his glasses back on. He grabs his flashlight from under his bed and turns it on beneath his space-patterned sheets. He opens up *The Lightning Thief* and begins reading. When he's about three chapters in, he shuts the book and gets out of bed.

The first step brings a soft creak ringing throughout his room, and he squints his face. He steps toe first until he reaches the door to the shared bathroom and opens it slowly. The cold floor shocks his feet, causing him to tiptoe quicker. He opens the second door cautiously. June is tucked deep in her sheets, grinding her teeth. Meeka spots some of her clothes near the closet and approaches slowly. He grabs her jeans and searches the pockets to find the crumpled-up note from this morning. He sits down inside the closet and closes its door before turning on his flashlight.

He skips over the sentences he had already read in the morning. His eyes zone in on the bottom of the note.

Do not ever read these at night.

The terror comes in the dark. With this note, we still do not yet know how.

Meeka hears June moving in bed. He opens the door slightly.

June shifts around and groans. "Meeka. Stop."

Meeka looks over a couple feet away on the bed and sees a small round bump inching toward June from under the covers. He blinks a couple times and still sees the shape as he moves his glasses up and down from his eyes.

June groans louder. "Meeka, I told you. You can't keep coming into my bed whenever you have nightmares."

"Junie." It barely comes out as a whisper, and Meeka stands up to move closer to his sister. "I'm not in bed with you."

June turns and sees the bump before feeling a rush of cold air escaping her sheets. She screams, its echoes vibrating the house. Sounds of footsteps running toward her room follow. Her door bursts open and the lights turn on, blinding both of them.

"June? Meeka? What's wrong?" Joe looks around the room. He approaches the window to check if it's locked, then makes his way to open the closet, finding nothing.

Min sits on June's bed and Meeka immediately goes toward her. He takes a seat on Min's lap and she holds him.

"Something came into my bed." June lifts her sheets and finds nothing but air gliding over her face.

Min feels her sheets and also finds nothing. "Are you sure it wasn't just Meeka playing around?"

"No, I was over there!" Meeka points at the closet.

"But that can't be possible. It probably was just in your dreams, dear." Joe checks the closet one more time.

"I know what I felt!" June crosses her arms and sees Meeka with the note. "You read it? Didn't you read what it said *not* to do?"

"It's not my fault. I didn't know until after. I saw the bump too!"

Min looks at both of them and checks the sheets again but is only able to feel June's body. "It might have just been June's body. It's hard to see clearly in the dark. Nothing's here."

Joe takes the note from Meeka and scans it. "Where did you find this? Was this from one of your books?"

Meeka shakes his head.

"We found it in the closet," June says.

He crumples the note and guides Meeka back toward his room. "Don't worry, kids. It's nothing. Probably just a silly prank from the last owners. Just go back to bed and it'll all be better in the morning."

Joe takes Meeka back to his room. Min stays in June's room.

"Mom, I know what I felt. There was a bump." June is lying down on her bed, and Min is still sitting on the edge.

"I'm not saying there wasn't a bump," she says. "But I don't think yelling at Meeka will help anything."

"Oh yeah, of course, we'll just focus on the fact that I yelled at Meeka."

"What's that supposed to mean?"

"Exactly what I said. I'm always doing something wrong against Meeka. He's only a kid. He can't do anything wrong." June turns to her side.

"June, he's your little brother. He's still learning, and you have to be patient. You're his big sister." Min gets up and walks toward the light switch.

"Yeah, Mom. Night." June says under her sheets.

"Night, sweetie." Min hesitantly turns off the light and heads back to her room.

Min immediately goes to bed and tries to shut her eyes for what sleep remains. Instead of being welcomed by a familiar darkness, she sees flashes of her children. Meeka is chewing on something until he's not. His eyes bulge out and his hands are around his neck. Something is preventing Min from running to help; all she can do is watch: Meeka, unable to breathe, and June, standing there watching. Min opens her mouth to try and yell, but nothing comes out. Min's body violently jolts itself awake and she's out of the covers, gasping for air. Death has always been close by, leaving Min feeling helpless when her younger sister passed away from an unknown illness, or when a neighbor drowned on a boat ride to Hong Kong. Min tries to shake these memories away. A strong gust of wind wakes her up to close the window.

June is rustling in bed, unable to shake the feeling that someone is watching.

She thinks she hears a whisper repeating one name in a familiar voice.

"Junie."

The whisper gets louder and sounds frantically helpless. She lifts her shoulders off the bed. She sees no one in her room and takes no notice of her curtains waving. She reaches for her phone and headphones. Every time her parents lecture her, they somehow tie the moment to her inability to protect her brother. But what about her? Who would save her in her time of need?

Joe is in Meeka's room and tucks him in. He looks at the book by Meeka's nightstand.

"So, what's this one about?" Joe picks the book up and turns it over to its back cover.

"Just some kids and the gods," Meeka says.

"Cool. Listen, Michael, you're growing up into a man. And that means sleeping in your own room," Joe says. He hasn't looked at the book and places it back on the nightstand.

"I know," Meeka says. "I just wanted to see the note. June took it away before I could read it."

"Ask her next time, in the morning," Joe says. "She's your big sister and you have to listen to her. That also means asking before going into her room. Okay?"

"Okay, Dad."

"Also, the back yard is almost done," Joe says. "We should play some ball this weekend. Maybe call some other kids from the neighborhood over." He is looking at his son. His brown hair is almost at his eyes. There's a freckle near his bottom lip. Michael looks almost like him when he was this age.

"I don't know, Dad," Meeka says. "I'm still the new kid, and I don't want to bother anyone."

"Do it anyway. This will be a good way to make some friends. Just think about it, buddy. Good night then." Joe switches off his light.

Joe goes downstairs for a glass of water. He opens a cabinet and takes out a glass to fill by the sink. His heart is racing quite a bit, and the cool water is a crash that gives him no relief. Meeka is growing up to be just like him, head in the clouds and eyes veiled by books. If only his father had taught him the difference between fiction and reality.

He looks out through the window for a moment. It's dark and he can make out the shapes of bushes in the back yard. He doesn't notice that when he blinks his eyes remain closed for longer than a split second. And in that moment, he almost sees a sunny day outside in the yard, with a basketball hoop set up. A large figure playing with a smaller figure. The faces are indiscernible, but Joe has a feeling who these figures are. He smiles, floating in his fantasy, as he walks himself back to bed.

The whole house catches a strong gust of wind that passes along its entirety, causing rippling creaks along the walls. A loose doorknob rattles.

After being tucked in, Meeka immediately reaches for the same book to read under his covers. He's trying to figure out what a diploma is again when the letters start to rearrange themselves. The "d" moves itself between the "p" and "l", and the "m" goes toward another word, making it hard for him to read anything. He blinks rapidly a few times and cleans his glasses. The words stick back on the page, but Meeka is unsure whether the words are the same. He's a little nervous because he heard his parents talking about the kid who failed a grade and was held back. His teacher from back home said he was ahead in his reading, but what if it's not the case in this new town? His dad already doesn't like him reading. Who is he outside of the books he reads? Meeka knows he isn't brave like Percy or funny like Captain Underpants.

He lifts his sheets and quickly runs into June's room. He huddles close to June under the sheets. June turns around and pinches Meeka's face.

"Ow," Meeka says, rubbing his cheek.

"Just making sure." June gives Meeka a quick squeeze. "Night."

"Night, Junie." Meeka squeezes back, still loosely embracing June as he falls asleep.

Time is the house's heartbeat; the clock's ticking pulses through the rooms, soft as a whisper. It is early and the sun's rays peek through the clouds. The first morning light shines through the curtains in the bedrooms, highlighting features of previously indistinguishable objects, like the piggy bank near Meeka's side of the bed or the memory box not completely tucked under June's bed.

In a note that will be found later, the same warning is followed by a question.

Were our dreams really that far away in this new morning?

— THE GHOST OF CREEK HILL —
by Aliya Chaudhry

My mother had been the first person to tell me the story. Hayward Manor stood between the children's hospital and the ice cream shop we would go to whenever I got a shot. One day, after a visit to the doctor, I asked my mother about the old house.

"The story is that there was a nurse who lived there. There weren't any hospitals back then, so sometimes she used to take care of people in her house. She was really hard-working and liked helping people."

"What happened to her?" I asked.

"When someone in the house is sick, the other people living with them might get sick too," Mom had said. "And so she got really sick, and because they didn't have the right medicines back then, she couldn't get better."

"Oh, that's so sad."

"It is," Mom nodded. "She helped a lot of people, though. That's why the house is still there. To remember her."

"And now it's haunted? By her?"

"Some people think so," she said. "Some people think they've seen her."

I looked at both the hill and the creek that had given Creek Hill its name. I couldn't see any sign of her. I hung my head. "How come I never get to see her?"

My mom laughed. "You want to see her? You're not scared?"

I shrugged. "She doesn't seem scary to me. You said she took care of people. She sounds nice."

A plaque in front of Hayward Manor read:

The Hayward family resided here for three generations. In 1845, Charles and Annabelle Hayward founded the local hospital. They died thirty years later, in 1875. They were survived by a daughter, Carolyn Hayward, who worked in the hospital. Her story became local legend. She is believed to have died in a fire at the hospital in 1880.

My mother had grown up near the cemetery, before it was open to the public. She told us stories about climbing over the fence and walking among the graves and weeds with her friends. Playing hide and seek behind the headstones and statues. Jumping out and making phantom noises, pretending to be ghosts. They would scream and laugh, more afraid of the living than the dead.

I had broken into this cemetery as a teenager. For most of my lifetime it had stayed open during the day but locked at night. I was staying at Amara's house a block away and we had told her parents we were catching a late movie before walking to the graveyard instead. They had made the fence a little taller by then, probably because of the trespassing children who now had children of their own. I had to give her a boost, then climbed up and clambered down the other side. We had the flashlights on our phones turned on, but the cemetery was already well-lit. I remember thinking it would be full of fog, but it wasn't. It was clear. We found a patch of grass to sit on.

"We should have brought snacks," she said.

"Do you think we're being disrespectful?" I asked.

"We're just sitting," she whispered, with a shrug.

Even back then, I didn't believe in ghosts. I just remember the cemetery being really quiet, and weirdly unexceptional in any way. Just a dark patch of grass at night. It didn't feel eerie or haunted or sad or scary. We could be sitting on my porch, or on Amara's lawn, or even in her living room, with the lights off, in our sleeping bags, like we would later that night.

I went for jogs around this cemetery during my breaks from college. I lived near a cemetery my junior year and would run there all the time, except it usually ended up being a much longer run because I would inevitably get lost and have to find my way out. Or I would underestimate how long it would take to get out, wouldn't budget enough time, wouldn't calculate when I was supposed to turn around. That cemetery was expansive, with winding paths and sections of different sizes. There were no maps and my GPS would always put me five yards away from where I really was. I'd just keep running until I miraculously ended up at the entrance.

After college, I visited home less often. This trip was a rare one, an exceptional one even, but I didn't last much longer than I thought I would inside the house. I decided to go for a jog on my third day back and walked to the cemetery. This cemetery was neater, more organized, more contained than the one I went to in college, or the one near my apartment building in the city. I just did laps around the area, didn't venture between the graves. It didn't feel any different than it had on any other jog, but I was trying hard not to get too close to any of the graves. Ultimately, my impulse to look won over my will to not see, and I caught a glimpse of the one part that had changed.

The flowers were still on Daadi's grave, only half decayed from when my mother had placed them there two days before.

My friends and I traded ghost stories at a sleepover in the fifth grade. When a friend started talking about Carolyn, I corrected her.

"Her house caught on fire," Rhea said. "No, that's not true."

"Yes, it is," she said.

"Her house is still there," I said. "It doesn't even look burnt."

"How do you know? You can't see it."

"She was a nurse and got sick and died."

"No, there was a fire."

I looked up the house on the city's website of preserved landmarks. It said:

After the deaths of Charles and Annabelle Hayward in 1881, ownership of the house and hospital passed to their only child, Carolyn Hayward. The death of Carolyn Hayward in 1883 resulted in the Hayward wealth being transferred to the hospital. Her death is a source of local legend, but the actual cause of death is unknown.

As a child, five minutes felt like an eternity. A year? Unfathomable. I remember noticing, after someone pointed it out to me, that time started passing quicker as you got older.

But nobody told me that time could collapse like an accordion. Nobody told me about those moments when you hear a sound that pierces through the years, that reaches out and grabs you and yanks you back to when you were eleven and you first heard that song on the radio. Or you see a bike and you feel shaken and suddenly you're five and that's your bike and you just fell off it and scraped your knee.

My parents had never moved. I had spent my whole life until the age of eighteen in that house. As I walked through, I could remember where I lost a tooth, where I fell down and broke my foot, where I stood when I opened my college acceptance letter, my parents on either side of me. I remembered being scared by the noise of the creaky step, slamming the door of my bedroom shut, lugging my suitcase up the stairs when I came for visits.

I didn't just remember these things, I felt them again, like it was the first time, all at once. As if I was stuck. And, at the same time, as if I was all of these people, all of these things and memories and feelings at once.

"Do you remember the story of Carolyn, from that creepy house on Creek Hill?" I said to Amara on a FaceTime call from my bedroom.

"Oh yeah, the Creep Hill Killer?" she said, from her apartment in Chicago.

"What?" I responded. "She didn't kill people."

"She totally did."

"That's absurd."

"Of course it is. This is a ghost story."

"So, she killed people while she was alive? Or after she died?"

"The first. That's why she became a ghost. Too much guilt."

From *A History of Southeastern Connecticut*:

Clifton Hospital was the region's first hospital with an entire section devoted to pediatric care. It was initially called Hayward Hospital, after the people who founded it, Charles and Annabelle Hayward. Their daughter, Carolyn, worked there and established the hospital's children's wing in 1859. All three died in a fire at their home, Hayward Manor, now a historic landmark, in 1877.

I had started seeing ghosts. Not in the sense that I saw my grandmother walking around the house, but I saw her in my face when I looked in the mirror. In my father's voice when he told us he'd see us later. In the curls on our heads. In my mother's turn of phrase when I knocked over a dish by accident. In my father's expression when he struggled to open a jar of olives. I wondered if, when other people saw us, they saw the dead as well. I wondered if we haunted them the way we haunted each other.

I messaged Jay. "How did that story go again?"

"She was a nurse," he wrote back.

"And?"

"Her patients all died and she blamed herself for their deaths. She hung herself."

"You sure?"

"That's what Wikipedia says."

I went on Wikipedia. "The Ghost of Creek Hill" rerouted to "Carolyn Hayward." It said:

In the spring of 1882, Carolyn accompanied her parents on a trip to Baltimore. They died as a result of an accident while traveling back. I clicked the link on the superscript number next to "back." An article from *The Chronicle* opened up. It was written twelve years ago.

The Haywards were some of Clifton's earliest residents. They were a wealthy family who, in 1849, built the first hospital in the town, Hayward Hospital, later renamed Clifton Hospital and now called Clifton Children's Hospital.

Carolyn Hayward, the daughter of the hospital's founders, Charles and Annabelle Hayward, was a nurse at the hospital until her death in 1883, while traveling with her parents to Philadelphia.

I don't think ghosts are nearly as scary or as powerful or as persistent or as upsetting as the things that actually haunt you. The things you said you would do and you didn't. The things you wish you hadn't done. The things you wish you had said. The things you wish you could take back. The memories you wanted but never had. The decision you wish you could make again. The one thing you would change if you could do it all over again.

If they wanted to make a movie about something truly frightening, they'd make one about regret.

"What's the version you heard?" I asked.

"She jumped out the window," Sairah said.

"What were the other versions?" I asked.

"I heard so many," Sairah said. "I think at some point I combined them in my head. Like I remember something about a fire. But then that was when we were little and they were teaching us about fire safety and we had that trip to the fire station."

"Yeah, I remember that."

"So, for a while I thought she jumped out of the window because there was a fire or something like that. But then I think that maybe an adult told me that as a child so they wouldn't have to discuss suicide." I scribbled in my notebook as Sairah continued. "I don't know what's real. I don't even know if she existed. People will construct almost anything."

From *The Founding Families of Connecticut*, Chapter 8, "The Haywards":

The Haywards were among the first settlers and founders of Clifton. Charles, the son of Henry and Julia Hayward, along with his wife Annabelle, turned their attention to philanthropy. They founded the first hospital in the town, then called Hayward Hospital.

The fourth generation consisted of only one member: Carolyn Hayward. She and her parents died of malaria in Hayward Manor in 1878. She did not marry or have children.

That time, on my jog, I kept going after I finished my loop of the cemetery. I ran out of the gates, onto the sidewalk and toward the Hayward compound. I didn't go inside. I stayed on the other side of the street. The house was obscured behind a wall of trees, but not as overgrown as I thought it might be.

Around that island of trees was a circular driveway, leading up to the gate of Hayward Manor. As I jogged, I caught glimpses of the wrought-iron gate, the lock probably rusted shut after having been kept closed for over a hundred years. I wondered if anyone else had wanted to open it.

I couldn't see them, but imagined the tall edges of the house, looming a distance past the gate. Big and imposing. I thought of Carolyn alone in there, in that huge house, hearing noises and wondering where they were coming from, echoes of footsteps, wondering if anyone had come in there, if she had left any windows open, forgetting things in one room and having to check three or four others before finding them, thinking the rooms should be filled with people and remembering them there. Finding memories of her family in every inch of the enormous house. Who knows, maybe she was haunted by something too. Maybe we're all just trapped in circles of haunting, of remembering and forgetting, of guilt and regret.

"Okay, so I've been doing research," I announced. Both of my parents looked up from their textbooks. "And by research I mean I've been calling or texting everyone I've known since I was thirteen," I continued. Dad nodded impatiently; Mom smiled. "And everyone heard a different version of the story of Carolyn Hayward. And they all think she died in some violent way instead of from a disease," I said.

"That's not how the story went," Mom said.

"What? That's what you told me when I was five," I said.

"You were telling her ghost stories when she was five?" Dad asked.

"I changed the ending." Mom dismissed Dad with a wave.

"Wait, so what was the actual story?" I said.

"The version I heard was that she drowned in the bath," Mom said.

"Wait, Dad," I said. "What did you hear?"

"That she died of old age," he said. "People just sensationalized it."

A pamphlet from the Children's Hospital read:

Clifton Children's Hospital was originally called Hayward Hospital, and patients of all ages were treated there. It was named after its benefactors, Charles and Annabelle Hayward, whose daughter, Carolyn, worked in the hospital as a nurse and, later, in management.

Hayward Hospital was renamed Clifton Hospital in the 1950s.The name was changed to Clifton Children's Hospital in 1981.

On the opposite flap there was a portrait of Carolyn, her dark hair wrapped into a bun. Her features were sharp, her nose slim, and even back then she looked like a ghost, pale white with grey eyes. The description read:

The daughter of two of the hospital's founders, Carolyn Hayward always had an interest in nursing and caretaking. She graduated at the top of her class from the New England College of Nursing before returning to Clifton. She created the children's wing of the hospital. She worked at Hayward Hospital and lived in Clifton until her mysterious death in 1876.

Sometimes it feels like people don't die at once but erode little by little. Fragment, dissipate, piece by piece. They die, their heart stops, they're no longer breathing. Their body is buried, stashed away in the ground. There's a death certificate. They smile in old photographs. They talk in videos. They laugh in flashbacks. Then, slowly, the people who knew them begin to forget about them, the memories get dimmer, blurrier, hazier, until you're not sure what's remembered and what's imagined. What's history and what are ghost stories.

"I'm always scared I'm gonna die in like some horribly stupid way," Amara said. "Like a piece of toast gets stuck in the toaster and I try to fish it out with a fork and electrocute myself in the process. And then when everyone asks how I died they'll be like, 'Oh, she stuck a fork in a toaster,' and at my funeral they'll say, 'She died making toast, which wasn't even a thing she loved.'"

"That's elaborate," I had said, aged fifteen. "And specific."

"It doesn't have to be toast," she shrugged.

"So you're more concerned with how you die than the fact that you will die?"

"Yeah, I think that's it. I think if I died of cancer or old age, I'd be happy with that."

"I don't know, I feel like that's more of a preference than a fear."

"I don't want some dumb mistake to be the last thing I do."

I nodded. "The last thing they remember about you."

She nodded and then looked at me. "Are you afraid of dying?"

"No, I've never been. I guess it just...missed me."

I was looking for articles on Carolyn and ended up on a creepypasta.

Carolyn of Creek Hill is a popular urban legend.

"Suburban," I muttered.

She was murdered at the age of twenty-three. She had studied to be a nurse but never got the chance to practice. On January 23rd, 1888, she went to bed. It was around 11:11 pm. She turned off all the lights and drifted off to sleep. An intruder snuck in at 1:23 am, crept upstairs, stood above her sleeping body and stabbed her twice in the chest. She was dead in five minutes. Her murderer slipped out into the night and was never caught. To this day, nobody knows the identity of the killer. Carolyn became a ghost to track down her killer and bring them to justice.

They say she still lives in her old house, Hayward Manor, and still regularly visits the children's hospital. People have seen her at Creek Hill Cemetery and Waybrook Elementary and there have been sightings underneath the Wishing Bridge at Grosvenor Park.

I laughed at the idea of Carolyn's ghost hiding under the bridge as Sairah and I walked over it, gossiping, or yelling, or throwing coins into the water. I wonder what she would have heard, and what she would have thought of us. Of me.

I think about death a lot. Not the act of dying. Not what it feels like. Not the biology of it. Not what happens to the body in the ground after years of lying there, how the skin and bone transform as they're broken down by the earth.

I think of what I'll leave behind. If I've made any contributions, done anything that will bring me to the attention of strangers. Which belongings go to which friends, who will be close with me at that time. And how they'll all remember me. If it'll be bits and pieces, or the whole. At my funeral and memorial service, will all their memories be obscured by a search for examples of my kindness, generosity, and what they'll no doubt call my "bright spirit," or will someone be annoyed, will someone have something awful I once said to them playing on a loop in their head, unable to get it out? Will they shake their head while a relative speaks, trying to forget, to think better of me in my death? Will someone suddenly remember that I owe them money, or forgot to return their book? Will someone remember a time I let them down, a time I frustrated them? Will someone think of me as completely unremarkable, or not think of me at all? Will they form new characters from selected memory? Will time cherry-pick the moments that determine the versions of me that live on?

And yet, I'd rather be completely forgotten.

"What stories do you think they'll tell about us when we're dead?" I asked and waited a bit. "I think I just want to fade away into obscurity. Be forgotten."

"I don't want to forget you," Sairah said.

"Who says you're gonna outlive me?" I replied. We walked for a few minutes in silence, as Sairah, a newcomer to the cemetery, examined the surroundings.

"What do you want your gravestone to say?" she asked.

"I don't know," I said. "That's way too much pressure. Something literally set in stone that will be there forever and you could never change it? No thanks." We walked a few more steps. "You?"

"Maybe if I have some unfinished work or like a really good line or title or something, we could slap it on there."

"In the event that I do outlive you, do you still want me to destroy all of your drafts?" I said.

Sairah nodded. "Oh definitely. Burn it all—every notebook, Word doc, post-it and scrap of paper—anything unpublished shouldn't survive me. I can't think of what people would do with that."

I laughed. "But after we pick an epitaph."

"Yeah, you go through everything, pick something to go on my gravestone, then torch it."

"What? You can't put that on me! That's too much responsibility!"

"It's just one line."

"It's the last thing you'll say."

"Won't be me saying it, just you quoting it."

"It'll be the last thing you'll leave behind."

Sairah tilted her head. "We'll see."

Women in Medicine, page 118:

Carolyn Hayward (1851–1889)

Carolyn Hayward was born to Charles and Annabelle Hayward, prominent Connecticut philanthropists. Her parents founded a hospital in her town, Hayward Hospital, later renamed Clifton Hospital.

Her family was wealthy, so her education was a formality. She didn't need to work, and therefore didn't need to get a professional degree or go to a vocational school. Nevertheless, she decided to go to nursing school, graduating at the top of her class. She went to work in the hospital her parents founded and was known for working hard and being truly dedicated to her patients.

In 1887, after the death of her parents, she took over the management of the hospital.

She died in 1889, at the age of thirty-seven, likely from complications relating to pneumonia.

The next day, after a lap around the cemetery, I jogged right up to the gates of Hayward Manor.

When we were little, and we had just learned how to ride our bikes, we used to ride by the house all the time. We liked to do circles in the entry driveway, around the patch of trees, careful to not go too close to the gate, for fear of the ghost.

There wasn't much of a reason to walk up to the gate anyway. I remember it covered in vines, leaves, and moss so thick you couldn't tell if there really was a house in the back.

We never saw the house, even when they cleared up all the foliage. Taking a break from my run to peer through the now bare bars, I couldn't see anything. The house was a distance away, the vegetation inside the compound more overgrown and unruly than the vines outside it. The gate was easily twice my height, flanked by stone columns. It was built to last centuries. From books, I knew the house was three stories tall and, from photos, I knew it had those big windows that are larger than a person. But I didn't know anyone who had seen the house.

I did see the stretch of the path leading up to the house, with oak trees lining the way, and for a second it felt like I was staring into a different time period, shut out, unable to go in. I checked the lock, the size of an orange and almost the same color with rust.

I felt disappointed, like I did the first time I visited the cemetery at night: I felt calm, normal, neutral, if anything at all. Not scared; I didn't feel any lingering presence.

I felt alone.

— EVERY SOUL WILL TASTE DEATH —
by Marwa Sarraj

Cities and cancer are alike. Both spread at rates that often take humans too long to process. And sometimes, if they are unlucky enough, by the time they have understood what's going on, it is too late.

Life passes similarly. Blink and it's gone.

It takes too long to understand how fleeting things are. It takes too long to realize how strongly to grip those around you.

Ismail did not have that problem. Everywhere he looked in his home—a home he built himself—were ghosts and memories. His wife floated in and out of rooms, muttering to herself. His little girl, pig-tailed and immortalized at six years old, giggled in one of the bedrooms, playing with the doll she was buried with.

Out in his own garden of Eden, his son, who had never come home from war, stared out at the cherry trees that swayed in the breeze. Every pet they had ever owned zoomed in and out of the one-floor, white stucco home.

Ismail was never alone, not here.

But he would be, soon. There had been whispers of the city's expansion for years, but he hadn't taken it seriously until five years ago, when city officials came to his door with an offer. A hefty sum of money for his lot. They wanted to bulldoze the whole neighborhood and replace it with luxury apartments.

The city could no longer contain its wealthy, and they were expanding, seeking novel places of refuge, new spots to discover like half-baked Ibn Battutas.

Ismail had refused, but each year the city officials came back with a higher offer. Each year, he refused.

Except this year.

He had been outnumbered—all the other homeowners in the area had agreed and he was the only hold-out. With such a backing, the city offered him an ultimatum: sign or fight it out in court. So, the eighty-year-old man had signed. What else could he do, at this age? And besides, he felt for his neighbors. They hadn't done as well as he had in life. Their homes were falling apart, and most couldn't afford to fix them. They spent their winters cold, having to choose between food and fuel for their furnaces.

This deal would allow them to buy better homes, in better locations. When they died, it would give them something of benefit to pass on to their children.

And wasn't that the whole reason they had become parents to begin with? To make sure their kids had better and did better than they had?

Ismail reached for his hourglass-shaped teacup with a sigh. He ruminated on the back porch, watching his son. He was the least talkative of the ghosts, but Ismail didn't mind. He knew the traumas of war were what silenced him. They had never gotten his son's body back—the army had said they couldn't find it. Officially, he was listed as MIA, but Ismail had known his son was dead as soon as he appeared in their home, looking confused and scared. What Ismail should have done was find a way to get his son to move on—his family had come from a long line of spirit-soothers, after all. But he just couldn't. So, his son joined his daughter.

Before she became one herself, his wife was always upset when a new ghost arrived. Throughout their entire marriage, Ismail had never been sure if he was happy that his wife could see the spirits as well. Eventually, though, as their other two children grew up and moved out, he was glad to have someone to share the ghosts with. When he and his wife sat for dinner, their ghost children would join them. It didn't matter that they couldn't eat. What mattered was that they still felt like a family.

And then his wife died.

It had happened in her sleep. Ismail hadn't even needed to turn his head. When he awoke that morning, he saw the shimmering white-blue shape of his wife at the foot of his bed and he knew.

Her funeral had been the very next morning.

It didn't take too long for his other children to figure out why he hadn't seemed as upset as they expected. They could see the spirits, too. It was the only reason they hadn't insisted he live with them now that he was alone.

Because he wasn't, not really.

His wife sighed beside him. "I would refill your tea but..."

"I know," he said with a chuckle. "I've been taking care of myself for ten years now. What's a couple more?"

"Don't say that. You could have many years left."

Ismail craned his head up. A solitary cumulus cloud moved sluggishly through the too-blue sky. "I don't need any more years. I'm not sure I want them."

His wife didn't say anything. She just gazed at him quietly, studiously. "Do you know," she asked in a soft voice, "what tethers us here?"

He had his theories, at the forefront of which was blood. Each of them had bled into this house one way or another: his daughter had cut her foot on a tile when he was remodeling the bathroom; his son had sliced his hand while they were finishing the attic; his wife had been the one to help him build the house and there were countless injuries between the two of them.

They would probably disappear once the house was bulldozed.

Ismail closed his eyes briefly, letting the ache wash over him. A burden of pain was waiting for him once they disappeared. He had never grieved their deaths like he should have because they had never really left him. Everywhere he looked was a ghost, a memory. A reminder that his life had been full. There had been love here.

"Ismail?" His wife's voice called him back.

He opened his eyes. "I'm not sure."

The look on her face was one he knew well. It was the same look she gave him when he low-balled the cost of fixing up the car or when he told her that he hadn't bought her a Valentine's gift, like they had agreed.

But she didn't say anything. She let it go and they watched the finches flit to and fro. It was a warm spring day and Ismail had put out water for the poor things. It hadn't rained in a while.

His old hunting dog perked up at the movement of the birds. Her tail wagged and she began to bark incessantly.

"Calm down," Ismail said. "They can't see ghosts either, old girl."

The dog whimpered, settling back down at his feet. He didn't know if she understood him any better now that she was a ghost, but it didn't matter much. At least her barking didn't bother anyone else anymore.

Why the animals stuck around was something he couldn't figure out. He wasn't even aware that animals could even become ghosts. What kept them here? Was it just a stubborn refusal to leave their human behind?

He reached down to pat the dog on the head. His hand passed right through her, much to both of their disappointments. Ismail had learned that, sometimes, if a ghost was disciplined enough, they could become more corporeal; it was how some spirits were able to manipulate objects in a room. There were times where Ismail would give anything to feel the touch of his wife's hand again, or to tousle his children's hair.

Ismail leaned back in his chair. This would be one of his last moments with his ghost family. The only one who hadn't quite understood the gravity of the situation was his daughter.

"Baba, baba," she shouted. Ismail's lips curved in a smile as he remembered a time, many years ago, when he would come home from work and she would run toward him. She had still been alive, then.

His daughter materialized in front of him, her eyes wide. "Is it going to rain?"

She asked him the same question every day. It was one of the last things she had asked before she died. His daughter had always been terrified of thunderstorms and storm clouds had rolled in the day she died. They had had to close the curtains to keep her calm until the rabies took her.

The disease had come out of nowhere—Ismail hadn't thought anything of it when one of the strays on the street had nipped at her, and, when she got sick shortly after, he had thought it was just the flu. But when the fever just wouldn't break, they took her to the hospital only to be told by the doctor that there would be no saving her now.

"No, sweetie," he said gently. "You see the sky? It's clear. No chance of rain."

The little girl looked up, eyes blinking. "Okay."

She skipped away to play among the fruit trees in the garden. Ismail looked over at his son, who watched his oldest sister thoughtfully. An ache grew in the old man's chest as he watched his firstborn and his lastborn. No parent wanted to bury their own child. And he had to do it twice. Even without the body, they had given his son a small service. Something to mark the occasion, to help with the grieving process.

He knew that the ghosts were why his living children no longer wanted to visit. They hadn't in a long time. They had been fine when it was just his daughter—they grew up with her. But with his son, things had been different. He carried a heaviness that his sister didn't have, and it made them uncomfortable. They would still visit on occasion, but then his wife died.

Now, the visits were limited to two or three times a year.

Ismail didn't mind it too much. His kids lived nearby, and he spent a great amount of time in their homes, among his grandchildren. But his children didn't want to bring them to his home to see their grandmother or their aunt and uncle. It was too weird, they had told him. The dead should stay dead. There were many times where his children had sat him down and asked him—sometimes gently, sometimes not so much—to get the spirits to move on.

He had always said that they would do so on their own accord. Spirits were ornery. Push them too hard and they only stick to this world more stubbornly. Now that the home was to be demolished, Ismail wasn't concerned that they would be here much longer. Hell, he didn't want to be here much longer. He envied the ghosts. At least they would move on to peace. What would he have once his home and his family of the dead were gone?

A strange apartment, devoid of memories and ghosts.

Tears stung his eyes. He blinked them back and reached for his teacup before realizing that it was empty. He could refill it, he thought. The double-stacked teapot still had plenty of tea left. He always made too much—he forgot that he, technically, did live alone.

How many times had he filled this particular cup? It must have been millions—the cup was the only one left from the set he had bought his wife when they first moved into this house, over fifty years ago. It was his favorite.

His thumb rubbed the outer ridge of the rim. He would have to take care to pack this cup so it wouldn't break.

"Shouldn't you be packing?"

His wife always did have a knack for reading his mind. According to her, his thoughts were written plainly on his face, and, as he had aged, the wrinkles only made his thoughts clearer.

"The moving company is supposed to do the packing too," he said, almost absent-mindedly.

His son got up to join his sister, who had been begging him to play with her. It was one of the few things he did, other than stare outside. Ismail didn't know what he had seen in the war, and he didn't want to know. All he had told his son was that he was there for him if he ever wanted to talk, and his son never did. He had a feeling, though, that his son spoke to his wife about it, from time to time. Ismail would look outside to see him talking to the ghost pets as well. If his son had still been living, that might have hurt Ismail's feelings, but he knew that spirits were often more comfortable with each other.

After all, they had all experienced the same thing.

"Arzu should be helping you," his wife grumbled. "She's the eldest. And has been for a while, now."

Ismail shrugged. "You know she doesn't like coming here. None of them do."

"Do they ever stop to think how that might make us feel? We might be dead, but we still have feelings."

"I know. But they're young. They haven't lived long enough to grow comfortable with death. It makes them uncomfortable to be reminded of the grave."

"Every soul will taste death," she murmured.

"You haven't finished the second half of your journey," he pointed out. "You still have to be returned. You can't stay here."

She scowled at him. "Now you worry about that? Ten years I've been dead, and this is the first time you've mentioned it."

"Well. I didn't want you to leave before. Now, though…now I think it might be better if you leave on your own accord. I don't know what it will be like for you if you are forced out."

His wife cast a long glance at their daughter. "She doesn't understand, you know. Time passes differently for her—she still has a child's mind. I'm not even sure she understands how much we've aged."

"You don't think she'll be able to go?"

"Not on her own."

"And you don't want to leave her behind."

"She's our daughter." His wife turned her head to him. "Would you leave her?"

Ismail's laugh was short and dry. "Isn't that what I'm doing? I'm leaving you all behind." His voice cracked and he looked away.

Silence slithered between them, growing as the seconds passed. Finally, his wife spoke.

"Yes. That is what you're doing. But you need to because you can't keep living for us. We're dead." His wife raised a near-transparent hand to stop him from interrupting her. "You spend more time with us than you do with our living children, or our grandchildren. Isn't that what we wanted for ourselves when we first built this house? What had we always talked about?"

He frowned as he answered. "We wanted a home where we could grow old together, among our grandchildren. But—"

"But nothing. Things haven't worked out the way we wanted them to. Two of our children died long before either of us. Our other two don't want to come here and that's fine. They're still *alive*, Ismail. There are still more memories to make. And don't our grandchildren deserve to have that time with you, too?"

Even dead, his wife was always right.

"You're telling me to quit feeling sorry for myself?" he whispered, looking down at his weathered hands.

She sighed. "I'm asking you to look forward. To remember that there *is* a forward. To live it for those of us who can't—to carry our memory with you."

The years had not erased the way Ismail could hear tears in his wife's voice before they came. If ghosts could cry, he was sure she would. He cleared his throat and nodded. "Okay, okay. But will you at least try to move on?"

"No," she said with a little smile. "The three of us are sticking together, like a family should. But you don't need to be here to see it. I don't want you to be here to see it."

"But—"

His wife materialized before him. She knelt in front of him, her hand on his. Instead of passing through him like it normally would have, it rested lightly on top. Ismail wasn't sure if he imagined it or not, but he could have sworn he felt the touch of her skin. "No buts. Let's count this as my death wish."

Mutely, he nodded. If that was what she wanted, then he would give it to her.

A week later, all his things were packed and on their way to his daughter's house. Arzu leaned against her SUV, arms crossed over her chest. "Ready to go, Baba?"

Ismail turned to look at his home one last time. His ghost family stood on the porch, arms wrapped around each other. Was there a choice? He supposed he could lay on the floor of his home, down a bottle of sleeping pills and wait for the bulldozer to take his life. That was an option. But his wife was right. There were more memories to make.

He turned to his granddaughter, two years old with wild black hair. She took after Arzu, and all of Ismail's daughters took after their mother—a blessing, he often called it. "What do you think, Melisa? Are we ready to go?"

"Yes," she giggled, trying to hand him the soggy biscuit that had been her snack. She had been named after her grandmother, his wife.

"Why don't you keep that?" Ismail said with a laugh, sliding into the backseat to sit with the little girl. As he stroked her soft hair, she careened her neck around him. Crumbs decorated the corners of her lips.

"Who is that?" she asked, pointing out the window.

In the rearview mirror, Ismail's gaze met Arzu's startled brown eyes. Clearly, she hadn't known that her daughter could see spirits. Out of all his grandchildren, Melisa might be the only one.

Arzu quickly pulled out into the main road as Ismail spoke. "The woman over there is your grandmother, and that is your uncle and aunt."

Melisa nodded and continued to eat her snacks. "Are they coming too?"

"No," he said softly. "They're going to stay there."

"Okay."

The little girl began humming to herself as she ate, her little feet swinging in the car seat. The movement sent him back through the years—when her mother would do the same. When his son would sit on the branches of their apple tree and stare out into the garden, chomping on the fresh fruit. When his little girl swung her feet on the edge of the bed before jumping down. When, many, many years ago—before she wore her wedding veil, her engagement ring, or even before he had confessed his feelings for her—his wife swung on a makeshift swing that hung from the strongest, oldest oak tree in their childhood neighborhood. She had turned her head to look back at him, her brown eyes sparkling, and that was when he knew he would love her forever.

Ismail leaned back as he watched her. His wife had been right. There were plenty of memories to make and so much more to share.

— ABOUT THE EDITORS —

LAUREN T. DAVILA is a Pushcart-nominated Latina writer currently pursuing her Ph.D. in English at Claremont Graduate University in California, USA. She holds an MFA in Fiction Writing from George Mason University and dual BAs in English and Creative Writing from Pepperdine University. After completing her studies, she plans to teach at the collegiate level while publishing poetry and fiction.

Her writing has appeared online in *Granada Magazine, The Paragon Journal, Ghost Heart Literary Magazine, Peach Velvet Mag, Voyage Journal, Second Chance Magazine, Headcanon Magazine, In Parentheses,* and *Poets Reading the News,* and in print anthology, *Hireath.* She is editing multiple short story anthologies.

She lives in Los Angeles where you can find her writing in coffee shops and swimming.

— ABOUT THE AUTHORS —

NISHA ADDLEMAN is a half-Indian, half-white writer and the daughter of an immigrant mother. Her stories vary from genre to genre and often address mental health issues, including ones she experiences herself, such as depression and anxiety. Growing up in a diverse community, Nisha's work also features an emphasis on inclusivity and diverse characters.

She was born and raised in Central Coast, California, where she still lives with her husband and dog. In her spare time you can find her cooking, sewing, and dancing.

ANGELA BURGOS is an Ecuadorian-American writer and researcher from Los Angeles, California, currently pursuing a Master's Degree in Social-Cultural Anthropology from Cal State, Los Angeles. Angela's writing is centered on community-based research and an anti-oppressive approach that emphasizes creating accessibility of knowledge through fiction and nonfiction pieces. Angela's work utilizes the intersectionality of her experiences as a first-gen Latine individual to showcase the complexities of her community. By taking a versatile approach, Angela is able to explore and write about topics that vary from gothic short stories to the shared experiences of POC in academia.

ALIYA CHAUDHRY is a fiction writer and journalist. As a journalist, she covers music and internet culture, and has written for *Billboard, Vice, Slate, Kerrang!* and *The Verge*, among other publications. She has lived in the United Kingdom, Pakistan, the United States and Kenya. She graduated from the University of Pennsylvania with a degree in English and a concentration in creative writing in 2018.The following year, she earned her Master's in Journalism from Columbia University. She is currently working on her first novel, which is about death, memory, and ghost stories.

D.C. DADOR is a Filipino-American science fiction and fantasy writer whose stories explore the unknown, whether the darkness of outer space or one's heart. Her day job supports space exploration and at night she devises ways to scare her protagonists. She resides in Virginia, where she enjoys exploring haunted sites.

MARGARET ELYSIA GARCIA is the author of *Graft*, a short story collection, published by Tolsun Books in October 2022. She's the author of the ebook *Sad Girls & Other Stories* and the audiobook *Mary of the Chance Encounters*. She writes and produces plays with her Latina theatre troupe Pachuca Productions in the northeastern Sierras. She's a Pushcart-nominated essayist who works as a staff writer for Feather Publishing as well as a poet associated with the Community Literary Initiative in Los Angeles, working on her first poetry collection. She teaches creative writing and theatre at California Correctional Center through the William James Associations Transformative Arts program and with the Artists in the Schools program in Plumas County. She's the co-editor of *Red Flag Warning*, an anthology about living with fire, to be published by Hey Day Books in 2024. She's a graduate of the University of San Francisco's graduate creative writing program.

EMILY HOANG is a Chinese–Vietnamese writer and editor from San Francisco. She is a first-generation college student who attended UCSD for her undergraduate studies and attained a MFA in Creative Writing at USF. You can find some of her work in *GASHER Journal*, *The Baram House*, and *Black Horse Review*. When she's not working on her short story collection, you can find her running by the beach or exploring new parts of the city.

ADALINE JACQUES is a young Black individual and a Native New Yorker living in Los Angeles who holds an interest in all things art. Jacques, whose real name is Amra-Adachi Jean, has a background in performance arts, having spread herself among multiple musical groups, whether they be educational or extracurricular. She is more than honored to be a contributor to *When Other People Saw Us, They Saw the Dead* and looks forward to contributing to many more projects akin to it.

C.M. LEYVA is a fiction writer and registered nurse who loves sharing her passion for science and medicine in her stories and exploring the what-if's around them. She enjoys writing character-driven fiction that provides representation for Latine women in science. When she's not working on her next short story or manuscript, you can find her attempting home improvement projects, losing herself in a good book, or playing video games.

DANNY LORE (they/them) is a Black writer from Harlem and the Bronx whose work in comics and prose runs the gamut of speculative fiction subgenres. They've written for *Marvel, DC, Vault, Dark Horse* and *IDW*, as well as *Fireside Fiction, FIYAH, Nightlight* and other short fiction venues. Most recently, they've written *Transformers* (IDW) and *Champions* (Marvel). They were also included in the *Unfettered Hexes* anthology (Neon Hemlock). Their wife and cat probably wish that they would take a nap.

ADAM MA is an avid fan of horror and fantasy, and has spent most of his freelance career building lore-rich worlds for adventurous strangers to be lost in. By day he manages customer support for a gaming company. Also by day (and mostly by night) he's dedicated to crafting stories. Adam has been a contributor for D&D-related editorial in a range of indie TTRPG publications, designed sandbox-style multi-group campaigns for local game stores, and is the writer behind the ongoing superhuman horror comic *Folklore*—which was voted by Sequential Magazine as one of the Best Webcomic of 2020.

LAUREN MCEWEN is a writer from the Atlanta area. A graduate of Howard University, her work has appeared in *The Washington Post, The Tempest, AJC.com, Bitch Magazine, Madame Noire, The Baltimore Sun, Ebony.com,* and elsewhere. When she is not staring at a blinking cursor, or trying to squeeze words out of her brain like blood from a stone, Lauren can be found trying to justify buying more books despite the fact that her to-be-read pile is over three feet tall.

MICHELLE MELLON has been published in more than two dozen speculative fiction anthologies and magazines. She is a member of the Horror Writers Association and the Science Fiction and Fantasy Writers Association. Her first short story collection, *Down by the Sea and Other Tales of Dark Destiny,* was published in 2018, and she's currently completing her second collection.

GERARDO J. MERCADO HERNÁNDEZ (he\they) is a Puerto Rican writer and poet. Currently working as a math tutor, he enjoys making art learning about world history and different spiritual beliefs. Gerardo's recurring subjects are the Caribbean, individuals and their community, and undefined, ever-protean, creatures. He is currently working on his first poetry book and other stories. Gerardo lives in Northern Puerto Rico while permanently catching up on physics and music.

A.M. PEREZ is a writer of speculative fiction with a Master's in Psychology completing her PhD thesis in the same field at the University of Central Florida in Orlando. She is Mohawk, Jewish, and Puerto Rican and grew up in Santiago, Chile. Her expertise in psychology and her mixed-cultural identity inspire the themes and elements in her dozens of novels and short stories. When she is not writing, she enjoys painting, teaching, running, and playing with her dogs.

DESIREE RODRIGUEZ is an Eisner-winning editor, writer and journalist who has been a featured voice in Latinx and queer representation in media outlets such as *The Washington Post, USA Today, The Nerds of Color, Color Web Magazine, SYFY Wire,* and *Black Comics Chat.*

She co-edited the Eisner-winning anthology *Puerto Rico Strong* in 2019, and has written in anthologies such as *Ricanstruction,* a collaborative charity anthology with DC Comics for which she wrote two original stories, and *Mañana: Latinx Comics From the 25th Century* from Power and Magic Press with artist Naomi Franquiz.

MARWA SARRAJ (she/her) is a Muslim Turkish-American writer. Her tastes lean heavily toward fantasy and gothic tales but she will read almost anything (especially true crime and narrative nonfiction). Through her own works, she utilizes her philosophy degree to form compelling fantasy worlds and intriguing characters. In addition to being a writer, she is a graduate student working on a degree in General Psychology. When she isn't writing or reading, she can often be found playing video games or binging true crime documentaries, and baking. She lives in Pennsylvania with her husband and two cats, Eevee and Ghost.

SHAKIRA SAVAGE is a poet and fiction writer from northwest Alabama. She holds a Bachelor's degree in Psychology and a Master's in Human Development and Family Studies from the University of Alabama.

In her work, Shakira makes it a priority to pay homage to her rural upbringing—from red clay dirt on white tennis shoes to sticky summer humidity that makes even the strongest lungs suffocate. Through a contemporary Southern Gothic lens, she explores both the beauties and complexities of surviving in the Deep South.

L.C. STAR is a Latina adult, young adult, and middle-grade writer with a focus on fantasy, witches, gothic horror, and identity. She is also the author of the upcoming novel series *The Servant Prince*. She is a Buddhist Mexican-Salvadorian American who currently lives in New Jersey, USA, with her Chinese-American boyfriend.

AMIAH TAYLOR is an editorial fellow at *Fortune* as of 2022. She enjoys writing about race, gender, and emerging technologies. Previously she served as the freelance technical editor for Blair Lauren Brown's book, *CBD for Dummies*, a reference book published in 2021. Her articles can be found in the Institute for Science and Policy at the Denver Museum of Nature and Science, *NBC LX*, *The Observer*, *Discover*, *Fortune*, *Well + Good*, *Yahoo Finance*, and elsewhere. Her work is also forthcoming in an anthology on Black womanhood, *Mamas, Martyrs, and Jezebels*, from Black Lawrence Press. Amiah grew up in Honolulu, Hawaii, and is pursuing her graduate degree in science writing from Johns Hopkins University. She loves baby lemurs, Claude Monet, and Rice Krispie treats, though not necessarily in that order.

ALICIA THOMPSON was born and raised in Los Angeles, California, where she has lived for the past fifty-three years, minus three at the end of the 80s when she jumped down a rabbit hole that took her to Humboldt County.

Alicia loves sci-fi, fantasy and horror and has written two YA novels about quantum physics and how hard it is being seventeen and the most destructive force in the universe. She is a human being, proud to be Black, and thanks you for reading her stuff! All love to all of you.

S.M. UDDIN is a London-born author of gothic fiction and a 2020 graduate. Her literature preferences lean more toward the dark, with an unusual affinity for eerie tragedies or the viscerally uncomfortable.

During her leisure time, her hobbies include not leaving the house, reading up on different psychological theories and admiring new K-pop videos. Whichever one requires the least talking.

ANUJA VARGHESE (she/her) is a Pushcart-nominated writer with a degree in English Literature from McGill University. Her work appears in *Hobart, The Fiddlehead, Corvid Queen: A Journal of Feminist Folklore & Fairy Tales, Plenitude Magazine, So to Speak Journal, Southern Humanities Review* and elsewhere. In 2021, she took on the role of Fiction Editor with *The Puritan Magazine*. She recently completed a collection of short stories, *Chrysalis* (House of Anansi Press, 2023) and is working on a debut novel. She lives in Canada with her partner, two kids and two cats.

JONAH WU is a queer, non-binary writer and filmmaker currently residing in Los Angeles, California. Their work is usually a deep dive into their Chinese-American upbringing and explores the intersection between mental illness, trauma, dreams, memory and family history. Their writing has been published in *Longleaf Review, Jellyfish Review, The Aurora Journal, Sinister Wisdom, Bright Wall/Dark Room, Cha: An Asian Literary Journal* and elsewhere.

— ABOUT THE COVER ARTIST —

MINA MARTINEZ is an illustrator and story artist based in Los Angeles, California. Her art has been included at Gallery Nucleus in Alhambra, California, as part of the *Warrior Painters Group Exhibition* in 2019.You can also find one of her donated sketchbooks, *Moments Well Spent*, at the Brooklyn Art Library in Brooklyn, New York. Naturally, she has been drawn to cultivating her artistic skills by collaborating with other artists and writers on zines, with topics ranging from picturesque landscapes, recipes and vampire lore. Much of Mina's interest in art came from exploring hidden parts of Los Angeles and cherishing nature.

— ACKNOWLEDGMENTS —

Creating a book takes a massive team effort. Outland wants to acknowledge the team behind the original Haunt publication of *When Other People Saw Us, They Saw the Dead*, without whose work, the North American edition would not exist.

Managing Director
Rebecca Wojturska

Editor
Lauren T. Davila

Copy editor
Ross Stewart

Cover Artist
Mina Martinez

Typesetter
Laura Jones

Contracts Consultant
Caro Clarke

Business Consultant
Heather McDaid